Mendoza's Dreams

Ed Vega

Arte Publ
Hous

Acknowledgements

The publication of this volume is made possible through a grant from the National Endowment for the Arts, a federal agency.

"Back by Popular Demand," originally published in *Maize,* No. 1–2, Fall–Winter 1979–80.

Lyrics quoted in "The Angel Juan Moncho" from "Marlene on the Wall" by Suzanne Vega © 1985 Waifersongs Ltd./AGF Music Ltd. Lyrics used by permission. All Rights Reserved.

Poem in "The Monument" and "Oye, Ronnie, Baby, What Really Went on Between You and Juanito Gwayne?" from *Bochornos and Bochinches: The Collected Poems of Potatoes Rivera*, Potatoes Rivera. Guaraguao Press, New York, 1984.
"Mayonesa Peralta," originally published in *The Americas Review* Vol. 14, No. 3–4, Fall–Winter 1986.

Anecdote in "The True Story Behind the Writing of the Conquest of Fructifera Soto" from *The Annotated Travels of Tiburcio Melendez: Physician and Pharmacist,* by Tiburcio Melendez. Barcelona: Sains i Fils, 1802.

Arte Público Press
University of Houston
University Park
Houston, Texas 77004

ISBN 0-934770-56-5
LC 85-073351

CONTENTS

***

This book is dedicated to
Dan Evans

We must, in the next place, investigate the subject of the dream, and first inquire to which of the faculties of the soul it presents itself, i.e., whether the affection is one which pertains to the faculty of intelligence or to that of sense-perception; for these are the only faculties within us by which we acquire knowledge.

Aristotle
On Dreams

That all the material composing the content of a dream is somehow derived from experience, that it is reproduced or *remembered* in the dream—this at least may be accepted as an incontestable fact.

Sigmund Freud
The Interpretation of Dreams

". . . and as I was thus deep in thought and perplexity, suddenly and without provocation a profound sleep fell upon me, and when I least expected it, I know not how, I awoke and found myself in the midst of the most beautiful, delicious, delightful meadow that nature could produce or the most lively human imagination conceive. I opened my eyes, I rubbed them, and found I was not asleep, but thoroughly awake."—Don Quijote

Miguel de Cervantes
Don Quijote de la Mancha
Part II, Chapter 23

If we shadows have offended,
Think but this, and all is mended,
That you have but slumber'd here
While these visions did appear.

—Puck—

William Shakespeare
A Midsummer-night's Dream

Back by Popular Demand

I had just finished touching up Mrs. Pantoja's dream of her daughter's wedding when Larry, Curly and Moe broke into my apartment and began yelling for me to get up. They were wearing business suits and their hair was styled and blown dry to confuse me. But it was them, all right. Up to their old tricks of hiding slapstick and shenanigans in doubletalk about social responsibility and satisfying the needs of the public. They were wearing gloves in the middle of June and that gave them away.

Larry grabbed a broom and began poking me in the ribs, yelling that a Mr. Layton wanted to see me. "Get up, get up," he was saying "We gotta be in his office at ten." Curly and Moe didn't jump around and hit each other on the head. They stood very still and stonyeyed, trying like hell to look serious in their expensive costumes. I couldn't help laughing. Curly said I better knock off the crap. He stepped over an oily pizza box and came closer to the army cot where, convulsed by their opening, I was bouncing up and down on my back. "I mean it, Mendoza," he said. "This is the chance of a lifetime." He wanted to know if I had gotten Layton's letters and said Layton was kind of annoyed that I hadn't contacted him. The name Layton meant nothing to me at that point. I assumed he was a theatrical agent. The whole thing was ludicrous.

My eyes began to sting from laughing so hard, but I urged them on. "Do some more," I said. "Hit him on the head with the broom, Larry. Hit both of them. Do some more stuff. I love it." Moe thought I'd had too much to drink and was hallucinating. "Jesus Christ," he said. "He's got the friggin DT's!"

Larry said I had diddley squat. "That's part of his act," he said. He dropped the broom, pulled up on his gloves and began shaking me. The more he shook the harder I laughed. Curly moved to the end of the cot, grabbed my ears and began pounding my head on the pillow. Their frantic attempts to amuse me, plus my tears, made everything blurry. It became impossible to enjoy their show and I began kicking my feet. In truth, what I was trying to do was walk on the ceiling to show them the lighter side of my character and therefore create a sort of humorous empathy with their plight as comics. They were obviously trying to recruit me as a fourth member of their act. I wanted no part of it and increased my attempts at the upside down stroll I had perfected from years of observing bugs. Hopefully, their realization that I could only perform as a single would dissuade them from insisting that I join them. Rather than creating empathy, my efforts angered the three. My kind of talent would no doubt upstage their act. They wanted simple slapstick from me. Moe ran over and pinned my feet. I finally stopped laughing after Curly missed the pillow and smashed my head against the metal pipe at the end of the cot. He said: "There, that oughta hold him for a while."

Larry stepped forward and kicked an empty can of ravioli against the wall. He took off his right glove, rubbed his nose with the back of his hand and said I smelled like an old tennis shoe. "Look at this place," he said. "It's like a garbage dump. I bet you haven't been out in the street for a month." He directed Moe to open the windows. Moe released my feet to carry out the order. The fresh air almost choked me. I suppose Larry was right about the place. When you dream it's nearly impossible to do housework consistently. Going out into the street, however, was another matter and boiled down to a question of esthetic preference. In the street all you find are gray shapes, definitely not the stuff for dreams.

Larry had put his glove back on and was pacing up and down the room, kicking cans and wine bottles to clear a path. I began laughing again but Curly moved towards the head of the bed and I stopped. There was a lump about the size of a brussels sprout in back of my left ear. I began to kick my feet once more. This made Larry pick up the broom and move menacingly at me. I held up my hands and told him that they had gotten me fair and square but that I wasn't joining their act. He said I was a fool. Rather than arguing over the merits of a show business career, I decided what I needed was a drink.

I threw my leg over the side of the cot and sat up. After a couple of blind thrusts of my right hand I came up with a half-filled or if you prefer, a half-empty bottle of wine. I make the distinction to allow for differing philosophical understandings of reality. It's like calling the kind of work I do, dreaming. It's hard to explain. Anyway, when I tipped the bottle to drink, some of the wine rolled off my lips, tickled the bristles on my chin and dropped to my pissed-stained shorts.

Larry went nuts. I thought he was objecting to my sloppiness, but he was concerned with the matter of hygiene. "Jesus, Mendoza," he said. "That damned bottle was open." He wanted to know why I hadn't checked for roaches before I drank from the bottle. I wiped my chin and told him I didn't have any French or Italian roaches in the apartment. "If it was rum," I said, "it'd be different." My humor was wasted on them. I took another drink, remembered my manners and pushed the bottle out to

Curly. "Go ahead and try it," I said. "Check it out. Not one roach."

"That's okay, *amigo*," he said, trying to disguise the nausea building up in his gut. I didn't interpret his disgust as a sign of rejection since, misguided as they were, they seemed sincere about my joining their act. Curly had turned away, gone to a suitcase leaning against the refrigerator and pulled out one of their costumes. Holding it out to me, he said, "Just get dressed and we'll get on the road."

"To hell with that," said Larry and snatched the costume away from Curly. "We can't take him up to Layton's like that. If we bring this mutt into that office, he'll stink out the joint. Christ, Layton'll have our ass in a sling." Putting the costume back into the suitcase, Larry said, "Let's go. Get him into the bathroom. God! Look at him! Move it! Let's go!"

"Go where?" I said. "I told you, thanks but no thanks. I ain't joining the act."

Moe said it was the new project I had talked to Layton about last year. I couldn't remember. He said it was a million dollar deal and the public was clamoring for the word. I again told them I had nothing to say, but Larry stepped up and told me that Layton said it was time for me to stop playing bohemian and move downtown and that if I didn't I'd be sued for breach of contract. I asked him what the hell he was talking about and he said that downtown I'd have more visibility, more accessibility to the public. I told him I was fine right where I was. "I don't bother nobody and nobody bothers me," I said. "The people knock, slip their orders under the door and go away." Larry didn't want to hear it. He said it was a disgrace for a man of my stature to live in such an environment. "Look at this place," he said. "Garbage all over the floor, mold four inches high and maggots the size of your big toes." He said I couldn't go on living like that because I had a social responsibility.

I said I was taking care of my social responsibility and pointed to my beat up desk where the old Royal sat like a black bird nesting among the stacks of papers on which I had recorded people's dreams. "As it is," I said, "I have a six month backlog. People are going crazy out there. I can't leave." Larry said I was being self-indulgent and that my head was full of romantic drivel. "Do you understand that?" he said. "It's all hopeless idealism, Mendoza."

I wanted to tell him about Mercado, the barber. He wants me to build him a dream about a thin wife who doesn't nag him and knows how to cook beans the way he likes them. And about Lydia Ramos, the checkout clerk at Met Foods, who wants a two story dream with six boy-friends on the top story and a rich *gringo* husband on the bottom one. I wanted to explain how nearly impossible dreaming was, but Larry wasn't having any of it. And I doubted seriously if he'd understand someone like Luciano Ponce. Luciano put in an order that almost made me quit all together. He's a nasty, mean, disagreeable bastard who beats his children, cheats on his wife, runs numbers, sells cocaine and helps the loan sharks collect their debts, but nevertheless is entitled to his dream. Ponce wants a dream about getting into heaven and becoming an angel after he dies.

Simple, right? I mean, in building dreams you can do anything. Wrong! Ponce, you see, wants a six month trial period to see if he likes the job. I have no choice but to scrape up whatever words I have left and put the thing together.

I also wanted to tell Larry about everyday kinds of dreams. I get ten or twelve a day. Heat in apartments, better jobs, less junkies, hitting it big with a number. And I wanted to tell him about the super dreams in which people go back to the island after thirty years behind a mop, or a clothes rack, or the counter of a bankrupt grocery store, and own a little yellow house up in the mountains, complete with banana plants and chickens in the backyard. I wanted to tell Larry, Curly and Moe about those people but knew all they'd do is laugh.

Instead, I began screaming that the people were going crazy. "Don't you know anything about dream deprivation?" I yelled. "Don't talk to me about social responsibility!" Larry wanted to know how much I was getting paid for my dreams. I said that wasn't important. "How much?" he insisted. I said he should forget the whole thing but he kept badgering me. I finally told him that dignity and self-respect were far more important than money. He laughed and said eating was more important. I said he was right, but that being around the people, I'd never go hungry." They bring me food and leave me alone to work on their dreams. "I told him the people were aware of my capacity to make them laugh or cry or take them back to the island or turn bums into angels and whores into princesses. Of course Larry had an answer for everything and said that there was eating and then there was eating. "Anybody can go to Burger King," he said, "but not everyone, purely on a whim, can get on a plane and go to Corfu's in downtown Athens and eat egg and lemon soup and french fried squid." I didn't follow the logic of his argument but I suppose he was implying I had these options if I joined their act. I told him I was quite happy where I happened to be and that I couldn't imagine why anyone would want to mix eggs and lemon into a soup.

Larry then asked me how I could justify my existence in such a complex society purely on the basis of building dreams. At that point I blew up and screamed that I didn't need to justify my existence. "Who else is gonna build the people's dreams?" I said. "Certainly not you guys. Bouncing around like life was a goddamn cartoon and making people forget where they live and who they are. Just get the hell outta here and leave me alone."

"Mendoza, Mendoza," Larry pleaded. "Let the people build their own dreams." I told him the people were too busy working and worrying to build their own dreams. He wanted to know who had chosen me. I told him the people had chosen me. Of course he wasn't satisfied and wanted to know how long ago this had happened and what process was employed in my selection. I told him I didn't know the answer to either question. His patience exhausted, Larry hitched up his gloves, picked up the broom and banged it on the cot. It was his turn to scream, this time about the public's need. I took another drink and tried to ignore him, but he kept on. "They're the ones who pay," he said. "Real dollars, too. *Pesos*, man. Not gratitude and respect." He said the public had a right to know what was going on with the people, why they couldn't pull themselves up by their bootstraps, why they couldn't straighten up and fly right, why they couldn't shape up or ship out. "Do you understand that, Mendoza? The public wants explanations, reasons, motivations, and answers."

I said I couldn't help them because all the public wants to hear were the same old things about the people. "Drugs, jails, prostitutes and gangs," I said. "They don't want to know about the people's dreams." Larry said the public was entitled to the reality. "It makes them feel safer," he said, and added that I had to reassure the reading public so they could take precautions against the reality. I told him that what he wanted was for me to rat out the people, to betray them and bust up their dreams. Larry shook his head and said there was no reasoning with me. He motioned to Curly and Moe and said, "Grab him. I'll start filling the tub."

Curly and Moe rushed over pulling on their gloves and sliding on newspapers and banging their feet on empty wine bottles. I tried to laugh at their slapstick but couldn't. I was beginning to get the message. They were determined to have me join their act. I struggled to get away but they picked me up under the armpits. I think they were surprised by how little I weighed. It was like picking up a scrawny kid. I also sensed that they didn't like the way I felt or smelled. They kept looking at the black streaks of dirt I get from lying down on the floor whenever I'm too tired to make it back to bed.

In the bathroom they placed me in the tub, underwear still on. They took off their black gloves, removed their jackets and rolled up their sleeves. As if they were about to tackle a sink full of dishes, Curly and Moe donned light green rubber gloves. With the desperation of a grade school kid erasing a mistake, they began scrubbing me and didn't stop until my skin felt tired, worn out and much older than it was. The water in the tub turned oily and gray. Larry, standing around to supervise my scouring, told me to remove my shorts.

Defeated by the indignity of their treatment, I did as asked. I wrung out the shorts so they didn't drip down into the Candelario's apartment and dropped them on the bathroom floor. Using the tips of the thumb and index finger of his gloved hand, Larry picked up the shorts and holding them away from his body as if they were a dead cat, put them on the window sill.

"Wash yourself down there," he said. "Esperanza's gonna be there. Mr. Layton got her to come back from the island."

"Esperanza?" I said.

"That's right, Mendoza," said Curly. "Your own true love."

All three of them laughed in unison. I wanted to join them but couldn't. The thought of seeing Esperanza again after so many years made my heart ache. Esperanza with her long legs and sweet mouth. With her at my side I could dream forever and catch up on the backlog. I scrubbed furiously, stood up, rinsed with clean water from the tap and made them put a towel on the floor. It was a regal image, me stepping naked from the tub and onto the towel. Hell, suddenly I felt regal. Esperanza could do that for me. Moe brought over a brand new bathrobe and held it out for me to slip my arms into. As I tied the robe my body felt alive and new. The blood rushed to the surface of my skin and my groin ached for the first time in years. Esperanza, Esperanza, Esperanza, my heart sang. It was all coming back to me. Who I was, my status, and why Layton wanted to see me. It would be so simple. I'd go see Layton, pick up his order, call Mrs. Candelario to come up and straighten out the apartment and take Esperanza to lunch. Afterwards we'd walk in the park and towards late afternoon we'd return to the apartment. There, with the last rays of the sun teasing her body, we would make passionate love like in the old days and then I'd conjure up incredible Indian battles, heroic pirate deeds and dreams of freedom for the people.

"How about a drink, fellas?" I said, feeling expansive, challenged once more by life and on top of the world, so to speak.

Larry motioned to Curly who rushed out of the bathroom. When he returned he was holding an unopened bottle of French champagne in one hand and four wine glasses in the other. He handed out the glasses, produced a corkscrew, seemingly from thin air, and with great ceremony opened the bottle and poured. Right there in the middle of my decrepit bathroom, with the plaster peeling off the walls, we toasted a new day, a new man.

"To Mendoza," said Larry, raising his glass. We clinked glasses and while we drank Moe began shaving me. When he was finished, he splashed Old Spice on his hands and patted my face. Curly came over, combed my sparse hair, trimmed my moustache and held up a mirror like Escobar does at his barber shop. To tell the truth, it was a shock. I didn't recognize myself. It scared the hell out of me and doubts rushed in like a flock of hallelujahs at the sound of a tambourine. I was old. Not aged but old. What the hell did they want with me?

Larry asked me to take off the robe so I could start getting dressed. I took it off and sat self-consciously on the toilet seat, crossing my legs against the nakedness. What with my scrawny limbs at odd angles, I probably looked more like a careless line drawing than a man. What the hell did they want? What more could I give them to feed their fantasies?

Out of their morbid fear and their need to see the people in a certain light, I had given them *Up From the Ghetto*, 185 pp. of a drug addict's harrowing journey from the degradation of his habit to the respectability of a social work degree; *Down to the Ghetto*, 256 pp. of a father's desperate search for his wayward teenage daughter, only to find she has become a beatific figure in a religious cult; *Return to the Ghetto*, the 457 pp. odyssey of an upwardly mobile, suburban family's obsessive concern with their roots; plus ten other minor works: *Dancing in the Ghetto, Ghetto Street Games, Gangbusting in the Ghetto, Ghetto Streetwalker, Ghetto Numbers, Ghetto Big Gun* and the ambitious but uninspired trilogy, *Ghetto Grass, Ghetto Coke, Ghetto Smack*. And of course my last work, the big *roman a clef* in which little known people became even less known, *Ghetto Mirror*. What else did they need to know about the people that they didn't already know? My tiredness of spirit returned.

"He's fading fast," said Larry. "Get him dressed and keep him away from the booze. If he gets bombed, Layton'll have puppies. After we get him up there he can drown himself in the stuff for all I care. Until then we gotta keep him straight." Curly and Moe brought me underwear and helped me put it on. They walked me back to the bedroom and began dressing me in their costume. They put silk socks on my feet and slipped them into soft leather loafers. When I stood up I felt like I was walking on feathers, but the feeling of despair wouldn't leave me. Every time I thought of Esperanza I cringed at the idea of touching her. Like me, she would be old, her face marred and wrinkled by time, her breasts dry and empty of love. I told Curly I needed another drink but Larry nixed my request.

"Jesus," said Moe, "he's starting to shake. Christ, give him a drink."

"Okay, Mendoza," said Larry. "One last drink and then we gotta go."

I told them to just give me the bottle and forget the glass. My voice sounded like a crow's cawing, cracked and broken by the pain. "Let me have it," I said, lunging desperately at them. Curly started to give me the bottle, but Larry grabbed his arm. "Put the robe in front of him, goddamit," he said. "He'll spill the stuff all over himself and we'll have to start all over again."

Moe bibbed me and, my hands shaking, I tipped the bottle. The wine was bitter and the thought of Esperanza's lips, dry and fleshless, her teeth long and yellowed with age, made me feel hopeless and without human worth. It was like I had been given license to fly only to find that my wings had been clipped beforehand. I drained the bottle, took off my bib and started to sit down on the cot. "Get away from that filth, you maniac," Larry shouted, and Curly and Moe were immediately on me. Larry said it was time to face the music.

Out the door and down the stairs we went, the four of us looking like cookies cut out of the same mold, indistinguishable one from the other. Except for my size, which was considerably less than theirs, my advancing baldness and my tottering legs, we could have passed for executives looking for cheap thrills on their lunch hour.

In the new haze brought on by the liquor, I suddenly knew what awaited me. After meeting with Layton and letting him flatter me about the importance of my work, I'd go to my studio with its comfortable chairs and potted plants. The desk at which I'd sit would be stylishly chic, a pine door supported by twin two-drawer file cabinets. On the desk there would be an enormous red, IBM, self-correcting Selectric. The typing paper would be the best. Although it would look like the perfect place in which to work, carpeted, well lighted, quiet and pleasantly decorated with book shelves and brightly colored file cabinets, it would be hell. Rather than being thirty floors above the city, or in a cozy loft in an artists' community, or perhaps safely tucked away in a cabin in the woods, my studio was in the display window of Layton Publishing Company.

In fact, the blank wall at which I would stare each day while I collected my thoughts before I began writing would be an illusion. Instead of mortar and brick, the wall would be glass, but I would not be able to see through it. Beyond this wall, on the other side, would be the street and the public; hundreds, perhaps thousands, watching me work, waiting for the word; needing to know how I live, whether I pick my nose or scratch my testicles while I search for the right word to fit a thought, a feeling. Every word typed by me would be projected on the large screen outside, for the public to keep tabs on my work.

Each day the crowds would increase and after a time Layton Publishing would give in to municipal pressures, lease the street from the city and erect stands to accommodate the overflow. The profits from the refreshments alone would climb into the millions.

In the background, beyond the four walls of my studio, I will hear Esperanza puttering around in her kitchen. She will not be the real Esperanza but an impostor: long-legged and sweet-lipped like the original but much too young to be her, there not out of love for me but at Layton's request, paid to satisfy my physical needs, minimal though they were these days. Her presence would, nonetheless, increase sales and improve my image.

Each day, shortly before I begin work, she will come in with a mug of coffee. We will kiss lightly, creating an image of subtle intimacy and mysterious domesticity. I may or may not fondle her breasts, depending on how the writing's going. If it's going well I'll thank her for the coffee and return to work. If not, I may do a number of sexually suggestive things, like licking my lips or arching my eyebrows and rolling my eyes lasciviously. To keep the crowds buzzing and intrigued, I may even leave the room with Esperanza for a time. At no time must I acknowledge the crowds. It had all been spelled out in the contract, agreed and signed by me as ransom for my eventual return to dreaming. Some mornings I will not fondle Esperanza's breasts. I will drink my coffee and ponder my existence and how I've come to suffer the indignity of being on display again. A faint suggestion of guilt will tiptoe across my consciousness to remind me of how long I've been away from dreams.

Unable to alter my future, resigned to my fate, I reach the bottom of the stairs. Curly and Moe usher me through the front door and out into the street. The air and everything in it is gray. On the way to Layton's limousine I pass people I know. They are gray and unsmiling. I greet them but they don't recognize me and look away. Some of the people stare at me with hatred in their eyes, perhaps suspecting that I am to betray them again. Larry holds the back door of the limousine open and I get in. I feel lifeless and empty of feeling. Curly starts up the engine and we begin moving through the canyons of crumbling tenements. The silent wailing of dreamless souls rings in my ears. I want to jump out, to shout for help, to scream that I'm a victim of circumstances, but I'm aware that it is too late and no one will come to my rescue.

The True Story Behind the Writing of the Conquest of Fructífera Soto

About fifteen years ago I suffered what people, in some circles, described as a nervous breakdown. I was in the middle of writing *The Conquest of Fructífera Soto*, a work fraught with social and psychological difficulties, since it deals with the seduction of a nun by a circus clown. One chapter into the book I was struck down by a most interesting malady. For me it was a quasi-religious experience, but the symptoms as observed by others appeared as those of a nervous breakdown.

I received a surprising number of letters from eminent writers, each with his or her own interpretation of what I was experiencing. None of them made the vaguest allusion to a nervous breakdown and all identified with my predicament, reassuring me that they had each gone through similar experiences in writing their major works, particularly those which dealt with criticism of a particularly powerful institution in their society.

Because I was involved in the literary exploration of such a controversial issue, I experienced extreme feelings of paranoia in which I was absolutely convinced that the Catholic Church was determined to punish me and would eventually kidnap me, throw me into a dungeon and subject me to incredible tortures not dissimilar to those employed by the Spanish Inquisition.

I should state that the book which I was writing was a fictional account of an actual event which took place on the island during the eighteenth century. I'm nearly finished with the project, but should you want to do your own research because you believe you can do a better job of documenting the events or simply because the story strikes your fancy and you'd like to adapt it to the musical stage, let me give you some of the facts concerning this bizarre tale.

The clown's name was Filiberto Casablancas, known in the circus world as Popoto. The nun's name was Barbara Almendros y Vizcarrondo, the youngest daughter of an immigrant silversmith from Valladolid, Spain. All of the action of the novel takes place in my hometown, Cacimar, during the ten days of celebration honoring the patron saint of the town, Our Lady of Perpetual Sorrows.

For people with a scant knowledge of the history of the island, it is important to point out that during this time the town of Cacimar was the site of the best known convent in the hemisphere. It was to this convent that the most dedicated of young women came to learn about Christ and prepare themselves for a life of abnegation and service. Set atop Punta Aguilar, to the northeast of the town, the stone and masonry structure which comprised the main body of the convent was visible from the town proper and stood like a sentinel, watching over the virtue of the young women of the town. Cacimar naturally gained the reputation of being the most chaste of towns on the island and because of its purity came to be known as the Village of Virgins. Of course whenever there are extremes there is always bound to be criticism and ridicule. In our culture the ridicule often comes in the form of amusing anecdotes. One in particular comes to mind and I pass it on simply to illustrate both my point and the type of humor which people enjoyed in the eighteenth century. I found this particular anecdote in *The Annotated Travels of Tiburcio Melendez: Physician and Pharmacist*, an obscure travel diary published posthumously in Barcelona in 1802 by Sains i Fils. It is likely that few people today will find any mirth in the tale. In fact, Esperanza, the love of my life, an incorrigible punster, suggested that I say that Tiburcio Melendez' diary was published posthumorously. But you be the judge.

> Maximo Ruiz, a ship captain plying the seas between the ports of San Juan and Cadiz, married late in life. From his union there issued three sons. One son died at sea, the other returned to Spain to study law and remained there and the last, Octavio, became a shoemaker, traveling from one town to another until he finally settled in Cacimar. In this town he met a beautiful young woman by the name of Mercedes Escobar whom he married after a short courtship. After their wedding they settled into domestic life.
>
> Octavio worked hard at his trade and soon was able to employ six men to help him in his shoe-making business. He received orders from all over the island and shipped some of his products off to Spain on his father's ship. Once a year his father came to visit him, bringing news of the continent and Octavio's brother, Rafael, who had also married.
>
> After three years of marriage Octavio and Mercedes had produced no heirs. This worried the old sea captain but he said nothing, happy to be with his son and his beautiful wife and grateful that Octavio's business was thriving. Rafael, his eldest son, was already the proud

father of two sons and a daughter. There was still time for Octavio.

Another five years passed and Octavio was still not a father. Already past the age of seventy the old sea captain sensed that his life was coming to an end. He was puzzled by his son's inability to sire an heir and on his yearly visit to Octavio's home, after a sumptuous meal prepared expertly by Mercedes, he sat with his son on the veranda of Octavio's newly built home on the edge of the prosperous and growing village of Cacimar. The old sea captain was offered a cigar by his son and after the two had settled into smoking the fine native leaf, the father broached carefully the subject of Octavio's barren marriage.
"I have no intention of prying into your affairs, but there is something which has been gnawing at me these past few years."
"Feel free to speak, Father."
"It concerns your marriage."
"It's a fine marriage. I thank the heavens daily that I was able to find such a good and industrious woman."
"Many men say that publicly in order not to bring disgrace upon themselves. Is she a difficult woman to live with, my son?"
"Not in the least. What makes you ask such a thing?"
"I constantly worry that there is no love between you."
"That is absurd, Father. We love each other dearly."
"I'm happy to hear that? But why are there no children if it is such a happy marriage?"
There was a pause and then Octavio answered.
"She's a very chaste and Catholic woman, Father."
The sea captain was puzzled.
"I don't understand," he said.
"She is still a virgin, Father," Octavio said, sheepishly.

The old sea captain did not speak again. He finished his cigar, retired to his room and in the morning was gone. He did not return again to Cacimar. It is not known whether Octavio and Mercedes ever consummated their nuptial vows, but it can be safely said that there issued no offspring from their union in more than forty years of marriage.

This may be an apocryphal tale, created simply to explain the times and juxtapose what had once been. Be that as it may, Cacimar did not remain a chaste town for long. In fact it soon became known for its scandalous reputation. Morality became loose and the Church merely an institution to be tolerated. It is said that much of the blame for the downfall of Cacimar can be attributed to the nun, Barbara Almendros or Sor Fructífera Soto, the name I've given her, and her obsession with Popoto's soul. In the novel Popoto is known as Calambre. In order to provide the necessary authenticity to what appears to be a bizarre set of circumstances in this narrative I shall continue to call the characters by their given names and not those which I've chosen for them in their fictionalized guise.

Raised on the southern coast of the island, Barbara Almendros was a stunning beauty. In fact by the time she was twelve years old she was so beautiful that her older sisters, themselves considered unnaturally beautiful, attempted to poison her. At that age Barbara already possessed a voluptuous body and a face which made even her own father lust for her. A righteous man, he saw himself burning in the fires of hell for all eternity for his incestuous thoughts. Barbara, on the other hand, was a quiet child, helpful and pleasant, given to flights of philosophical fancy in which she composed acrostics for calling angels to her side. She studied her catechism incessantly and prayed fervently no less than six times a day, keeping an almost austere, or without wishing to create an unnecessary pun, an unconventional practice of Catholic ritual. Young men came each evening to stand below the veranda of the Almendros's home under the pretext of courting her sisters but in truth hoping to get a momentary glance at Barbara.

Attempting to capture in verse the sensual beauty of this maddening creature, young men wrote poetry constantly. My own great-grandfather, Alejandro Mendoza, a budding poet at the time, who later turned to wholesaling dry goods, was reputedly one of these young men. Overwrought and frustrated, they argued over her, insulted each other, broke off life-long friendships and even fought duels to establish rights of courtship. Barbara was oblivious to the controversy surrounding her. She was slightly hurt by her sisters' apparent rejection, but explained it simply as a test of her soul.

Her mother, a devout, loving supporter of her daughter, not only because of her physical beauty, but because of her goodness, grew also alarmed. No matter what clothes Barbara wore, she appeared immodest, so pronounced were the fullness and curves of her body. She began designing and sewing dresses which would hopefully disguise her charms. This did little to solve the situation, because one was now forced to concentrate on her face which was startling in its symmetry and beauty. Unlike her sisters, who had brown eyes, Barbara's eyes were the color of amber. They were indescribably large and bright, bisected by a nose so fine as to recall classical statuary. When she smiled, her lips revealed small even teeth, not unlike those of a young child. She had high cheek bones, a dimpled chin and her skin was a light golden color accented by a rosy tint which made men recall sunsets. It was a face that begged one love the rest of the person. Her hair, like her eyes, was a most unusual color, somewhere between dark blonde and red, but shimmering and thick as if it had a life of its own independent of Barbara. It combed easily and, even when in disarray, appeared to lend itself perfectly to the face it so gracefully adorned. If she had a physical flaw it was her rather large feet.

As if her physical beauty were not enough, Barbara Almendros was possessed of a keen, introspective intelligence which made her the envy of every woman she met. To counteract the strife which was quickly developing in the family, her father isolated his daughter, built a separate wing to the house, brought in tutors and exposed her to music and letters. By the age of fifteen she was an accomplished pianofortist and composer of sonatas of uncommon sophistication and beauty. Her teacher, Maestro Sebastián Villafañe, the noted Spanish pianist and conductor, labeled her a genius, "a reincarnation of Scarlatti in an angel's body." At the age of sixty he fell madly in love with Barbara, who innocently aware of the ardor in the maestro's words, had not discouraged him, seeing his professed love as an affirmation of her own belief that God loved all that He had created and she could do no less. Barbara's father, confused, himself madly in love with his own daughter, turned Maestro Villafañe down when he asked for her hand in marriage. The maestro, dishonored, bereft, returned to the capital and, after a recital at the governor's mansion three evenings later, put a gun to his head and ended his life. When Barbara learned of the maestro's death she said: "Poor man. May he rest in peace. I shall always pray for the repose of his soul." She immediately sat down and wrote Opus 57, an elegaic composition of unequaled sadness, rarely played today because of its deathly beauty.

In mourning Maestro Villafañe she took to wearing black clothing and going daily to church to pray, lighting dozens of candles and spending countless hours kneeling in front of the main altar. It was here that the revelation came to her that she had a supreme mission to accomplish in this lifetime. She made a vow then to meet the Devil and convert him to the teachings of Christ and the love of God the Almighty.

That evening she went to her father and expressed her wish to enter a religious order and devote her life to the service of Christ. Her father was opposed. He cried and despaired at the thought of not seeing his daughter again. Knowing the weakness of the flesh, he acceded and went to see the priest the following morning, finally confessing his onanistic sins concerning his daughter. He asked for forgiveness and posed the question of where he should send his daughter. The priest suggested a number of convents, describing each in detail. At the dinner table that evening the convents were described to Barbara. She chose the Convent of Our Lady of Perpetual Sorrows on Punta Aguilar, outside of the Village of Cacimar.

A week later Barbara Almendros y Vizcarrondo was accepted as a novice into the Order of the Sisters of Perpetual Sorrows. The mother superior was stunned by the young woman's beauty and keenness of mind. She made her a special project, knowing that for someone so beautiful and talented to give up a worldly life could only mean that she was destined for sainthood.

Barbara took to the rigorous training as if she had been born to it. For the next five years she worked, studied theology, medical nursing and animal husbandry. She prayed and said not one word except to raise her voice in supplication of forgiveness for the sins to which she might fall prey. She prayed fervently that she would someday meet the Devil and be able to convert him to the faith. "In that way," she wrote secretly, "all the evils of the world, the trials and tribulations of humanity will be eradicated."

By the 1750s Cacimar had become, because of its fame as a chaste town, the center of religious activity for the island. A shrine was erected outside of town to which people came to offer their prayers, mostly to be released from sexual torment. Women flocked there daily, walking on their knees for miles, their faces emaciated from fasting, their bodies tortured from flagellations. Hopeless, they threw themselves at the foot of the shrine to wail and ask forgiveness, wishing for perpetual sorrows so they would not feel their hungering torment.

It was the custom of the convent to assign to the shrine a sister of particular virtue to attend to the women who came there. In 1795 at the age of twenty-two Sor Barbara Almendros, fully a member of the order, was given the responsibility for the shrine. She came down from the Punta Aguilar convent riding, not as had been suggested by the Mother Superior on a donkey, seeing that act as pretentious and potentially sacrilegious, but in the back of an ox cart filled with vegetables and presented herself to the town's priest, who, himself a saintly man, averted his eyes lest he fall prey to her beauty.

"Go with God, Sister," he said, after speaking with her. In his mind he prayed for the souls of the men of the town.

"Thank you, Father," she said.

And with that she retired to the small stone house beside the shrine, where she counseled women to pray fervently and ask forgiveness for past, present or future sins.

Nothing untoward occurred during Sor Barbara's first three months at the shrine. She rose early to perform prime and do her chores, which consisted of caring for a pig, a cow, a duck, some chickens and a vegetable garden. When she finished she again prayed and then had warm milk, some bread she had baked and a boiled egg. When she was finished eating, she read theological commentary, prayed and asked God fervently that He allow her to convert the Devil.

In May of that year the town began to stir, as it did each year, in preparation for the upcoming celebration of Cacimar's patron saint feast, or as they are called it in Spanish; *Las Fiestas Patronales*. Booths were built within the square, Lorenzo Conde began mixing his colored powders for the rockets which made up the nightly fireworks displays and the grounds of the church were spruced up in preparation for the arrival of the circus and the death-defying trapeze artistry of the Flying Batatinis who were once again touring the island after an absence of three years.

The Gordils Circus, originally from northern Cataluña but now firmly established on the island, featured no animal acts, but was famous for its trapeze artists, tightrope acts, magicians and clowns.

Among the clowns was the little known Filiberto Casablancas, known professionally as Popoto, a Canary Islander with a sad dark face and faraway eyes which frightened people and reminded them of stories they had heard of the times when the Moors ruled Spain. It could not be said that Popoto was an ugly man, but there was something disfigured about the way he looked. If one examined each feature of his face one found nothing amiss. Their combination, however, gave him a sinister look, one of suspicion and dread. Perhaps he had suffered too much, as Sor Barbara eventually decided.

Popoto had come to the island some ten years before and began working with the Gordils Circus. He enjoyed the climate and the easy relaxed way of the creoles. Going from town to town gave him the opportunity of avoiding extensive human interaction, an activity which had always pained him because of his inability to establish a long term relationship with a respectable woman.

For Sor Barbara the meeting with Popoto was inevitable. The closer the celebration of the patron saint grew, the more women came to the shrine to wail and writhe in front of the statue of the Virgin of Perpetual Sorrows. Tortured by real and imagined sins, they clutched at their breasts and sexual organs as if they were threatening to detach themselves and escape to eternal perdition. Her days became waking nightmares of suffering for the souls of the women and caring medically for their bodies, which carried the ravages of infected self-inflicted wounds, boils and sundry mutilations attempted in order to find release from their torment. Her nights were no better. They were filled with anxiety over her own mortal soul which had taken on the task of converting the Devil.

On the night of June 11th, while the Gordils Circus' caravan camped in a field twenty kilometers from Cacimar in preparation for their grand entrance into the town, Sor Barbara had a frightening but nevertheless revealing dream. A bright and courageous woman, she did not succumb to the fear. The following morning she confessed herself. The priest granted her forgiveness and prayed the entire day to rid himself of the images which Sor Barbara had left with him. She related how she had been walking totally naked in a beautiful field of wild flowers when she met up with a serpent who spoke enticingly to her. Her response had been to kneel down and pray.

Eventually, unable to get her attention, the serpent had grown angry, said foul things about her person, urinated sulphur on the ground, and writhing in front of her, had reared up and spit on her face. She confessed to the sin of pride which had made her derive pleasure from being so defiled by what was obviously the Devil.

This dream proved to be prophetic in a most uncanny way once she had met Popoto and decided that here, in the smallish body of this man, she had finally encountered the Devil himself. After confessing herself regarding the dream, Sor Barbara returned to her duties of ministering to her tortured women.

Days and nights blended into each other as she kept pace with the maddening pitch which preceded the celebrations. Deeply troubled, she prayed constantly and warded off evil, her soul soaring with religious ecstasy. As she worked she grew more radiant, her beautiful face, encased by the tight habit of her order, revealing nothing of the torment which had begun to build up in her soul. Rather than detract from that exquisite beauty, the turmoil seemed to feed it, making her grow spiritually and thus enhancing her allure. Men began coming to the shrine to catch a glimpse of her magnificent beauty and in that way ease the pain of being married to fat, hairy women.

For Popoto, coming to Cacimar meant nothing special. It was just another town with people who stared at him and treated him as a stranger. He wore his sadness concerning life with stoic resignation. At the age of thirty, unable to withstand what he perceived to be the ridicule of women, and constantly in fear of having them find out that he desired them, he had renounced the pleasures of the flesh to live as monastically as was humanly possible without being interned.

It seems indelicate to speak of these things, but in the interest of veracity and in order to understand how a woman who had committed her life to the service of God could become corrupt enough to allow herself communion with someone like Popoto, it is my duty to disclose the circumstances surrounding this event.

Parenthetically, I would like to point out that people like to think of writers as daring and unscrupulous when it comes to the difficult business of iconoclasm. I would like to dispel this myth. Most writers, despite what anyone may say, play it safe. They do not survive long if they don't. Unromantic as it may seem, I've only taken courage to divulge the true story behind the writing of my book, because just last month I was in a bookstore in midtown Manhattan—a place which I try to avoid whenever possible—when I ran across a book entitled *Secrets of a Nun, My Own Story* by someone called Elizabeth Upton. By most standards I am considered a worldly man and no less prudish than the next, but I must inform you that I found myself blushing while leafing through this book.

This was no mere fictionalized account, but an actual auto-biographical narrative of a woman who had spent considerable time in a religious order. Nun or not, the author is quite explicit about what she experienced sexually. I am not ashamed to tell you that, besides blushing, I found myself uncommonly aroused, a rare occurrence for me these days.

Discussing a subject such as the seduction of a nun, whether by a circus clown or an insurance salesman, is also fraught with great literary peril, for critics and others involved in the creative process will read many erroneous meanings into the particulars of the narrative and accuse the author of personal lack and therefore infer some sort of psychological over-compensation in dealing with such a subject. If it is any comfort to those people, I reveal here and now that, although I am not meagerly endowed as a man, I have always felt lacking and at times wished that Providence—not Providencia Porrata, the woman who introduced me to the pleasures of love and who nearly dismantled my manhood at the tender age of sixteen, may she rest in peace, but true Providence—from which all gifts flow, had been more generous. I have no regrets, however, for I chose to dedicate myself to the craft and to the love only of my once faithful Esperanza, who experienced always profound satisfaction in sharing herself with me. So, as indelicate as a subject of this nature may be, in the interest of accuracy I must relate it exactly as I have uncovered it.

Of equal concern and the main reason why I did not scrap the project as I had originally thought of doing is the well known fact that a good and true friend, a craftsman of superb imagination and skill, was already writing adequately on the subject of enormity, and he felt no threat whatsoever because I had uncovered a historical character of perhaps greater monstrosity. It is quite possible that his character and mine share a common ancestor and therefore a similar genetic aberration. This possibility came to light when I ran across a letter written by an old Sevillian prostitute, Bienvenida Iba$_{6}$nez, to a friend in Galicia about an experience she had with a young man whose sexual organ emitted whistling sounds.

Literary critics should understand that in no way am I documenting these facts in order to upstage a Nobel laureate. These very same critics should be careful about making metaphoric comparisons between the two of us. I, Ernesto Mendoza, am in no way saying that my pen or any part of my anatomy is larger than my friend Gabo's.

With that in mind let me continue this narrative and inform you that when Popoto was born he was a normal healthy infant in all respects but one. So large was his male organ that the midwife nearly snipped it off with a scissors thinking she had forgotten to cut his umbilical cord. His mother was not alarmed and instead marveled at the size. A half gypsy, she saw the size as a sign of great fortune for her son. As Popoto grew, so did the organ. By the time he was five years old it was as large as that of a grown man. It was thick and veined and, invariably as she was dressing him, she would fondle it playfully. His mother soon realized that he could not wear the short pants worn by other boys so she made him long, baggy trousers which would conceal the enormity of his male organ. His baggy trousers eventually became his stock in trade when he decided to become a clown. In fact he was the first clown to adopt baggy trousers, a common trend in clownsmanship today.

What is even more indelicate, and I hesitate to mention it, is that the glans of young Popoto's organ was twice the width of its trunk. At the age of fourteen, while collecting crabs in a rocky cove near the beach where his parents lived, Popoto undressed and decided to go for a swim. He dove into the water and swam for some fifteen minutes, his organ keeping pace as would remora a shark. He did not find the size of his organ unusual and as a matter of fact had grown rather fond of it, treating it as a companion. No lustful thoughts ever invaded his mind nor had he ever experienced even the intimation of an erection. He dutifully followed his mother's instructions not to allow people to see him without his pants and relieved himself only when he was alone.

That day, however, as he came out of the water he found what he later swore was a Canary Islands mermaid waiting for him. She was sitting on a rock, her fish tail waving gently in the eddies of water made by the waves further out on the cove. The mermaid had beautifully shaped breasts and seaweed in her hair. She called him forward and behind a rock she seduced him, teaching him about love and praising him for his prowess as a man.

That day he also found out, after the mermaid pulled back the prepuce of his organ, that its orifice rather than running vertically, as did that of other males, ran horizontally, giving it what appeared to be a smile. This pleased the siren. More curiously, as he became more aroused, the orifice emitted a beautiful whistling sound. The mermaid found this quite pleasing as well and she sang a beautiful mermaid song as she made love to Popoto. The whistling of his organ and her song stopped the waves and made all manner of sea life, including dolphins, lobsters and sea urchins come out of the water to listen.

When they were finished making love, Popoto fell asleep on the sand. He woke up as the sun was setting and looked for the mermaid, but she was gone and he felt overwhelmingly sad.

Each day he went to the same spot in the cove but the mermaid never returned. He called her incessantly by the name she had given him: Caterina. He called her and thinking of her aroused him so that his organ whistled, but Caterina the mermaid never returned and from then on Popoto cried each time he saw the sea.

Of greater importance, although quite difficult for me to believe, whether through some sort of genetic disorder or because of his contact with the mermaid, Popoto's organ developed silvery-green scales similar to those of fish, but perhaps more akin to those of reptiles; that is, they did not peel off but, based on existing accounts, appeared to form part of a pattern on the skin. The scales, from all indications, did not feel rough to the touch, yet their appearance filled women with primal repugnance at the sight. As another anatomical aside, according to Popoto himself in recorded accounts of confidentialities that he revealed to Jordi Gordils, owner of the circus which employed him, the vaginal canal of a mermaid is located roughly in the same place as that of a woman except that a mermaid has no legs and therefore cannot open them. One can only gain sexual access to the creature by gently stroking her armpits.

I had never heard of anything as ridiculous, nor do I believe there are such creatures as mermaids, in the Canary Islands or any place else. It is important, however, that one include these things in order to evaluate the condition of the character's mind, the myth involved and perhaps understand how it was possible for Popoto to seduce Sor Barbara Almendros y Vizcarrondo, a nun.

As he grew older, Popoto tried to establish contact with young women in the village, but failed miserably in even the most insignificant of social contacts. On an island where whistling was not uncommon, it being used as a mode of communication, Popoto's whistle, caused by his constant desire, became known and women ran from his presence so distinct and enticing was its sound. They all knew what it meant because Popoto had gone to the harelip whore, Manuela, to relieve his misery and, because he had hurt her in his desperate lovemaking, so immense had been his desire for release from the torment of wanting the mermaid, that she cursed him and afterwards told everyone she met that Popoto had the organ of a monster and that it whistled. More distressing yet, his ejaculations filled the air with the smell of the sea. Within minutes, however, the fresh smell turned into the stench of decayed fish. Within a week the entire village knew about Popoto's musical organ and every woman was warned to shun him. Before the year was over, every village in Spain and more than a few across the border into Portugal and over the Pyrenees into France had heard of the famous whistling organ of Filiberto Casablancas. Ribald songs and limericks were composed and jokes told to deal with the dread of such a calamity. The name Filiberto became a verb and men spoke of filiberting women, of leaving women totally filiberted, or of attributing the temperament of difficult women to a lack of adequate filibertation. The euphemism for the male organ became the filiberto and men who carried that name quickly changed it to avoid becoming the butt of jokes. One elderly judge, Don Filiberto Castro Astudillo, from the province of Burgos, chagrined over the constant references to his name in a sexual context, hurled himself one evening into the Ebro River and perished. This produced a comic elegy called "The Double Suicide of Filiberto." The Church became alarmed and sermons were preached on the evils of filibertinage. The situation became so severe that word reached the Pope in Rome and he went as far as writing an encyclical called *Populum Filibertinagium*, which at the last minute, being let in on the joke by a French cardinal, he did not publish.

By the time he was nineteen, Popoto had left his village with a freak show. He had visited the show, seen the fat woman, the dog man, the two headed cannibal, the eight-legged pig and identified with their pain. He asked the owner if he could join his troupe. The owner said that his show was a display of misery and that he seemed like a perfectly stupid country boy who would know enough misery if he simply lived out his life. Popoto said that he was filled with enough misery for ten lifetimes because women were frightened of him. The owner asked him why and Popoto explained. The owner did not believe him, so Popoto was forced to display himself. The owner was overjoyed and took him on. He informed him that what he was doing was against the law and could get him in trouble with the authorities. He said that his only reason for hiring him was the fact that his show was performing a true service for humanity in showing others the true senselessness of life.

The freak show left the Canary Islands and crossed over to the mainland. Popoto remained with the freak show six months, encountered his first circus in Seville and decided to become a clown. He painted his face blue and drew large red teardrops under each eye. On his head he wore a flowered hat. The rest of his outfit consisted of large baggy red trousers with suspenders, oversized shoes and a cape. He carried an umbrella and a watering can, making of watering flowers an act of unusually tragic comedy, for the flowers would not remain alive no matter how much he watered them.

In Barcelona he met María de las Mercedes Batatini who was the daughter of Rodolfo Batatini of the world famous trapeze family, recuperating from a fall which broke her arm. Popoto fell hopelessly in love with the muscular but lovely flyer. She rejected him outright, not because of his anatomical aberration, since she was unaware of it, he having devised a way of wrapping a leather thong around his thigh and thus tethering his organ so that it would not become erect and whistle, but because she found him too somber and withdrawn and not at all pleasant to be with. Rejected once more, Popoto took up drinking and reading religious texts. He arrived quickly at the conclusion that God did not exist. One evening in Seville, after a particularly brilliant performance in which people could not tell whether they were laughing or crying, he drank himself into a rage, went to a gypsy tattoo artist and threatened to kill him unless the gypsy tattooed two sinister eyes, two nostrils and a moustache above the smile on the glans of his organ.

The gypsy protested to Popoto, that he had never before attempted such a delicate feat, that it would be more painful than swallowing hot lead, if he could imagine that, that he was certain it was close to a mortal sin to do such an operation and that if he did so it could lead to horrible inflammation, infection, illness, possibly death or worse, amputation. Popoto roared with bitter laughter and said all those possibilities were slight compared to the pain he had endured in feeling so much love for women and having them avoid him as they did. He insisted and the gypsy resigned himself. He asked Popoto if he wished eyebrows and eyelashes to be included on the tattoo. Popoto apologized for the oversight, thanked the gypsy and said he definitely should include them. Reluctantly, the gypsy went to work with his needles. Popoto did not cry out once and in fact bore the pain with remarkable calm, almost as if the pain were an affirmation of his suffering.

It took weeks to complete the coloring of the tattoo and months for the scabs and swelling to disappear. What Popoto was left with was a work of art, an awesome figure so sinister that it inspired fear in the most hardened of prostitutes, who began by laughing at the whistling of his organ and ended up initially being awed by the imposing sight, their hearts beating faster at the weight and magnificence of it and then fainting when taking the enormous organ in their hands and pulling back the hooded monstrosity were faced with evil incarnate, smiling, its pained eyes mocking the folly of their existence. For the gypsy, out of his own suffering or perhaps because he was forced to absorb Popoto's suffering in the defacing of his organ, had poured every ounce of pain into those eyes. Veiled, nearly on the verge of tears, but violently defiant, they dared the gaze they met to argue that life was not indeed cruel.

The circus arrived in Cacimar on June 12th. The municipal marching band greeted the caravan on the edge of town and escorted the troupe to the square. A crowd of children and adults, all of them singing and shouting, followed the costumed performers: trapeze artists, jugglers, tightrope walkers, magicians, fortune tellers, musicians, exotic dancers and, of course, clowns. Rockets were fired, dogs barked, birds were flushed from their nests and Popoto dressed in his baggy trousers and cape, his blue face and tear-dropped eyes macabre in the brilliant sunlight, pranced and gamboled merrily, taking pratfalls and threatening to water flowers atop people's heads.

The fact that the Flying Batatinis had joined the Gordils Circus for this tour of the island, pained Popoto immeasurably, for he still felt the twelve year old rejection by María de las Mercedes Batatini, now a world famous trapeze artist and wife of the equally famous El Alhazar, The Master of Moorish Magic, who was viewed by Popoto as a charlatan who relied on cheap tricks of the most meager prestidigitation, but who in Valladolid had once caused 388 doves to appear from his breast pocket handkerchief and in Segovia darkened the skies for a full three hours, and once in León, turned a man into a lion to honor that city, and in Córdoba made, not once or twice but three times, six children fly above the rooftops on a magic carpet and who, Popoto had learned from a whore, possessed the organ of a child, barely the circumference of a string bean, another fact to confirm for him the senselessness of life and to further provide undeniable proof that God did not exist and, if He did exist, was enjoying himself totally at his expense.

That evening after the rigging for the trapeze and the tightrope acts and the tents for the show had been erected in preparation for the opening of the celebration of the Feast of the Virgin of Perpetual Sorrows, Popoto wandered the cobblestoned streets of Cacimar cloaked in his profound desolation. He stopped in La Fonda Gallega, ordered a meal of steak and salad and rice and beans and drank two glasses of beer. Afterwards he sat back to smoke a cigar and drink rum. By ten o'clock that evening his desolation was so profound that he considered suicide. It was then that Radamés Uribe came and sat at his table and informed him that he knew of a fine looking woman on the edge of town who was so amorous that she could cure any ills.

Through the haze of rum Popoto looked at Uribe suspiciously.

"I thought that sort of thing didn't go on in this town," he said.

"It doesn't," said Uribe. "Not so you can notice. Are you interested?"

"It will cause nothing but trouble," Popoto answered. "Don't you know who I am?"

"Yes, you're with the circus."

"Yes, but I'm Filiberto Casablancas."

"Shh, don't say that word in here," said Uribe looking quickly behind him. "I only know that I see a man in need of an amorous woman. Come with me. It will only cost you a few coins. I promise that you won't regret it. She is young and willing. Believe me, you won't regret it."

"I always have," said Popoto sadly.

"Not this time," countered Uribe, grabbing his arm and helping him up. "This time you will leave your desolation with Rosa María. Trust me."

Popoto rose and followed Uribe out of La Fonda Gallega and through the streets, the air sweet and the sky filled with stars. They walked to the edge of town, past the shrine of the Virgin of Perpetual Sorrows where people had camped out and several bonfires lit the night, and to a small house on the edge of a field. A candle burned in the window and, as they approached, Popoto felt a huge ache which traveled from his groin upward and threatened to break his heart. Next to his thigh his organ strained to snap the thick leather thong which held it captive.

Uribe knocked once and there came to the door a plain, thin, hard looking peasant girl, her eyes filled with hatred. Uribe greeted her but she did not respond. He introduced Popoto and told him to leave his payment with her. Popoto nodded but he could see nothing but the body of a woman. He was beyond recognizing beauty and only wished release from his agony. When Uribe left, Popoto stood in the middle of the small two room house, paralyzed more by the fear of what would take place after he disrobed and the woman saw his organ than by the enormous amount of rum that he had consumed.

"Are you with the circus?" asked the woman.

"Yes, I am. Do you live here alone?"

"That is not your concern. Where is your money?"

Popoto went into his trousers, extracted several coins and held them out to her. She took them greedily and motioned to the inner room with her head. A candle burned in a dish.

"Your name is Rosa María, isn't it?" he said sadly as he entered the room, his voice trembling from the emotion of being with a woman.

"That's what they call me," she replied. "What of it!"

She removed her dress, revealing a body nearly devoid of distinguishing feminine physical characteristics. She lay on the bed and whispered hoarsely for him to undress. Popoto removed his shoes and stockings, his shirt and then his pants. He unstrapped the belted leather thong and immediately his organ let out a long sorrowful whistle which made Rosa María sit up on the bed.

"What was that?" she said. "You're not one of those whistling farters, are you?"

"No, I'm not."

"Then what was that? I heard it. Is it a circus trick?"

"It was nothing," Popoto replied. "I'm sorry. Please close your eyes."

"I will not," said Rosa María firmly.

"Please, I won't hurt you."

The urgency and sadness in Popoto's voice touched Rosa María momentarily and, muttering a curse, she agreed. Popoto approached the bed, fighting his organ at every moment. He lay down next to Rosa María and asked her not to be frightened, explaining quickly that whatever happened it was not his intention to hurt her, but that what he had between his legs was monstrous. Rosa María laughed heartily.

"Every man likes to think that he is a horse," she said, positioning herself to receive him. "Please don't concern yourself with my discomfort and commence your filthiness. I am very tired and desire to sleep. Do you wish me to blow out the candle?"

"Yes, perhaps darkness would be best, but you should know that I'm not like other men," Popoto said.

"Oh, you're not?" said Rosa María sarcastically. "Then I will not blow out the candle. I wouldn't miss something like that for silver or gold."

"I am speaking the truth," said Popoto firmly.

"Yes, yes," said Rosa María, boredom dripping from her voice. "Come in and tell me about it, but quickly. I'll even close my eyes as you wished," she added, placing both hands over her eyes.

Popoto became infuriated and taking his organ in his hands, pulled back on it and knelt between Rosa María's legs.

"All right, open your eyes and feast on true filth," he said.

What next took place has had many versions over the years but none is more descriptive in detail than the one recorded privately by the Captain of the Guard of the Village of Cacimar in his diary. By that account, the night was pierced by the most horrifying scream he had ever heard. Within the scream there was an eerie whistling which set dogs howling and cocks crowing as if it were morning. The next day the hibiscuses, roses, marguerites, jasmines and lilies in all the gardens of the town had wilted and earthworms appeared everywhere as if they had poured from the heavens despite it not having rained the previous night. The screaming went on and on and the whistling grew louder until the soldiers burst into the house as Popoto was climbing out the window. They managed to grab him and dragged him off into the field in back of the house where they beat him and kicked him until their fists and feet were sore. When Popoto was a bloody mess and moans no longer issued from his tortured body, thinking that he had expired, they threw him into pile of pig manure.

He lay unconscious in the pig manure nearly two hours before he finally came to. Severely bruised and barely able to move, he determined to leave Cacimar as soon as he could.

What the Captain of the Guard found and heard in Rosa María's bedroom left him impotent for life. The woman was sitting up on the bed totally naked and in shock, repeating over and over that she couldn't believe what she had witnessed. Her face and hair were caked by Popoto's viscous seed, her entire chest coated with the now dry ejaculation. The Captain felt as if he had been plunged into the depths of the sea and was drowning. Holding a handkerchief to his face to ward off the powerful stench, he stepped forward to question the young woman.

"Please tell me what transpired here in your domicile tonight," he said.

"Who wants to know?" she replied, angrily. "Who are you? I can't see you, the bastard's blinded me with his filth. Who are you? Answer me!"

"I'm Leonardo Camacho, the Captain of the Guard. What happened?"

Rosa María began screaming again and Captain Camacho called for two of his men. When they arrived he told them to take Rosa María out of the house to the rain barrel and wash her. The two men looked at the naked woman, looked at each other, shrugged their shoulders and moved to the bed. When Rosa María felt their hands on her arms she began screaming again. The Captain reassured her that she was not blind and they simply wished her to wash her face. Rosa María calmed down and the men took her outside.

Left alone in the room with the candle nearly extinguished, the Captain inspected the room in the failing light. What he next saw made him so angry that he drew his sword and went searching for the culprit himself. Above the headboard of Rosa María's bed was a foot square, scarlet, padded embroidery of the Sacred Heart of Jesus, he learned subsequently, done over a period of more than a year by Rosa María's mother. The heart emitted a powerful incandescence which made the Captain grow closer. He lit a match and held it up to the embroidery. Popoto's massive ejaculation had reached the padded cloth, coating it unevenly so that it seemed opaque in the places it had been defiled. What shocked the Captain into impotence was the distance which the seminal fluid had traveled to reach the embroidery. By his calculations the powerful stream had to have traveled more than six feet at an almost ninety degree angle to hit the heart.

When his men returned with Rosa María, who was still complaining of not being able to see clearly, the Captain asked his men to wait outside the house and then, after urging her to get dressed, he questioned her extensively. She swore that the man who had been in her house had the organ of a horse, but that the size had been of no importance since she could handle even something like that. What had truly frightened her was that she was convinced for a moment that the man did not really have an organ but was accompanied by an elf and was about to force the *duende* into her.

"And then he let go with his filthiness," she said. "It was like being scalded with oil. I doubt that I will ever fully regain total vision. And the smell was awful and foul."

"Yes, I know," the Captain said. "Like putrefaction."

"Exactly."

The Captain and the prostitute talked for nearly two hours, at the end of which the Captain vowed to find the criminal and kill him for his infamous crime. He said goodbye to Rosa María, went outside, spoke with his men and together they went into the field to search for Popoto, whom the soldiers had reported was quite dead.

"We must be sure," the Captain said.

Popoto had come to a half hour earlier and with great difficulty he began walking out of the field, hobbling away from the prostitute's house and toward a distant structure around which there burned the last vestiges of two bonfires. Whatever he did he must reach the circus and explain to Jordi Gordils what had taken place. Gordils knew of his problem and would help him. He was convinced that he would certainly be killed if the soldiers found him again. When he had almost reached the edge of the first dying bonfire, he heard voices in the distance, one voice urging the others on. With each step his body ached more and more and he almost gave up and allowed himself to sink to the ground. But he went on, hoping with all his might that whoever lived in the house would take pity on him. The voices grew closer and he pushed on in the dark, slamming into trees and tripping over bushes. As he grew closer to the house he saw a candle burning in the window and he regained some hope. Whoever lived there was awake. He wouldn't have to shout.

When he reached the house, he knocked on the door and in a whisper called out for help. The Captain and the soldiers were no more than forty feet behind the house when the door opened and Sor Barbara Almendros, up early to begin her morning prayers, opened the door and gasped at the sight of Popoto's bloody and swollen face. Popoto, upon seeing the nun, was reminded of the siren Caterina and grabbing his organ so that it did not whistle, stumbled inside and fainted. Sor Barbara pulled him further inside and closed the door.

Fighting the overpowering stench of the pig manure which clung to his clothing, she dragged the unconscious Popoto out of the front room, through her kitchen and with little effort, since she was young and healthy and Popoto was slight of body, got him up on her bed. But there appeared to be a stronger smell present and it puzzled her. An extremely perceptive young woman, she immediately deduced that he had been drinking and had eaten codfish that evening. But how had the smell of codfish remained on him for so long and how was it able to overpower the stench of pig manure? This was most odd. Had he spilled food on himself? Perhaps in his drunkenness he had done just that.

A minute later there was again a knocking at her door. She drew a curtain across her bedroom entrance and with candle in hand opened the door.

"Please be so kind as to excuse our imprudence, Sister," said the Captain, detecting immediately the stench of pig manure.

"It is no imprudence at all, sir," said Sor Barbara. "I am up early to begin my prayers. How may I help you?"

In the candlelight the young nun's face looked radiant and more beautiful than ever. The Captain, a secret admirer, who often went out of his way to pass the shrine in the hope of seeing Sor Barbara, stared ecstatically at the face for a moment. Unlike other times he did not feel the slightest bit of desire. Instead, he felt repugnance at the sight of such perfect beauty. The men behind him shifted around to get a better look at the nun. The Captain coughed.

"We're looking for a man. He's committed a most serious crime, one which has not only defiled womanhood but the Holy Mother Church and all it stands for. Have you seen a man about?"

Sor Barbara smiled kindly and shook her head.

"No one has come here tonight," she said. "Have you checked around the bonfires near the shrine?"

"No, we haven't yet done so, Sister," the Captain replied. "We only wished to warn you. He's a foul, dangerous man. We believe he is with the circus."

"You are the only ones to have come to my door tonight," Sor Barbara said. "Will you please excuse me. I must pray. It will be light soon. May God go with you."

"One more thing, Sister," the Captain said.

"Yes, of course."

"Do you keep a pig?"

"Why, yes I do. He's being fattened for the feast of the Nativity to feed the less fortunate of the town."

"Thank you, Sister," said the Captain. "Good night."

Sor Barbara closed the door and through the window watched the soldiers make their way past the shrine and head for the embers which had been the bonfires. Her heart beat wildly now and instinctively she seemed to know that this man who had come to her would play an important part in her religious development. What foul crime had he committed against the Church? What an odd idea. What were human beings if not sinners? Who needed salvation more than those who were lost?

She returned to her bedroom, held the candle above Popoto's face and shuddered. The swollen and disfigured features, the nose slightly askew, eyes and lips swollen, blood caked where steel-tipped boots had cut into the skin produced in the young nun an outpouring of compassion such as she had never felt. Turning quickly away she drew the curtain aside and went into the kitchen to boil water and take an inventory of her medical supplies.

The man was badly hurt and she must heal him. It was her duty and responsibility. Of what use was healing someone's soul if the body ached? She must wash him and help him rest his body. If he had committed a foul crime against the Church, his soul was in mortal danger. Punishment was not the answer. Christ himself had suffered enough for us, so there was no need to punish man for his weaknesses. Her mission was to save human beings from suffering, not to aid in their punishment. She loved the Church and knew her position was a rebellious one, but the Inquisition was a travesty of the basic teachings of Christ.

Not waiting for the water to boil, she carried the kettle back into the bedroom, opened her medical kit and began ministering to Popoto. She did not once consider the nakedness that would be produced by removing the man's clothes, nor were there sinful thoughts in her pure mind. Gently, she washed his face and applied salve to the swelling. She then removed his shoes and stockings, unbuttoned his shirt, turned him over and removed his shirt. Popoto moaned but did not wake up. As she prayed she washed his entire back, swabbed it with witch hazel and applied unguent.

When she was done with his back she turned him back over. It was then that she noticed the enormous bulge in his trousers.

Alarmed at the enormity of the swelling, she panicked momentarily. Her medical skills were far too limited to deal with such an injury. Not once was there any connection in her mind between the apparent swelling and the man's sexual anatomy. Those thoughts had never entered her mind, and although she had briefly glimpsed the sexual organs of farm animals and stray dogs, she was certain that men as well as women had been created equally in God's image. Men, as well as women, she thought, undoubtedly possessed the same type of anatomy. The only distinguishing characteristics between the two were facial hair on men and breasts on women, the latter simply to nourish the newborn.

She touched the swelling gingerly and Popoto moaned again. He must truly be hurt, thought Sor Barbara. She unbuckled his belt, carefully undid the buttons on his pants and then became more fully aware of the pungent seminal smell which she quickly identified with advanced infection, as she had been taught at the convent. So it had not been codfish that she had detected after all. She must work more quickly to stem off further progress of the putrefaction. Did she have sulfuric unguent? She checked quickly. Yes, there was still some. She turned Popoto on his side, and sliding her hand under his hip, tugged at the pants and undergarment until she had removed both, avoiding any notice of his meager buttocks.

When she turned him over, ready to inspect the source of the swelling and possible illness, Sor Barbara Almendros y Vizcarrondo nearly fainted from the shock. Staring at her with utter contempt was Popoto's organ, the prepuce retracted and the organ slightly tumescent. She swooned momentarily and stared unbelievably at the silver-green enormity before her. What did this mean? Other than the largeness of the breasts on a woman, men were no different than she. Her medical training at the convent had not included such phenomena. What had happened to this man? How had this aberration occurred? Had God a part in this? And if so, what was the divine reason for such an abnormality? Were all men like this? Was Father Barrientos? Her own father? The saints? Christ? Was man truly made in God's image? And if so, was God such as this man? Impossible.

Popoto moaned once more and his organ moved. He opened his eyes, looked momentarily at Sor Barbara, thought Caterina the mermaid had appeared to him and that perhaps he had died, and his eyes rolled back into his head and he passed out again. Sor Barbara looked once more at the swelling and a weak, painful whistle issued forth from the organ. What did it mean? Was this a gastric disorder? Had this man's intestines escaped through an opening in his torso? She had never read of anything such as this. She was fascinated by the green-silvery skin of Popoto's organ and horrified by the mocking face, the malevolent smile and eyes suggestive of she knew not what. She noticed a few bruises but no apparent sign of putrefaction. There was no doubt, however, that what she smelled were signs of advanced illness, perhaps a gangrenous condition. Did she have the courage to lance the growth, to amputate the malignancy?

She reopened the jar of sulfuric unguent and began gently to apply the medicine to Popoto's organ with her fingers. This made Popoto moan loudly and within minutes, to the young nun's surprise, the organ had grown even larger and was pointing at the ceiling, pulsating in quick even spasms as Popoto repeatedly called out Caterina's name and moaned as if he were in pain, his hips alternately undulating and thrusting forward. Sor Barbara was now on the edge of hysteria, her kind heart filled with Christian concern for this very sick man. Was he about to have an attack of some sort, a seizure? In attempting to calm him, she grasped the organ firmly in her right hand, and under the mistaken belief that she would do well to return the wayward growth back into the abdominal cavity, she pushed downward. Popoto emitted a powerful moan, the bed shook mightily and his organ produced another weak whistle. Once again his seed escaped in rapid and powerful spurts, barely missing the nun's face and splattering the wall of her bedroom. This was most amazing. Quite apart from the odd appearance and behavior of this man, her own heart was beating strangely, her face was quite warm and her underpants felt as if she had wet them.

Within seconds the room was filled with the stench of decayed fish. There was no doubt. The putrefaction was within the man and her ministrations were bringing out the desired effect of ridding him of the poison. This filled Sor Barbara with a great deal of satisfaction and she prayed in thanks that she was able to help the unfortunate Popoto, who was now sleeping soundly, his swollen and disfigured face seemingly more at ease. At least whatever had been paining him had subsided and the swelling on the strange protuberance in his groin had diminished considerably. She finished applying salve to his legs and then covered him with a sheet, closed her medical bag, and getting up from the bed, wiped the wall with a rag, went quickly outside, burned the soiled rag and washed her hands.

She knelt down and prayed fervently but her mind would not remain on her thoughts. She asked for forgiveness but even then all she could do was see the odd, sneering face of Popoto's organ and the spurting putrefaction. What did it mean? And why was she so drawn to the strangeness? The sun came up and she hurried outside to tend to her animals. On the other side of the fence women were already lining up to pray at the shrine, their faces marred by the torment of their pain. What was she to do with the man? She could not turn him over to the authorities. She would have to keep him there until he was well enough to travel and then she would help him escape. Until then he would be treated as having sought asylum from the Church. The Church was after all supreme in these matters.

She worked feverishly through the morning, tending to the self-inflicted wounds of women who had lost all hope. Nearly a hundred women knelt at the shrine daily, reciting Hail Marys repeatedly hour upon hour, beating their breasts and crying torrents of sorrow. By noon, Sor Barbara was spiritually exhausted and yet her body tingled strangely and her every thought centered on the well being of the man now lying on her bed.

She went to the chicken coop and collected a half dozen eggs, entered the house and checked on her patient. He was still asleep, part of his body revealed where the sheet had slipped off him. She returned to the kitchen and began preparing an omelet. When she was done she returned to the room and attempted to wake Popoto. She was extremely eager to find out how she had fared with her ministrations, but decided to wait until her patient was fed.

"Sir, please wake up," she said, touching Popoto's arm.

After several attempts, Popoto slowly opened his swollen eyes and peered at the woman before him. When he was able to focus he stared at her for a brief moment and then closed his eyes and shook his head violently.

"I'm dead," he said. "It can't be, it can't be," he added. "I thought I had dreamt it, but it's true."

"Calm yourself, sir," Sor Barbara said. "You are not dead but you've had a dreadful time. Please open your eyes. Are you hungry? I have made an omelet and I think you should eat. Please open your eyes."

Popoto slowly opened his eyes. What he saw was too unbelievable. How had a mermaid become a nun? Because there was no doubt about what he was seeing. His body hurt immensely but his mind was quite clear. Before him, sitting on the bed, was Caterina the mermaid, except that her eyes resembled a sunset and Caterina's eyes had been the palest blue, almost colorless, as if being underwater had bleached them. But there was no mistaking the face. There was no doubt in his mind as to her identity, even beneath the habit. What was happening to him? If he wasn't dead, what was going on?

"You're a nun," he said.

"Yes, I am. Are you hungry?"

Popoto shrugged his shoulders. He was hungry but the puzzle before him concerned him much more. And had he dreamt of making love to Caterina? It had all been so real.

"You're a very sick man," Sor Barbara said. "And in considerable trouble. The authorities came here last night looking for you. You must eat."

"All right, if you insist," Popoto replied. She was hiding him, then. But why? It had to be the business with the whore. He now recalled the soldiers and how mercilessly they had beat him. It didn't matter. What troubled him was how Caterina had become a nun. Were mermaids Catholic? Were there churches beneath the sea?

Sor Barbara stood up, left the room and within minutes had returned to the room with a tray of food: a green pepper, onion and potato omelet, freshly baked bread, salad and wine.

"Here we are," she said, happily. "Tonight I will make a fine soup with vegetables and a freshly killed chicken. How would you like that?"

"Thank you very much, Sister," Popoto replied. He hated the Church, but if Caterina was in its service he could tolerate its idiocy. He had never forgotten Caterina and now she was here, more beautiful than ever. He strained over the bed to see the bottom of Sor Barbara's habit, half expecting to see the fish tail, but fell back on the bed and let out a cry of pain. "Is your name Caterina?" he said, gasping for breath.

"No, it is Barbara Almendros," she said. "Last night, in your delirium you called this very woman's name. Is she your wife?"

"Unfortunately, I am not married," Popoto said.

Sor Barbara's heart tumbled strangely inside her chest. Her hand went to her face, as if grooming herself. She felt lightheaded and all at once she had the urge to examine her patient.

"You must eat before the food gets cold," she said, nervously.

He made an attempt to rise but fell back on the bed, the pain attacking him anew. Sor Barbara placed the tray on the night table near the bed and began feeding him. Now that he had tasted the food, he ate hungrily, his jaw and face hurting from the soldiers' blows but he taste of the wholesome food nevertheless overpowering the pain. As she fed him, Sor Barbara attempted to learn what great crime he had committed against the Church, but Popoto was reluctant to talk about it. He would never dare to make love to a woman again, and then he became aware that beneath the sheet he was naked and that his organ could at any minute begin whistling and this poor and saintly young woman would be horrified. But what the hell was he talking about? What kind of hypocrisy had he fallen prey to?

"Why were the authorities so interested in you?" she said.

"It was nothing, Sister," he said. "Nothing of great concern to you. These are strange times. Any breach of the law is attributed to offenses against the Church."

"Yes, these are trying times, but our town is a most upright one and rarely charges people for minor infractions. Are they fabricating these things for ulterior motives?"

"That is possible, Sister. But I'm curious. What made you take pity on me? Aren't you risking your position?"

"You were hurt. I have been trained to care for the sick, the wounded and the infirm. And in answer to your second question, the Church is empowered to extend its help to anyone and offer asylum to those in need. What is your name?"

"I am called Popoto. I am with the circus. A clown. A painful and unrewarding profession."

At mention of the word clown, Sor Barbara smiled innocently.

"I love clowns," she said, in a child-like voice. "When I was a little girl my father always took me to the circus and I loved the clowns. Do you juggle?"

Popoto shook his head.

"No, I don't. I simply wander around skipping and falling and making out of the ordinary the ridiculous. I carry a water can, but no matter what flowers I water, they die."

The sadness in Popoto's voice felt as if someone had taken a knife and stabbed her in the heart.

"Do you love Christ?" was all she could think of saying.

"No," he said, taking a long draught of the wine. "I have never held much belief in religion. I see no order in the world to indicate that it is of any more importance than my clowning."

"From the way you speak, you have evidently read considerably," Sor Barbara said.

"Some, but not nearly enough to make sense of the world."

"You need not worry. All of it is God's doing. I have also read some but have come to the conclusion that certain things are God's design and no one else's. Only He understands them. Would you like some more omelet?"

"No, thank you," Popoto said, holding up his hand. "I am quite full. Are my clothes available?"

Sor Barbara explained that they had been washed and were now drying in the kitchen.

"I did not dare hang them outside for fear that the soldiers would see them and report this to the priest. They cannot enter this house to harm you, but it is best that they do not learn of your presence. Let me tend to these dishes and I will come back and treat your swellings."

In a few moments she returned with her medical bag and a basin of water and began gently washing his face and applying salve to his cuts and bruises. Popoto watched her beautiful, slender fingers at once strong and feminine and a languor overtook his body. The more he looked at her the more beautiful she became.

"Please turn over," she said.

He did as she asked and she treated his back before asking him to again face her.

"There is a major infection in your abdominal area," she said. "I have never seen or read of anything quite like it."

Popoto was perplexed by her words.

"An infection?" he said. "I wasn't aware of any infection."

"Oh, yes. A rather virulent one. I treated it last night and a good deal of the putrescence was released. Have you had the condition long?"

"What condition?" he said, growing more alarmed.

"The growth."

"Growth?"

"Yes, it is as if your intestines had escaped from your abdomen."

There was an interminable pause and then it was as if the room had been bathed in brilliant light as they both realized what had taken place. He, that somehow in her innocence she had seen his organ, touched him and perhaps even caused him to release his seed which must have been why he thought he'd dreamt that he was making love to Caterina. She, on the other hand, had an enormous philosophical realization. Her prayers had been answered and she had come face to face with the Serpent, attached to this sad, tormented man. The dream in which the Devil in the form of the Serpent had appeared to her and spit on her face was now a reality. She had met the Devil and now she would fulfill her promise of converting him to the true faith.

"Sister, I must leave here at once," Popoto said. "Please forget anything you may have seen last night."

"You cannot leave. It is out of the question," she said, firmly. "Your infection is far more serious than I thought."

"Please, Sister," he said. "I have no infection. Please believe me. These are things which a sister of the Church should not witness. As much dislike as I have for the Church, I have no wish to soil the purity of its womanhood."

Purity? thought Sor Barbara. It was he that was pure. She was overcome with gratitude for being able to witness a mortal soul struggle with the forces of evil. Even with the Devil attached to him, he was still able to exhibit nobility and defend the honor of womanhood. Her heart expanded and for the first time in her life she felt boundless love. The feeling seemed to extend from the middle of her being and take in all of creation. Such, she imagined, must have been the love of Christ for all of humanity. She must convert the Devil and release all of God's children from suffering. But how?

"Have you had this condition long?" she said.

Popoto's face reddened and he looked away.

"Let us not discuss this matter further," he said. "I beg you, Sister. It is a topic which should not be discussed by religious persons."

"Please do not be concerned, Señor Popoto," countered Sor Barbara. "All subjects are God's doing and there is nothing of God which is not the concern of the Church. Your condition is most serious. Answer me now! Did this condition come upon you recently or have you suffered it long?"

Her insistence angered Popoto. Was she no better than a common whore! She was no different than any other woman. If that was so, he would shock her beyond anything she could have imagined. What did he care. He was in enough trouble as it was.

"Sister, what I have to tell you may affect your nerves," he said.

"Do not concern yourself with my nerves," she said.

Popoto looked at her beautiful face and felt a great desire to relieve her of her virginity, if she was indeed a virgin, since she was behaving like a common harlot.

"I have had this condition since I was a child," he said.

Sor Barbara's eyes opened up in disbelief.

"Oh, you poor, poor man," she said, reaching to take his hand. "Then the Devil attacked you at birth."

"The Devil?"

"Yes," she said, pointing at the bulge under the sheet. "It cleaved to you as soon as you entered the world."

He was ready to agree, but all at once he felt as if he were walking on the beach back in the Canary Islands and that, if he walked to the cove of his boyhood, he would find Caterina waiting for him and once again he would experience love and hear his mermaid sing and the waves would stop and his heart would no longer ache as it did. He couldn't go on with the charade. She was truly an innocent and it would serve no purpose to take advantage of her.

"Sister, I must reveal something of which you may have no knowledge. All men, my dear Sister, have such appendages. Some unlucky ones have tiny ones which resemble a child's finger, others more fortunate have normal apparatuses . . ."

"Apparatuses?" she said, looking confused. "I don't understand. Is that what they're called?"

"Yes, that is what they're called," he replied. "Apparatuses, although they are given many names."

"For instance?" she said, peering into his face to make sure that he was telling the truth.

"It is not important," he said.

"You are wrong. It is very important. I wish to acquaint myself thoroughly with this matter. Please."

Popoto thought a moment and then shook his head several times.

"I cannot," he said.

"Please," she said. "You are in great danger and you must let me help you."

"Very well," he said reluctantly, already feeling the embarrassment. "Every male, whether animal or man, possesses this apparatus, this curse. It is called variously a stake, a club, a mace, a sword, a lance, a musket, even a sausage."

This made Sor Barbara laugh and her face reddened.

"A sausage?" she repeated, and laughed once more.

"Yes, a sausage."

"I am very sorry," she said. "I suppose you're right, but the thought produces laughter in me. I must be more serious. Go on."

"You're not alone," Popoto said, said somberly. "The entire matter is conducive to laughter."

She composed herself and then thought for a moment.

"It is hard to imagine that all men have this growth, this appendage," she said, after a while. "But you called it a curse, why is that?"

"It's very simple," Popoto said. "It makes otherwise good and sane men behave crazily in their desire for women."

"For women?" she said, suddenly alarmed.

"Yes, for women."

"Whatever for?"

"To use them."

"Now I've heard everything! Don't women do enough as it is? What more could men want from them? They cook, they sweep, they wash, iron and mend clothes. They bear children, take care of them and of animals. They plow, seed, weed, gather, haul. What more could men want? Please clarify this for me."

"Please, Sister."

"Tell me. What is this thing that men want from women?"

"I cannot tell you that, Sister," Popoto insisted. "It is a great ugliness which young women such as yourself should not hear. Even if you were not of the Church it would be an impropriety for me to speak of these things and soil your innocence."

"But I wish to know," she said. "It is my right to know these things. Women come to me every day tormented by their lives. And in any case, how am I to help if charges are brought up against you! If you wish to further endanger your life I will not be part of it. I cannot force you to be honest, but please understand that my curiosity is simply a religious one. Let me understand clearly what you're saying. You say that all men have this appendage?"

"Yes."

"Are there men with more than one?"

Popoto shook his head violently as if the thought was too painful.

"No, not that I know of."

"And do they come in different colors or are they all like yours?"

"No, certainly not like mine."

"But it varies in size from man to man?"

"Yes, that is correct. Unfortunately, I was born with a monstrosity of an apparatus. It is too large for women and therefore they shun me as if I were myself a monster. Sister, I confess this to you. To me, women are the most beautiful beings in nature. Even those who are not attractive to look at hold something precious within them. I would give anything to share my life with a woman, but no woman has ever wished this. The ones with whom I've shared moments recoil when they see my nakedness."

The words poured out of him in a torrent, the emotion cascading over her so that she felt his every pain. Tears came to her eyes and she nearly swooned from the emotion. Her heart expanded further and she felt waves of pleasurable love emanating from the depths of her being. This is how Christ must have felt upon seeing human suffering, she thought. She knew the Devil had tried to overpower this man's soul, but he was steadfast in his resolve to retain his nobility.

"Tell me something," she said. "Do these, what shall I call them? Yes, apparatuses. These apparatuses, do they have faces such as there is on yours?"

"No, they don't," he said, with absolute certainty that no man would have dared undergo the pain he had. "At least, it is doubtful."

"Aha! And are these apparatuses sometimes called serpents?"

"Yes, but how did you know this? I had forgotten, or perhaps wished to spare you further unpleasantness."

"So they are called serpents?"

"Yes, *the* Serpent in fact."

"Aha!" she said once more. "*The* Serpent. It is just as I had suspected. I know you have told me several names, but does this so called apparatus go by any other name. Please tell me everything."

Popoto thought a moment.

"Does the name Filiberto mean anything to you?"

"No, not at all. It is a Christian name. There was a cabinet maker in my town by the name of Filiberto Barrientos, but he moved away. Why do you ask?"

"No reason," he said, shuddering at mention of the name. "Sometimes things pop into my head. No reason at all. I'm very sorry."

"That's quite all right. And only yours has this face?" "Yes, Sister. As far as I know I am the only who has such an atrocity."

"Uhm! Please explain."

"I am quite ashamed of this, but a gypsy performed a . . ."

Upon hearing the word 'gypsy, she cut him off.

"A gypsy?"

"Yes, I was despondent . . ."

"Aha!," she said once more, no longer listening to him, but having answered a question which had been troubling her since she vowed to meet the Devil and convert him to the faith in order to rid humanity of evil. "Gypsies, the Devil's own handymen," she said, resolutely. "You need say no more."

Her eyes appeared transfixed, distant, beatific, her golden complexion shining with an inner glow causing Popoto to feel a monumental desire welling up in his groin. In a moment his organ would begin whistling and he wouldn't know what he'd do. He watched the front of Sor Barbara's habit rise and fall, her full breasts rounded and firm and he wished he were dead. In order to quell his desire all he could do was think of the beating he had received at the hands of the soldiers. Thinking about the previous evening made his entire body ache anew and his organ quiescent.

"One thing puzzles me?" she said, coming out of her trance. "You have not answered why it is that men so desire women? I know that there is love between men and women, but that it is given mutually and it is necessary in God's eyes. Please explain."

"There is nothing to explain, Sister," Popoto replied. "You must know what happens in order for women to have children."

"Yes, of course, women are blessed with children because of God's grace."

"But don't you know how this happens?"

"It is a miracle," she said, innocently.

"Well, yes . . . but . . ."

"But, what?"

"I cannot tell you."

"You must, you must. If it is so important, then you must tell me. If not for myself, then for the hundreds of women who come here daily seeking release from their torment."

"I'm sure they know."

"How can they, if I, a woman dedicated to God's work, do not. You're being unjust and I demand to know."

"All right, I will tell you everything," Popoto said, angrily. "But it is likely that you will not believe a word of what I'm saying and, even if you do, you will hate me for robbing you of your innocence."

"I am prepared to undergo any trial to learn this. If it will help others relieve their suffering, I am willing to sacrifice anything."

Popoto shook his head despairingly and looked pityingly at the beautiful Sor Barbara. What had possessed such a beautiful creature to seek a religious life? Was she a saint? She was certainly an angel. Her eyes were half closed and small beads of perspiration had collected on her upper lip. Every so often she let out a small breath and the delicate wings of her nostrils flared slightly . What lips she had! Slightly opened now, they reminded him of luscious, ripe, summer strawberries, cool and sweet to the taste.

"Dear Sister, I am not a religious man, but I am certain I am committing a mortal sin in telling you these things. This appendage which men have, this apparatus, as it were, hungers for the innards of women."

"The innards?," she said, grimacing.

"Please forgive me," Popoto said, shaking his head. "I cannot go on."

"Oh, you must not spare me. I will be brave," she said, setting her shoulders, straightening her back and in the process making her breasts more pronounced behind the black habit. "Continue."

"All that it thinks about, this foul beast, is entering women to deposit its seed. That is how women become pregnant with child."

"Seed? Child? What seed? How did children come into this?"

"A fluid shoots forth from the apparatus and within it is the seed which produces life in the woman."

"That is preposterous! What causes this fluid to emerge?"

"Passion, Sister. Untamed, unbridled, animal passion which makes the blood boil, the head spin and the heart ache for the touch of a woman. The apparatus grows and pulsates and wants to enter a woman."

"But how? That is impossible," she said, casting a glance down at the sheet beneath which Popoto's organ lay as would a cat awaiting a mouse, ready to pounce on its helpless victim. "Does a man cut a woman in order to enter her?" The question puzzled her and then she recalled overhearing a conversation which her mother had with a neighbor when she was a child. They had spoken of blood on the wedding night and how the woman had gone over to her daughter's house and how difficult it had been to remove the blood from the wedding sheets. She had always thought it was blood such as appeared from her each month, but now she knew that it was different blood. This was what men did to women in order to enter them. "Oh, that is too horrible," said Sor Barbara, bursting into tears. "No wonder my poor women suffer so much. Men mutilate them. No wonder men are so attached to knives and swords and call their apparatus by those names. Oh, my poor women," she wailed. "My poor defenseless women. Every time men want to they cut them and they bleed."

Popoto looked helplessly on.

"No, it is nothing like that, Sister. Men do not cut women. It happens naturally. The blood only happens when a woman has not had a man enter her before."

Sor Barbara stopped crying suddenly and looked at him in great wonder. How could this be? If men did not cut women, how were they able to get their apparatus into them. Even if they were not as this man before her, it seemed an impossibility. Aha, she thought. She had it. A knowing smile came over her face and she nodded happily.

"I understand perfectly," she said. "I know exactly what happens."

"You do?" said Popoto, now equally perplexed by the change in her expression.

"Yes," said Sor Barbara, opening her mouth and pointing at it.

"What?"

"The women swallow the man's seed . . ."

"Stop, stop!" he nearly shouted. "What are you saying! Do not repeat such a blasphemy. I implore you, be still!"

"I will not," she said, resolutely. "I now understand perfectly. It makes absolute sense. The men put their apparatus in the woman's mouth, release their seed, the seed travels down the alimentary canal and when it reaches the woman's belly she is with child."

Popoto shuddered. He had heard of such things being done by French women, but could not imagine what sort of woman would subject herself to such an indignity. The French were true pigs, there was no doubt about it.

"No, nothing like that takes place. How could you think of such a thing? Men are brutish, but we can also be gentlemen and when it comes to lovemaking we do our best to ease a woman's pain."

"Lovemaking? What are you talking about! I am totally confused. First you tell me that the apparatus is introduced into a woman, but not in the mouth and then you talk about lovemaking. This is madness. Are you sure about all of this?"

"Oh, yes. Very sure."

"Then explain yourself."

"It happens when a man loves a woman."

"Oh, you mean what takes place when a young man wishes to marry a young woman and he goes and stands outside her window and speaks to her, or brings her a serenade and eventually he is allowed into the house if she so wishes and he is a desirable suitor, and as long as the mother or an aunt is in attendance while the young man and the young woman speak, and eventually the young man asks the father of the young woman for her hand in marriage?"

She said all of this very excitedly, her face becoming flushed and her eyes animated. Popoto closed his eyes patiently and shook his head.

"No, Sister, that is called courting. Lovemaking is different."

"I don't understand."

Popoto thought for a moment. How much longer would he be able to control himself. He was angry and the more he looked at her the more he wanted her. Did he dare hope to make love to such a beautiful creature. How his heart ached for her! He realized that what was taking place was quite remarkable. He was growing warm with desire and yet it was originating somewhere in his heart. He soon identified the feeling as the same one he'd had for Caterina, the mermaid, and for the treacherous María de las Mercedes Batatini, who had married that charlatan of a magician. This time he was doubly doomed. Not only was this love even more impossible but he stood a good chance of dying for it. It was at that moment that all that has been written and sung over the centuries depicting the Spanish as masters of romance overcame Popoto. He knew that if it was a question of death he need no longer worry. What was life without the pleasure of a woman! And a woman like this one was worth a hundred, nay a thousand deaths. He would have her or die.

"Lovemaking is a serious matter, dear Sister," he said, confidently. "One best left alone for it creates dangers which innocence cannot prevent."

Sor Barbara was stunned by the new tone in the clown's voice. The words reverberated inside of her.

"Explain yourself, Sir Clown," she said.

"It is best left alone," he said, again drawing back. "If you wish to turn me over to the authorities, please do so, but I will not under pain of death reveal anymore of this subject."

"Oh, cruel man," she cried. "So many lives are at stake and you have the answer and will not reveal it. Cruel, cruel man."

His heart throbbed with desire and love for her.

"It is best that way. I do not wish to hurt you."

His nobility made her heart ache and she cried quietly, hiding her face and turning away from him.

"You could not hurt me," she said, looking up slowly. "You are a kind man. Nothing you could do would ever hurt me. Please, tell me about lovemaking so that I may explain this to the women. I am sure they know nothing of it. You are no different than me. I know this now. We appear different, you a clown, me a nun, but our souls are quite alike. Don't you see that? I must tell you something. I have devoted myself to the service of God and I am willing to do anything to advance His reign here on earth. I have chosen this life and therefore receive His protection. But you, from the time of birth have been invaded by the Devil and have fought, retaining the nobility of your soul, thinking not of yourself but of others, in this instance me. I will explain something to you. What you call your apparatus, or more rightly *the* Serpent, is nothing but that very same beast which in the Garden of Eden corrupted Eve and made Adam aware of sin and therefore doomed them both to eternal damnation. My mission has been to meet the Devil and convert him to the true faith and therefore eradicate all evil from the earth. At every turn all that you have uttered is concern for my person and I am deeply grateful for this. I fear nothing that you may say to me or anything you may do in my presence."

She paused a moment, removed a handkerchief from a pocket of her habit and wiped her face. Popoto was suddenly taken aback. This was going to be harder than he'd thought. His conscience troubled him. She was making it so easy for him. She now thought his organ was the Devil. Well, she wasn't far from the truth. Or was it indeed, the truth? She went on, explaining about the dream she'd had the day before the circus had arrived in town and how the Devil in the form of a serpent had appeared to her and how similar his apparatus had looked to the serpent in her dream. She said she had been frightened when she was ministering to him, but she had been able to calm the serpent down instinctively, as it had been once again angry and attempted to spit on her. She laughed momentarily.

"I thought it was part of your intestine," she said. "You're right. I am rather innocent. But I learn quickly. Tell me more about lovemaking." She was happy again, her face radiant. "We know now that the curse of God upon man was to cleave the Serpent to him as a reminder of his sin. But now what you're saying is that this serpent has a constant desire to be inside of the woman and this makes perfect sense since Eve was the one who was originally enticed by the Devil in the form of the Serpent. It is nothing but God's reminder to women of her own sin. I am sure this is why she must suffer so much."

Popoto nodded and watched her smile and digest the information which her quick mind seemed to produce effortlessly. He had never been in the presence of such a brilliant and at the same time innocent woman. His heart expanded and contracted in prolonged rhythms which made his entire body feel as if no pain existed.

"One thing which is not so clear is the manner by which the serpent enters the woman?" she said, almost to herself. And then it was as if someone had stuck a sword at her back. She bolted upright and he knew she understood exactly how men entered women. Her face became very red and she immediately extracted her handkerchief and began wiping her forehead. "Oh, I see," she said, to herself. "Please excuse me, Sir Clown. It has grown late and I must pray and then tend to the women at the shrine. I will return tonight with your supper. Please rest."

And with that she exited from the room, carrying the tray of dishes, not looking back over her shoulder but hurrying and rather worried.

As I mentioned before, the public likes to think of writers as being daring and courageous, always on the point of the arrow, pricking society's balloons, prodding the collective conscience of the masses forward from its lethargy, battering the walls of institutionalism and much more. Such is not the case. Writers, for the most part, hide behind allegory, metaphor, structure and style. From there, they peek out and then like mischievous little boys toss firecrackers out at the unsuspecting public, frightening it momentarily until the public realizes it is only a boyish prank and laughs at the foolhardiness and innocence.

If the writer has an engaging smile and a harsh, disagreeable personality, he is given, much as a boy will be given candy or a few coins to quell his desire for attention, prizes and awards. Once in a while one of these writers will get carried away and toss not a firecracker but an entire stick of dynamite. When this happens the writer in all cases blows himself up along with the public and becomes a casualty. If this happens in a totalitarian society he is jailed, or worse. If, on the other hand, it takes place in a so called free society he is lionized and thus, because large felines are dangerous to the overall populace, he is caged and put on display. I have been put on display but I cannot say I have been lionized, for all that I have done is betrayed my people and their dreams and therefore, to coin a phrase, what can best be said of my caging and display is that I have been tabbified or worse, pussyfied.

You see, I am of the former category of writer, that is, timid and fearful of public disapproval. For example. In writing *The Conquest of Frucítifera Soto* I did not dare tell what took place between Popoto and the nun, Barbara Almendros. Instead I chose to employ a philosophical debate between the two of them in which Popoto develops the argument, based on the extensive writings of Ben Al Muhazim, the famed 15th century Moorish philosopher, to prove to Sor Barbara that as a social system the idea of a theistic religion robs the human being of freedom. Rather than a large sexual organ, in the novel I gave Popoto a keen, inquisitive mind, something quite rare these days.

Al Muhazim, the Moorish philosopher, had traveled extensively, was in contact with eastern scholars and philosophers and had access to the secret diaries of Marco Polo and others who had found their way to the Orient. He knew that rather than a supreme being there existed in the universe a law of causality, unfathomable and absolute in its strictness and that it was this law which governed what occurred on earth and that men in their haste to answer the unfathomable could only find a feasible explanation for creation by assigning a supreme being to that most unfathomable of tasks.

For many years Al Muhazim pondered and wrote, wrote and pondered until he was faced ultimately with the question of first cause. In both a theistic system and a system in which a law is absolute, the question still remained unanswered. How did it all come about? Did God initiate all of it? And if so, who created God? The answer to that question was a question in itself. God has always been. He is without beginning or ending. He is Alpha and He is Omega.

In the Eastern system, developed in India and through trade routes brought to China, and then to the rest of Asia, the law of causality which holds every human being responsible for all of his actions, including his own animation based on causes made in previous lives, even to the point of the choosing of his parents, the question of who created the Law needs also to be answered. The answer, however, is the same and so there exists no difference between the two systems in that respect. The Law has always been and will always be.

In both systems, argued Popoto, the devout is faced with the unfathomable as a driving force towards his or her ultimate enlightenment or salvation.

"Yes," said Sor Barbara, in her guise as Sister Fructífera Soto. "I follow your argument."

"With one distinct difference," said Popoto, who is called Calambre in the novel. "In the theistic model, be it that of the Christian, Jew or Moor,

God is the maker of all. The question is answered and the only thing the common man is left with is an anthropomorphic image of an all powerful being who rules at times benevolently, at times tyrannically, but always imponderably erratically, so that when natural disasters occur they become part of 'God's plan,' and when there is discord and strife among men, 'it is their doing,' since they have free will. This is at best a contradictory system, and at worst one which renders man guilt-ridden, in fear of divine punishment and therefore impotent to determine his destiny."

"And the Law?" asked Sor Barbara, leaning forward from her side of the fence which surrounded her yard and across which she and Popoto conducted their daily dialogue each afternoon before the evening's circus performance. "I see no difference, Sir Clown."

Popoto goes on to explain that the Law presents a similar predicament as to its origin, but that it is resolved by accepting that there is a law, impersonal and without either benevolence or malevolence.

"Just as there is day and night and there are seasons, there is also the Law, with its own rhythm. It is man's choice to be either in harmony with the Law or not. In either case his success or failure is totally dependent on the causes he makes. Whatever course he chooses he cannot blame anyone but himself. There is no pleading, begging or cursing some being as there is in the case of a theistic faith. Instead there is a growing understanding of the Law. Much as a child is educated to certain norms, a human being can be educated to observe the causes which he makes and the effects which he receives. In time if he truly wishes to live in rhythm with life, he will choose to make those causes which create harmony."

"Are you saying that life is impersonal, that there is no design?"

"No, I don't think so. There appears to be an order to things, but I don't think that we have the wisdom to fathom that order."

"Yes, of course. That is God's area of responsibility."

"No, it's a question that does not require an answer. That is how things are. There is no need to assign responsibility to anyone, including God. Man must learn to live in harmony with his surroundings."

And on it went like that for ten days until in the end the nun capitulates to the argument, leaves her order, moves to Spain, disguises herself as a man, becomes a Mason and returns to the town as Bartolomé Cordero Blanco, a newspaperman, who eventually founds the *Clarión*, a newspaper which champions free thought. The newspaper lasts only three years before Cordero Blanco, in reality Fructífera Soto, is shot coming out of a cafe down the street from the Municipal Hall for an editorial in which the *Clarión* advocates the abolition of the Catholic Church. Cordero Blanco's death causes an uproar, splitting the town into detractors and supporters, but more to the point causing a wave of wantonness such as had never been seen. At night it was sufficient to walk into a home where a woman was alone, for a man to be able to sate his desire. Some said it was the unusual amount of rain that had fallen, bringing with it bad humors which disagreed with women, but in the final analysis the town becomes infamous for its loose morals.

But none of the above took place other than my hometown of Cacimar becoming sexually loose and unconcerned with morality.

What really happened follows. That evening, after spending the afternoon tending to her women, Sor Barbara killed a chicken, chopped vegetables and made a rich stew. She cooked rice and boiled plantains and made a wonderful meal which she served on her small table in the kitchen.

The smells of cooking awakened Popoto from a long sleep. He felt quite rested and, although his body still ached, he felt a renewed energy and determination. Upon waking, his first thoughts were of Sor Barbara. As he lay on the bed he saw her face clearly, each feature lovely and enticing. She had placed his newly cleaned and ironed clothes on a chair near the bed and he now got dressed, ever conscious of the bulge in his trousers. He had lost the strap but it would not matter. He could control his desire. He must in order not to frighten her. When he was dressed he walked out of the room and toward the appetizing smells emanating from the kitchen.

"Oh, you're up," said Sor Barbara, immediately shaken by Popoto's presence. "Perhaps you should lie back down and rest. The food will be ready any moment."

"No, I'm fine. You're a wonderful nurse. Thank you."

The compliment unnerved her and she did not answer. All she had thought about that day was the Serpent, the apparatus, the Devil and how it entered women. She must experience this, but it seemed to her an impossibility. How could this be? How did women subject themselves to this thing?

She set the table and they sat down to eat. Popoto ate as he had never before. She in turn hardly touched any of the food and was having a difficult time looking at Popoto. Unusually open in talking to others, she found herself retreating into herself and becoming girlishly shy. Finally, after ladling a third helping of the chicken stew into Popoto's bowl, she set her shoulders and addressed him.

"I have prayed and have decided to learn all there is to know about this matter of men entering women. Somehow there is something which remains a mystery to me. I now realize how men enter women and feel thoroughly embarrassed that it had not occurred to me before now. Be that as it may, it must be a very painful thing for women. My only consolation is that this only takes place a few times in a woman's life, that is, in order for her to conceive."

Popoto looked dubiously at her and she was immediately aware of his reaction.

"Am I not correct in what I have stated?" she said.

"Yes and no. I hate to tell you this but that is exactly where the problem lies. A woman does become pregnant from a man entering her but there is such great pleasure in entering a woman that a man is not content in simply doing this once or twice. The beast, the Serpent, is ever hungry for a woman. He craves her day and night."

A look of distress came over Sor Barbara's face.

"Are you saying that a woman must undergo this torture more times than she has children? And that men draw pleasure from this tormenting of women?"

"Yes, but for some women it is not a torment."

"Impossible. How often does this take place? Monthly?"

"When a man is young it is said that he can enter a woman every hour or so each day."

Sor Barbara's face went immediately pale and she covered her face with her hands. Popoto nearly stood up and went over to her, such was his concern. What was he doing to this lovely creature? Was the Devil really operating in him?

"This cannot be," she said. "Poor, poor women. I have seen young men and women together and it all seemed so innocent. I had no idea. I have read of carnal sins but I merely thought these things had to do with greed and jealousy. I truly had no idea of the extent of Eve's transgression. For it was she who was initially tempted by the Serpent. I have been so utterly stupid about these things. Now I understand better what these women are saying. They say their bodies are tortured by something inside of them wishing to come out, and I tell them simply to pray, that it is the Devil tempting them and they cry and tear at their hair and breasts, writhing on the ground and calling the Lord's name. Please help me. I don't know what this is about. You, who have more contact with the Serpent, must help me with this problem. What must I do?"

Popoto watched her intently, wishing for all his life that he had not come to her house. What was he to do now? And then it occurred to him that all he needed to do was go along with her interpretation of what his organ represented.

"The Devil must not win," he said, calmly.

"I know, I know," she said. "But how are we to combat him?"

"There is only one way, Sister," he said. "It may be painful but there is only one way. We must render him helpless. Each time the Serpent rears its ugly head we must sate its desires and keep him dormant. I have been a fool in my rejection of the true faith. As long as we are pure in spirit I believe we can overcome the Devil."

"Oh, Sir Popoto, you don't know how happy this makes me. I did not want to ask this of you, but this afternoon during my prayers I decided that anything my poor women undergo I too must suffer. I did not know how to ask you this but I wish you to help me and have the Serpent enter me. It seems the only way to convert it and, as you say, sate its appetite. I understand more than ever my dream. Don't you see? I've had a revelation and you have been sent to me by God precisely so that I may fulfill His wishes in capturing the Devil and converting him to the faith. I know it will be painful, but I am willing."

Popoto looked at her tenderly and she lowered her eyes.

"Are you sure you are willing to subject yourself to this?" he said. "It may be very painful."

"I will pray. Please don't concern yourself. Why it is called lovemaking is becoming clearer and clearer. How could I have been so blind. Eve betrayed the Lord. The Serpent gave her the forbidden fruit, she ate of it and enticed Adam to do the same. While he ate the Serpent cleaved itself to Adam. Her destiny, to make amends for her transgression, has been to capture the Serpent and render it still so that it may not tempt others. And yet, I believe, we teach abstinence of this greatest of virtues. It is odious that the Church would prevent women from fulfilling this most sacred of tasks. Of course my women cry for release from their sorrows. They are being made to feel unclean for wishing to fulfill their sublime mission of capturing the Serpent. Oh, what a fool I've been! Now I see it all. At first I thought men wished to hurt women, but they are simply under the influence of the Serpent and it is women's holy mission to extinguish the evil fire in the Serpent. It is the only way that women can repay for their betrayal. Of course it would be called lovemaking! What greater labor of love is there than sacrificing oneself for the faith! Where does this lovemaking take place, Sir Clown?"

Popoto was overcome with emotion. Beneath the table his organ was rising as would a leviathan from the depths, its body gorged and ready. He held it down with his hand for fear that it would emit one of its horrid whistles and frighten Sor Barbara.

"It usually takes place in a bedroom," he said. "But it could be most anywhere. And I must tell you this. Usually, it is more easily accomplished if the people involved have no clothes on their bodies."

"Yes, of course," she said. "I understand perfectly. It is a replication, an enactment of the Garden of Eden. Everything fits so perfectly now, everything makes sense now that I've seen my error. We must begin immediately. Let me attend to these dishes and I will be there in a moment."

Popoto swooned at the prospect of making love to this beautiful creature. He stood up from the table, looked into the kitchen and with his hand firmly holding down his organ he returned to the bedroom. In a few moments Sor Barbara entered the room. In the candlelight the skin on her face shone with a remarkable incandescence. It was a glow which made her more radiant and enticing to Popoto. Her eyes, generally bright, now seemed on fire beneath the heavy lids of desire which had begun, unbeknownst to her, to build up inside her body.

"Is there anything I need to do?" she said.

"Yes," Popoto replied, the words catching in his throat. "Please remove all your clothing."

"Very well," answered Sor Barbara, and proceeded to undress.

She removed the tight headpiece and collar, letting her once luxuriant hair now cropped close to her head, show for the first time in several years. Rather than detract from her beauty, the shortened tresses added to her allure, making her high cheek bones more pronounced and therefore her eyes deeper and more exciting. Placing her headpiece and collar on a chair, she now began to unbutton her habit. As she did so she wore a look of profound confidence and delight, much as if she were deep in prayer. When she had finished undoing the last of the buttons she stepped out of the habit, folded it and placed it on the chair. She was now dressed in a long sleeved undergarment also buttoned to the neck but clearly outlining the shape of her incredibly beautiful body. Popoto's organ could no longer be restrained and it let out a mournful whistle which startled Sor Barbara.

She turned quickly and looked at Popoto, who explained that the Serpent was hissing and needed to be sated immediately.

"Please remove your shoes and the rest of your clothing," he said.

"Please, not my shoes," she said. "I am deeply ashamed of my feet," she added, bowing her head.

"There is no need for shame," he said, going to her and holding her in his arms. "You are a lovely woman, young and more beautiful than any woman I have ever seen."

"But my feet are so ugly," she said, almost inaudibly.

"No, no. That's not true," Popoto said, undoing the buttons of her undergarment and cupping one of her lovely breasts. "You have a beautiful body and no doubt your feet are beautiful as well."

"You have not seen them," she said. "But I must be brave."

And then, as she sat on the bed and crossed her legs to untie her shoes, he saw that rather than the dainty shoes which should have gone with the rest of her body, she wore large brogans almost the width of a broom. When she had taken off both shoes and pulled down her stockings, she stood up with her head bowed, her breast rising and falling as she breathed. It was then that Popoto understood her concern. Although her legs were extremely well shaped, when the eye reached the ankles it was assailed by monstrosity.

The feet were long and wide and between each toe there extended a membrane, not unlike that of webbed aquatic birds.

"You see?" she said, suppressing a sob.

Popoto knew immediately that his every wish for a woman had been answered. He recalled that idyllic afternoon so many years ago when Caterina the mermaid had come to him and the sea and wind had accompanied her siren song.

"You have lovely feet," he said, gently.

"You are simply being kind," she replied, blushing deeply from shame.

"No, I am telling the truth. I have heard of only one other occurrence such as this one. You have the feet of a mermaid, a siren, and feet such as yours are a sign of great love."

She looked at him, her eyes pleading for a sign that he was not mocking her. He returned her gaze openly, the love he felt enveloping her until she sighed and smiled shyly at him.

"You told me both people had to be undressed," she said.

Quickly, Popoto removed his clothes, baring his monster organ which was now fully erect, extending itself more than a full foot out from his body. At the sight of it Sor Barbara now gasped and held her hand to her mouth. She shook her head involuntarily at the thought of having the giant organ within her.

Nature in its impersonality is not as cruel as people often think. In fact oftentimes nature displays touches of such great logic that it defies description. The historical Buddha of India writing in his *Kama Sutra* spoke about the need for men and women to be matched sexually. He warned of horse men coupling with elephant women, or of bull men coupling with horse women, for it would diminish the pleasure of both. As luck would have it, Barbara Almendros would have made any normal man unhappy because she possessed an equally enormous "yonni," as the Buddha would say. So that if Popoto was an elephant man, so was Sor Barbara an elephant woman.

Popoto did not become aware of this until he himself had undressed and motioned for Sor Barbara, now fully naked, to lie down on the bed. As he caressed her body and kissed her face, which she questioned but once understood as part of the lovemaking, she found most enjoyable, he came to her pubic area. She was immense. Nonetheless, his organ was so large that the defloration pained Sor Barbara enormously.

The pain did nothing to interfere with her resolve. She endured the initial anguish, imagining Christ on the cross as he suffered endlessly the spears against his ribs and the nails in his hands and feet. The episode lasted at the most three minutes from the time Popoto entered her until, in a frenzy of passion, he exploded, driving his organ deep into Sor Barbara. Her reaction was a shock to her. She felt an immediate pain which traveled from the middle of her body upward into her head making her black out and then sending waves of pleasure throughout her body so that she clung to Popoto, her legs pinning his slight body to her.

He lay atop her for a few moments and then tried to rise. She held him, whispering that they must make sure the Serpent was dormant. He agreed and remained within her, watching her lovely face now flushed, her full lips ripe, her eyes heavy lidded with abandon. A minute later he was erect again.

"I'm sorry," he said.

"No, please don't be. I can feel him stirring. He must be sated," she said, resolutely. "I must tell you something. I have heard and read of religious ecstasy, but I never imagined it would be like this. I can understand perfectly why our Christ would subject himself to crucifixion. Beyond the pain there is an area of pleasure which is truly the essence of love. I am most grateful to you, Sir Clown. Sate the beast!"

Once, during a lull in their lovemaking, Barbara Almendros sat up in bed and very thoughtfully requested that he answer one more questions.

"Anything you wish," he said.

"Beneath the beast there appear to be two sacks. What are they called and what is their function?"

"Eggs," he said. "That is what they are commonly called and it is there that the desire and passion reside."

"Uhm!," she said. "Eggs. I see. Passion and desire." She thought for a moment and then nodded several times. "But of course," she said, smiling knowingly. "They are the apples."

"Apples?" Popoto said, amused.

"Yes, apples. There wasn't just one apple. There were two. One for Adam and one for Eve. If only Adam had participated in the act of betrayal there would have been only one apple, but it was also Eve that the Serpent wished to corrupt and she too partook of the forbidden fruit. It all makes perfect sense."

"Do you think so?"

"Yes, there is no doubt about it," she said. "Does the beast presently sleep?"

"Presently, but I doubt that he will remain so," Popoto said outwardly serious, but amused by her innocent curiosity.

"Aha!" she said. "Do not hesitate to inform me if he stirs."

"Of course."

And so it went for most of the night until, in a stupor, Popoto lay spent, his mind traveling beyond time into eternity, such was his joy. As for Sor Barbara, she rose early the next morning and began the long arduous task of exhorting the women who came to the shrine on the purity of sating the Serpent. She saw her mission now and she explained patiently to each one how to defeat the evil which resided in men. At all cost they must sate the desires of the beast and understand that beyond the pain there was pleasure. Within days word traveled from woman to woman, friend confiding in friend, mother instructing daughter, so that before the end of the week only a few old women, regretting their loveless lives, came to the shrine to pray.

The disappearance of Popoto from the circus created a minor crisis, but in time things went back to normal and, after the celebration of the town's patron saint, the Gordils Circus left Cacimar. Jordi Gordils, its owner, explained to everyone that Popoto had decided to leave circus life after meeting a young woman in the mountains. The circus people spoke about him for a week or so and then were happy to forget his dark countenance.

One dark, drizzly night Sor Barbara and her clown lover, the two of them dressed in nun's habits, left the house with their belongings and simply vanished. They left the island for the United States, and in 1797 ended up in Connecticut. Through a complex series of events Popoto became involved with the Connecticut Western Reserve Land Company, at that time surveying several large tracts of land north of the Ohio River. Although by birth neither of them were native to the island, each being a transplant from the Iberian Peninsula, Sor Barbara and Popoto the clown became, technically, the first Puerto Ricans to settle in Cleveland.

The bond between the clown and the nun grew stronger and their lovemaking no less intense. In time the whistling of Popoto's organ disappeared as did the silvery-green coloration and the offensive odor. Sor Barbara saw this as final proof that she had accomplished her life mission in meeting the Devil and converting him to the faith. They eventually married and had seven children, four boys and three girls, all of them with their mother's looks and bright spirit, a factor which Popoto attributed to her strength of character and her goodness. None of them had webbed feet nor unusually large sexual organs, although all of them were highly sexed and produced for the couple 56 grandchildren, none of them Catholic, for religion became unimportant to Barbara Almendros and Filiberto Casablancas. They lived to the ripe old age of 92 and 90, respectively. They engaged in sexual relations with each other until that last night in November when Popoto, after spending himself on his wife, fell asleep with a smile on his face and never woke up again. In death he still wore the smile, which led to jokes from his offspring and their offspring that made the then octogenarian Barbara blush.

And so there you have it. I hope that when the novel is eventually published, that you enjoy the philosophical debate between the nun and the clown, but understand that it was cowardice on my part which kept me from writing the truth about what turned my hometown of Cacimar, up to that time a haven of purity, into a snake pit of sexual abandon, a place where the smell of copulation was more prevalent than wood smoke.

Collazo's Diet

When one becomes a famous writer he is invited to speak at the most unlikely places. Literary expression is a noble endeavor but one replete with frustrations and unpaid bills. Financial remuneration, therefore, is a primary consideration when accepting a speaking engagement. Last November I was asked to address the local Dieting and Literary Club of Brooks' Landing, New Jersey. When I arrived the Hamilton Room of the Maxwell Brooks Hotel was filled to capacity with two hundred or so matrons feasting on cottage cheese and lettuce. On my way to the podium I said to myself: Mendoza, you're in for it. These ladies may smile and wish to know about the craft, but their main interest is not looking like rejects from a New York Jets tryout. If they go off their diets because of you, forget them as readers. As much as they may want to know about the people and their struggles to overcome adversity they won't buy your books if your influence makes them get fat.

With this in mind I told them what I believed to be a touching story of weight loss. This story actually took place in El Barrio and concerns the manner in which Victor Collazo got Marcelina Puente to reduce. You see, Marcelina lost weight and she did it in record time. It seemed to me a natural assumption that my audience would enjoy the story. Throughout my narration the women nodded, smiled understandingly and occasionally eructated discreetly into their paper napkins. At certain points in the story their faces registered mild shock. When I finished speaking, however, they applauded and seemed pleased. Some even came up and asked me questions about writing and the veracity of the story. One or two even expressed an interest in getting to know me more intimately. The latter is always flattering to a writer, even one advanced in age such as myself.

As it turned out, the story had displeased most of the women. The following week I received strongly worded letters from the president of the club, the manager of the hotel, the Chamber of Commerce of Brooks' Landing, the National Association for the Prevention of Cruelty to Animals, the Daughters of the American Revolution, the Department of the Army and my agent. He, rather than accusing me of attempting to undermine the American Way of Life, hinted at the possibility that I derived sadistic pleasure from watching middle aged women struggling to keep trim. He suggested I be more careful about the topics I discussed in front of certain groups, adding that if I thought there was the slightest chance that a misogynous streak had surfaced in my character I ought to seek professional help. On a separate sheet of neatly typed paper he included a list of "reputable" New York City psychiatrists.

I immediately telephoned my agent and argued vehemently with him. A writer, I explained, needs to describe life exactly as he sees it. I told him I planned to answer every letter thoroughly, invoking artistic integrity and reaming my detractors good and proper for their attempt at censorship and for their prudishness. My agent listened patiently and then said that literary suicide took many forms and that if I wished to cut my throat a letter was a cowardly way of doing it. I hung up the phone and began drafting the first letter. After a few paragraphs I changed my mind. My agent was right. What would I accomplish? The damage had been done. As one of the letters said, I "had contrived to tatter and besmirch (sic) the fabric of American rules of decency and fair play," an often used cliche, but a confused metaphor if ever I heard one. Who the hell would bother besmirching after tattering a fabric of any kind. If my purpose were to screw around with American rules of fair play I would choose solely besmirching, never tattering. What gall! It still angers me that such an uproar was created over what is in essence a love story.

You see, when Victor and Marcelina became engaged to be married she was a wisp of a girl, as thin and delicate as the *guajana*, the sugar cane flower of their parents' homeland. Victor, entranced, would watch her lovingly as she'd cross the living room of the Puente's apartment, or when they went to the beach and she'd run toward the water. There was music in the graceful, long-legged way of her movements. He often wished they were already married and she was naked before him. But she was a "good girl" and had informed him early in their courtship that there was to be no "freshness" before the wedding. Such a staunch defense of her virginity made Marcelina that much more desirable and deepened Victor's love for her. She was a haven of morality along a moteled highway of abandon. Or as I said in front of my audience at Brooks' Landing: Among the dunes of wantonness, Marcelina Puente was a puritanical oasis of virtue. A little too flamboyant for my taste, but the ladies loved it. Literature buffs like to be included in the creative process.

Like any normal, healthy Puerto Rican young man, Victor Collazo continued making advances on Marcelina's virginity, but would have been shocked had she relented. Had she been one of those women who enjoy having power over a man, Victor would have been a willing victim. But Marcelina was not one of those women. She was thoughtful, kind and full of hope for the future. She never complained, was thrifty and cooked marvelous rice and beans and stewed codfish. She enjoyed doing little things which made a home attractive and comfortable for a man and had no other ambition than to make Victor happy.

Everyone agreed they were the ideal couple. He, tall and dark, and she, small and fair. Friends and relatives on both sides longed for the day when the young lovers would be joined in holy matrimony. Men chuckled and made oblique jokes about the wedding night, jokes which usually dealt with food or getting caught in the rain or else baseball. Women, on the other hand, wore out their rosary beads, praying fervently that this time marriage would be different.

Unfortunately, before the marriage could become a reality, things took a turn which transformed Marcelina from a thin, attractive young woman into a human dirigible. One day, upon returning home from his job as a checkout clerk with Associated Supermarkets, Victor Collazo was presented with a letter by his mother. The letter was from the U.S. government and requested his presence at Whitehall Street for immediate induction into the U.S. Army. After a tearful goodbye, in which Victor and Marcelina swore undying love for each other, he was gone.

When he returned after three months of basic training, his body more solid than ever and his manly resolve to wed Marcelina made greater by the separation, he found that she had filled out a little around the face and that her breasts appeared fuller. In fact, when he walked into the Puente's apartment, he mistook Marcelina for her older, married sister, said hello and walked by her.

Marcelina grabbed his arm, turned him around, clucked her tongue and threw her arms around him. This surprised him and he finally recognized her.

"Oh, wow," he said. "I thought you was Olga," he added, amused by the change in Marcelina.

Marcelina laughed, kissed him passionately and hugged herself to him. There was an appealing womanliness to her which Victor had not seen before. She is maturing into a fine *hembra*, he thought, employing the gender counterpart of *macho* in Spanish. She's going to be a fine, honest to God female. Visions of their wedding night goaded his imagination.

"Let's go up on the roof and check out your brother's pigeons," he whispered amorously in her ear. "I bet they had babies."

"Not now, Victor," she replied nervously, aware of his increased passion. "I have to help Mami with dinner."

Victor's fifteen day leave went well. It was summer and he and Marcelina wandered the city, going to movies, attending outdoor Latin music concerts, walking along the East River and talking about decorating their apartment when they were finally married. Subjects such as the pros and cons of plastic covers for the living room furniture, buying on credit and the design and color of linoleum became the foundation of their dreams. On weekends, during his leave, Victor accompanied the Puente family to Orchard Beach and nearly drove himself crazy gazing at Marcelina's body, each curve and rise adding to his torment.

Another tearful goodbye and Victor was off once again, this time for paratrooper training. On his return he was tanned and even more muscled, his body straining against the form fitting uniform. He had been promoted and walked proudly, his jump boots shining and the paratrooper wings a subtle sign of the rigorous training.

When he saw Marcelina she was returning from her job at a downtown discount store. Victor took her in his arms and kissed her hungrily. This happened in front of the Valencia Bakery on Lexington Avenue. People in the street cheered the lovers. It was war time and everyone knew Victor might never return after he left the next time. When he broke off the embrace and held Marcelina at arms' length, he was overwhelmed by the width of her hips and the ampleness of her bosom. My God, he thought, she looks like Iris Chacon. He took a step back and whistled loudly. Marcelina blushed and lowered her eyes. Taking her hand, Victor twirled her around to the music from a restaurant jukebox. The sight of her mare-like buttocks confirmed his comparison to the richly endowed Ms. Chacon.

At this point in my narrative to the Brooks' Landing Diet and Literary Club, I explained that Iris Chacon is a Puerto Rican entertainer and television personality and the quintessence of that which seems to drive our men into helpless tizzies of passion. "When she dances," I explained to my ladies, "she wears dangerously cut leotards which highlight the enormity and perfect roundness of her gluteal anatomy." There was considerable whispering and passing on of decoded linguistic information, followed by some gasps and a scattering of titters. There is no doubt that my choice of words, genteel as I strove to make them, displeased my audience. Also it is quite likely my description of such a shapely woman upset the dieting ladies and produced the subsequent barrage of poisonous missives.

I continued my tale and explained that during the thirty days Victor spent in New York before shipping out for Vietnam, he pleaded and begged for release from his sexual torment. Marcelina, although quite passionate when they embraced, remained steadfast in her resolve to maintain her chastity until their wedding night. The pain to Victor's body became so great that he sought relief with previous girlfriends in other parts of the city. He lied and swore undying love for them, insisting that he had received a vision of his death from the Almighty, so that the girls cried and allowed Victor to take full liberties with their bodies. But as willing as they were, it wasn't enough and Victor was left longing for Marcelina.

"Oh, Marcy, I love you," he'd say, when he found himself alone with her. "Please, *mamacita*. I can't hold back, honey."

And there, alone in the Puente's apartment, with the afternoon sun sneaking into the room to give the air an opaque glow, the two of them, fully dressed, struggled with the demons of temptation. During their nearly demented groupings, Marcelina's mind would recall all the tenets of maidenly behavior which her mother had learned growing up in her hometown of Cacimar and had passed on to her. "*Cuando un hombre está enamorado*," her mother was fond of saying, "*no piensa con la cabeza de arriba*."

For the ladies in Brooks' Landing I translated this ribald morsel of maternal wisdom as: "A man in love knows no reason," and left it at that. In retrospect, had I translated the true intent of the phrase, that is, the inherent drive of an aroused male to think with the lower component of his duocephalic anatomy, I truly believe I may have been tarred and feathered on the spot.

Her mother's words, rather than lending some comfort to Marcelina, set up incredible images in her mind. As her curiosity increased, she wished to determine the accuracy of the maxim. The more she thought about a miniature of Victor's strong, handsome face entering her, the weaker she grew. Her heart beating uncontrollably she would push him away and cry disconsolately.

Victor finally left for the West Coast without success. He was not embittered by the experience but filled with a new resolve to survive the war in order to win his prize. In his letters to Marcelina he spoke of his dreams of a life together, of their children and their names, of attending college upon his return and of the house which they would eventually purchase in Queens. Marcelina's letters were equally optimistic, full of love and tenderness. Only one thing seemed amiss to Victor. Whenever he asked for a photograph of Marcelina, rather than receiving new snap shots, he received old ones. The day to day routine of life in the battlefield, however, did not leave much room for speculation. Instead of dwelling on the issue, Victor concentrated on remaining alive.

At the end of his year in Vietnam, having seen death in varied forms and having received a bullet wound that nearly shattered his left shoulder, Victor returned home for good. He stopped off to see his own family and without changing rushed over to Marcelina's house. When Mrs. Puente opened the door of the apartment Victor was shocked by how coldly he was received. Even Coco, the Puente's cocker spaniel, friendly in the past, seemed to be avoiding him.

"*Marcy salió,*" Mrs. Puente said, looking down at the floor. "She went out."

"I'll wait for her," Victor said.

"She went to her aunt's house in Brooklyn," Mrs. Puente said.

"Didn't she get my letter? I wrote her I was coming," Victor said.

"She got it," said Nancy, Marcelina's younger sister. "But my aunt had an emergency and Marcy went to take care of her."

They were obviously lying but Victor was not one to create strife and confront people with their weaknesses.

"Well, tell her I came by," he said politely as he left.

The next day he returned and was received similarly. Marcy was still in Brooklyn. Perhaps they could give him the address and he'd go and see her. No, it wouldn't be a good idea. The aunt was suffering from nerves. She'd lost a son in the Korean War and seeing the uniform would upset her. He'd change. No, she'd recognize him from Marcy's pictures. Finally having lost all patience Victor appealed to Mr. Puente who sat impassively in front of the TV set.

"Mr. Puente," Victor said respectfully. "What's going on? I'm engaged to your daughter. I'm gonna marry her. Why don't you let me see her?"

Mr. Puente looked towards his wife and painfully, as if the matter were out of his hands, shrugged his shoulders. Puzzled and hurt, Victor left the Puente's apartment, vowing to himself never to return. Perhaps during his time in Vietnam Marcelina had become pregnant out of wedlock and they were protecting her from his wrath. His own family was of no help. All they said was that they hadn't seen Marcelina in the street in the last six months.

In spite of his vow Victor could not stay away long. After a week he began going to Marcelina's block. Forlornly, he'd spend hours looking up at the windows of the Puente's apartment, hoping to catch a glimpse of her. One morning toward the beginning of spring, when he had almost given up all expectations of seeing Marcelina again, Victor thought he saw a large shape peeking out from behind a window shade in the living room. Mr. and Mrs. Puente were both at work, the younger children were in school and Olga lived with her own family in the Bronx. It couldn't be a burglar because it seemed to be a woman's shape. Perhaps, Victor surmised, the sick aunt had been brought to stay at the apartment and Marcy was up there taking care of her.

Full of anticipation, his heart filled with renewed hope, Victor raced up the six flights. He knocked on the door. No answer. He knocked again, this time calling out Marcelina's name. Still no answer. In a rage he pounded on the door several times. Nothing. Frustrated, his mind on the verge of snapping, he kicked at the door, making locks and hinges strain from the blows. With little success other than leaving some ugly marks on the wood, Victor stopped his attack and listened. Not a sound issued from within. Perhaps in his anxiety he had imagined seeing someone. Similar things had happened in the jungle when he'd been on patrol.

He wanted to give up but instead found himself racing up the stairs to the roof. Once there, he climbed down the fire escape to the Puente's floor. The living room window leading to the fire escape was locked and protected by a gate, but the one next to it was opened slightly. Not caring that he was six stories up Victor inched his way along the ledge of the building until he was able to reach down and raise the window. Without looking over his shoulder he tumbled inside. He got up, took a look down into the street and decided no one had seen him. When he turned around Coco was sniffing at him, but when he reached down to pet the usually playful cocker spaniel it ran away yelping. Was Coco trying to tell him something? Was he warning him of some danger?

As if he had been thrown back in time and was once again in combat and had been asked to secure part of a village, Victor crouched and began going through the apartment, ready to karate chop the enemy. After searching every room and finding no one, he sat down in the kitchen. For a few minutes he pondered the dilemma. Again, as if he had been transported once more to Vietnam, his sixth sense told him someone else was indeed in the apartment.

Driven by animal instinct, Victor stood up and went directly to the Puente's bedroom. He got down flat on the floor and there, beneath the four poster bed, he found Marcelina with a box of Ritz crackers. She was whimpering softly and Victor immediately said he was sorry he'd frightened her. He asked her to come out, but she shook her head and whimpered more loudly. This time Coco joined her, the two of them bewailing he didn't know what. In the semi-darkened room Victor decided that the bloated face staring back at him was caused by Marcelina's crying.

"Please come out, Marcy," he repeated.

"You'll hate me," she cried.

"No, I won't," Victor reassured her.

"Nooooo," she wailed.

"Please, Marcy. I love you, honey. I don't care if you're pregnant. I saw you in the window."

"I'm not *pregnant*," sobbed Marcelina. "I can't come out."

"Are you stuck?"

Marcelina's next emission of grief filled Victor with greater sorrow than he had experienced when close friends had been cut down in combat. He crawled under the bed, got hold of Marcelina's wrists and began pulling gently on her. Rather than being stuck she appeared to be resisting him. Like a man possessed, Victor stood up and removed mattress and box spring from the bed and leaned them up against the wall. Only then did he realize why Marcelina's family had gone to such lengths to deceive him and why his own family had not seen her in the street for six months.

Marcelina looked like a beached whale. It was impossible that anyone could have grown so fat in so short a time. The thin delicate face he'd found so much delight in had become a puffy caricature of itself. Her large dark eyes had become slits and now peeked out pig-like from the dough-colored fat. As if they had been pumped full of air, her arms and legs had tripled in size. The rest of her body, encased in a sack-like housecoat, looked like a giant sausage.

"Please stand up," Victor said, suppressing his emotions and extending his hand to her. "What the hell happened?"

With great difficulty Marcelina sat up, held up her pudgy child's hand and allowed Victor to help her up and climb over the bed frame. Avoiding his eyes Marcelina smoothed her housecoat, brushed the crumbs from her face and attempted to put her hair back in place. God, Victor thought, even her hair looks fat. Disappointedly, he noticed that the slightest motion made the fat on her arms jiggle like human jello. He followed her as she waddled into the kitchen, her once-thin ankles swollen and without differentiation from the rest of her leg. She reminded him of an elephant and his heart nearly broke from the pain. She sat at the kitchen table and hiding her face began crying again.

"My God, Marcy," Victor said. "Tell me what happened? Did someone put a curse on you? Tell me who did it and I'll kill him."

"I was worried about you," Marcelina said, through her tears.

"So? That was no reason to go see a spiritualist."

"I didn't," she said, stamping her foot.

"What then?"

"I don't know. I was just nervous and worried. I didn't wanna think about you all bloody. Whenever Papi turned on the news and I saw all the stuff going on over there, I thought of you all bloody. The next thing I knew I was opening the ice box. It was horrible, Victor. You can't imagine."

"Go on."

"What do you mean?"

"Well, it didn't all happen in one day, did it?"

"I didn't say it did."

"I know, but couldn't you tell what was gonna happen if you kept stuffing your face?"

"I couldn't help it," cried Marcelina. "I couldn't. It was like I was blind. Anything I found I'd put in my mouth. Sometimes the only thing left in the fridge was rice from the day before and I'd just pull the pot out and without even heating it I'd take large handfuls and stuff them in my mouth. Anything I found. Old bread, pieces of dried up meat, whole boxes of cereal, cake mix, jello. Anything!"

"Jello? Without cooking the stuff?"

"Yeah, I'd just open the box and put the powder in my mouth. It was horrible, Victor. I thought you was gonna die. One time I found some of Papi's Ex-lax. I thought it was chocolate until an hour later."

"That should've helped," Victor said, growing angry for the first time.

"Don't joke about it, Victor. I couldn't help myself. Almost every month somebody would hear about a relative or a friend getting killed. Word always got back to me and I'd think you'd be next. When Israel Pagan from 102nd Street came back and was missing an arm and his left eye was sewn up I almost died. I found out about it at work. He and his girl Migdalia came by the store to say hello and Israel looked terrible. I had to ask my boss to let me leave early. I got home about one o'clock in the afternoon. Mami had asked me to cook supper so I started doing that to take my mind off Israel. I finished the whole thing about 2:30 and before I knew it I had eaten everything. A whole pot of rice, a pot of beans, a whole fried chicken with french fries and a big salad."

"What, no dessert?"

"Victor!"

"Well, what do you expect me to say? Go on. What happened?"

"I had to go buy the same things and cook all over again."

"You're kidding! Did you eat again?"

"Yeah, I didn't want Mami to think there was anything wrong. I'm sorry. I know you don't wanna marry me now, but don't hate me too much. I couldn't even stop when I found out you were gonna be okay and coming home and everything. The doctor at the clinic said it was nerves. I tried a couple of diets, but they didn't work."

Victor looked at Marcelina but still couldn't believe his eyes. Her words were lost on him. He wanted to take her in his arms, comfort her, tell her everything would be all right, but couldn't move from his seat. A mixture of love and violent nausea churned about in his stomach.

"I still love you, Marcy," he said with some difficulty. "Don't worry, we'll work it out."

Marcelina's eyes hinted at gratitude and she smiled weakly. Only a semblance of the old Marcy appeared on her face. Victor didn't know how they would work it out, but like any other challenge he had faced, he would rise to the task. That much he had learned about himself in the Army. Perhaps he would have to grow fat himself in order to be able to stand looking at her. He had seen fat couples and both partners had appeared happy. Looking once more at Marcelina he rejected the idea. She looked like a pale hippopotamus. By the time he said goodbye to her that afternoon, however, and unbeknownst to Marcelina, Victor Collazo had devised a plan which would bring her back to the normalcy he had found so attractive in the past.

"I'll pick you up at eight o'clock tonight," he said.

"Where are we going?" Marcelina asked happily.

"Oh, just walking," Victor replied off-handedly. "Don't get dressed up or nothing."

When Victor returned that evening, the Puente family was all smiles and apologies. Everyone laughed at his or her part in the matter. The only member of the family reticent to join in the reunion was Coco, who evidently had been traumatized by the scene earlier in the day and remained under the Puente's bed. After about an hour or so, during which Victor answered the family's questions about his experiences in Vietnam, Victor led Marcelina out of the apartment, down the stairs and out into the street.

As they walked, neighbors whispered and shook their heads sadly. It was the suffering, they said. Nerves. Maliciously, some even whispered that she had gotten pregnant while Victor was away. Marcelina was oblivious to the stares. She had not been happier in all the time she had known Victor. He truly loved her and even though she felt awkward and ashamed of her weight, she held her head up as she walked beside him. Strolling in the cool of that spring evening, she allowed herself to think once more about their first home.

When they reached Central Park they found a bench near the lake at 106th Street and sat down. The sun had gone down entirely and the lights from the lamp posts reflected languidly on the still water of the lake. It was as romantic a setting as two young people could find in el Barrio. Marcelina was panting from the walk and long rivulets of perspiration rolled down her face and into the folds of her thick neck.

Very slowly and gently Victor began telling Marcelina about his more harrowing battlefield experiences: the awful mangling of bodies ripped apart by mortars, bombs, machine guns, rockets, land mines; the burned flesh of peasants hit by napalm; the tortured bodies of Viet Cong, their genitals seared by electrical wires; the bloated rotting corpses lying in the fields for days; the decapitations; the amputations, both surgical and accidental; the mass graves and the earth swamp-like from the blood, so that when you walked on it you did not hear a liquid sound but the agonized screams of the dying.

Victor spared Marcelina no detail. When he was finished with that end of his experiences and she was nearly in shock, he began talking about vietnamese cuisine, going into great detail about the variety of ways in which dog meat could be prepared.

"Dog?" she said.

"That's right," Victor said wistfully, as if something dear had been removed from his life.

"My God, Victor," said Marcelina.

"What?" he said surprised by her tone.

"Is that why Coco was so scared of you?"

"I'm sorry," Victor said. "I didn't know you were home. They told me you went to Brooklyn to take care of your aunt."

"You lied to me. You really didn't wanna see me and snuck in to get Coco. That's why he was crying and so scared of you. You were gonna grab him and eat him."

"I'm sorry," Victor said. "It's just that stray dogs . . . I mean, you never can tell if they're sick of something."

Marcelina fainted.

After Victor revived her she began gasping for air. It was as if someone had gotten hold of her windpipe and wouldn't let go. When she was once again breathing normally, Victor began telling her about his skill with a knife and how he would never take any prisoners, choosing instead to disembowel his victims.

"There was a bunch of us useta to do that," he said seemingly crazed. "Their guts would come spilling out with the food they had eaten and everything.:

"This time Marcelina leaned over and began vomiting. At this point in my narrative to the Brooks Landing Dieting and Literary Club, nearly three quarters of the audience brought paper napkins to their mouths and at least a dozen of the ladies left the room. It didn't help matters any that I described Marcelina's condition as anorexia ponderosa. Art is a struggle, no doubt about it. How can one retain artistic integrity if he has to constantly pull punches and worry about how people are going to react. People think an author makes money on books and movies. Very little. It's all speaking engagements and seminars, if he's lucky and his book has gotten some publicity. It's depressing.

Anyway, Marcelina continued her regurgitations for a full five minutes, with Victor holding the back of her neck as if he were trying to empty her out. When she was finished, he walked her to the bench across the way, sat her down, took out a handkerchief, and in the process let two dried apricot shells drop out of his pocket.

"What's that?" Marcelina screamed peering down at the ground.

Victor quickly picked up the apricot shells and put them back in his pocket.

"Here, let me wipe your face," he said.

She pulled back from the handkerchief.

"What was that in the handkerchief, Victor?"

"Souvenires," he said. "C'mon, let me wipe your face."

"Don't," she screamed. "Souveniers of what?"

"*Orejas*," he said.

"Dog ears?"

"No, silly," Victor said, laughing and taking one of the apricot shells out of his pocket. "People ears. We'd cut them off the gooks after they were dead."

"Oh, my God," Marcelina said, hiding her face in her hands. "And people ate them?"

Aha, Victor thought, another opportunity to attack the fat. He fell silent and waited.

"Well, did they?" Marcelina squealed, her entire body wracked by hysteria. "Did they?"

"Only when there was nothing else," Victor said, seemingly ashamed of the confession.

"Did you?" Marcelina said, hyperventilating.

"I don't wanna talk about that," Victor said, turning away from her.

"I wanna go home," Marcelina said. Her voice was like that of a child's, pleading. "You're trying to scare me because you hate me."

"No, Marcy, I love you," Victor said turning back to her. "I'm sorry, but I had to tell someone."

And he was sorry. It hurt him to tell Marcelina such things. He had never used a knife or a bayonet on anyone. For whatever it was worth, the times he had shot his rifle, it had been at long range, with no certainty that his bullets had reached their intended target. Most of his time, in fact, had been spent preparing for combat and being shot at. And tasty as others had sworn it was, he had been as nauseated by the idea of eating dog as she was.

"Can't we go home?" Marcelina pleaded. "It's too dark in the park."

"We can't leave yet," Victor replied.

"But why?"

"We're gonna play hide and seek."

"What? Are you crazy?"

"We used to call it search and destroy."

"I don't wanna play, Victor."

"I'm gonna count to ten and you go hide. If I can find you in less than ten minutes I get to rape you. If you scream I'll tell everybody in the neighborhood that we've been doing it."

"You're crazy," Marcelina screamed. "What'd they do to you over there? You're really crazy."

"One," Victor said.

"Don't," cried Marcelina.

"Two."

"Stop it. It's not fair."

"Three," he said, reaching down and unsheathing a bolo knife from under his pant leg.

Marcelina stood up and waddled into the darkness of the park, the counting receding as she climbed up the side of the hill. Victor put his knife away and as he followed her began to create the illusion of tracking Marcelina down. He allowed her to stay well ahead, but each time she stopped to rest he made it obvious that he was getting closer. When she reached the top of the hill and the open spaces of the baseball diamonds, he remained hidden and watched her fat body working laboriously to get away.

At the end of ten minutes he caught up to her. Without the least sympathy he brought her back to the Puente's apartment. In the hallway he warned her about telling anyone what had happened. If she refused to go out in the evening, he would sneak into the apartment and rape her. Marcelina nearly passed out.

"That's right," Victor said roughly. And if that isn't enough, there's always Coco."

"Oh, Victor, don't even think about that again."

"I don't know."

"Please!"

"Well, I got a couple of buddies up in the Bronx. They say they miss it. Either you keep your mouth shut or it's Cocoburgers."

"All right, all right," she said, her head spinning and her eyes closed. "I won't say nothing."

Victor knocked on the door, helped her inside and explained sweetly to Mrs. Puente that Marcelina had become nauseous on their walk. Mrs. Puente said she understood and asked Marcelina if she was hungry. Marcelina made an exceptionally ugly face and ran into the bathroom.

Each evening for the next two months, in fair or foul weather, Victor brought Marcelina to different areas of the park, gave her instructions and turned her loose, each time increasing the time she was to be "out in the field" before he caught her. The only complaint Victor ever received from the Puente family was that Marcelina would not each much anymore and would he speak to her because she was becoming too thin.

When he was not with her, Victor spent hours at the 42nd Street Library, poring over books which might speed up the reducing process. His research skills were minimal, but while there he happened upon a theme which suited his purposes perfectly. Once a week before her run, Victor would subject Marcelina to greater and greater dosages of deviate human appetite: The Donner Pass party, the Uruguayan rugby team's ordeal in the Andes, the cannibalism of the original inhabitants of the British Isles, the ritual anthropophagy of New Guinea tribes, which according to Victor had consumed Nelson Rockefeller's son, were all detailed to the distraught Marcelina.

As the pounds continued to disappear and people began commenting on how well she looked, they inquired as to her secret. Smiling wanly she would say, "*Estoy a dieta*, you know. It's a new diet."

One night late in May, when Victor had chased Marcelina for over an hour and was beginning to feel his own exhaustion, he decided that the job was complete. He caught up to Marcelina near Belvedere Lake and called out her name. Marcelina did not look back. Instead, she clambered cat-like up the rocks surrounding the castle above the lake. In the light of the moon Victor watched her lithe body silhouetted against the background of rocks. Everything he had ever felt for her before their separation swelled his heart with longing.

He climbed the rocks and caught her as she reached the castle. There, against the cool of the stone, he told her of the pain he'd endured being away from her. She touched his face and they cried together. Their tears made them feel as if they were embracing the sea.

"You finally caught me," she said, her body seemingly fitting into his. The tone of her voice embarrassed Victor and he found himself avoiding her embrace. Shyly, he tried to explain but she placed a long finger to his lips. Taking his hand she led him to the back of the castle and into the thick spring shrubbery, pulling him down on top of her on the fragrant turf.

"We should wait," he said meekly.

"You promised," she replied, unzipping the jacket of the jogging outfit she'd purchased the previous week. "You caught me, right?"

"Yeah, but . . . like, what about your parents?"

"Shhh," she said, putting her finger to his lips again. "If you don't wanna, I'll tell people on the block that you came back from Vietnam funny and dig guys."

"What? Me?"

"I mean it," she said.

Victor roared with laughter. When he had laughed himself out he took her face in his hands and kissed her with all the pent-up passion he had suppressed since returning home. Afterwards, as they lay touching each other, watching the stillness of the park, she asked him if everything he'd told her was true.

He did not answer.

"None of those things really happened to you, did they?" she said.

He shook his head.

"No, none of them really happened," he answered. "But it worked," she said sitting up, zipping up her jacket and pulling on her sweat pants. "It could work on somebody else."

Victor was shocked.

"Are you crazy?" he said.

"It could," she insisted. "All those exercise studios and diets are all bull. I don't wanna work in no discount store for the rest of my life, Victor."

As they walked out of the park they discussed the subject, Marcelina explaining how many fat girl friends she had and how they would do anything to reduce and how Victor could get his Army buddies to help out and they would be employed.

"On commission," she said enthusiastically. "You know, like Avon ladies. Search and destroy missions against fat. They'd go to the girl's house and pick them up and everything. We could make up a little cookbook of really messed up things with a special section for dogs and even cats and gerbils and they'd have to read it and make written reports like in school."

Victor thought a moment, nodding as he walked out of the park with his arm around Marcelina's slim waist.

"Yeah, maybe you're right," he said.

The Angel Juan Moncho

One day late last fall when the days were growing shorter and colder and I was preparing to lock myself up for winter to catch up on a backlog of dreams, some of the people came to me and said, "Mendoza, you're too serious when you tell our dreams. Although what you write about us is true, there are times when we would prefer hearing something humorous." I nodded and explained that the recounting of dreams was a serious matter and that there were inherent difficulties in turning dreams into comedy. They replied that words were words and since I was supposed to be the expert, it was my responsibility to produce some humor from dreams. Arguments are useless once the people have made up their minds, so I asked what they had in mind. They said Christmas was approaching and tradition dictated they listen to the story of the Three Kings and the Infant Jesus, which was a very spiritually uplifting story except that a few months later they had to make promises which they never kept anyway, which made them feel very badly. Patiently, I explained to them that the story of Jesus was part of the yearly cycle of death and rebirth. "It's a metaphor of the seasons, part of ancient myth and therefore extremely important to the collective psyche," I said. They said that I certainly talked beautifully but that they weren't interested in philosophy.

Instead, they wished me to recount a miracle. I said the birth of the Child Jesus was a miracle and that the resurrection was most certainly a prime example of the same. They agreed but said they wanted to hear about a modern Christmas miracle, but one which would not frighten them like most miracles tended to do. I attempted to explain that germane to the idea of a miracle was the awe which the miracle inspired. They said that awe or not most miracles frightened them. I was silent, hoping they would recognize the futility of their quest and allow me to return to the recording of their dreams.

But they remained and insisted that the least I could do was explain what had taken place last year with Paulino Camacho, the butcher. How was it, they said, that after spending all his money drinking, Camacho was able to place such beautiful gifts under the Christmas tree for his wife and children? Gifts like no one in the neighborhood had ever seen? Like beautiful electric trains, expensive bicycles, fire engines and trucks with real rubber wheels and hoses; and oh yeah, white dolls that seemed more alive than any white person they had ever seen, and doll houses with better furniture than the furniture in their own apartments, stuffed toys bigger than the children themselves, and clothes like they had never worn, and mind you, we're not jealous, they said, but to see his wife, Marta, in that mink coat Camacho gave her for Christmas just to go to the laundromat or the supermarket when it was 80 degrees was a little bit too much for any human being to have to endure. And how did that happen? they wanted to know.

I said I had no idea but that whatever had happened it certainly had the makings of miraculous intervention. "Well, there you have it," they said. I asked them if upon finding out that Camacho had been able to accomplish this seemingly impossible feat, which had all the makings of a miracle, they hadn't been frightened. They said they had not, but that plenty of people had been angry with Camacho and some even began whispering that perhaps he wasn't really a butcher but spent his spare time dealing in drugs. I said I didn't know anything about that but that I seriously doubted it. "Well then, how do you explain Camacho's good fortune?," they said growing annoyed.

I again said I could not explain it, certainly not rationally, but that I thought perhaps an angel may have had a part in the matter. They then wanted to know if this angel I was talking about would frighten them. I said that angels were not generally intended to frighten people. They disagreed and were more annoyed than ever, insisting that angels, for the most part, came down to take people away and that the only reason they were dressed in white was so that people would be fooled and accompany the angel wherever it was he wanted to take them. "It's like doctors," they said. "As soon as you see them dressed in white, you think you're going to be all right and then before you know it they're sticking needles into you and cutting you open and who knows what else and that's the way angels are." I told them I disagreed, that angels were inoffensive, ethereal beings and that I couldn't guarantee that Camacho's story would be as humorous as they wanted. They said that just as long as the angel wasn't frightening and they could at least smile a few times I could do whatever I wanted, as long as I finally explained how Camacho had gotten away with what he did. I said I'd do my very best.

* * *

So, I began by saying that it was the night before Christmas and all through El Barrio everybody was stirring, including Camacho. Especially Camacho and most certainly Camacho. Because, I mean, Christmas only comes once a year and what the hell: *Felicidades y Japi Nu Yial*. Right? You see, you have to understand something about Camacho. Camacho enjoyed drinking. Not to excess but in the tradition of comradery, which dictates that whenever and wherever men gather bottle and glasses be on hand. So on this most festive of nights, Camacho was sitting at the long brown bar of *La Estrella de Borinquen*, on Lexington Avenue up the street from the subway station, and things were heating up. He was what we call *picao*. Somewhere between feeling mellow and passing out.

If you had seen Camacho you would've loved him immediately. He'd remind you of your father, all chubby and brown, sporting his big moustache and looking out into the world through those serious, sad eyes which used to make you shake when you were a child and made you say, penitently, "*Sí, papi*," and "*No, papi*." So, there was Camacho hitting on a bottle of Bud and saying things like: "Dis Bod for jew," and laughing and every once in a while one of his *panitas* would buy him a shot of Bacardí and down the hatch it went. And Camacho would feel so grateful for his friend's generosity that he'd slap a ten or twenty dollar bill on the bar and buy everyone a drink. No doubt about it. It was absolutely the best of nights, this *Nochebuena*. The jukebox was playing *salsa* and *aguinaldos* and one time when the disco version of "I'm Dreaming of a White Christmas" came on, Camacho got silly and danced, his belly hanging out and sweat rolling off his face.

About nine o'clock, as if everyone were hooked into the same circuit, men started making excuses about having to get home and be with their families. Snow was falling quite heavily and the streets gleamed brightly. Words went back and forth and in each one there was the aroma of *pernil, arroz con gandules, pasteles, salmoreja de jueyes, empanadas, alcapurrias, morcillas, mofongo, arroz con dulce, majarete, tembleque, almendras, nueces, turrón de alicante, turrón de jijona de mazapán* and to top it all off *coquito*. *Ay, madre santísima*. You couldn't believe how tongues were watering as men wished each other *Felicidades*.

Camacho snapped to. Oh, man, he thought. I've done it this time. He looked into his pockets and extracted three crumpled up dollar bills and some change. His stomach turned over a few times and he felt as if his legs would buckle and he'd fall over in a faint. All at once the Christmas decorations on the bar window became blurred and Camacho's eyes rolled up into his head. Holding on to the bar with both hands, he tried to steady himself. A feeling of complete desolation and regret hit him, tears came into his eyes, and then a long sobbing sound, which to the remaining patrons of the bar sounded like the flushing of the toilet, escaped from his chest.

One of Camacho's buddies, Epifanio Marrero, whom everyone knew as Ponce, came over and put his arm around Camacho's shoulder. Ponce was a worthless drunk, a piece of human driftwood, but the best guitar player in all of El Barrio. He lived for his art and if anyone had ever suggested that he take money for his music he would have been insulted.

"What's the matter, Camacho?" he said, tipping back a bottle of beer. "Don't cry. If it's a woman, forget her. If it's money, we'll rob a bank. Cheer up! It's *Nochebuena*, man!"

All Camacho could do was shake his head and another agonizing sob escaped from his chest. Why had he been so careless? The children were expecting so much this year. He had meant to get them all something earlier in the week but he'd never had a free moment at the butcher shop to get away and buy the presents. He should've let Marta buy the gifts but she always complained that whatever she bought for them they were never satisfied. The kids would just say Santa Claus was cheap. But that wasn't it. It was all his fault and, rather than being a man and doing his best, he had squandered all his money on drink.

"What am I going to do?" he said holding his head in both hands.

"You're drunk," said Ponce peering into Camacho's face.

"Yes, I know," said Camacho. "Leave me alone, Ponce. I'm no good. No good at all. I feel like dying."

"Well, in that case, let me have the rest of your beer and I'll sing at your funeral. What would you like me to sing? A *bolero*? Maybe a *guaracha*? I know, I know. You're from the mountains, right? Good, good. *Un seis chorreao*." And having said this, Ponce kicked off his shoes, removed his socks, rolled up his pants to the calves and began singing a *seis*, introducing the song with that high pitched nasal *lelo-lai-lelo-lai* of the *jíbaros*. For Camacho all it did was to give him a headache and make him feel as if his friend were mocking him.

"This is no laughing matter, Ponce," said Camacho regaining some of his composure.

"No, of course not, *compadre*," Ponce replied. "When it comes to my music I'm very serious. It's a pity that just this morning I had to hock my guitar."

"I'm in trouble," said Camacho.

"We all are, my friend. Plenty of trouble. Each day I'm faced with the same question. Should I go on living or should I step out in front of the Lexington Avenue Express and get it over with."

"Do you think that's what I ought to do?"

"Are you crazy? What kind of a man are you? What will people say. 'Camacho? He was a coward.' That's what they will say."

"Well, maybe they won't. You can be my witness. You will tell them I was very drunk and fell on the tracks."

Ponce held up his hand and shook his head violently.

"No, I will not be a part to deceiving people. I will not join you in this scheme to make them believe that you died accidentally. How would I face Chu Chu Barbosa down at Florindo's bar. He takes his job seriously. Suppose it is he that is driving the train and you jump out in front of it. Am I supposed to make him believe it was an accident? No way. *De ninguna manera*."

"But he drives on the D Line, not the Lexington."

"It doesn't matter. He will ask questions. No, I won't do it. It is nothing but cowardice to kill yourself. Have another drink. Whatever it is, it will pass. It always does."

"You're no help," said Camacho, and stumbled forward out of the bar and into the snow, his jacket open. "No help at all," he yelled as he skidded on the sidewalk.

The snow was coming down harder, the wind blowing in wild gusts that made the snow drift up against cars and buildings. Camacho staggered forward, oblivious to the cold and snow. Which way was home? Yes, First Avenue. He must walk towards Third. No matter what happened he had to get home. What time was it? Ten o'clock. Should he pray? Maybe if he prayed hard enough a miracle would take place. What was he talking about? He didn't believe in any of that stuff. That was for old women. What did he care if Paco Miranda had seen a vision of the Virgin holding up a piece of cardboard with a number and then played it and hit for almost $600. Or stupid Gloria Franco, ugly as sin, praying every single day at Saint Cecilia's for 20 years to get married, and having that rich Cuban with the two restaurants up in Washington Heights courting her like she was a princess and then marrying her and buying her a damn condominium downtown. Everybody said that was a miracle. Maybe he should pray.

Rather than going down the subway stairs and perhaps as a deterrent against his original plan to do away with himself, he began walking towards what he thought was First Avenue, where he had grown up, but not where he now lived. He also walked west rather than east. He crossed Park Avenue and then Madison. Halfway down the block between Madison and Fifth Avenues, near an empty lot next to an abandoned building, Paulino Camacho slipped and fell banging his head against an iron railing and passing out in a deep snow drift. The street was deserted and no one saw him.

No one that is, except Juan Ramón Burgos, scanning the city of New

York, at the Puerto Rican Department of the OFFICE FOR THE PROTECTION AND SALVAGE OF WAYWARD MORTALS. Dressed in his blue velvet V-neck robe, his beautiful blue wings tucked safely in a non-flying position, he was sitting at his monitor when he caught a brief glance of Camacho slipping and falling. Damn, he thought, another drunk. He'd come back to him later. He went on further south where in the Lower East Side a woman was threatening a man with a broken beer bottle and further on in Brooklyn someone was about to pass out on his bed with a lighted cigarette. What the hell were they doing down there! Christ Almighty they were worse than ever this year.

He pushed a couple of buttons and made the woman throw down the bottle in disgust and walk away. He then pushed another button and the man with the cigarette suddenly sat up and started screaming for his wife to hurry up and come to bed. Finally, he came back to Camacho but couldn't find him in the snow. He tried a closeup but still couldn't locate him. The scanner showed that he was there but he couldn't see him and therefore couldn't help him. He pushed a button and Camacho's data showed up on the screen.

Son of a bitch! He'd have to go down there.

He picked up the phone and dialed his supervisor's number. The phone rang a few times before he got an answer. He then explained that it was imperative that he go down.

"It's an emergency, Tillary," he said.

"Emergency? What kind of emergency?" his supervisor said.

"I got a drunk that fell into a snow drift in Manhattan. It's really coming down hard. There's a blizzard down there. What the hell are those people in weather doing! Tell them I don't appreciate their humor."

"I have nothing to do with the weather department," Tillary said.

"Well, I gotta go down and help this guy out."

"Maybe he got up?"

"Tillary, the scanner goes right to the spot. The board's lit up. It's an emergency. Take my word. He's there all right. I just can't see him."

"Can't you just scrape the snow away?"

"Scanners can't do that, Tillary. The Old Man's inventing all this electronic stuff but somehow he hasn't figured this one out yet."

"Have you tried everything?"

"Everything, Tillary. Bad dreams, sirens. Nothing. If every red light on my board's lit up, he's in trouble. It's all in the regulations. I have to go down."

"I can't let you go. There's nobody to run the scanner in your department."

His supervisor's response made Burgos angrier than he'd ever been in all the time he had been in heaven. It made him reflect again on why he had ever volunteered for this kind of duty. It was all guilt about the way he had lived down on earth and how just before he had died he had promised to reform. He died anyway and rather than going down he went up. Big deal! Boring and thankless work. Day and night rescuing idiots from their stupid mistakes.

"Give me a break, Tillary," he said. "This guy's gonna die. He'll freeze to death."

"Maybe I can put in a call to the old man and He can talk to him. He'll repent, die and you got somebody you can train."

"Tillary, this guy's got five kids to support. We're not talking about some worthless drunk. He's a hard worker, loves his wife and worships those five kids. He just screwed up, period."

"Worships?" Tillary said.

"Cut out the doctrinal stuff, okay? You know what I mean."

"Is he worth saving?"

"Goddamit, Tillary! What in the hell . . ."

"Careful, Burgos."

"Sorry, Tillary. I know, I know. Language. Regulations and all that. Okay, okay. Yeah, he's worth saving. He just screwed up and spent all his money drinking and now he can't buy anything to put under the Christmas tree. He's really a good guy. Just got carried away. Can't you get Blaisdell from the Wasp Department to help out. God, they're. . . . Sorry. I mean, they're overstaffed over there."

"I'm sure you can understand that," Tillary said. "There are a lot more wasps than there are Puerto Ricans."

"Sure, I'm not gonna deny that. You don't even have anybody covering Puerto Ricans in Boston or Philly."

"They're covered. We got them split up. The Polish department's got some and the Irish, the rest. We're doing our best."

"But a 1 to 3 ratio, Tillary? One damned angel . . . oops . . . one angel to watch every three wasps and I gotta bust my hump watching all the Puerto Ricans in New York City to make sure they survive all this holy day crap . . ."

"Burgos!"

"Okay, okay. So it's the Kid's birthday and the Old Man's not gonna like it if I talk that way. But have a heart. I did the computations, and even if I'm at my best, I'm gonna lose at least a hundred people before the New Year comes in. People leaving kids alone and the building going up in flames, arguments that turn into murder, overdoses, people falling into subway tracks. A hundred souls and the way they're carrying on not one of them's got a chance to make it up here. It isn't easy, Tillary. Get me one of the guys from the Wasp Department. Some sociology professor that would enjoy slumming."

"They don't understand Spanish. It's in the regulations. The guy that runs the scanner has to speak Spanish. Your people got the thing passed last year as part of that affirmative action package."

Burgos thought for a moment.

"What about Sinclair?" he said. "He was a Peace Corps volunteer in South America. Some guerrillas blew him up."

"Speaks Quechua."

"Yes . . ., sorry. What about Garrison? I've spoken Spanish with him. He was with the Lincoln Brigade. Got killed outside of Madrid back in the thirties."

"Burgos, you're jeopardizing the welfare of an entire community. The man is not well. Still carries on conversations with Hemingway, even though we have no communication channels with those people below."

"He'll have to do. Just send him down and I'll explain the whole scanning procedure to him. I'll have to take my chances."

"Okay, he'll be at your shop in five minutes."

"Five minutes? He's gotta be here now. I'm leaving."

"I'll do my best."

"Thanks, Tillary. Just keep me posted on who else is down in New York in case I need help. Log me off in five minutes."

A few moments later a pale young man entered the glass enclosed quarters where the giant Puerto Rican scanner was located and greeted Burgos in Spanish. Burgos explained everything very quickly, patted him on the back and thanked him.

"Just make sure that on each ten minute round you scan The Bronx, Manhattan and Brooklyn first. Don't worry too much about Staten Island. We don't have too many there. In Queens most of the people are pretty middle class. Once in a while there's the makings of a traffic accident or a faulty wire on a Christmas decoration, but nothing major. Just keep your eye on the upper and lower ends of Manhattan, the South Bronx and the four different locations in Brooklyn marked in blue. All right?"

The young man saluted and Burgos went off running into the decompressing chamber. He pushed several buttons for dress and stepped into the converter. Within seconds his blue robe and wings were off and he was dressed in the same clothes he'd worn that fateful night ten years before when, after celebrating his third round knockout of Bobby Russo in his fifth pro fight as a lightweight, he'd gone drinking and stepped out in front of a car going 80 miles an hour on the Grand Concourse and that was the end of Juan Moncho, as his mother had called him. He looked in the mirror and felt ashamed of the raggedy clothes, torn by the scraping metal, but he felt the blood pumping in his body and a fraction of a second later he was standing on the corner of Madison Avenue and 111th Street.

The snowfall was now a blizzard, obscuring objects no more than a foot away. Looking down through the snow at his locator he finally found the spot where Camacho had fallen and began shovelling away the snow with his bare hands. After a few minutes he found Camacho's chest. His heart was still beating but he was already stiff. He got him out of the snow and slung him over his shoulder. As he walked he called his own number at the Department and Garrison answered.

"*Teniente Garrison a sus órdenes*," Garrison said.

"Garrison, this is Burgos. Screen up the file on Paulino Camacho, butcher."

"I'm afraid I would need a direct communication from control in order to do that."

"Garrison, knock off the shit. This is life and death."

"Regulations are regulations and I really don't feel I should jeopardize this operation by bending the rules."

"Garrison, screen up the fucking file or I'm gonna spread it around that you got shot in the back outside Madrid because you were scared shit and were running from the fascists, damnit. Screen up that information."

"Yes, sir," Garrison said.

"Thank you."

"Here it is. Camacho, Paulino. Occupation, butcher. Age 38. Born, Cacimar, Puerto Rico. Married. Wife, Marta. Five children. Address, 405 East 6th Street, Apt. 4. Last Mass attended 4/17/77."

"Jesus Christ. He's all the way down there? I thought he lived in El Barrio. Thanks. I'll see you later."

As he walked he applied heat to Camacho's body with the hand resuscitator. By the time they were back on Lexington Avenue, Camacho was moaning. The angel Juan Moncho looked for a cab but there was no traffic at all on the street. They would have to take the subway. As they reached the subway stairs Camacho came to and began struggling.

"Let me down, Ponce," he said. "I can make it down the stairs by myself. What the hell are you doing, anyway? You're right, I would be a coward to kill myself. Are you gonna throw me in front of a train, you idiot? Let me down."

The angel Juan Moncho propped Camacho up against the wall and Camacho all of a sudden opened his eyes and peered into Burgos' face.

"Hey, you're not Ponce," he said. "Who the hell are you and where were you taking me? You were trying to mug me and then throw me in front of a train, right? You're a junkie."

"Just take it easy."

"Bullshit, you little bastard," said Camacho, and took a wild swing at the angel Juan Moncho.

Juan Moncho slipped the punch easily and pushed Camacho up against the wall.

"Hey, I told you to take it easy, Ace. You're in a lot of trouble and all I was doing was trying to help you. You fell in the snow and I'm trying to get you home."

The liquor having worn off somewhat, it once again dawned on Camacho what he was facing when he arrived home. He burst out crying and began pounding the wall near the token booth.

"I can't go home," he bawled. "My kids. I got nothing to put under the tree. I don't care what Ponce said, I'm gonna jump in front of the train."

And off he went crawling under the turnstile with the angel Juan Moncho behind him after slipping two dollars into the booth's window. He grabbed Camacho and pushed him down on a bench with the specific instructions that if he got up he'd feel a lot worse than if the train had run over him.

"Hey, I don't wanna hurt you, but if I have to I'm gonna knock you into next year if you keep it up. Now get a hold of yourself and stop behaving like an asshole. Okay?"

"Okay, okay. Boy, you're pretty strong for a little guy. What's your name?"

"Juan Moncho," said the angel.

Camacho peered into the angel's face and then at his clothes.

"You look familiar as hell. Like you was in the newspaper or something. Ain't you cold in those summer clothes?"

"I'm fine. Don't worry about it."

"Hey, I'm in trouble, man."

"I know all about it. Here comes the train."

They got on the Lexington Avenue local, changed at 86th Street and got on the Express train, and all along Juan Moncho reassured Camacho that everything was going to be all right.

"How? Man, I spent all my money and those kids are gonna be disappointed as hell in the morning."

"Don't worry about it," Juan Moncho said. "We'll pick something up on the way there. There's gotta be a toy store or two down in the Village."

"Everything's closed right now, man. I really blew it."

"We'll find a way. Just leave it to me."

"What you gonna do, break into a toy store?"

"Just don't worry."

At that point, as the train was leaving 59th Street, Juan Moncho got a call from Tillary. He closed his eyes and concentrated on silent receiving and sending.

"Yeah, Tillary?"

"How's it going with the job?"

"Pretty good. We're going down to the Village and see if we can transmit some stuff to his Christmas tree. Another hour or so of work and I'll be back up there. How's Garrison doing?"

"No complaints yet. He hasn't called in any emergencies, but I had to send O'Brien from the Irish Department to show him how to operate the console. There was some party up in the Bronx and a bunch of people crashed it and all hell broke loose. Guns, knives, the whole works. O'Brien patched the cops and they just happened to show up in time to put a stop to the whole thing."

"Good, good. Well, I'll see you later. Thanks for calling."

Juan Moncho was about to click off when all at once Tillary was talking very fast and giving him orders.

"Slow down, Tillary. Slow down. Who?"

"Mandlestein. Mandlestein," Tillary said. "He's gotten himself involved with those idiotic Guardian Angels. Go see what's going on."

"I can't do that! Where the hell is he?"

"Two cars down from yours."

"On the same train? You sure?"

"Of course I'm sure. Go! I'll monitor and send help if it's needed."

Juan Moncho clicked off, shook Camacho awake and told them they had to go.

"Where? We getting off?" Camacho said.

"Let's go. Follow me."

They went through a couple of nearly empty cars and then into a third one and there was six foot one Bryan Mandlestein, dressed in gold lamé from head to toe, cape and all, bleached blond hair to his shoulders and made up like he was being photographed for the cover of Vogue. Around him six red berets in feathers and buttons, all of them with logoed t-shirts over their winter clothing, were shoving and pushing as they tried to get at Mandlestein. As soon as Mandlestein saw Juan Moncho coming he began clapping his hands. He then jumped up on one of the seats of the train.

"Oh, thank goodness you've come, Robin," he said, sighing. "Please explain to these cretins that they're tastelessly and abominably dressed.

Tacky, tacky, tacky," he added, turning to them and pointing his finger at the startled Guardian Angels. "Tell them, okay? I mean you speak their language. Oh, and add that if they're Guardian Angels, then I'm Marlene Dietrich." And then oblivious to their growing anger he went into the singing of some current popular song while gyrating sensuously atop the subway seat 'Marlene watches from the wall, her mocking smile says it all . . .' "

"Let me at him, José," said one of the Guardian Angels. "I'll kick his faggety ass."

"Word," said a couple more.

"Yo, what's going on, brother," said Juan Moncho. "Chill out."

"Hey, mind your own business, shorty," said one of the Guardian Angels. "Or ama bust you upside the head."

"Just take it easy," Juan Moncho said.

Two of the Guardian Angels moved towards Juan Moncho, adopting karate stands, their fingers curled as they crouched.

"My, my," said Mandlestein from his perch. "How grossly butch. Let me turn them into Michael Jackson teeny boppers, Burgos."

Juan Moncho waved Mandlestein off and as soon as the first one made his move, consisting of a high kick, he stepped under and inside, jabbed three times with his left, crossed over with his right and knocked the Guardian Angel out before he hit the floor of the subway car with a thud. The other five Angels rushed Juan Moncho, but as he was getting ready to deliver his next blow, the five turned into young screaming teenage girls made up in punk outfits, their hair chopped in mohawks or dyed the most awful shades of green, orange and red, and their clothes looking like they had shopped at the Salvation Army. The subway car doors opened and Mandlestein jumped off the seat.

"Let's go, you beast. You could've hurt that boy. You Latins are so impulsive."

Out the three of them went at Grand Central Station. Camacho was totally sober but nearly in shock. He kept looking from Mandlestein to Juan Moncho, unable to say anything. He was sure the little guy was Johnny Burgos, the lightweight that had gotten killed about ten or eleven years ago.

Mandlestein explained how he'd been sitting up in his cubicle, monitoring the gays in the Village when all of a sudden a friend he knew from fifteen years before when he died was about to commit what amounted to suicide by getting involved with somebody who had been diagnosed as having AIDS.

"Like I couldn't blame him because this boy was divine. I mean, can we talk? Tab Hunter move over, okay? But I couldn't let my friend, Donald, do it and he wouldn't respond to anything I sent down and Tillary told me under no circumstances was I to come down and I told him to buzz off, know what I mean? And now I'm in all sorts of trouble and he's going to report me and I'll probably have to go in front of the All Powerful and all that other garbage. Oh, I'm getting so depressed. Look at me. Still dressed in this tacky outfit which is strictly passé. So, what brings you down here?"

Juan Moncho explained about Camacho.

"I'm just gonna stop off at a toy store and get some stuff for his kids. We'll just beam it under their Christmas tree and then get a dress or something for his wife and get him home."

Mandlestein was shocked.

"You have to be kidding. I know what you're thinking. Just cheap stuff and get it over with, right? I know you got it hard with so much responsibility but, puleeze. Okay? Can I speak frankly without you going into your Rocky or Rambo thing, or whatever fantasy it is you think you're playing out?"

"Sure, go ahead," Juan Moncho said.

Camacho couldn't take it any longer.

"Say, who are you guys?"

"Quiet, Pancho," Mandlestein said. "Everything's under control."

"My name's not Pancho," Camacho said.

"Okay, then Cisco," Mandlestein said. "Just don't get your panties in a wad, all right?"

"What?" Camacho said, feeling insulted.

"That's okay, Camacho," Juan Moncho said. "Let me handle this," and turning to Mandlestein, told him to go ahead.

Mandlestein explained that part of the reason Puerto Ricans were in such bad shape was because they felt all this guilt about one thing or another and therefore didn't believe they deserved the very best the society had to offer. And that here Juan Moncho had a chance to do it up big and really bring about a miracle and he was settling for some cheap toys and a $19.95 dress for Camacho's wife.

"What did you have in mind?" said Juan Moncho.

"Don't get me wrong, Sheena of the Jungle," Mandlestein said. "I know I'm being a bit selfish because I haven't been shopping in so long but, like how does FAO Schwarz, Bergdorf Goodman, Bloomies and Fred the Furrier sound to you?"

"Are you crazy?" Juan Moncho said.

"Of course I am, but it's your holyday not mine. I'm already in trouble, so let them put it on my tab. Come on. Get out your scanner and get sizes on Lola or Conchita or whatever her name is. What's your wife's name, darling?" he said, turning to Camacho.

"Don't call me that, okay?" said Camacho, going into an extremely awkward boxing stance. "I don't let *patos* talk to me like that."

"Oh, my!" said Mandlestein, backing off as if he were frightened. "Mucho macho! Get out your scanner, Burgos. Although Pancho Villa here doesn't seem to appreciate our effort."

Juan Moncho went into his pocket and retrieved his miniature scanner and punched in Camacho's address. Immediately the screen showed Camacho's living room with the kids sitting around the Christmas tree in their pajamas and Marta Camacho sitting on the sofa crying. Mandlestein snatched the pocket scanner away from Juan Moncho and shoved it at Camacho.

"Take a look, big man," he said.

"Oh, my God," said Camacho. "I'm gonna jump in front of a train."

"No, you're not, sweetie," said Mandlestein. "You're going shopping, whether you like it or not."

"What's he talking about?" Camacho said, turning to Juan Moncho.

"Just do as he says. Don't worry. We'll have you home in less than an hour."

"Oh, goody," said Mandlestein. "Let's get out of here and get a cab. Burgos, make sure they all go to sleep before we start."

Juan Moncho pushed a couple of buttons on his pocket scanner and watched as the kids kissed their mother and went off to bed. Unable to resist the angel induced sleep, Marta Camacho turned off the lights and also went to bed.

Within minutes they were inside FAO Schwarz and Camacho was going crazy picking out toys for Alicia, Betty, Rodolfo, Kevin and the baby, Nilsa. He couldn't believe it. He picked out a stuffed elephant the size of a great dane for the baby. Juan Moncho aimed the transporter at the gray form and it disappeared.

"See," Mandlestein said, pointing to the scanner.

"Wow," said Camacho, watching as the elephant ended up against the couch where Marta had sat. "You guys are too much! Listen, I'm sorry about what I said about *patos*," he said to Mandlestein.

"That's okay, ducky," Mandlestein said. "Just keep shopping."

From the FAO Schwarz they went to Bloomingdale's and then to Bergdorf Goodman, then to Cartier's where they picked out a watch for Marta and then off to Fred the Furrier where Mandlestein chose a full length sable for her. He wrote down a name and address on a piece of paper and gave it to Camacho.

"Your wife's not half bad," he said, "but she's got to do something about her hair and makeup. Have her go see my friend, Alonzo in the Village. We do miracles, but what he does with women is truly heavenly, okay, sweetie?"

"Sure," said Camacho.

And so it went. When they were finished they stood out in the street with the snow still falling. Juan Moncho told Mandlestein that he had to get Camacho home. Mandlestein said he was absolutely exhausted. Since they should both be getting back up, Juan Moncho said, why didn't they use the transporter to get Camacho home. Mandlestein agreed.

"Okay, Camacho," Juan Moncho said. "We gotta go. Merry Christmas and Happy New Year."

"But who are you?" Camacho said.

"If anybody wants to know, just tell them, you met your guardian angel," Juan Moncho said laughing.

Before Camacho could say another word, the angel Juan Moncho pushed three buttons and Camacho found himself in bed next to Marta. He slipped quietly out of bed, tiptoed out of the bedroom, looked in on the children and then peeked into the living room. By the light of the lamppost outside the window he saw dozens of boxes next to the Christmas tree and against the sofa, the outline of the huge elephant.

Sometimes, If You Listen Closely, You can Hear Crying in the Zoo

A few years ago, one week before his fortieth birthday, my nephew Gregory Sandoval, assistant to the head of the art department for Russell, Thomason & Layne, woke up, looked at his wife of sixteen years, the former Gayle Auerbach of Racine, Wisconsin, and decided that his marriage, if not over, had reached its terminal stages and, like a comatose patient with little hope of recovery, was either to be tolerated or put out of its misery. Hardly ever given to emotional outbursts, having conquered that handicap many years prior in his search for stability, Sandoval felt a twinge of regret. With great care not to disturb his wife's angelic repose, he reached over her Rubenesque body, turned off the alarm on the clock radio before it could intrude into his thoughts and slid quietly from his side of the bed onto the carpeted floor.

At seven o'clock in the morning the sky blue walls and the white furniture, gilt-edged and delicately crafted, made him feel as if he had woken up in the bedroom of a great and beautiful actress, something which the former Gayle Auerbach was not, having devoted her entire adult life to early childhood education. Sandoval lit a filter-tip cigarette, inhaled deeply, squeezed his eyes with thumb and index finger and let the long, slender digits travel down the bridge of his equally long, thinly chiseled nose before exhaling the smoke. The combined sensation brought him away from the sleepy morning haze and into another day.

Seventeen stories below, on Riverside Drive, he could barely hear traffic already moving, the horns moaning in agonized mortification muffled by the distance, the engines idling as the cars moved at a snail's pace. Sandoval went to the window and stood looking out forlornly. Almost every tree had bloomed and the park, stretching north and south along the river, appeared as inviting as the day when he and Gayle and the children had moved into the apartment ten years before. Once again he felt a strange tugging at his heart. He was reminded of a mournful solitary note plucked on a string. His mind went immediately through the family of string instruments, searching for the origin of his sorrow. He hesitated between a balalaika and a medieval lute before deciding what he had heard was a mandolin. The melody of a nostalgic Italian song full of melancholic trills overwhelmed his awareness. He shivered in disgust at the treacle and rejected the notion of anything but his desire to be away from his wife.

There was no need to return to Sorrento since he had never been there, entertained a visit or had the least curiosity where on the map of Italy it lay. Those had been his words to Dr. Feinstein. From that bit of insight, Sandoval had decided that his fascination with Italians was a negative one. There had always been in him a need to be accepted and his experiences among Italians were filled with unresolved anxieties.

Each morning, walking to school, he had had to contend with the possibility of attack simply because he lived on the other side of Third Avenue. There was no consolation in people's insistence, his mother's among them, that he looked Italian and had nothing to fear as long as he remained quiet. For as long as he did not utter more than a few words at a time no one could detect those long double e's, or the lack of them, that once in a while crept into his speech to denounce him as a Spanish speaker and which kept him up nights preoccupied with such words as chin and fink, feel and reel, and numerous other elusive English sounds. Those fears had driven him to develop the clear enunciation which made Gayle Auerbach, at the time of their first meeting, inmersed as she was in a course called "Fostering Correct Speech Among Pre-kindergarten Children," initially feel more than a mild attraction to him, but which the passage of years and hour after waking hour of guarding against that tell-tale accent had caused him to develop a laconic and seemingly pessimistic personality.

In high school the fear of physical harm at the hands of the feared duck-tailed, pegged-trousered toughs in club jackets of wool and satin with gladiators, jokers or winged insignia had brought on frequent rashes and cold sweats. Once or twice he had been stopped in Jefferson Park but nothing had come from the encounters. In time he had managed to establish his identity among the rough talking gang members by drawing beautiful girls in seductive poses whenever a class became too boring. He had proudly allowed his drawings to be passed around and at times had incurred the wrath of several teachers for producing mass inattentiveness in their classes. The teachers' reactions further established his position among the tougher and more rebellious of the students and in that way Sandoval was able to forge an identity quite separate from other Spanish-speaking students, who, although in attendance at the school in small numbers, were driven enough to handle themselves on the basis of their own physical toughness, athletic ability or connections, either in fact or through elaborate rhetorical bluffs, to powerful and feared Puerto Rican gangs from the other side of Third Avenue and had no need of props such as the semi-pornographic drawings which he drew at the risk of possible disciplinary action. They, the others, strutted the halls speaking Spanish, jostling each other and keeping to themselves in tight hierarchical unity. They joked with him, called him a "guinea lover" and pitied him because they knew, somehow, that he had a problem and was weak. He had nurtured a deep hatred for his own people those years, the emotion kept alive by dreams of becoming an artist and an instinctive knowledge that he was different, smarter, more talented and above all, he realized later, caucosoid, a term which finally united him with Italians, Irish, Jews and all other chosen people.

And yet something painful and dark had remained with him from those years. Lately, a renewed obsession with Italians, almost bordering on the morbid, had crept back into his life. Each time an item turned up in the media in which there was mention of an Italian involved in underworld activity, he listened carefully or read the account several times, wrote down the name and checked assiduously through ten years of yearbooks from his high school to see if here at last some measure of retribution had been visited on his tormentors. Instead of corroborating his need for revenge he periodically received bits of information which negated his expectations: Mancuso had become a school superintendent in Rochester, N.Y.; Satriano was doing obscure research in genetics; Conte headed a police precinct in Queens; Buono had an undefeated season as head football coach of a Division III college in Iowa; DeSpina was an Air Force major and Lucca, who'd frightened him more than once with his temper and imitated his supposed accent every time he needed to get a laugh, had become a Franciscan Brother and was now somewhere in the Brazilian jungle. Once, someone whom he barely remembered from school was arrested in a union dispute. Upon reading about it he felt a surge of vengeful pleasure, a shortlived sensation quickly replaced by feelings of remorse and an almost paralyzing fear that he was to be executed gangland fashion, as the newspaper so colorfully put it.

When the book, THE GODFATHER, became a best seller, Sandoval stayed up all night reading. He pored over each word for a clue as to his safety, convinced that years back he had committed a great and unforgivable breach of Sicilian ethics and eventually would have to pay the ultimate price. The day after he finished reading the book, he became ill at work and left the office after lunch. When the movie was released he went to the theater alone and sat with his hands on his thighs, periodically wiping the perspiration from his palms as the actors convinced him that not only was his person in great danger but that his whole way of life was about to be obliterated. He left the theater, hopped into a cab, praying that the driver had not been employed to take him for his last ride. Riding through Central Park on his way home he kept looking out of the back window of the cab to make sure a black limousine was not following.

He was terror stricken for several weeks. They were all around him: in restaurants, trucks, subways, buses, cabs, in lawyers' offices, disguised as doctors, dentists, teachers, statesmen. All of them wearing that surface respectability but underneath sworn to *omerta*, the sinister code of silence which bound them to each other. Even in his office, up there, thirty stories above Madison Avenue, sitting around the conference table discussing an advertising campaign for a new cereal, he had not been able to keep his eyes off of Mike Russo, with his thick glasses and business suit, so meek and unassuming that nobody but the most paranoid of individuals could suspect him of anything more sinister than keeping a secret about an upcoming birthday party. Nevertheless, Sandoval saw in him the makings of a future don, wielding power over the lives of thousands of people, controlling the advertising agency and him through intricate business deals, legitimized by suave men with degrees from the Harvard Business School.

Sandoval turned away from the window, took one last drag from his cigarette and put it out. He looked at his wife, still sound asleep, her blonde hair spread out on the pillow, her rosy, porcelain-like arm resting beneath it, and wondered if she was aware of his unhappiness. He doubted that she had ever given much thought to his need to get away from the city and live out in the country and paint. He wished he could pick up and go and like Roger Briggs get his trip together. WANDERING PARISIAN STREETS. NOTHING AT ALL LIKE MICHEL LEGRAND. EVERYTHING NEW AND ALIVE. VISITED MOULIN ROUGE SECTION YESTERDAY. ROGER.

But Gayle could not imagine what it was like, the anguish. Nor was she expected to, he thought. Nothing in her background had prepared her for such a life. He resisted an urge to go to the bed and kiss her. It would be an act devoid of sincerity and brought on by guilt. He would then have to deal with the subsequent feelings of rejection of himself as a conformist, a word he had never examined thoroughly until it came into common use by his daughter the past year. With controlled rage he ground his right fist into the palm of his left hand. There was no question about it. He would have to talk to Gayle. That evening after the children were in bed he would sit her down and explain why he had to move out and start over. Perhaps it would all dissipate before the day was over. No, that was a copout, a way of wishing that the problem would go away without his taking action. His brow was suddenly furrowed as he considered that perhaps something else other than his relationship to his wife was disturbing him. He shook his head several times. Nothing surfaced. Chuck Thomason's personal investments had increased miraculously in the past month, the Art Department had once again received praise and everyone was happy. Maybe the new account would take his mind off the problem for a couple of weeks. No, there it was again; his need to escape this confrontation with Gayle was amazing, his cowardice enormous.

Sandoval lit another cigarette, began to go into the bathroom adjacent to the bedroom, realized running water would wake up his wife, and after opening the door of the bedroom, walked through the apartment to the larger bathroom, utilized exclusively now by his two children. He lifted the seat from the light blue toilet bowl, which along with the bathtub and sink, his wife had had installed after his promotion four years before, and urinated into the clear, sea-like water. He watched the clouded, milky liquid and wondered again, although he felt no pain in his kidneys, whether something was the matter or it was merely a sign of middle age. He decided not to mention the clouded urine to Gayle. Her response would be mild chiding on his avoidance of vitamins and a good natured suggestion that he take an extra dosage of Vitamins E and C, drink a strong cup of rose hips tea with alfalfa honey and eat some wheat germ with yogurt, not to mention dissolving or attempting to dissolve some lecithin into his orange juice.

When he was finished at the bowl he walked to the sink, examined the graying stubble on his chin, fought the urge to make up a joke about Grecian Formula, an account which the agency had lost, and wondered if at some point in the future there would be an ad for a similar product which could be applied to the pubic area. Instead of dwelling on such an event and how it would be treated esthetically, Sandoval began shaving, amusing himself with mentally drawing pictures of shaving cream commercials which would discredit other firms. In his fantasies he would sneak into another agency's art department and, working quickly, efficiently, he would draw, photograph and lay out ads with just the subtlest hint of failure in them. Perhaps a slight touch of gay insinuation in the eyes of the shaving he-man. The company would come to Russell, Thomason & Layne to be rescued and the rival ad agency would be discredited, ruined. He would become a vice-president and in time, perhaps, his name would be added to the firm. It was no wonder that he felt such fear of Italians and their alleged secret organizations. He was himself a master of industrial espionage.

After shaving, Sandoval turned on the shower, began to do his limbering up exercises, stopped after no more than a minute and, after removing his pajamas, stepped under the shower. There seemed to be little need for the exercises. He never overate. What had he to prove anyway? His weight never varied. Winter or summer he had remained trim. A little flabbiness around the middle was expected once a man reached his age. Not everyone was Hank Aaron.

As he closed the sliding doors of the shower, Sandoval dug his toes into the yellow rubber daisies which Gayle had the Cuban super, Mr. Gonzalez, glue to the bottom of the tub. He began to sing "Sergeant Pepper's Lonely Hearts Club Band" as he stepped under the water. It was the only time of the day when he felt totally uninhibited.

Sandoval was at the top of his voice as he trod up and down on his wife's daisies. He marched and strutted as he imagined himself singing at the head of the band. His entire body shook with abandon.

He sang the song four times from beginning to end, each time becoming wilder and more exaggerated in his movements. It was the only song he knew by heart. When he finished belting out the last line, he applauded and then began to sing in Spanish. Not recalling words or tune, he made up melody and words as he went along. They were not the real words but they sounded authentic, so that he was not sure whether they were or not.

When he was finished showering he dried himself vigorously and, with a towel wrapped around his middle and his pajamas in hand, came out of the bathroom only to be confronted by his eldest offspring, Barbara, aged fifteen, high school freshman at Bronx High School of Science, and resident authority on Elton John, Cindy Lauper, Sid Vicious, W.C. Fields, Star Trek, yoga, belly dancing, camping, astrology, Buddhism (both Zen and True), scientology, cybernetics, T.M., EST, J.R. Tolkien, *Mad Magazine, The National Lampoon, Rolling Stone*, the legalization of marijuana, the situation in Latin America, the Middle East, South Africa, abortion and the Women's Liberation movement, the latter, through the devout, comprehensive and diligent study of *Cosmopolitan, Ms* and several other publications to which she subscribed. Still wearing her full length, electric blue, satin robe in which she slept, her long brown hair hanging over half of her face in an 80's version of Gloria DeHaven, she looked at Sandoval and shook her head disapprovingly.

"What's the matter?" Sandoval asked.

She regarded him condescendingly before speaking, pitying him, he thought.

"Did you know that for every minute you spend under the shower you use up over twelve gallons of water? And even though it generally takes less water to take a shower than to fill a tub, any time beyond seven to eight minutes proves counterproductive?" she said, adding as always, he didn't know why, a question mark to her every sentence. "You've just finished using over 360 gallons of water?"

"Com'on, I didn't," he shot back, momentarily defensive and at the same time amused by his daughter's candor. "Where did you read that?"

"I didn't read it, okay?" Barbara said, haughtily. "Francine Cohen and I measured it out at her house? It's true, okay, Greg? You were under the shower exactly twenty-seven minutes and you turned on the water three minutes prior to that?"

"What are you leading up to?" asked Sandoval, no longer amused. "I pay for the water. I'm entitled to take a shower."

"It's really not a question of rights, Greg?"

"What is it, if it isn't rights?" he tried again.

"Awareness, concern, empathy, humanness?"

"You're kidding!"

"No, I'm not? Are you aware that there is currently a drought in Africa?"

All the tension he had been able to relieve through his morning ritual had returned and his shoulders began aching. The muscles in the back of his neck tightened and he felt his stomach turn over.

"What are you talking about, Barbara! Africa, droughts! What is this, anyway? What am I supposed to do about a drought in Africa? Should I take a sponge bath and send them a case of Perrier?"

"It's no joke, okay, Greg? Millions of people are starving because of it?" Her head was bobbing up and down, nodding patiently at him. "The least you could do, sort of to express your sympathy with their plight, would be to conserve water? The exorbitant amount of water you used this morning probably has no effect on having the drought end, but it certainly augurs badly for America and its disregard for the environment?"

"It what? Look, I'm not going to stand here and be made to feel guilty about taking a shower. Jesus!"

"That's a copout, Greg."

Sandoval ignored his daughter and began walking back to his bedroom. Halfway there he realized that she had been calling him by his first name. He turned and called her in a sort of growled whisper. Barbara Sandoval walked defiantly to him and stood, hands on hips, looking up into his face. He prided himself in never having to worry that his children were afraid of him, but the look of rebellion in Barbara's eyes made him want to slap her.

"What's this Greg stuff all of a sudden?" he said.

"Isn't that your name?" she said.

"Yeah, it's my name but where do *you* get off using it?"

"You call me by my first name?"

"I'm your father."

"Merely a genetic accident? Having sired me doesn't give you the right to hold me in bondage . . .?"

"Bondage? Sired? Genetics?" The words had no meaning when spoken by his daughter. All he heard was defiance in her voice.

". . . The parent-child relationship is oppressive to both parties and is rapidly on the way to becoming obsolete?"

Sandoval's mouth literally hung open.

"Obsolete, right?"

"Yes, outmoded, passe?"

"I suppose allowances have gone the same way?" he said.

Barbara shrugged her shoulders at the implied threat.

"There you have it?" she said.

"What?"

"Another reason why it's important to abolish this type of sick dependency, this symbiotic attachment which exists between us?"

"Sick! You call the time your mother and I spent nurturing you, catering to your whims, sick!"

"Yes, I do? Sick? Diseased?"

"Barbara, cut it out!" pleaded Sandoval, fast becoming exhausted by the argument. "Don't test my patience. Where are you getting all this stuff from? I know your mother and I are pretty liberal people but you sound like a fanatic . . . some throwback to the sixties. What are they teaching you at that school?"

"This has nothing do to with school? This is a personal confrontation between you and me? As a matter of fact, schools are also on their way out? About the only benefit in schools is that at least there's a chance of finding people who might share your dilemma?"

"Don't you mean, *one's* dilemma?"

"Semantics?" said Barbara, waving her hand to shoo away Sandoval's argument.

"Now it's semantics, right?"

"Yes, linguistic excess and purist priggishness?"

"Forget it," Sandoval said, shaking his head. "You want to call me Greg? Go ahead. Be my guest."

"Okay, so be resentful? It'll improve our relationship? You'll see me not as a daughter but as a member of the community at large, with as much input into the general well being of the environment as the next person?"

"Yeah, all right, kid. Whatever you say."

"Greg?"

"Yeah?"

"Billy Nelson's sleeping over this weekend and I'd appreciate it if you kind of made him feel welcome? We'll be seeing a lot of each other in the next few years and the better you get along with him, the better it'll be all around? I've told you and Gayle about him?"

Sandoval couldn't contain himself. He wanted to scream at this caricature before him. He closed his eyes, counted to ten and through clenched teeth informed his daughter that until the matter was discussed thoroughly between himself and her mother no one was coming over to sleep.

"And that is final, Ms. Sandoval," he said. "Now go and wake up your brother and don't get *him* started."

Sandoval turned and walked into the bedroom. Ripping the towel away, he threw it up against the wall and in the process knocked over a bottle of perfume sitting on his wife's vanity. The bottle clattered around the vanity, lost its top and spilled over onto the floor, perfuming the air.

"Gayle, wake up!" Sandoval screamed.

Gayle Sandoval sat up in bed dazed, and looked in shock at her husband.

"You're naked," she said. "The shade's up."

"Sure the shade's up. Is that all you can say! What is it with you? I suppose you think every peeping tom across the Hudson River in Jersey keeps a twenty-four hour watch on this apartment?"

Seeing that her husband was not about to cover himself, Gayle Sandoval did the next best thing. She pulled the sheet up to her neck and sat in the middle of the bed, her lower lip quivering.

"What's the matter, Greg?" she said, after a few moments of watching her husband pacing back and forth across the room, puffing on a cigarette. "Is something the matter? There isn't a problem with the plumbing, is there?"

"No, nothing's the matter with the plumbing," he shot back angrily. "Not here in New York, anyway!"

"What is it, then?"

"Tell me something. And don't cover up for her. Have you been taking Barbara to those silly New School classes? What the hell's gotten into that kid?"

"What do you mean, Greg? That was last year. And it was Bank Street, not the New School. It was a seminar on kindergarten free time."

Over her initial fear Gayle Sandoval had gotten out of bed, gone directly to the chest of drawers on the other side of the room and, deliberately avoiding having to look at her husband's nakedness, extended him a pair of jockey shorts. Sandoval stepped quickly into them and in a torrent of words explained what had taken place.

"Africa yet!" he said, smacking his forehead theatrically. "Can you believe that! Africa! What the hell's gotten into her? Why Africa? Why not Nicaragua or Afghanistan? You know, start small and build up. Jesus Christ!"

"She's merely expressing her need for independence, Greg. It's a natural stage in a child's development."

"Yeah, yeah. Everybody goes through that. Some kids don't want to pick up their rooms, others are ashamed to be seen with their parents, they wear funny clothes and hardly ever change them, they cut their hair in ridiculous hairdos and tie up the telephone for hours on end. Some even turn to drugs. All that seems pretty normal in order to declare your independence. Our Barbara, however, isn't satisfied with some mundane kind of rebellion. She wants to topple the regime right now. She's a regular friggin Gloria Steinem."

"Greg!"

Sandoval watched his wife's hand shoot up to her mouth and her eyes widen. But he wasn't through and no amount of outrage or shock on her part was going to prevent him from having his say. Dr. Feinstein was right. He had been passive far too long.

"You shouldn't use such language when referring to the children," Barbara said.

"Purist priggishness," Sandoval said, going up to his wife and spitting the words at her as if they were an insult.

"What did you say?"

"No, not me," Sandoval said sarcastically. "I didn't say it, she did."

"Barbara?"

"Yes, Barbara. Our daughter. Yours and mine."

"She didn't!"

He was sure she had no idea what 'priggishness' meant, but it sounded sexual and therefore her shock.

"Yes, she did. And what's all this stuff about Billy Nelson sleeping over?"

"I'm sure it has nothing to do with what she said. I told her it was all right, if you approved."

"Well, according to her it's all settled. She wants me to be nice to him. Which one the hell is he?"

"A friend. Nothing serious."

"Well, he's not coming into the house to sleep."

"He's black, Greg."

Sandoval had gone to the closet for a pair of pants but the word "black" turned him around. He looked at his wife as if he had not quite heard her and walked very slowly in her direction.

"He's what?" he said, pants in hand. "Black?"

"Yes, black. Negro. Call it whatever you want," Barbara said, walking backwards until she was flush with the wall.

"Is that supposed to make a difference?" asked Sandoval, still holding his pants. He paused for a moment. "Of course, now the picture becomes clearer. Africa. The drought. It makes all the difference in the world. If we don't let him into the apartment the NAACP will picket our building. Eldridge Cleaver will give up religion and reunite the Black Panthers. Jesse Jackson will go on TV and accuse us of economic discrimination. Minister Farrakhan will call us white devils. Is that it? Well, I don't care if this pubescent Andrew Young is green with purple polka dots. Since when does a fifteen year old girl have boys coming over to sleep at her house! For that matter, eighteen, nineteen or twenty! What the hell is this, anyway! Does Spock mention that in his book? What does Dear Abby say? What about Bruno Bettlegeuse?"

"Bettleheim."

"Bettleheim, Bettlegeuse! What's the difference. Jesus Christ!"

"Greg?"

"What?"

"Did you take your vitamins yet?"

Sandoval stood in the middle of the bedroom, frozen by his wife's words. A feeling of overpowering guilt swept over him. It threatened to turn every bone in his body to liquid. Who was this woman? Who was she? He stared at the floor, unable to speak or move. When he finally said something it came out like the squeak of a broken mechanical toy in its death throes.

"Please, Gayle," he said. "Listen to me."

But as she often did when things became too difficult, she didn't listen and instead reached into herself for proven remedies, a good old fashioned saying, a word of encouragement, a suggestion.

"You haven't taken your vitamins in a couple of days," she said now. "Have you? The stress formula's very important, you know. It contains the B complex."

He could not listen. She was going on and on about how if one stopped taking the B complex it created a greater vitamin deficiency; and did he know that particular ethnic groups were more prone to certain kinds of vitamin deficiencies than others; and how Vitamin C, for example, is needed by everyone because human beings and anthropoid apes are the only animals which cannot synthesize their own. As she spoke she edged herself along the wall and away from him.

Sandoval walked to where his wife stood babbling and ceremoniously placed his pants over a chair and then put his hands firmly on her shoulders. A pretty woman with an ever hopeful look in her large brown eyes, Gayle Sandoval suddenly looked as if her husband was about to commit an unnatural sexual act upon her person. A U.S.A., as she had categorized it in her mind in order to euphemize its impact, was her greatest fear and one which she had not been able to bring up in six years of analysis.

"Greg, please don't," she said, her knees becoming weak and her voice cracking. "Don't, please."

Sandoval said nothing. He looked into his wife's eyes and held her shoulders until the anger subsided. He sighed deeply and letting go of her shoulders he let his arms dangle helplessly at his sides. Having expected the inevitable, she had sunk to her knees and remained there with her mouth half way open staring at his jockey shorts.

"What's happening to us, Gayle?" he said.

Gayle was now totally spooked. Her husband had finally cracked under corporate strain. Everything she had feared about his upwardly mobile drive was coming to a head. She got quickly back on her feet and tried to find words with which to soothe him.

"Would you like me to get back into bed?" she said.

"What?" Sandoval said. "What did you say?"

"You know, Greg," she answered, attempting to sound seductive. If she could achieve as much, it would save her once more from his more unexpressed animal Latin instincts. "You know, sexual tension."

"No, no sexual tension," Sandoval said.

He wanted to laugh but could not. He turned away and began dressing. As he did so he muttered unintelligibly to himself. His wife followed him around the room at a discreet distance, not yet certain whether it was safe to turn her back on him. When she saw that he no longer seemed interested in pursuing, neither the argument nor her person, and that he was quite absentmindedly knotting his tie, she asked him how he wanted his eggs.

"Eggs?" said the startled Sandoval.

"Yes. Poached with cheese sauce?"

Sandoval turned away from the mirror and looked suspiciously at his wife. She was trying to kill him.

"What about the cholesterol?" he asked.

"The Vitamin E takes care of it. Vitamin E dissolves . . ."

"All right, all right. Poached, then. Just don't go on and on with the vitamins."

He was not quite sure what she was up to but he might as well find out.

"Good," she said. "I'll get started as soon as I slip into something. Okay, darling?"

Gayle Sandoval, once more in control of her life, made the innocuous poaching of eggs sound like something out of an x-rated movie. Nothing was further from her mind, but now Sandoval was suddenly aroused. He watched her go to the closet, select a light yellow dress and disappear into the bathroom. He tiptoed to the locked bathroom door and listened. In a moment he heard the cassette being inserted into the tape recorder and several seconds later Dvorak's "New World Symphony" was drowning out the sound of the shower. How did she manage to be so sterile about everything? Sandoval was convinced she timed her flatulations to the crash of the cymbals. He walked away from the bathroom door, retrieved his wallet and keys from the dresser, put on his wristwatch and NYU class ring and headed for the dining room.

There he was confronted by another of the agonies of his life. His son, Christopher, was already seated, reading a new sugar frosted cereal box and stuffing its contents into his mouth with amazing rapidity. Sandoval could not fathom any of it. If his daughter had been blessed with a glib mouth and an overly developed sense of social consciousness, his son had been damned by slow wits and limited interests. At age eleven Christopher's interests were sports and space travel. Already well over five feet tall and weighing nearly one hundred and fifty pounds, Sandoval was sure the boy would grow up to be a thick-necked, mammoth National Football League lineman. Little doubt existed in Sandoval's mind that his son's progress was being monitored by some giant computer and that scouts were already feeding the data to sundry coaches around the nation.

Fate had certainly dealt harshly with Sandoval. For if it were not enough that he had suffered the injury of being a strange child, an insecure adolescent and a frightened adult, one thing had been constant in his development. Bar none, short of actual physical handicap, Gregory Sandoval was the worst athlete ever created by nature's erratic hand. There had always been little things which he could not master and had caused him to be ridiculed. Things like running to third base after hitting a ball. As hard as he tried he could not cure himself of the disgusting habit, much as he could never overcome having balls bounce off his head when the game was not soccer, or prevent himself from shooting a basketball clear over the backboard whenever he got his hands on it. And now this. A son who ate, breathed and lived sports and who was superb at whatever he attempted. What could he teach him? What exquisite bit of knowledge about life could he impart on him when all the boy thought about were statistics, game plans and trades. When he was not involved in those he was throwing, catching, kicking, shooting, batting, saving, sliding, tackling, blocking, dribbling, stick handling and dozens of other intricate athletic moves too complex for Sandoval to even follow.

He noted the movement of the boy's eyes as they shifted over the written words. His hand moved mechanically from bowl to mouth in absent-minded and incomprehensible response to what he read.

"Good morning, Chris," said Sandoval, sitting down across from his son and doing his best to sound in command.

"Morning, Greg," mumbled the boy, through a mouthful of cereal and milk.

"What did you say?"

"I said, 'good morning.' "

"No, after that."

"Nothing."

"Are you sure?" Greg said, positive he had heard his name.

His son looked up and faced him with a look that would have made Mean Joe Green or Lyle Alzado wish they had taken up bull riding, alligator wrestling or something similar but less dangerous than football.

"Yeah," he said.

Sandoval tried staring him down but finally gave up.

"Christopher, would you go out in the hall and get me the *Times*?"

"Sure," said the boy, jumping up, still looking at the cereal box and moving laterally with remarkable agility. He was a replica of his mother. Dark blond hair, large wondering brown eyes and the same Germanic corpulence. When he was gone Sandoval turned the cereal box around and read the offer which was so thoroughly engrossing to his son. BE THE FIRST IN YOUR NEIGHBORHOOD TO EXPLORE SPACE. COMPLETE WITH LUNAR MODULE AND LANDING INSTRUCTIONS. Sandoval studied the layout, looking for flaws. Nothing. Who was he? He reached inside the cereal box, scooped a handful of the spaceship-like bits of cereal and tasted them. His face contorted into a grimace at the taste. Once through the sugar the cereal tasted like saw dust. The guy was a genius if he could layout the back of a cereal box that way and kids gobbled up the stuff like Christopher was doing. Perhaps he should have taken the job with General Mills ten years before. Where would he be now? Michigan? Wisconsin? Maybe he would have been happier out there in Middle America. Perhaps he would've blended into anonymous tranquility. There were fewer Italians there. Was that true? At least the pace was slower, more suitable to his generally placid disposition.

But it was too late. The die had been cast long ago and he was destined to spend a life of agony as he strove to achieve his goals. And that was important. How many of his people had achieved as much as he had? Sure, a congressman, a couple of baseball players, a golfer, an opera singer, three or four actors, his uncle and a couple of other writers, some lawyers and doctors. Out of how many? Two million of them living in the U.S. Some of his old friends were still doing the same thing they were doing twenty years ago. Pushing carts in the garment district, or brooms and floor waxers. The Post Office, some firemen and cops, a couple of dozen teachers and hundreds of social workers, as if they served any purpose other than making people even more dependent.

Goals were important. But what were they? That was it, he thought. He had lost sight of his goals. He had gone off half-cocked in search of financial security and had lost sight of his goals. Had his goal been to become the head of the Art Department at some ad agency which sold junk to people? What had been his rationale? What was the needed economic function of advertising? Of course to keep money flowing. If people didn't buy, the economy would stagnate. How easy it had been to rationalize everything back then.

But that had not been his reason for existence. No, long ago he had dreamt of Greenwich Village lofts and wine and large wide canvasses brilliant with color and the long sweet caress of a woman totally naked before him; naked in body as well as being; a woman who gave herself totally to him and his art. He had dreamt of the Seine; of the French and Spanish countryside; of windmills and bullfights; of incandescent suns and wheat fields and golden faced peasants breaking bread and smiling toothless smiles which he could capture in all their reality, using his palette as the lens of a camera.

Those had been his goals and now he did nothing more than push a pencil and order others to draw and paint cans and boxes of junk. He did not even get his hands full of paint anymore, was not able to exercise his talent even in painting junk. Deodorants, soaps, cereals, baby foods, detergents, cars, frozen foods, all of them harmful not so much to the body but to the psyche. There was a concept. The pollution of the environmental psyche. Barbara would understand that.

Christopher had returned to the dining room and after placing the newspaper in front of his father, turned the cereal box around and proceeded with the task of obliterating its contents. He refilled his bowl, shook the box to make sure there was nothing left and, putting his head down as if he were going into a three point stance, attacked his breakfast with renewed determination.

"Christopher?"

"Yeah?"

"Where's your sister?"

"I think she's still on the phone."

Sandoval wanted to ask what she was doing on the phone that early in the morning, decided to ignore this latest bit of intelligence and instead turned to the *Times*. He scanned the front page, reading the headlines to find something of interest. Nicaragua, Libya, AIDS, Space Program, Gay Rights Bill. He turned the pages of the newspaper, going up and down the columns, looking for some sign that indeed this great institution printed news and not esoteric argumentation between a chosen few.

He stopped to read the Op Ed page, saw something about municipal bonds and gave up. He turned another page and there, staring at him, was the saddest picture he had ever seen. Sandoval was immediately overcome with grief. All of his heartache, his shattered dreams and faded hopes flooded his chest at the sight of the forlorn, misty-eyed gorilla.

REJECTED BY MATE, BONGO REFUSES FOOD

Sandoval was transfixed by the picture. He read the story as if it were a world-shaking event. Every couple of paragraphs his eyes darted up to look at the grief stricken animal. When he was finished reading, Sandoval looked up and was surprised to find that his son had finished eating. He was alone in the dining room. He looked around and for a fraction of a second did not recognize his surroundings.

The sun had come into the dining room suffusing it with clear morning light. Warm, gentle breezes rippled the curtains and smells of growing things were in the air. The sadness within him had not subsided and a heaviness had now taken over his body. Sandoval got up and went to the window, not with a conscious effort but more as if a force outside himself were pulling him.

Like a dark blue ribbon beyond the canopy of trees, the Hudson River seemed to beckon to him. He felt the ache deep in his heart and wished he could fly out of the window, wished he could stretch his arms and like a great, majestic bird soar above it all. The image of his body striking the sidewalk set the hair on his arms on end. His wish to fly was a suicidal urge and he knew it. Making a mental note to discuss the incident with Dr. Feinstein on Thursday, Sandoval turned away from the window, crossed the beautifully furnished living room and went into the kitchen.

Almost commercial perfect, Barbara Sandoval stood poised at the bronze colored stove with its matching grease and smoke removing unit, preparing to dish up his eggs onto a bright orange enameled dish. Her yellow dress, her hair done in a French twist, she seemed to be waiting to receive a cue and begin selling a marvelous and revolutionary new product. She turned as Sandoval entered the kitchen and smiled cheerfully at him. It was as if she were seeing him for the first time that morning.

Through some miraculous process she had been transformed. Somewhere between their bed and the kitchen she had passed through a machine which changed her into an efficient, loving, hard working career woman, housewife, mother and muse to the American male. What have I done? thought Sandoval. I loved her at one time. No, it was my greed, my need to possess America, to make her mine and now that I have her, I don't want her and I'm lost.

"Good morning, dear," Gayle said, as she set the dish on the white surface of the round, poured plastic, modern table in the middle of the kitchen. How far had he come from the metal dinette set of his boyhood? His wife kissed his cheek. She smelled of Camay and Johnson & Johnson baby powder. "My, don't we look spiffy this morning!" she added cheerfully.

"Good morning, Gayle," Sandoval said. He sat down at the kitchen table and watched his wife remove her apron, fold it neatly, return it to a drawer and sit opposite him. She was a stranger. He began eating, drinking his orange juice and feeling the granulated lecithin stick to his teeth. With the last of the orange juice he swallowed the five vitamin pills which his wife had placed on a demi-tasse saucer. She could easily poison him one of these days, thought Sandoval. All she would have to do was inject one of those glycerin capsules with cyanide and he would be a goner. The Tylenol killer did it. Why not Gayle Sandoval, Upper West Side matron. But why? He had given her no reason. Perhaps she had found out about Nancy Fergusen and the lunches on the East Side, the ice skating at Wollman's, their brief ineffectual affair. Nancy had pressured him immediately to move in with her, her whole being full of the impetuousness which he now fantasized about but was unable to produce in himself. It was too late for him. Too late for him to have followed her through that bohemian Village, Soho and Tribeca labyrinth she knew so well: the apartments reeking of incense and grass; the homemade loftbeds; the wonderful conversations about art and life and seeing oneself as the guardian of something precious. But they were all boring neurotics and he really did not want to associate with them. My God, what was he saying! He was talking like an over the hill conservative. It was the Nixon curse again. But he had hated Kennedy's smugness, his wealth, his ease and the appeal he had with women. He had never told a soul about his vote. It was the lot of every immigrant, but how to capitulate gracefully, how to admit that some made it and some did not and he was in the latter category. It was useless. He began the mechanical process of eating his eggs and toast. The cheese sauce was a little too thick.

"Gayle?"

"Yes, dear."

"When was the last time we went to the zoo?"

"The zoo, dear?"

"Yes, the one in Central Park."

"Let me think."

Sandoval watched his wife as she pursed her lips, rested her elbow on the table and with her fork aloft, reached back into her storehouse of memories. If it had to do with the children she would have no problem recalling the event. Chances were that the trip to the zoo had been for Barbara and Christopher's benefit.

"I think it was three years ago this coming summer," she said. "Christopher was just eight years old and you gave him *Winnie The Pooh* for his birthday. Barbara was eleven and she went off to that Quaker workcamp for the rest of the summer.

"Ethical Culture."

"Yes, that was it. Well, that's the last time I remember."

Sandoval thought for a moment before asking the next question. Any way that he phrased the thought it sounded ridiculous.

"Do you remember the gorilla?" he finally said.

"The gorilla, dear?"

"Yes, Bongo. The big, arrogant male and how he'd stomp up and down his cage and every once in a while he'd stare back out like he recognized somebody. Bongo. That was his name, wasn't it?"

"I don't remember, Greg. Was he Pattycake's father?"

"I don't know if he was her father. But he's stopped eating."

"That's terrible," she said, making a concerned face as if one of her charges at the school had just reported that he had offered one of the classroom rabbits a carrot and the animal had refused it. "Where did you hear that?"

"It's in today's paper. The female won't let him come near her and he's stopped eating."

"You're kidding?" she said, suddenly agitated. She wiped the corner of her mouth with her napkin, turned quickly behind her and coughed as if to indicate that the children might be listening.

"They've had a couple of specialists in but there's nothing physically wrong with him. The last time she was in his cage she became violent and threw a water pan at him."

"Really?" she said, turning her head towards her shoulder to indicate interest.

Every time Sandoval added another detail, his wife's eyes opened wider, her face turned more to the side. In a few moments she would resemble a broken-necked marionette. Sandoval doubted that she was really interested, but went on.

"You won't believe this but she bared her teeth, beat her chest and growled at him. Bongo made no aggressive moves toward her. Do you think that's normal?"

"I don't know," she said, suddenly straightening her head as if the conversation had taken a safer turn. "If you compared a child's behavior to that of an ape I suppose there could be something to it."

It was obvious she had become bored with the subject and, in making the connection, made one of her unimaginative transitions into her area of expertise and began talking about her kindergarten class. He listened for a moment and then asked her again if it was normal for a female gorilla to behave so aggressively.

"I don't know what to say," she said. "I'm trying to remember something from anthropology. All I have is my own experience to draw on. For example, in my class little girls can be just as aggressive as little boys." She was in her glory as she spoke. Sandoval watched her face light up and a quick animal intelligence, such as one sees in frisky dogs, invaded her eyes. "I mean, studies have been made to prove this. It even confuses *me* at times and I've been with them the whole year. You can't really tell with children until they reach puberty and go through it. Look at Barbara. She used to be such a proper little girl."

Sandoval didn't want to discuss his daughter.

"So the same thing could be happening to Bongo. Is that what you're driving at?"

"Bongo?"

"The gorilla."

"Oh, yes. The gorilla. I suppose so. I never thought of it that way."

"Which way?"

This was Sandoval's way of checking to see that his wife was paying attention to his part of the conversation. He was convinced that the problem with his daughter's generation was that it had been allowed unlimited freedom of speech without anyone paying much attention to what they said. At least as a child he was hardly ever given the opportunity of speaking. And when he spoke adults would scrutinize his every word for signs of disrespect, insinuation or malice. What was it his mother would say, drawing on her island wisdom? Children should speak when chickens begin riding bicycles.

"Which way?" he repeated.

Gayle Sandoval was the picture of understanding. That it was understanding at the-end-of-the-year-kindergarten-level did not go unnoticed by her husband.

"Which way what, dear?" she said, smiling stupidly at him.

"Why don't you listen to me, Gayle?" he said, practically on the verge of tears. "This is important to me."

Gayle Sandoval suddenly remembered that her husband had been talking about a gorilla.

"Well, maybe he's trying to punish her," she said.

Sandoval was astonished.

"She's not his mother. These are gorillas I'm talking about, not people. For crying out loud!" He could feel his anger surfacing. "What the hell do you have between your ears, anyway! He's trying to screw her and she doesn't want anything to do with him. He's stopped eating. How the hell does that prove he's trying to punish her, dammit! Can you explain that! She doesn't cook for him. It doesn't make any sense. Can't you see that? Hell, she could be punishing him for just being a male. Isn't that possible? Maybe the women's liberation crap of the sixties and seventies finally filtered down the evolutionary scale to the anthropoid apes." He knew he was cracking up but he didn't care. "Maybe those free love, no bra broads running around the zoo, obviously not giving a damn about the animals but just there to get picked up for a quickie influenced that damned female gorilla. They were hairy enough."

She did not answer him. He had wounded her, questioned her intelligence. Sandoval watched her rise regally from her chair, push it against the edge of the table, put her dishes in the sink and with delicate little moves begin to clean up. She wiped the table, drawing a damp arc around the area where he was eating. Sandoval felt as if he were one of her pupils and had just been ordered to a corner of the room. He now sat, ostracized from the rest of human society, the dunce, a potential kindergarten dropout. Her face was a mask, the nostrils flared and the brow furrowed in suppressed anger. She was frightening then, although she never said anything.

He imagined her in a Nazi uniform interrogating terrified prisoners before sending them off to receive deadly, massive injections of vitamins or else to be forced-fed pounds and pounds of sauerkraut mixed with lecithin: OVERFUHRER EVA AUERBACH, THE HEALTHNUT BEAST OF WEST END AVENUE.

"Hey, Gayle," said Sandoval, timorously. "I'm sorry."

Gayle Sandoval turned and stopped wiping the stove.

"About what?" she said, her eyes opened in a remarkable imitation of genuine surprise.

"What I said. It was a low blow. I didn't mean to imply that what you do, your career, doesn't require sensitivity and intelligence."

Sandoval had spoken sincerely. He did not enjoy hurting others and, whether out of self-preservation or because of his somewhat sensitive nature, he always felt enormous guilt after doing so. But as soon as he had finished apologizing he realized that he had put his foot in his mouth. Without meaning to he had said exactly what had been on his mind each time he brought up the subject of her work. He loathed the change which had taken place in her. Rather than teaching six year olds to become seven and keeping it at that, she had managed to absorb their mannerisms and simple ways of dealing with life. In the space of twelve years she had been swallowed up by the kinder-garten subculture.

"I mean it, Gayle," he said. "I'm really sorry."

"Well, we'll just pretend it didn't happen and continue with our work, won't we?" she said, and gave him one of her understanding looks. "Now, finish your breakfast and off you go to your office."

She was back to her cheery, All-American self. She had won again. Once more, she had assumed responsibility and had bested him. What did she draw on for patience? His own mother had a similar kind of patience. Many had been the times, however, that her patience exhausted, she had lashed out in Spanish and broken English, berating him, pitying herself for her lot in life, blaming his father for leaving them to fend for themselves.

His wife, on the other hand, never accused, always understood, held her ground quietly until she won. Was that what America was all about? It didn't seem likely. The history was contradictory. Action. Always action. Movement. Forever advancing against all odds. Raucous and full of energy, leaping headlong into danger. Always new frontiers. Ready to accept the challenge, to pick up the gauntlet at a moment's notice. Indians, the British, Indians, the French, the Spanish, the Germans, the Japanese, the Koreans, the Chinese, the Viet Cong, more Indians. Taking on all comers with wild abandon, shooting from the hip, no holds barred. Where did the patience come in?

Sandoval took another bite of toast, pushed at the white and yellow mess which had begun congealing on his plate and put his fork down. Gayle Sandoval had sat down again. This time she was writing a note. She looked up and asked him something vague about a cauliflower. In his mind the word reverberated wildly, seemingly out of context with his thoughts.

"I don't know," he said. "It doesn't matter."

But it did matter, he thought. The cauliflower was a joke on human beings. It looked like a brain, like somebody's head had been cut open, the brain extracted and elmered to a green stalk to create a deception.

"How about a nice salad? I can have Florence pick everything up at the new Korean fruit store on Broadway. It'll give her a break in the cleaning. Everything's fresh early in the day. How about two different lettuces and a nice watercress? Boston? Romaine?" She sounded like a stewardess. They were all the same. They came out of a mold and some were stamped teachers, others models and actresses, but they all had that same deceptive sweetness. She went on but he had tuned out.

"That's good," he finally said, and got up. He looked at his watch. It was 8:15. "Where's Barbara?," he said from the entrance to the kitchen.

"She's gone, dear. She left while you were in the dining room. What if we get some escarole instead of Boston?"

Sandoval did not answer. The words seemed far away and in his mind he imagined the female gorilla lumbering over to the male and asking what he wanted for lunch. "Uga-uga escaroluga?" And the male gorilla pounding his chest and shaking his head. "Nuga-nuga, escaroluga! Bostonuga! Bostonuga!" And then the female, her eyes downcast, acquiesing and sweetly asking again: Uga-uga Romainuga, Caulifluga?" His nerves frayed by the simpering idiocy of the female, the male would roar: "Nuga, nuga godamnuga! Nuga, nuga caulifluga!"

Sandoval smiled sadly to himself, walked to the bathroom, brushed his teeth, gargled with mouthwash, ran a brush over his semi-long black hair and smoothed down his moustache. When he was done he headed for the front door. His wife, holding their briefcases, was waiting for him.

"Are you ready?"

"Yes," he said, but he did not know for what. Another day of misery, of counting lost years and faded adventure.

They walked out of the apartment and into the elevator, saying nothing to each other until they walked out of the building, and up the street to West End Avenue.

"Have a good day, dear," Gayle Sandoval said to her husband. She offered her cheek for him to kiss. He did so obediently and watched her move away down the block. She was still attractive and he imagined not knowing her. A surge of sexual desire welled up in him and he felt like calling her back. As she walked her hips swayed beneath her dress and Sandoval imagined undressing her for the first time, amazed at the smoothness of her skin, each gentle curve of her body, its fullness delightful to all of his senses. He tried to recall times of passion between them and raised his hand as if to call her but she was too far away. The yellow dress moved anonymously down the incline of the street.

Sandoval began walking toward Broadway and the subway station. As he walked he thought about Bongo, the gorilla. What did he see in the female? What did she see in him? Was it an instinct, a smell, a time of the year? Which one drove him to want her? Did he feel guilty if he was attracted to another female? Did he suffer from homosexual fears? As he walked in the spring sunlight, the trees planted by the block association dappling the sidewalk, he wished he could turn back time and start again.

The aching he felt when he had first gotten up had intensified and, as he moved mechanically up the street, he imagined walking down a Parisian boulevard to have coffee and *croissants* with his lover, a delicate gamin-faced creature whose eyes saw no one but him. The idea had always appealed to him and with each passing year he had embellished upon it. It was a romantic notion and he was flooded with shame if even the slightest part of the fantasy was mentioned. To see Leslie Caron on a television screen was tantamount to being stripped of all defenses.

But it was the *croissants* which provided the mood. The word was magical. There would not be the heaviness of an American breakfast sitting in his stomach to interfere with the love making. No fears of diminishing energy because *croissants* possessed a magic ingredient. French bakers were in reality magicians of love, injecting each *croissant* with a fabulous elixir which supplied men with unlimited passion.

He thought about Briggs and a violent, irrational hatred passed through him, making him almost swoon. He was smug, Roger Briggs. Picture post-cards and cryptic messages. Had he made love to Gayle? There had never been the slightest chance. All her time was accounted for and she had never expressed the slightest interest in him. She would have bored him inside of an hour. Her sterile, closed little mind would have driven Briggs crazy, much as he was being driven crazy.

Sandoval went down the stairs to the subway, inserted a token in the slot, descended to the platform and, when the train came, boarded it. Strap-hanging, he tried to prepare himself for the day. But it was no use. He found himself changing trains and in another fifteen minutes he was entering Central Park. His pace quickened as he passed the seal pond, his heart beating with anticipation. He dodged a couple of dogwalkers and Scandinavian nannies as he searched desperately for Bongo's cage.

And then he saw him, huge and magnificent but hunched over in a corner of the cage. Large tears began welling up in Sandoval's eyes. He checked around for an attendant. When he was certain none were in the vicinity he went under the protective railing in front of the cage and grabbed the bars of the gorilla's cage. With every ounce of his frustrated being he screamed the gorilla's name at the top of his lungs. "BONGO! BONGO! BONGOOOOO!" Big salty tears ran down Sandoval's face. "It isn't worth it, buddy. They don't give a good goddamn," he screamed. "They don't. They don't. They don't, BONGOOOOOOOOOOOOOO!"

All at once the gorilla rose up and rushed at Sandoval, roaring and pounding his chest, his eyes filled with incredible anger. He released his grip on the bars as the gorilla reached for him. His heart pounding, Sandoval slid back under the protective railing.

Even angrier now, Bongo, himself, grabbed the bars of the cage and began trying to shake them from their foundation in the concrete floor. It was unbelievable and Sandoval cried and cried and the attendants came and wanted to know what was happening, but when they saw the gorilla flexing his muscles and roaring, they laughed and patted themselves on the back and Sandoval was suddenly laughing while Bongo went on pounding his chest and emitting horrible, frightening cries of triumph and stomping around the cage fully erect.

Sandoval finally walked away feeling twenty years younger. Every young woman he passed smiled at him. He found a phone booth, called his office and spoke to his secretary.

"Yeah, tell Anderson I'm taking the day off. I'll see him tomorrow morning. If anyone calls just take messages."

He spent the rest of the day looking up numbers in the yellow pages and calling until around one o'clock that afternoon he finally found what he was looking for. They told him the price and he went to his bank cash machine and took out $200, went to Kaplan's Theatrical Outfitters and bought himself a magnificent gorilla suit.

That night when his wife and children were asleep he got out of bed, went to the spare room they used for a storeroom and brought out his gorilla suit. With a pair of scissors he cut a small opening above the crotch and going into the bathroom he removed his pajamas, donned the suit, then put on the headpiece, secured it with the velcro strip and smoothed the fine hair around the neck. He looked in the mirror and smiled behind the gorilla face, his eyes filled with tremendous excitement.

He turned the lights off in the entire apartment and walked down the hall to their bedroom, his gait becoming more and more simian as he went. Once inside the bedroom he locked the door and in the dark he began a rhythmical pattern of breathing and uttering of gorilla-like sounds: "Uga-uga wanna fugga! Uga-uga wanna fugga! Uga-uga wanna fugga!" until he was in a frenzy and ready. He heard his wife stir in her sleep and emit a low moaning sound. Simultaneously, as he turned on the bright ceiling lights he let out a deep roar much like the ones Bongo had emitted and watched his wife sit up in bed and freeze in utter panic. He ran to the bed and pounced on her, ripping at her negligee with his gorilla hands until she was completely naked. He then pinned her to the bed as she struggled under him. When he was done he rolled off and lay contentedly for a few seconds listening to his wife whimper before he fell asleep.

The next day he woke up at 9:45, walked around the apartment in his gorilla suit and felt even better than the previous day. In the bathroom he relieved himself, unaware of the color of his urine, and then walked to the kitchen. On the table there was no orange juice and lecithin, which Gayle Sandoval always left on days when he slept in after a long night at the office; neither were there vitamins on a demi-tasse saucer.

Instead, there was a note in his wife's handwriting.

The children and I have gone to mother's in Racine. Frank Lauder, our family lawyer there, will be contacting you about the divorce. You're a very sick man, Greg. Please get help as soon as possible.

—Gayle—

"Nuga, nuga waspauga. You sickuga," he said, and pounded his chest before taking his son's baseball bat and smashing the round, mushroom-like, molded plastic, white kitchen table and letting out a tremendous roar of delight.

I spoke recently to Gregory. He did not contest his wife's claim for a divorce on the grounds of mental cruelty and is living in San Diego, has a job with the zoo, is painting and living with a twenty-seven year old Mexican-American potter by the name of Aurora.

The Barbosa Express

Several years ago, at the tail end of the big snowstorm, I was in Florindo's Bar on 110th Street and Lexington Avenue when Chu Chu Barbosa walked in cursing and threatening to join the FALN and bomb the hell out of somebody or other. Barbosa's name is *Jesús* but nobody likes being called Gee Zoos or Hay Siouxs, so it's convenient that the nickname for *Jesús* is Chu or Chuíto because Barbosa was a motorman for the last seventeen years with the New York City Transit Authority.

Barbosa is your typical working class stiff, bitter on the outside but full of stubborn optimism on the inside. He has gone through the same kind of immigrant nonsense everyone else has to go through and has come out of it in great shape. In spite of ups and downs he has remained married to the same woman twenty-two years, has never found reason to be unfaithful to her, put one kid through college and has four more heading in the same direction. He owns a two-family home in Brooklyn and on weekends during the summer, he takes Bobby and Mike, his two sons, fishing on his outboard, "Mercedes," named after the children's mother.

Usually even tempered and singularly civic minded, he lists among his responsibilities his serving as treasurer of the "Roberto Clemente Little League of Brooklyn," vice-president of the "Sons of Cacimar Puerto Rican Day Parade Organizing Committee," Den Father for the Boy Scouts of America Troop 641, Secretary of the "Wilfredo Santiago American Legion Post 387" and member of the Courtelyou Street Block Association.

That night Barbosa was out of his mind with anger. At first I thought it was the weather. The snowstorm was wreaking havoc with the city and it seemed conceivable Barbosa was stranded in Manhattan and could not get back to his family in Brooklyn. Knocking the snow off his coat and stamping his feet, Barbosa walked up to the bar and ordered a boiler-maker. He downed the whiskey, chugalugged the beer and ordered another one. I was right next to him but he didn't recognize me until he had finished his second beer and ordered another. Halfway through his third beer he suddenly looked at me and shook his head as if there were no reason for trying anymore.

"This does it, Mendoza," he said, still shaking his head. "It makes no sense, man. The whole town is sinking."

"Yeah, the snow's pretty bad," I said, but it was as if I hadn't even spoken.

"The friggin capital of the world," he went on. "And it's going down the d-r-a-drain. I mean, who am I kidding? I put on a uniform in the morning, step into my little moving phone booth and off I go. From Coney Island to 205th in B-r-o-Bronx. Fifteen years I've been on that run. I mean, you gotta be born to the job, Mendoza. And listen, I take pride in what I do. It isn't just a job with me. I still get my kicks outta pushing my ten car rig. Brooklyn, Manhattan and the Bronx. I run through those boroughs four times a shift, picking up passengers, letting them off. School kids going up to Bronx Science, people going to work in midtown Manhattan, in the summertime the crowds going up to Yankee Stadium. And that run from 125th Street to 59th Street and Columbus Circle when I let her out and race through that tunnel at sixty miles an hour. Did you know that was the longest run of any express train between stops?"

"No, I didn't," I said.

"It is," he said. "Sixty-six b-l-o-blocks."

"No kidding," I said, suddenly hopeful that Barbosa was pulling out of his dark mood. "That's amazing."

"You're damn right it's amazing," he replied, his face angry once more. "And I love it, but it's getting to me. How can they friggin do this? I mean it's their trains. Don't they know that, Mendoza? They don't have to shove it down my throat. But who the hell am I, right? I'm the little guy. Just put him in that moving closet and forget about him. Jerónimo Anónimo, that's me. I don't care what anybody thinks. For me it's like I'm pulling the Super Chief on a transcontinental run, or maybe the old Texas Hummingbird from Chicago to San Antonio along all that flat land, eighty, ninety miles an hour. I give 'em an honest day's work. It's 'cause I'm Puerto Rican, man. It's nothing but discrimination."

I could certainly sympathize with Barbosa on that account. I had met severe discrimination in the publishing world and had been forced to write nothing but lies about the people. I was curious to find out what had taken place to make Barbosa so angry.

"I know how you feel, Chu Chu," I said.

"I mean you're a writer and it might sound strange, Mendoza. But I'm not a stupid man. I've read, so I know about words. When I'm in my rig going along the tracks and making my stops, it feels like I'm inside the veins of the city down in those tunnels. It's like my train is the blood and the people the food for this city. Sometimes there is a mugging or worse down there, but I say to myself, hell, so the system ate a stale *alcapurria* or some bad chittlins or maybe an old knish. Do you understand what I'm saying?"

"Of course I do," I said. "Subway travel as a metaphor of the lifeblood of the city."

"Right. It's the people, the little people that keep the city going. Not the big shots."

"Exactly."

"Then how can they do it? The trains belong to them."

"The grafitti's getting to you," I said, sympathetically.

"No, that's a pain in the ass but you get used to it. Those kids are harmless. I got a nephew that's into that whole thing. I wish the hell they'd find someplace else to do their thing, but they're nothing compared to the creeps that are running the system these days. Nothing but prejudice against our people, Mendoza."

I asked Barbosa exactly what had happened and he told me that nearly a thousand new cars had arrived. "They're beautiful," he said. "Not a spot on them. Stainless steel, colorful plastic seats and a big orange D in front of them for my line. Oh, and they also have this bell that signals that the doors are gonna close. Have you seen 'em yet?" I told him I had not since I avoid subway travel as much as possible, which he doesn't know nor would I tell him for fear of hurting his feelings. He then went on to tell me that even though he had seniority on other motormen, they didn't assign a new train to him.

"Why not?" I said.

"Discrimination," he said. " 'Cause I'm Puerto Rican. That's the only reason, Mendoza. Just plain discrimination. Even *morenos* with less time than me got new rigs and I got stuck with my old messed up train. I'm not saying black people are not entitled to a break. You know me. I ain't got a prejudiced bone in my body. Man, I even told them I'd be willing to take an evening trick just to handle one of the new trains, but they said no. I'm burnt up, Mendoza. I feel like blowing up the whole system is how I feel."

I immediately counseled Barbosa to calm down and not be hasty in his response. I said that there were legal avenues that he could explore. Perhaps he could file a grievance with his union, but he just kept shaking his head and pounding his fist into his hand, muttering and ordering one beer after the other. At the end of an hour he began laughing real loud and saying that he had the perfect solution to the problem. He patted me on the back and said goodbye.

Of course I worried about Chu Chu for three or four days because you couldn't find a nicer guy and I was worried that he would do something crazy. Every time I stopped by Florindo's Bar I'd ask for him, but no one had seen him around. Once, one of the bartenders said he had seen him in Brooklyn and that he was still working for the Transit Authority. I asked if he had gotten a new train, but the bartender didn't know. I didn't hear from Barbosa or see him again for the next six months and then I wished I hadn't.

About a week before the Fourth of July I received a call from Barbosa. He was no longer angry. In fact he sounded euphoric. This made me immediately suspicious. Perhaps he had taken up drugs as a relief from his anger.

"How you doing, Mendoza?" he said. "How's the writing going?"

"It's going, but just barely," I said. "My caboose is dragging," I added, throwing in a little railroad humor.

He let loose a big roaring belly laugh and, speaking away from the telephone, told his wife, Mercedes, what I'd said. In the background I heard his wife say, "that's nice," and I could tell she wasn't too pleased with Barbosa's condition.

"Your caboose, huh?" he said. "Well, I got just the right maintenance for that. Something to get your engine going again and stoke up that boiler with fresh fuel."

"What did you have in mind?" I said, fighting my suspicion.

"A party, Mendoza. A Fourth of July party. We're gonna celebrate our independence."

This didn't sound too strange since Barbosa believed in the American Way of Life. He was a Puerto Rican, but he loved the United States and he wasn't ashamed to admit it. He didn't go around spouting island independence and reaping the fruits of the system. His philosophy was simple. His kids spoke English, were studying here and there were more opportunities for a career in the U.S. Whatever they wanted to do on the island was their business. "I don't pay no taxes there," he'd say. "I don't live there, I don't own property there, so why should I have anything to say about what goes on. Don't get me wrong. I love the island and nobody's ever gonna let me forget I'm from P.R., but it don't make no sense for me to be a phony about where I earn my rice and beans." I personally thought it was an irresponsible political stand, but I don't meddle in how people think or feel, I simply report on what I see.

"What kind of party?" I said.

"That's a surprise, but it's gonna be a party to end all parties. Music. Food. Drink. Entertainment. Fire works. You name it, we're gonna have it."

"At your house in Brooklyn?"

"Naw, too small. Up in the Bronx. Ralph, my nephew, can come pick you up."

"I don't know," I said. "I got a backlog of stuff and I'm not too good at celebrating the independence of this country," I found myself saying, even though I like to keep politics out of my conversations. He knew that and sensed that I was simply trying to get out of it.

"Aw, com'on, Mendoza," he said. "It's gonna be great. I wouldn't be inviting you if I didn't think you'd enjoy it. I know how hard you work and what your feelings are about this whole American and Puerto Rican thing, okay? Trust me. You'll never forget this. You're gonna be proud of me. Everybody's coming. The whole clan. You never seen my family together. I don't mean just my wife and kids, but my eight brothers and five sisters and their husbands and wives and their kids and my aunts and uncles and my parents and grandparents. And Mercedes' side of the family which is not as big but they're great. You gotta come."

I couldn't help myself in asking the next question.

"Where are you holding this party, Yankee Stadium?"

"That's funny," he said, and again laughed so loud my ear hurt. "No, nothing like that. You gotta come. My niece, Zoraida, can't wait to meet you. She's a big fan of yours. She's doing her, what do you call it, to become a doctor, but not a doctor."

"Her PhD? Her doctorate."

"That's it. She's doing it on your books. She's just starting out, so she wants to talk to you and get to know you."

All of a sudden I felt flattered, even though most of what I've written doesn't amount to much. I felt myself swayed by the upcoming adulation, but I truly wish I hadn't participated in what took place between early evening on the Fourth of July and some time around four o'clock in the morning when all hell broke loose on the elevated tracks near Coney Island.

"Where is she studying?" I said.

"Some college in Michigan," Barbosa answered. "I don't know. You can ask her yourself. Ralph'll pick you up about 6:30 on July 4th, okay?"

"All right," I said, suddenly experiencing a strange feeling of foreboding about the entire matter. "But I can't stay long."

"Don't worry," Barbosa said. "Once you get up there and the party starts you can decide that."

"What does that mean?"

Barbosa laughed and said he'd see me on the Fourth.

So on the Fourth of July I got ready. I put on white pants, polished to my white shoes, got out one of my *guayaberas* and my panama hat and at 6:30 that afternoon Ralph Barbosa knocked on the door and down I went to one of my infrequent social activities.

I got into the car and off we went across the Willis Avenue Bridge into the Bronx. I asked him where we were going and he replied that his uncle had told him to keep it a surprise, but that it was up near Lehman College. I relaxed for a while, but still felt that feeling that something not quite right was about to take place. Some twenty minutes later we drove under the Woodlawn Avenue elevated line tracks and into the campus of Herbert H. Lehman College. Ralph parked the car, we got out and walked to a grassy area where a number of people were seated on blankets. Around them were boxes of food and drink, ice coolers, paper plates and cups, coffee urns and several other items that indicated we were to have a picnic.

I felt relaxed at once and as I was introduced to different members of the family I noticed that there were very few men. Out of the over 100 people gathered around several trees, most of them were women and children. I asked Ralph where I could find his uncle and I was informed that Barbosa was making final preparations. I was offered a beer, which I accepted gladly, was offered a beach chair which I also accepted, and then was introduced to Zoraida Barbosa, the PhD student, a lovely, articulate young woman with a keen intellect and, unfortunately, a genuine interest in my work. So enraptured and flattered was I by her attention that more than an hour and a half passed. I then realized that the sun was going down and Barbosa still had not shown up. I once again began to worry.

Another half hour passed and now we were sitting in the dark and some of the younger children began to get restless. And then the word came that we were ready to move. "Move where?" I inquired. "It's all right, Mr. Mendoza," Zoraida said, taking my hand. "Just follow me." Such was her persuasiveness and her interest in me that I allowed her to take my hand and followed her as we crossed the grassy field. We walked for nearly a half mile until we were at the train yards. At that point I knew I was heading for a major catastrophe, but there did not seem to be any way of turning back.

I soon found out why the men had not been in attendance. I saw the plan clearly now. We were to descend into the train yards, a rather hazardous undertaking from the place where our crowd had stopped. The men, however, had constructed a staircase, complete with sturdy bannisters. This staircase went up over the wall and down some fifty feet into the floor of the train yard. I followed Zoraida and as we went I looked down on the nearly forty rails below, most of them with trains on them. This was the terminal of the Independent Subway System or IND as it is popularly known, a place where trains came to be cleaned and repaired or to lay up when they were not in use. Down we went and then guided by young men with flash-lights we walked along, seemingly dangerously close to the ever present third rails until we arrived at an enclosure where a train had been parked. I suspected this was where trains were washed.

Again, utilizing a makeshift staircase I followed Zoraida as we climbed up into a train. Although the light of the flashlights being employed by the young men was sufficient for us to find our way, it was impossible to see what I had walked into. I was directed to a place on the train and asked to sit down. Expecting to find a hard surface when I sat down, I was surprised to find myself sinking into a plush armchair. Moments later I recognized Barbosa's voice asking if everyone was on board. Word came back that everyone indeed had boarded the train. Then quite suddenly the motors in the car were activated. I heard doors close and lights came on. I found myself in a typical New York Puerto Rican living room, complete with sofas, armchairs with covers, little tables with figurines, lamps, linoleum on the floor and curtains in the windows. I thought I would have a heart attack and began to get up from my chair, but at that moment the train began moving slowly out and a loud cheer went up.

I turned to Zoraida sitting on the arm of my chair and she patted my shoulder and said I shouldn't worry. A few moments later we were moving at fairly rapid rate and then the music came on, at first faintly but then as the volume was adjusted it was quite clear: Salsa, I don't know who, Machito, Tito Puente, Charlie Palmieri. I didn't care. This was outrageous. Moments later Barbosa came into our car and smiling from ear to ear greeted me.

"How do you like it?" he said, after I explained to him that my heart was nearly at the point of quitting. "It's pretty good, right? My nephew, Ernest, he's an interior decorator, did the whole thing. Wait till you see the rest of it. It's not a new train but it'll do."

I wanted to tell him that I had seen enough, but was too much in shock to protest. With an escort of his two brothers who, to my great surprise, were members of the police department undercover detective squad, we went forward as the train began picking up speed. I asked who was driving and Barbosa informed me that he had another nephew who was a motorman on the IRT Seventh Avenue line and he was doing the driving. From the living room car we moved forward into the next car, which was a control center laid out with tables, maps and computers. I was introduced to another nephew, a computer whiz working on his PhD in electral engineering. Several young people were busily working away plotting and programming, all of it very efficient. The next car, the lead one, was laid out as an executive office with a switchboard connecting the other cars by phone. There also were several television sets and radios, all tuned to the major channels and radio station. "We're gonna monitor everything that happens," Barbosa said, and introduced me to yet another nephew, an executive from AT&T, dressed in a business suit, seated at a big desk with wood paneling on the walls around him. Off to the side a young woman was transcribing from dictaphone onto an IBM Selectric. My shock was indescribable.

We retraced our steps through the train until we came out of the living room car into the bar car. How they had managed to get a thirty foot oak bar with matching wall length mirror on the train is beyond me, but there it was, stools riveted into the floor. I was introduced all around to the men and women at the bar, all of them relatives of Barbosa and all of them grinning from ear to ear about this adventure.

"I hope you're doing the right thing," I said.

"Don't worry, Mendoza," he said. "Everything's under control."

The next car was a kitchen with six different stoves, four refrigerators, two meat lockers, cutting boards, kitchen cabinets. Here I was introduced to Monsieur Pierre Barbosa, the chef for the Lancaster Hotel, on leave especially for this occasion. Dressed in white and wearing a tall chef's hat, he greeted me warmly and invited me to taste one of his sauces. I did so and found it quite agreeable, if somewhat tart. "Too tart?" he said. I nodded and he spoke rapidly in French to one of his assistants, another Barbosa nephew who moved directly to the sauce with several condiments.

In the next car there was a nursery with cribs and beds for the children and a medical staff headed by Dr. Elizabeth Barbosa, a niece who was a pediatrician in Philadelphia. There were also bathrooms for ladies and gentlemen in the next car. Two cars were devoted to dining tables with linen and candlesticks, each with its own piano. The last car was the most magnificent and modern dance establishment I've ever seen. The floor gleamed and there were lights beneath it and on the ceiling colored lights were going on and off and young people were dancing. "Our disco," Barbosa said, proudly. "With D.J. Mike, my son." His oldest son waved and Barbosa laughed. "I hope you know what you're doing," I said. "But I have to hand it to you. How did you do it?"

"This is a family, Mendoza," Barbosa said. "We'd do anything for each other."

Ten subway cars decked out for partying were moving now through the Bronx, making stops but not letting anyone on, the Latin music blaring from loud speakers above four of the central cars. Every stop we made, people laughed and slapped their thighs and began dancing and very few people seemed angry that they couldn't board the train. All of them pointed at the train. I asked Barbosa why they were pointing and he explained that the train was painted. He described it but it wasn't until the following morning when the escapade came to an abrupt end that I truly was able to see what he was talking about. Each of the cars had been sprayed a different color: orange, red, yellow, pink, green, several blues, white (I think that was the nursery) and the disco which was black and even had a neon sign with the letters *El Son de Barbosa.* All along the cars in huge graffiti letters each car said *The Barbosa Express* and each one, rather than having the Transit Authority seal had BTA or Barbosa Transit Authority on it. All of them were decorated with beautiful graffiti "pieces," as I learned these expressions were called when I was introduced to Tac 121, the master "writer," as these young men and women are called. Tac 121 was in reality Victor Barbosa, another nephew, studying graphic design at Boston University.

The party began in full and we kept moving through Manhattan and then into Brooklyn and the elevated tracks. Everyone had eaten by now and it was then that all hell began to break loose. It was now close to midnight. At this point one of the dining rooms was cleared and converted into a launching pad for a tremendous fire works display. I was introduced to yet another nephew, Larry Barbosa, who was a mechanical engineer. He had managed to restructure the roof of the car so that it folded and opened, allowing his brother, Bill, a member of Special Forces during the Vietnam War and a demolitions expert, to set up shop and begin firing colored rockets from the car so that as we made a wide turn before coming into the Coney Island terminal I could see the sky being lit up as the train made its way. The music was blaring and the rockets were going off in different directions so that one could see the beaches and the water in the light from the explosions.

I was exhausted and fell asleep while Zoraida was explaining her project and asking me very intricate questions about my work, details which I had forgotten with the passage of time. Two hours or so must have passed when I woke up to a great deal of shouting. I got up and went to the control car where Barbosa, dressed in his motorman's uniform, and some of his relatives were listening to news of the hijacking of a train, the announcers insinuating that the thieves had gotten the idea from the film "The Taking of Pelham 123." One of the television stations was maintaining continuous coverage with interviews of high officials of the Transit Authority, the Mayor, pedestrians, the police and sundry experts, who put forth a number of theories on why the people had commandeered the train. They even interviewed an art professor, a specialist on the graffiti culture, who explained that the creation of art on the trains was an expression of youths' dissatisfaction with the rapid rate at which information was disseminated and how difficult it was to keep up with changing developments. "Using a mode of transportation to display their art," he said, "obviously keeps that art moving forward at all times and ahead of change."

In another corner a couple of young men and women were monitoring the communications from the Transit Authority.

"We gotta a clear channel, Uncle Chu Chu," said one of the girls. "They wanna talk to somebody."

Barbosa sat down and spoke to some high official. I was surprised when the official asked Barbosa to identify himself and Barbosa did so, giving his name and his badge number. When they asked him what was happening, he explained how the hijackers had come to his house and kidnapped him, took him down to the train yards and forced him to drive the train or they would kill him.

"What do they want?" said the official.

"They wanna a clear track from here to the Bronx," Barbosa said. "And they want no cops around, otherwise they're gonna shoot everybody. They grabbed some women and children on the way and they look like they mean business."

"Can you identify them?"

"The women and children?"

"No, the perpetrators."

"Are you crazy or what!" shouted Barbosa, winking at me and the rest of the members of the family around him, most of whom were holding their sides to keep from laughing. "Whatta you wanna do, get me killed, or what? There's a guy holding a gun to my head and you want me to identify him?"

"Okay, okay," said the official. "I understand. Just keep your cool and do as they say. The Mayor wants to avoid any bloodshed. Do as they say. Where are you now?"

"Kings Highway," Barbosa said.

I was amazed. The train had gone to Coney Island, backed up, turned around and had made another trip to the end of the Bronx and back to Brooklyn. I looked above and saw news and police helicopters, following the train as it moved.

"Okay, we'll clear the tracks and no police," said the official. "Over and out."

"Roger, over and out," said Barbosa, clicking off the radio. He raised his hand and his nephew, leaning out of the motorman's compartment, waved, ducked back in, let go with three powerful blasts from the train whistle and then we were moving down the tracks at top speed with the music playing and the rockets going off and people dancing in every car.

"We did it, Mendoza," Barbosa said. "Son of a gun! We d-i-d-did it."

I was so tired I didn't care. All I wanted to do was go home and go to sleep. I went back in to the living room car and sat down again. When I woke up we were up in the Bronx and Barbosa's relatives were streaming out of the cars, carrying all their boxes and coolers with them. There were no policemen around. Zoraida Barbosa helped me out of the train and minutes later we were in Ralph's car. A half hour later I was in my apartment.

The next day there were pictures of Barbosa dressed in his uniform on the front pages of all the newspapers. The official story as it turned out was that graffiti artists had worked on the old train over a period of three or four weeks and then had kidnapped Barbosa to drive the train. Why they chose him was never revealed, but he emerged as a hero.

Unofficially, several people at the Transit Authority were convinced that Barbosa had had something to do with the "train hijacking."

A month later I was in Florindo's Bar and in walked Barbosa, happy as a lark. He bought me a beer and informed me that shortly after the train incident they had assigned him a new train and that in a year or so he was retiring. I congratulated him and told him that his niece had written again and that her dissertation on my work was going quite well. One thing still bothered me and I needed to find out.

"It doesn't matter," I said. "But who thought up the whole thing?"

"I thought up the idea, but it was my nephew Kevin, my oldest brother Joaquin's kid, who worked out the strategy and brought in all the electronic gear to tap into the MTA circuits and communication lines. He works for the Pentagon."

"He does what?!" I said, looking around behind me to make sure no one was listening.

"The Pentagon in Washington," Barbosa repeated.

"You're kidding?" I said.

"Nope," Barbosa said. "You wanna another beer."

"I don't think so," I said. "I gotta be going."

"See you in the subway," said Barbosa and laughed.

I walked out into the late summer evening trying to understand what it all meant. By the time I reached my apartment I knew one thing for certain. I knew that the United States of America would have to pay for passing the Jones Act in 1917, giving the people automatic U.S. citizenship and allowing so many of them to enter their country.

As they say in the street: "What goes around, comes around."

Mayonesa Peralta

Apparently, whoever had tagged Nemecio Peralta with the incongruous nickname of Mayonesa had long ago left the neighborhood. Peralta did not seem bothered by the name and, in fact, during those rare moments when he stopped his mad race with time and hovered around the edges of normal sociability, he appeared pleased by the familiarity of the name and the glee it produced in other people.

Well past sixty years of age, Peralta was still spry and energetic, a barrel-chested, powerful little man, who was forever on the move, his tree-stump limbs pushing at the air in front of him as if it offered unconquerable resistance when he walked. Driven by private demons, he appeared at war with life. On the infrequent occasions when I spoke with him I was surprised by his keen intelligence and sensitivity.

As for all people who dedicate their lives to creative endeavors there were apparent disappointments in his life. But of all the vicissitudes to which men of art are subjected when they insist on living life on their own terms, Peralta's greatest struggle was the manner in which he earned his living.

Each weekday he rose early and traveled by subway to the depths of Brooklyn, a trip of nearly two hours. Once there, he labored eight to ten hours, some days twelve hours, at turning bedposts for the Isadore Kaplan Furniture Company, Inc.

As Sisyphus, he began his upward struggle each day only to have it culminate in wasted effort. And yet he had to eat, had to clothe himself and continue working at his art. More importantly, I truly believe his powerful, scarred and knotted hands had a life of their own and would have withered and died without the feel of wood, of suffering cuts and bruises and painful splinters.

The first time I had the privilege of visiting his apartment I was moved deeply by the austerity and orderliness of his life. In a railroad apartment on top of the hill near Lexington Avenue he had fashioned a world so wondrous that I was spellbound for days afterwards. I also felt understandably ashamed that I had chosen to fashion images out of words when there was an existing physical reality around me which was more concrete and Peralta had captured it in his work. It is rare to be awed by a contemporary, but on that occasion awe is what I felt.

The front room, which faced the street, was his living quarters: a single bed, neatly made; a bureau, singular in its beauty and crafted by him; a small table with two matching chairs; a refrigerator; cabinets filled with cans and boxes of food; a double hot plate and some pots and pans. The rest of the apartment had been given over to his art.

One room held his wood, mostly chunks and pieces which he found or asked for at lumber yards, never from Kaplan Furniture; the pieces were arranged by size and type of wood. The next room had floor to ceiling shelves along three walls and on these he had placed finished pieces, polished but as yet unpainted. The next room was the painting and drying room. Although well ventilated, there was a strong aroma of paints, shellacs, varnishes, turpentine, benzine and other spirits. My first reaction upon entering the room was to deduce that Peralta's odd reactions to the world around him had been caused by constant exposure to these toxic materials. Such was not the case, as I was subsequently able to learn.

The one fact which struck me about Peralta was his lack of pride in the fine wood carvings which stood on shelves and drying racks: saints, The Three Kings (in different sizes), nativity figures, doves, roosters. The pieces were articulated in odd cuts from his carving knives, but possessed that quality which a fine artisan gives a medium so that one has to stop and wonder why man, consciously or unconsciously, must seek to immortalize himself, to infuse his lifeblood into dormant, insentient material, marry it with nature and animate it after it has died.

Peralta believed odd things, gathered from conversations and snatches of philosophy which he had read, but they formed a clear view of life which drove him to suffer the indignity of working at Kaplan's so that after work and on weekends he could coax from the wood images of life. As some Buddhists, he believed all things possess life. Even when organisms die they do not entirely disappear but enter into a dormant stage to be awakened into future incarnations. So his job at Kaplan's was at once a way of keeping his passion alive by earning a living and a consternation, since the metaphor of turning bedposts lent itself to making inanimate matter more inanimate, dormant and in this case a vehicle for helping human beings themselves become dormant.

He seldom spoke to anyone and was rarely seen in the street, except when he went to and came back from work or when he shopped for necessities. The rest of the time, he carved. People came from all over the city to buy his carvings, which sold for paltry sums; often, he simply gave them away as if to cement a secret pact that he had made with himself. I liked to think that he deemed it more important to send his work out into the world than to be paid for it. I so much admired his altruism. It was as if the primary consideration was to set his work free.

People in the street mocked him. They greeted him with the name Mayonesa and laughed as he strode past them, his gait simian and short, his eyes blazing with a fire seen only in madmen or the holy.

Once a year, during his vacation from Kaplan's, Peralta would disappear from the neighborhood. Some people said he returned to Cacimar to visit his family, but no one was sure of this, because those times when he was seen leaving the block he had no suitcase and upon returning he looked as if he had spent his time with derelicts in the Bowery. This I found out is exactly what Peralta did. Why he chose this course of action for two weeks out of the year became a mystery to me.

One year, in the middle of writing the final draft of *The Tragedy of Cacimar*, the story of the great chieftain of the Taíno Indians, who slaughtered his children and flung them from a cliff into the sea rather than see them become slaves of the Spaniards, I was suddenly seized by a passionate urge to uncover the mystery of Mayonesa Peralta.

Driven by my own madness I began asking questions. Why was he called Mayonesa? No one knew, but old timers, like Sinforoso Figueroa, who owned *Bodega Cacimar* on the block where I lived, swore the name dated back to the end of World War II and that Peralta was already in the neighborhood. This was established early on. Peralta spoke English with only the slightest trace of an accent. He had served in the infantry during the war and was wounded slightly. As I researched further, I learned that he had been married to an American woman from New Bedford, Massachusetts, an heiress of considerable beauty, whom he had met while they were both in Italy, he as an infantryman and she as a Red Cross nurse.

Had anyone ever seen her? Ramón Aguirre, the old baker, had.

"She was blonde and had very good manners," he told me. "Very good looking, even though she had hardly any lips. They lived on 116th Street in a brownstone which she bought. They had a Hudson with whitewalls and Mayonesa always dressed in a suit. Everyone thought he was a gangster, but he wasn't."

In talking with the old timers I learned that her name was Constance Bickford and that she knew pupils of Rodin and had introduced Peralta to them; that Peralta had studied sculpting in Europe after the war and that the backyard of the brownstone was filled with large pieces of stone at which Peralta worked.

And what had gone wrong? This no one knew. One year the two of them disappeared and eight or ten months later Peralta returned to the neighborhood, disheveled and bearded, his eyes wearing that look of fury which he still retained nearly forty years later. But why the name? Everyone I asked laughed and shrugged his shoulders. It isn't uncommon for our people to give each other odd names, but if one looked deep enough it was possible to find a logical answer to why the person had been rechristened: a predilection for a food, an idiosyncrasy of behavior, a word spoken incorrectly or at the wrong time, a certain look. In Peralta's case, each time I turned in a different direction I met a dead end.

I struggled on with my work until finally one day in late spring, I finished the final revision and shipped it off to be read or not read, but most likely to be rejected, for it was a work filled with anger that we, as a people, must still undergo ritual suicide in order not to be enslaved by our present "masters."

It was then that I made a conscious effort to befriend Peralta and find out directly from him why he had been tagged with such an odd name. A week of timing his arrival from work with a walk in his area of the neighborhood proved useless. I inquired as to his whereabouts and was told that he had disappeared. "Probably on vacation," said Manrique, the superintendent of his building.

It was useless and I nearly gave up trying to find him. I imagined all sorts of incredible romances. She had passed away and each year Peralta would travel to Massachusetts to place flowers on her grave and pray for her eternal repose. Or else they had produced a beautiful mentally deficient child which they both loved but had to institutionalize and each year they journeyed to some secret hospital and visited their thirty year old infant. As in all chimeric matters I was absolutely wrong. Somehow in nearly giving up I found myself mystically encountering Peralta in the most unusual and tragic of circumstances.

One day, after meeting with my good friend, Bertrand Saddler, the internationally known law scholar, in order to check a fine point of law concerning the Spanish Courts of the time of the conquest of the island, I came out of his apartment house on Park Avenue near 70th Street when I heard an overwhelming torrent of the foulest language I had ever heard, all of it in Spanish. I turned and, across the street, through the shrubbery and tulip gardens of the center dividers which adorn Park Avenue in this section of the city, I saw Peralta, his winter coat on and a purple woolen hat on his head. He was gesticulating wildly and shaking his fist while spewing forth a continuous stream of obscene epithets wholly directed at women for the ease with which they could lie back and give themselves freely without having to concern themselves that they were not fully aroused. Peralta was drunk beyond redemption and totally unbalanced as to his mental state. Of the latter there was little doubt in my mind.

I crossed the street and saw that Peralta was carrying a large white jar. As I drew closer I saw that it was a restaurant-size jar of Hellman's mayonnaise and that every once in a while he would dip his hand in the jar and attempt to fling the contents at a window on the second or third floor, all the while screaming at the top of his lungs that American women were frigid and dry and what they needed was lubrication in the form of mayonnaise. More obscene yet, he proclaimed that the reason they had developed this condition was that mayonnaise was made from the collected vaginal fluids of American females in order to please American males, who were more interested in a well-made sandwich than they were in satisfying their women and that he didn't care how many books the son of a bitch had written or how many bulls he had fought or fish he had caught, it didn't give him the right to impose himself on his woman and that he would go on challenging him to a fist fight even in death and how come, since he thought he was such a great boxer and such a brave macho, he had to go and blow his brains out without first giving him satisfaction in the field of honor.

All of this in Spanish so that the Cuban doormen in front of the buildings ducked back inside in order not to be identified with this madman, who, they explained to the affluent tenants, was not Cuban or even Dominican, or any other Latin type, because no one would behave this way except Puerto Ricans. This attitude on the part of the doormen I learned about from my friend Bertrand Saddler a few days later.

But at that point I could no longer endure the pain of watching this great man, who worked so well with wood, demean himself in such a fashion. I thought of walking up to him and suggesting that he come with me back to the neighborhood, but I knew that he would feel doubly ashamed to be found under such conditions now that he knew we shared common ground as artists.

Instead, I walked sadly away and returned to my apartment troubled by what I had seen. I had learned why he was called Mayonesa, but now a bigger puzzle was confronting me. There was no doubt that Peralta was referring to the great Ernest Hemingway in his attack. What was the connection between Peralta and Hemingway?

When I reached my apartment I immediately called Saddler back and, without going into elaborate detail asked, if he knew anyone nearby who would have known Hemingway. He wanted to know what I meant by nearby and I said within a block or two of where he lived on Park Avenue. He said he did not but that he would inquire and get back to me if he found anyone.

A few days later Peralta returned to the neighborhood, again disheveled, dirty, haggard, his beard matted and more pained than ever. He remained in his apartment several days and then emerged sober and returned to his routine of traveling to Brooklyn to work and then come home to devote his spare time to his carvings.

A month or so later I received notification from Houston that my novel *The Tragedy of Cacimar* had been accepted and that upon publication I would fly there for a book party and several public readings. I was overjoyed and forgot about Peralta. Sometime in late June Bertrand Saddler called me and said he had found a widow who had known Hemingway and would I be interested in meeting her. At first I didn't make the connection between my interest in Peralta and the phone call, but as soon as I realized what Saddler was referring to I felt the same urgency that I had felt several months before.

"At your earliest convenience, Bertrand," I said.

"Very well, Ernesto," he said. "I shall get back to you within the hour."

An hour later Saddler called back and asked if it was possible for me to come to his home the following Friday evening. I said it would be no problem at all. That entire week I could do no work. When Friday came I dressed in my old summer suit of white linen, my white shoes and Panama hat and went to Saddler's home, a large, elegant apartment befitting my friend's stature.

I was shown to the library by his butler. Seated there was a woman of some sixty years of age, quite delicate and still very beautiful.

"Ernesto, may I present Mrs. Constance Bickford Clay," Saddler said. "Constance, this is my dear friend, Ernesto Mendoza, novelist and raconteur par excellence."

I bowed solemnly and kissed her hand, barely brushing the skin with my lips.

"How do you do, Mrs. Clay," I said.

"Very well, thank you, Mr. Mendoza," she said. "It is a pleasure to meet you. Bertrand has told me many wonderful things about you."

We had drinks before dinner and then we went into the dining room and had a light seafood meal with superb wines. All through dinner we talked about literature and painting and the world situation but never once was the subject of Hemingway broached by the three of us. When dinner was over we returned to the library and then Mrs. Clay asked me directly, while she was stirring her coffee, about my interest in Hemingway, that yes, she had known him briefly in Paris *and* Spain after the end of the Second World War, while she was a correspondent for a Boston newspaper, but that after that time she had lost contact with him.

"Are you doing some type of research on him?" she said.

"No, not really," I said.

I went on to explain my concern and said that I had a friend who was very troubled and perhaps it was possible that she might have known him. She asked me his name and when I told her she readily admitted that she had been married to him. I thought I detected a slight pained expression cross her face, but she quickly regained her composure and went on to say that what had happened between them had been unfortunate but in many ways made her realize how foolishly romantic she had been.

"Please, don't misunderstand me," she said. "Nemecio was an extremely talented man. A man of boundless energy and an enormous appetite for life."

Candidly, she went on to explain that she had been head over heels in love with him, would have given the world to remain with him, but that she could not endure his obsession with Hemingway and his insistence that she and the famous author had had an affair. She laughed heartily and wiped her delicate mouth with her napkin.

"In truth," she said, "I despised the man. He was a braggart and a bully. If you did not worship at his shrine, you became his mortal enemy. I," she added, haughtily, "do not worship anything but life itself. Certainly not a man like the late Mr. Hemingway, in spite of his literary success. He was a troubled man, driven and without spiritual substance. Much weaker than Nemecio. And yet poor Nemecio could not see that. He was driving himself mad with jealousy."

She explained how they had moved from New York to Martha's Vineyard and attempted to live there. She had tried everything in order to restore Peralta's self-esteem but nothing had worked. In time her love for him withered away when he became abusive and began using foul language against her, which she could not tolerate.

"To the end he insisted that I had been Hemingway's lover," she said.

"Are you aware that he often comes to this neighborhood and behaves quite abnormally?" I asked.

"For a number of years," she replied. "At first I thought of calling the police, but then I realized that he was quite harmless."

"Yes," I said.

We were silent for a long while and then she spoke, but her tone was not as formal.

"You care for him a great deal," she said.

"He's a fine artist," I said.

"Does he still work in stone?" she asked, her voice quivering slightly and her eyes suddenly misting.

"Wood," I said.

"Yes, he always spoke about wood with great longing."

Her words trailed off and we were once again silent. Bertrand Saddler excused himself from the room and then Constance Bickford asked me if I thought he was well. I explained all that I could about his life and his work and how each year about the same time he went on a drinking binge, but that the rest of the time he simply went from his job to his apartment and his carvings.

"Is he married?" she said.

"Not that I know of," I said.

Silence once more. This time much longer than previously. I became uncomfortable and finally said that he was in good health and remarkably strong for his age.

"Yes, he always had a strong constitution," she said, and laughed for the first time. "Please answer me truthfully."

"If I'm able," I said.

"Do you think I could see him sometime?" she said. "What I mean is, do you think it would upset him to see me?"

"I truthfully don't know, Mrs. Clay."

"Please find out."

"Very well."

We said goodnight and I returned to my apartment more troubled yet. How was I to approach Peralta? I thought it over for nearly two weeks before I decided on a direct approach. One Thursday in July I went to his building and sat on the front steps until he arrived. When he saw me he frowned and then greeted me. We spoke in Spanish.

"You made a mistake, Peralta," I said.

"What are you talking about?" he snapped at me.

"That Hemingway business," I said, sternly, but quaking inside since I was no match for his physical strength.

"Come upstairs and have a cup of coffee," he said.

I followed him up the stairs and watched him as he made coffee. We didn't speak until he had set the cups on the table and we were sipping from the strong, sweet *café con leche.*

"What's this about Hemingway, that son of a bitch," he said. "What in the hell do you know about it?"

"Constance told me," I said.

"Where do you know the whore from?" he said.

"Quiet, you old fool," I said.

"Watch your mouth, Mendoza," he said, menacingly, his eyes on fire, his huge hands opening and closing. "I could kill you with one blow."

"I know you could, but you still made a mistake and that's all there is to it. She never had anything to do with Hemingway. She loved you and you were too blind to see it. She probably still does."

He was stunned and sat there looking beyond me at the street outside his window, his eyes growing cloudy and his powerful body visibly shrinking with shame.

"I thought she was sleeping with him," he said. "I wanted to kill him. Not her, though. We came back to New York and things got worse and worse. Did you see me outside her building?"

"Yes, I did," I said, feeling all of his shame and all of his pain. "It's all right. I understand."

"You understand about the name, then?"

"Yes, I understand." I said.

"I haven't cared about my life," he said.

"I know, but you should. You're a fine artist."

"Thank you," he said, and nodded several times. "Thank you very much. You are a man of great courage."

"A man of great stupidity," I said. "You could have destroyed me."

He laughed and shook his head.

"No, I'm all bluff," he said. "All I care about is making things, not destroying them."

He then asked about Constance and I told him what I knew. When I told him she was a widow, he seemed relieved and when I said she wanted to see him, he became embarrassed and said it would be impossible for him to face her.

"It's never too late," I said.

"Perhaps you're right," he said. "But I must have time. Tell her that for me."

I said I would and we said goodbye. We became good friends after that and I began urging him to get out more. Although I am somewhat of a recluse myself, I found that for his sake I would spend time walking around New York City with him, stopping off at sidewalk cafes and discussing life. Each time I asked him if he was ready to see Constance, he said he wasn't. And then one day in late fall when the trees had shed all of their foliage and the days had grown shorter, he announced without my broaching the subject that he was ready to see Constance.

"At my place," he said. "Next Saturday."

I immediately conveyed the message and the following Saturday, Constance Bickford Clay emerged from her limousine, climbed the steps of the tenement building where Nemecio Peralta lived and I escorted her upstairs to his apartment. They greeted each other cordially, a certain familiar warmth apparent but held in reserve.

In the middle of the front room draped with a sheet there stood what I surmised was a sculpture. After she was seated at the table and he had made coffee for the three of us, Nemecio stood up and pulled the sheet away from the sculpture. It was a beautiful polished wooden carving of Constance as a young woman, her naked body so sensuous and inviting that I turned away quite embarrassed by the life-like quality of the piece. When I turned Constance was blushing. Her reaction made me even more uncomfortable.

Peralta was smiling.

"Do you like it?" he said to her.

She nodded ever so demurely and I announced that I had several matters to which I had to attend. They did not hear me so I let myself out of the apartment and immediately decided to contact Esperanza on the island. Wherever she was I had to find her and convince her that it was not too late, that she need not feel she was too old to share her life with me. I felt lighter and happier than I had felt in years and knew then that no matter what happened to my life from that moment on, I had lived fully and with a certain measure of courage and, ultimately, that is what counted.

Mercury Gomez

People may say a great many complimentary things about me as a person or even as a writer, but these accolades are without justification because I lack common sense. I don't know how many times Esperanza told me to always check the weather before going out. I seldom remember and end up over dressed or without enough clothing to protect me from the elements. At my age I can ill afford nagging colds or a bout with pneumonia. So there I went one Monday morning to see my lawyer, Harold Gunderson, of the firm of Silverstein, Gunderson ¿ Estes, about the business of translation rights for my non-ghetto novels which Layton Publishing refuses to grant on the grounds that I have maligned my own writing and therefore damaged their reputation.

I was fuming and, of course, did not listen to the weather report. Although it was June and the weather warm, the forecast had evidently included rain and out I went without either a raincoat or an umbrella. As I waited for the Second Avenue bus the air grew heavy, there was a thunder clap to the south, lightning streaked the darkened sky and quite suddenly it was pouring and the wind was howling, sending sheets of driving rain into the bus shelter. Even if the bus had arrived at that moment, I would have been soaked before I was able to board it. As I stood there cursing my stupidity for letting Layton push me around, a gray, stretch limousine, the word MERC on the licence plate, pulled up. Out of the driver's side there emerged a young white man dressed in livery, carrying an umbrella and urging me to get in.

Of course I refused, but then the window in the back seat of the limousine was lowered and one of the smallest, blackest faces I had ever seen on a man grinned out at me and motioned for me to get in.

"Come on, Mendoza," the man in the limousine said. "The meter's running. Get in!"

The man looked familiar but it couldn't be the person I was thinking about. My curiosity got the best of me. He evidently knew me. I had no enemies, other than Layton with his vendetta regarding my books, so I got under the umbrella, into the limousine and off we went through the downpour.

"How's it going, Mendoza?," the little black man said. Wet out there, ain't it? Want some coffee?"

I said I would, and a young, red headed woman seated across from us poured coffee, asked me what I wanted in it, and after I said cream and two sugars, executed the order, handed me the cup and returned to her work on a portable lap computer.

"I know you, don't I?" I said to my host, after taking a sip from my coffee. "How do you know my name?"

He chuckled and said of course I knew him and I had better remember quickly or else he'd put me out of the limousine and he wouldn't care how wet I got. I don't know whether he meant what he said or whether he was joking, but his manner was quite firm and intimidating. I immediately knew who he was. The incongruity of the situation, however, made me feel as if I were dreaming the entire episode.

"You're Solomon Gomez," I said.

"In the flesh," he said, grinning and extending his small black hand. "But nobody calls me that anymore."

"Evidently from the looks of things," I said, "they call you Mr. Gomez."

"That too," he said. "But most people call me Merc. How you been? You see the plates?"

"I did, Merc," I said, uncomfortably.

"So how you been?" he again said, grinning.

"I've been all right," I said. "How about yourself?"

"Can't say I have any complaints, except maybe some stock I bought last month that just sits there like a lump. My broker wants me to hold on to it. Other than that, everything's copacetic."

I said I was glad to hear that.

"You look like you're taking care of yourself. How's Mrs. Mendoza?" he said.

"You mean, Esperanza?"

"Yeah,"

"She's back on the island," I said. "Couldn't take the cold anymore. Went back about five years ago."

"So where are you headed?"

"Madison and Forty-Fifth. My lawyer's," I said, and gave him the address.

"No problem," Solomon said and spoke to his driver. Hear that, Vincent?"

"Yes, Mr. Gomez," the driver said.

Solomon Gomez grinned, turned to his secretary and began dictating, using words like satellite, micro chip, and rattling off Japanese company names. I listened but felt very uncomfortable. I didn't want to ask what Solomon Gomez was doing dressed in a six hundred dollar suit, riding around in a stretch limousine with a secretary, talking about stocks and yields and Japanese companies. But I was curious how the oldest but the runt of the litter of my old friend Baltazar Gomez had managed to attract such fortune into his life. I shuddered thinking of the possibility that he had come by his wealth illegally. Although I'm not generally concerned with the morality of people's life styles nor do I pass judgement on them, I, in all cases, keep my distance from people whose criminal activity brings about the destruction of others. If Solomon Gomez was a big time drug dealer and the words he was using were code words I had to find out. His father, Baltazar, was a hard working man, a man who did not tolerate sloth and corruption of any kind. He swept and mopped and janitored buildings for the rich in exchange for a small salary and a huge basement apartment where he and his wife, Altagracia, could raise their ever increasing brood, twelve of them at the time when I lost touch with him some twenty years ago. Solomon had to be close to forty and his father in his sixties. Baltazar Gomez was a few years younger than me. Solomon finished dictating and appeared to be thinking, his tiny black face, filled with nooks and crannies from his concentration.

"How's the old man?" I said, breaking into his thoughts.

"Great," Solomon said, once more grinning. "I set him up in business down on the island. Bought him and Mom a big house. Swimming pool and all. Remember how he always talked about wanting to be a radio announcer?"

"Of course," I said. "He had a great voice and spoke Spanish with great care."

"*Un negro inteligente*, right?" said Solomon, chuckling. "Read a lot. Cervantes, Unamuno, everybody. And all the Latin Americans. Rulfo, Quiroga, Fuentes and all our people. Laguerre, Soto. And all the black writers. Met Langston Hughes and Zora Neale Hurston through Arthur Schomberg, who was from the island. There isn't one he hasn't read. He could be a literature professor." He stopped talking and looked directly into my eyes so that I felt as if he were reading my mind. He nodded several times and then said: "By the way, I read your last book. *Ghetto Mirror*. It was pretty good. I recognized everybody in it. Badillo and the rest of the politicians and ball players and even the people from the old neighborhood. You gonna put me in your next book, right?"

"Absolutely," I said, convinced that if I didn't my life would become very difficult.

"Anyway, I bought the old man a radio station down on the island."

"The whole thing?"

"You got it. Got some of the best people managing it. Pop's got a one hour interview show every weekday. He's had the governor on and Jose Ferrer, Raul Julia, Rita Moreno and all kinds of celebrities. You know, ball players and people in the news. Wednesday nights is devoted to writers, his other love. He always asks about you, but you're very hard to find these days. We're thinking of buying a television station or just starting our own and putting him on a talk show format. Maybe two hours late night. But something classy. 'Cause once in a while the producers screw up and go along with some of the sponsors who want to put on people in the news. You know, whackos. Like the lady down there that was pregnant and had a bunch of puppies and they all looked like the governor. You remember the old man. He didn't pull any punches with any of us kids and he hasn't changed. If it's bull, he'll get it out of you. That's the way he runs his show. If you try to snow him, he's got you. He goes right for the jugular."

"Amazing," I said, referring to my friend, Baltazar. "What does he think of your success?"

"He's proud as hell," Solomon said. "You know, his oldest kid and everything." He chuckled once more. "Tried to get me on his interview show."

"And?"

"Had to turn him down."

"How come?" I said.

"I don't give interviews," he replied.

I was about to inquire further when his secretary looked up from her work and gave me a warning look. Ever alert to the subtleties of a changing human environment, if not the weather, I understood immediately and withdrew from the conversation. We were turning up Forty-fifth Street and a few moments later we were in front of my lawyer's office building.

"Here we are, Mr. Gomez," said the driver, getting out of the car with his umbrella even though the rain had stopped and only a slight drizzle now fell.

"Well, it's been nice seeing you, Merc," I said, extending my hand to Solomon.

"My pleasure, Mendoza," said Solomon, shaking my hand and then handing me his card. "Give me a call tomorrow and we can have lunch. I'm calling the old man as soon as I get into the office. I'm gonna ask him to schedule you for an interview. The station'll pick up the tab for air fare and hotel. Everything first class. I think there's an honorarium. We'll do a whole hour on your work. How's that?"

"Sounds all right to me," I said, somewhat embarrassed by my lack of enthusiasm. At least I'd get a chance to look in on Esperanza and talk to her about coming back. It would probably end up being another long drawn out discussion of climate and politics and why I would insist on being in New York rather than on the island.

"Tomorrow, then?" said Solomon.

"Tomorrow," I said, and stepped out of the car.

The driver held the umbrella and walked with me until I was inside the lobby of the building. He then nodded politely and went back out.

In the elevator going up to see Harold Gunderson, I looked at Solomon Gomez' card. The first thing which struck me was the logo, a silhouetted figure of Mercury with his arm raised as if in a passing stance holding a package. Next to the logo, in slanted letters which instantly conveyed speed: MERCURY COMMUNICATIONS. Below that, Mercury Gomez, President. Down near the bottom edge, a Third Avenue address and a telephone number. My heart skipped a beat and I found myself smiling and shaking my head in disbelief. How had he done it?

Inside Gunderson's office I was greeted, as always, warmly and with great respect by Mrs. Fazio, Harold's secretary. She said Harold would be with me in a moment. I sat down and began looking through a magazine, flipping the pages absently, when I saw a big flashy ad for MERCURY COMPUTERS. "When accuracy is not enough," the ad said, and went on to compare the IBM PC and the Apple with its own and in the end touted the MERCURY PC as the state of the art computer. "Combine accuracy with the speed of 21st Century technology." Next to a computer, on whose screen there was a six color graph, a statuesque blonde, with a bust big enough to feed the City of Boston, was smiling warmly, encouraging everyone to buy a MERCURY PC and she would forsake that fair city for whoever was reading the ad. On the corner of the computer, the little black Mercury passer. Damn, I thought, he's really done it. My friend's son had taken the American dream seriously and turned it into a full scale Hollywood extravaganza.

At that moment Harold Gunderson came out of his office and I stood up. We embraced and then went into his office, with the plush carpeting, the view of Manhattan facing west, the beautiful mahogany desk, matching conference table and chairs; the shelves filled with law books, the walls displaying diplomas and awards and pictures of Harold in all types of athletic gear from when he was a collegiate star at Princeton University. Mrs. Fazio came in and served coffee and a couple of assistants came in to discuss my situation with Layton.

As much as I tried I could not concentrate on the business at hand and kept thinking about Mercury Gomez. I could no longer call him Solomon. He had transformed his life to the extent of completely obliterating my consciousness of him as the diminutive teenager I had known. At noon, Harold suggested we send out for lunch and continue our discussion. By two o'clock we were finished and it had been decided that we would sue Layton Publishing and that when Silverstein, Gunderson ¿ Estes were done with Layton he'd wish he'd gone into ladies apparel rather than publishing.

"There's no way they can force you to honor that contract," Harold Gunderson said. "Enough is enough."

I felt quite good about taking on Layton and once and for all I would begin chipping away at the damage I had done in writing those ghetto books, but I still felt an enormous curiosity about Mercury Gomez. I asked Harold if he'd heard of him. He thought a moment and then shook his head. I told him the story and he found it remarkable. He buzzed Mrs. Fazio and asked her if Irving Silverstein was in his office. Mrs. Fazio said he was, Harold thanked her and then dialed Silverstein's number.

"Irving, Ernesto Mendoza's here in my office," Harold said, when Silverstein had picked up. "He wants some information on someone by the name of Mercury Gomez. Burgess handles his outfit, right?"

Harod listened intently, nodding several times and then breaking into a big smile. He thanked Silverstein and then, laughing uncontrollably, which for him was uncharacteristic, said I should go and see Silverstein.

I thanked Harold, we shook hands and I walked down the hall to see Irving Silverstein. His office was similar to Harold's, perhaps less formal. Silverstein greeted me and asked me to sit down. When I was seated he asked me about my health, said he was thinking of retiring and moving to Florida for good and letting his son take his place in the firm and then he mentioned Mercury Gomez.

"Little guy, right?"

"Four foot ten at the most," I said.

"Yep, some piece of work that kid was. You know him?"

I told him his father and I had known each other but that I hadn't seen him in more than twenty years. And then I told him how he'd picked me up in his limousine and how he'd set up his father in business on the island.

"Oh, sure. That's Fortune 500 stuff he's got there," Silverstein said. "Multinational corporation. Offices in London, Paris, Tokyo. You name it. Five years ago they were just electronics but now they've diversified and have their hands in everything you can name that's developing. There's even a rumor that they're ready to launch their own satellite."

"So buying that radio station for his father was no big thing," I said.

"Like going to Nathan's for a couple of hot dogs," Silverstein said. "A tax write off. My God, he owns more media stock than Ted Turner."

"How do you know him and how did he do it?" I said.

Silverstein shook his head.

"I don't know the answer to the second question, other than to tell you he's sharp. You've heard Harold talk about Bill Burgess and his firm, right? They handle big corporations and sometimes assign a hundred or more lawyers to work with one company. Well, they handle Mercury Communications and Bill says there isn't one thing that goes by the little son of a gun. He's on top of everything. Like a black Napoleon as a strategist and like Patton determination-wise. Any damn thing he puts his mind to turns to gold and they say he negotiates with the intensity of a starving cobra. I don't know anybody that's got the best of him. If they have, they're probably working for him right now."

"And the first part of the question?" I said.

"Yes, right. I don't know if I ever told you but my uncle Seymour used to have a messenger service," Silverstein said. "This is going back twenty, maybe twenty five years. The little guy worked for Seymour for two or three years. We'd use Seymour's firm to get stuff down to Wall Street in a hurry. You know, contracts and that. Light stuff but stuff you couldn't trust to the post office or needed to get to a client in a hurry."

"He was just a messenger?".

"Right," Silverstein said. "But what a messenger. That's how he got his name. Seymour's the one that started calling him that and I guess it stuck."

"What do you mean?"

"Well, Seymour says that for about a year and a half he was just an average messenger. You'd give him something and he'd deliver it and come back two hours later and make another delivery. Never any problems. Always on time. No complaints from his clients. No disrespect. Always got the right signature. Never lost anything or damaged it. No accidents."

"And?" I said, growing anxious.

"Relax," Silverstein said. "I'm getting to it. All of a sudden, Seymour says, the kid's a whiz. Seymour would say, 'here, kid, this is gotta be picked up down on 34th Street near Macy's and it's gotta go across town to 666 Third Avenue, The Kent Building, 9th Floor.' 'No problem, Mr. Silverstein,' the kid would say. 'Be back in no time.' And off he'd go. Ten blocks from Seymour's business down to 34th, another twelve to the Kent Building and five blocks back to Seymour's. How much time before the kid's back?"

"I don't know. Maybe . . ."

"Wait, don't answer right away. Think about it. Consider midtown traffic on both the streets and sidewalks in the middle of a weekday. Sometimes there's rain, sometimes snow and then slush. How much time?"

"An hour, maybe an hour and a half," I said.

"Fifteen minutes," Silverstein said. "Fifteen minutes before he was back in front of Seymour, grinning and telling him that he was ready for another delivery."

"You're kidding!"

"Nope. The first couple of times Seymour checked the clients and they said they'd gotten their deliveries. No problems at all. 'Who picked up?' Seymour would ask. 'Little black guy,' they'd say. And then he'd call the people the package was going to and ask who had delivered it. 'Little black guy,' they'd say. After a while he just gave up trying to figure it out and anything that needed prompt attention went to the little guy."

"Incredible," I said.

"That's not the end of it," Silverstein went on. "Inside of a month Seymour's business had doubled. If you wanted something delivered in a hurry, who did you call? Silver Streak Services. Three black S's with a white arrow through them."

"Symbolic," I said.

"I don't know from symbolic, but the following month business quadrupled. And then one day the kid walked in and asked Seymour for a raise. Seymour offered him fifty dollars more a week. He thought he was being fair and magnanimous. From what Seymour says the kid looked at him and shook his head. 'Seventy five?' Seymour says. More shaking of the head. 'So, what do you want?' says Seymour. 'My heart? My liver? What?' The kid grins and says he wants to work on commission. Seymour says it's totally out of the question. The kid grins some more and tells Seymour thank you very much, Mr. Silverstein, and walks out never again to be in the employ of Silver Streak Services. So now Seymour's down again to two and three hour deliveries and clients are calling up asking for the little black guy and Seymour's going nuts looking for him and can't find him anywhere and then his clients start dropping off and pretty soon his business is down the drain because, guess what?"

"The kid went into business for himself," I said.

"With a vengeance, my friend," Silverstein said. "It served Seymour right. He died about ten years ago still trying to figure out the whole thing. We used Mercury for a while and then we heard he was getting out of the messenger business and that was it."

"Amazing," I said. "I'm having lunch with him tomorrow, maybe I can find out."

"Let me know."

We said goodbye and I went home totally obsessed with the riddle of Mr. Mercury Gomez. I woke up in the middle of the night after a terrible nightmare in which I was placed in a manila envelope and was being delivered from one office to another not knowing where I would go next.

The next day I called Mercury's number and his secretary said he was expecting me at noon. I wore my only dark suit and at eleven thirty I was on my way downtown. At noon I was met downstairs by one of Mercury's executives. The Mercury Building, a new glass and steel structure on Third Avenue, reeked of efficiency and wealth, two phenomena which have eluded my grasp for as long as I can recall. In the lobby, part of which was an arboretum, there was a thirty foot smooth black stone statue of the Mercury logo.

On the 60th Floor we went into a suite of offices and there was Mercury Gomez, seated behind a desk, signing papers. As if he had a secret, he came forward and greeted me with that ever present grin. He asked if I preferred going out or if I wanted to eat in his office, which had a dining table already set up for lunch. I took the hint and said the office would be fine. He pushed a button and moments later a waiter came in and went over several menus with us. I finally chose a light meal of chicken and wine.

Once we were seated Mercury thanked me for coming and told me he'd spoken with his father, Baltazar, and everything was set up. He gave me three or four possible dates in the fall and said I should decide which one suited me, but to let the producers know with at least three weeks notice so they could take care of the advertising. He added that Baltazar's television show was a certainty, although Mercury would most likely have to start his own television station down on the island. Four hot dogs, two knishes and a couple of orange sodas, I thought.

I then asked him how he'd achieved his success. I told him I was very impressed but rather intimidated by all the affluence. Mercury suddenly grew sad. He smiled and said he sometimes wished he were back at the beginning.

"With Silverstein?" I said.

He looked at me sternly and then seemed to think it over and relaxed. He chuckled and nodded several times.

"I don't do interviews," he said, mocking himself. "But the old man said I should trust you. I know you're dying to find out how I did it. By the way, who told you about me and Silverstein?"

"His nephew."

"The lawyer?"

"Yes."

Mercury Gomez nodded and then the food came. When we were seated and had been eating a while, he said I could ask him anything I wanted. I told him that although I would be interested in learning how he had managed to multiply his wealth, I was certain that he'd achieved it all through hard work, developed talents, risk taking, some luck and an indomitable will to triumph, and that he would have to forgive me, but that my primary concern was how he had managed to make those deliveries as quickly as he had when he first began.

He thought for a moment, mulling over, it seemed, how to answer my question. He chuckled and then began telling me what it was like working for Silver Streak Services, how grateful he was to have a job because his father had instilled in all of them the value of hard work, but how demeaning it had been to be treated with contempt and to hear all the racial jokes and the word "nigger," even though growing up he never thought of being black, notwithstanding the fact that both his father and mother were both blacks from Loíza on the island. And that this problem was what all of the people here in the United States had to confront.

"On the island," he said, "and even up in El Barrio you're black but it's no big thing. But once you get out into the world they make you decide. Even if you're a little bit black, they make you choose."

He said no matter how many years go by the people are gonna keep speaking Spanish and eating the same food and listening to the music and they're always gonna say they're from the island. "That's why being P.R.'s such a big thing. This society wants you to choose. Black or white and we refuse. It's a messed up system."

"I agree a hundred percent," I said.

And then he said that after working for about a year for Silver Streak Services he realized he was pretty much anonymous. "Just another black guy. And worse than that I was small. 'The little black guy,' I useta hear people say and I useta feel like saying, '*puñeta, váyanse pa'l carajo, coño! Yo soy boricua! Negro pero boricua y si no le cae bien, cáguense en su madre!*' Know what I mean?"

"Of course," I said. "I've suffered similar discrimination."

"Everybody does. If you're real white, then you kinda slide in and become anonymous too, but there's little rewards here and there. But if you're black, forget it. That's it."

He became pensive again and then went on to tell me that back then he had spoken with his father and his father told him to just keep going and he'd figure it out because he had the brains and the courage to win and that he shouldn't feel sorry for himself because that's all they were waiting for. And then one day he was in Brooklyn visiting his girl friend and he went by a playground and saw a small black young man playing basketball, dribbling and scooting around and driving the other players crazy and then passing or shooting but always coming out on top and all of a sudden he had an idea. He waited until they were finished playing and spoke with him.

"Luther Robinson was his name," he said. "A little bit taller than me, but pure black and smart as a whip. High school dropout and part-time numbers runner. Street smart, that is, 'cause there's a difference. No matter how street smart you are, if you ain't got certain fundamentals for dealing in the bigger society, you're gonna get jammed somewhere along the way. Luther's been with me ever since. He lives in Nigeria right now and runs the entire African Mercury division from our offices in Lagos. I knocked all the NBA fantasies out of his head, made him go back to high school, graduate and then we both went to City College at night. I'll be damned if in his junior year he doesn't suddenly get a bug up his ass that he wants to study law and after we graduated we got him into Columbia Law and it was like a breeze. A genuine born legal mind. Photographic memory from the numbers racket."

He continued and said that for the next month he combed the city of New York, going into every neighborhood looking for small black young men. Five foot five and under, because as long as they were black and small they were totally anonymous in the greater society and nobody paid much attention to them; that he explained the scheme, informing them that at first they wouldn't make much money but that after a while nobody would be able to compete with them. Some of the young men thought he was crazy but that about a dozen or so figured it might work and stuck it out for the first few months while he was still at Silver Streak Services; and that they didn't make much money but had a lot of laughs at Silverstein's expense when he'd send him out and he'd be back in ten or fifteen minutes, when in the past the job would have taken at least an hour, if not more.

"So how were you able to accomplish this?" I said.

"I'd post them at different corners in midtown," he said. "Near telephones and I'd call in the address and off they'd go. Like the pony express."

"They must've been tired at the end of the day," I said.

"That's right and that's when Luther had a brainstorm and he said why didn't we start using real tall guys."

"Because they have longer strides," I said.

"No, nothing like that," Mercury said.

He explained how they started recruiting tall fellows in the playgrounds, only people with good hands and when they had a fair number of them they bought cheap footballs and cut them open and put zippers on them and used them as courier pouches and issued everyone whistles, so that now all he needed to do was get an order and phone it to one of the little guys near the pick up location. The little guy'd run up and get the letter or package, stick it in one of the footballs, blow the whistle and up the street one of the tall guys would blow his whistle and stick up his hands. "The little guy," Mercury said, "would let fly with a forty or fifty yard spiral that the big guy would catch and pass to the next guy until the package was delivered by another little guy."

"You're kidding, of course," I said, truly finding it hard to believe. "It didn't really happen that way."

"I swear to my mother," Mercury said.

That was enough for me. When the people swear on their mother there's no need to question a person's integrity. But that wasn't the end of it. Ideas continued to emerge from all the members of Mercury Gomez' messenger crew.

"One day Andre Covington, he's my West Coast man, shows up with his cousin on roller skates and tells me that Louis, that was his name, wanted to become a roller derby skater and he needed all the practice he could get and could we put him to work since he could really sharpen his skills skating in and out of Manhattan traffic. No problem, I said. So now we had passers, catchers, runners *and* skaters. And then it escalated and word got around and everybody thought it was a big joke and they all wanted in. At one point I had a hundred and fifty of these guys. About twenty-five of them roller skaters. It was unreal. All of us that delivered always dressed the same. Day in and day out. Same pants, same sneakers, same jacket and cap. Three or four basic outfits. I bought them wholesale in the garment center. And then I decided to talk to Silverstein."

"You wanted a raise and he turned you down," I said.

"No, he didn't. He offered me raises but I turned him down. I wanted a partnership, but he wouldn't go for it and went into this song and dance about my wanting to deprive his children of an education and was I after his heart and so I figured I'd go into business on my own. I put on a suit and went back to our clients and promised to deliver in record time. MERCURY MESSENGERS 'On Time, Every Time' That was our motto. For a while we worked out of phone booths around Grand Central Station and then I got my first office. I bet Silverstein, the lawyer, told you his uncle gave me the name, Mercury."

"As a matter of fact, he did say that," I said.

"Wrong. The fact is he started calling me Speedy Gonzalez. It pissed me off no end but I didn't show it. No, by that time I was at City, studying business at night. I had to take a humanities course and ran across Greek mythology and then I saw the Western Union logo. I had Bootsie Powell draw up our logo. He couldn't roller skate, run, pass or catch, but was a hell of an artist and we all dug him because he really wanted to be in on everything we did. I had business cards printed up and the rest is history. Bootsie's in charge of all our advertising and owns half of San Francisco's real estate. And that's the whole story. Bootsie began calling me Merc and it stuck."

"Amazing," I said. "What happened to the original messenger service?"

"A couple of years later I sold it to some smart ass types from Wall Street for a couple of hundred thousand and I took the whole amount and bought Polaroid and Xerox stock. The fellas that wanted to keep improving went off to go to school, came back and are still working for Mercury Communications. Luther and I went into the copying business all over the city. The Wall Street guys ruined the messenger service and six months later I bought the company back for peanuts. Just to have use of the name."

"You bought Polaroid and Xerox, before they went big?" I asked.

"You got it."

"How did you know?"

Mercury thought for a moment, shook his head and then chuckled.

"I guess I musta figured out two things about this country. They want everything in a hurry and they want everybody to kinda be the same. You know, carbon copies. Polaroid and Xerox. Fulfilling industrial fantasies for the American people. We always got a kick outta delivering. Nobody could tell the difference between us. It was always the little black guy that picked up the package or delivered it. It didn't matter whether it was me or Luther, Raul, Dolores or Cynthia."

"What?"

"Oh sure," Mercury said. "We began getting more and more business and couldn't find enough little black guys, so we started using little black girls. No makeup, no earrings, no giggling and no falling for guys while on the job. And they had to wear the same clothes as the other messengers, hair tucked in. No exceptions."

"And the people in the offices still couldn't tell," I said.

"Nope," Mercury said. " 'The little black guy already picked it up,' they'd say."

"You've accomplished more than ten men do in a lifetime," I said.

"What's next?"

Mercury Gomez was once again the super shrewd businessman. A stern look came over his face, his eyes took on their frightening look and his body radiated power.

"The electronics industry has unlimited potential," he said. "The sky's the limit."

My heart skipped several beats.

"Silverstein, the lawyer, said there was a rumor that Mercury Communications was planning to launch its own . . ."

I stopped speaking and watched Solomon Gomez bring the index finger of his right hand to his lips and silently issue a request that I keep my counsel. A knowing grin broke out behind the index finger and then he winked at me.

He offered to have me driven back to my apartment but I thanked him and told him I needed time to think and that I thought I'd walk for a while, but to be sure and tell his father that I would definitely be coming down to the island.

Out in the street I couldn't stop smiling. Those Rough Riders had definitely made a mistake back in 1898 when they landed in Guanica and annexed the island.

Boy, had they made a mistake.

La Novela

As someone who, because of his destiny, has been chosen to set down in coherent fashion the peregrinations of the people, their travails and sorrows, I must retain the utmost objectivity concerning the human flaws which I encounter. It is not my position to pass moral judgement and cast disapproving glances in the direction of others. Having more than my share of human failings I've always thought moral nearsightedness to be a blessing in disguise. Some things, however, cannot go unnoticed nor can they be simply passed up as isolated events. Instead, these incidents form a pattern in the persistent weakening of our cultural fabric as a people.

What took place between Rogelio Valenzuela and Dorcas Conde was reprehensible and beyond anything which I had ever encountered. They were both wonderful, dedicated people who gave unstintingly of themselves without ever a thought of sacrifice. That they chose to give themselves to each other is shameful and for me an incomprehensible scandal. That they were also from a fundamentalist Protestant background creates even more chagrin in me, because in recounting what took place it makes me appear to be accusing that faith of hypocrisy, which is not in the least my intent.

Please understand that as an artist I am responsible for taking the most radical positions in order to advance human knowledge and sensitivity. Because I've chosen to live on the point of the arrow, so to speak, I've never had the opportunity to experience married life, nor to father children, at least, none that I know of. But I have the utmost respect for the family. It is within the family that culture is kept alive. For this reason to cause any type of disruption in this most important of institutions seems to me, without seeming extreme or allowing hysteria to confuse the issue, cultural suicide.

We, as men, are weak and fall prey to the charm of women, oftentimes without regard to consequences. But most men, as they grow older, temper their need to conquer, or to put it more aptly, to be conquered, and content themselves with surreptitious liaisons which protect their conduct and safeguard the sanctity of the home. Would that this had been sufficient for Rogelio Valenzuela.

It all began last spring when Awilda, Rogelio's oldest daughter, met the

Condes' son, Bobby and they fell in love. They were both seniors at Hunter College where I had been invited to speak on my views concerning the state of the novel. Both Awilda and Bobby were devoted literature students. So involved were they in their pursuit of their studies that they didn't notice each other until they ended up together in a course called "Contemporary Ethnic Literature," which, because of their "sociological" significance, chose to include my now infamous ghetto novels as part of its fall syllabus. When Professor Pfeiffer, who designed and taught the course, called me in September, I was at first reluctant, but after discussing the matter with him and explaining my views, he reassured me that perhaps my visiting his class could help to clarify whatever misconceptions students had about my work. It was with this in mind that I accepted.

After my lecture there was a small reception and, as often happens, several students appeared most eager to engage me in dialogue concerning literature. I'm always willing to discuss the subject and help anyone who is interested in the thankless task of documenting the people's dreams. My message to them is always the same: find useful employment in an industry which will offer you the maximum benefits and under no circumstances entertain ideas of becoming an artist. Most students listen and come to their senses. On occasion there are a few who are adamant and insist on pursuing a writing career. Awilda Valenzuela and Bobby Conde said they were willing to sacrifice their lives for the sake of literature. I told them they ought to seriously think over their stance, but they insisted that they were committed to the craft.

In a small compartment of my heart I was touched by their resolve and although I did not envy their future, I was glad to meet such courageous young people. There was a fire in their eyes which I mistakenly interpreted as artistic fervor. In truth they were madly in love with each other and for the past semester, and in true bohemian fashion, took every opportunity they had to make love. They had reached a point of ecstasy which remained etched on their faces whether they were aroused or not.

Looking at them made me think of literary couples: Robert Browning and Elizabeth Barrett, Jean Paul Sartre and Simone de Beauvoir, etc. Except that these two were not consumptive nor did they look as if they were at all wrestling with any type of dilemma, existential or otherwise. They looked the picture of health. I subsequently learned that they rose each morning at 6 a.m. to jog, worked out with weights twice a week and swam three times a week. On weekends they spent endless hours in paddleball tournaments. They smiled easily, were extremely polite and seemed to handle their professors with remarkable aplomb. It struck me that they had the artistic temperament of somewhat aroused koala bears. If the phrase "cute couple" needed an example they would have served as the best. They reiterated, however, that they were committed to the extremely unrewarding and often difficult task of writing. Between their love making and their athletic schedule I found it difficult to believe that they could do much else other than perspire a great deal.

But I could find no fault with them. Sadly, they had read every word I had written, had absolutely no problem recalling characters, plots and settings and *she* could quote *verbatim* long passages from my work, effortlessly. Needless to say, I was intrigued.

And yet it was her father and his mother who caught my attention when I met them at the Christmas party to which I was invited by the young couple. The gathering was to serve to announce their engagement.

At six o'clock on December 22, Bobby Conde rang my door bell and a few minutes later I was in the back seat of his car speeding out to Queens with Awilda in the front seat explicating the symbolic element of the heroine's struggle in *Return to the Ghetto*, insisting that what I was writing about was the decadence of American society and extrapolating that metaphor to a universal one in which I was predicting the destruction of the earth. I told her that I wasn't aware of dealing with such a profound subject, but she insisted and Bobby backed up her argument, citing various examples such as the scene in which Gloria Campos, the heroine, as a sixth grade teacher in a ghetto school, becomes frustrated with her class as she attempts to teach them geography and with her ruler totally obliterates the classroom globe, repeating, as she strikes the rapidly disintegrating orb: "The hell with Oslo, the hell with Prague, the hell with Buenos Aires, the hell with Cairo, the hell with Peking," and so on, naming each of the capitals of the world as her students cheered. I said that perhaps there was something to their theory. Inwardly, however, I thought the young couple rather pedantic and did not feel like explaining that I was simply dealing with the benighted nature, both in students and teachers, so prevalent in ghetto schools.

But they went on like that until we were in front of the Valenzuela home, a beautiful English cottage type structure with a landscaped winter garden dominated by a large pine tree, decorated, perhaps too gaudily, for Christmas. At the foot of the tree a Nativity scene sat illuminated by a flood light on the snow-covered lawn. The figures were two feet tall and the animals quite life like, particularly one of the cows. As it turned out, it was not at all a cow, but the Valenzuela's dachshund, Goethe (so named by Awilda, who had a love-hate relationship with German literature), which evidently had been influenced by the family's religious devotion and enjoyed sitting for hours in the manger in adoration of the Child Jesus. I, for one, found the dog's dedication remarkable. Awilda, however, did not appreciate his religious zeal.

"Oh, that dog," she said, getting out of the car. "*Goethe, warum wieder schlafst du mit Jesus? Kommen du hier, schnell.*" When the dog didn't deem it necessary to respond to why once again he was sleeping with Jesus and kept looking from Joseph to Mary for direction, Awilda gave up. "*Ach!*" she said, and shook her head. "*Dumm, zwiebelkopf, schumtzig Hund.*"

Having a soft spot in my heart for animals I resented her designation of the family pet as a dumb, onionhead, dirty dog.

"*Ah, sprechen sie Deutsch*?" I said.

"*Ja, Ich studiere Deutsch seit vier Jahren,*" she said, explaining that she had studied the language for four years.

"*Gut, aber der Hund schlaft nicht mit Jesus. Der Hund bewacht Jesus,* I said, pointing out that rather than sleeping with Jesus, the dog was watching the Babe.

She laughed and let go with a perfectly accented barrage of Germanic words, which in spite of my having studied the language for a time during my brief soujourn in Europe after the Second World War, I could not follow. When she saw that I had become lost, she said, "I'm sorry. I get carried away when it comes to Goethe. He is obsessed with that manger. Quite dense and without much canine sense. Please come in, Doctor Mendoza," she said.

They both called me Doctor Mendoza. I wanted to tell them that I did not have a PhD, nor for that matter a Master's and had barely managed to earn a Bachelor's degree from New York University many years ago, but recalling those days made me think of Esperanza, whom I met in Washington Square Park one lovely spring morning while she was pushing a carriage with a small blond child in it. I asked her if it was her child. She laughed and said it was not and that she was working for a judge and his wife and was simply a maid in their employ. I fell immediately in love and rescued her from menial labor for pay and not for love. I made a conscious effort not to think about my beloved, lest I grow morose and mourn her absence.

I followed Bobby Conde and Awilda Valenzuela into the house and was introduced to each member of the family as Dr. Mendoza, the famous writer. We sat down immediately to a Christmas feast which left me wishing I had not accepted their invitation. Each time my plate was half empty more food was forced upon me.

Dorcas Conde, Bobby's mother, was a pretty woman, perhaps a bit too plump as she approached her fortieth birthday, but possessed of an engaging smile and large, heavy-lidded brown eyes which gave her a languorous, albeit bovine, appearance. She sighed often and spoke in almost a whisper, her voice sweet and airy. Her husband was a large beefy man, who drove Greyhound buses across the country. He enjoyed telling stories of his days and nights on the highway. The Valenzuela couple were quite different. Rogelio, the father of the bride-to-be was a gentlemanly type, very polite and quite elegant. His wife, however, was a thin, high-strung woman who complained incessantly about various ailments and the cures which she had attempted. Her husband comforted her often, reassuring her that the treatment she was presently receiving would cure her of the malady.

My first indication that something was amiss in the lives of Rogelio Valenzuela and Dorcas Conde was the fact that not once during that evening at the Valenzuela home did they look at each other. At first I did not find this unusual since familiarity between men and women is not customary among our people until they have known each other a while. But then I learned that the two families had known each other for several months and had visited with each other on numerous occasions. They had, in fact, picnicked together and more than a few times had gone to the beach to please their children, recognizing that their love for each other was not a passing thing and the two families would be joined in the future.

My second clue that something was drastically wrong took place when, after dinner was over and people were sitting around talking, I excused myself and climbed the stairs to the second floor to use the bathroom. When I emerged from the bathroom I saw Rogelio going down the stairs and, as I walked down the hall, I saw Dorcas Conde leaning against the wall, smoothing her dress and hair and breathing quite heavily, much as if she had finished running.

"Oh, there you are, Dr. Mendoza," she said. "I came up to tell you that we're about to take some photos. These stairs are such a bother and me with this asthma."

"Thank you, it was kind of you to go to the trouble," I said.

Of course, the next time I saw Bobby Conde I asked him if his mother suffered from asthma. He said he didn't think so and thought my question rather ridiculous.

"She's as healthy as a horse," he said. "You probably heard her discussing that idiotic soap opera she watches on the Spanish channel every day."

"She watches *novelas*?" I said, stupidly, knowing that most of our women watched soap operas. "I didn't know that."

"Oh, sure," said Bobby. "Her favorite one's called *Más alla del olvido* and the heroine suffers from asthma."

I didn't want to discuss the subject any further fearing that I would create suspicion in the young man's mind concerning his mother and future father-in-law. I returned to my apartment and began working on my new experimental novel *The Duel* in which I set up a western type confrontation between a gang of presidents of the United States and island patriots. It was no use. I could not concentrate and ended up calling Camilo Marquez, an audio technician at Channel 45. I asked him about the soap opera.

"The one in which the heroine has asthma," I said.

He snickered at my interest in a *novela* and then apologized and said that as a matter of fact it was quite good and that if I was willing to travel to New Jersey I could view as many episodes as I wanted. I couldn't help myself. I called up my friend, Alejandro Cordero, who is pastry chef at a country club near Secaucus, New Jersey, and asked if he minded a visitor for a few days. He had become a widower the previous year and was more than happy to have a house guest since he lived alone. I told him I would take the bus out the next morning and he graciously volunteered to meet me at the bus station in his car. As soon as I hung up the telephone I had a terrible anxiety attack. I took out a map of New Jersey and checked to see how far Secaucus was from Brooks Landing, where I had once lectured disappointingly to a dieting and literary women's club. Brooks Landing was quite a ways from Secaucus and I relaxed.

The following day I took the bus to New Jersey and had Cordero drop me off at the television station. Camilo Márquez immediately set me up in a room with a large color television set and nearly twenty hour-long cassettes of the soap opera. "When you finish one, just take it out and put the other one on," Cordero said. "They're numbered." I thanked him and began watching "Beyond Forgetfulness."

The story takes place in a small town on the island. The heroine, Elena, a beautiful but poor peasant girl, working as a cashier at a Burger King, goes to visit her beloved, Armando, a poor but ambitious bank clerk, in jail where he has spent the last four years after being unjustly accused, tried and found guilty of embezzling nearly a thousand dollars. Armando is handsome, soft spoken and totally devoted to Elena, swearing to remain true to her no matter how long he has to stay in jail. She cries, implores God, wrings her hands, wheezes, coughs, becomes short of breath and confesses bitterly that the doctors have not been able to do anything for her asthma, but that she too will remain true to him.

For the next three days I returned to the television station and sat mesmerized by the unfolding plot and shocked by the buried emotions which began surfacing in me. How could such chicanery take place. The son of the bank president, Mario, a suave but evil looking young blade, begins plotting to seduce the helpless Elena by befriending her with plans for obtaining Armando's release through his political connections with the mayor of the town, Don Bonifacio.

Lauro, the mayor's gardener, a troubled young man whose mother, on her deathbed, has confessed that he is the illegitimate son of an American homosexual who did not wish to ruin his status in the artistic community by having it be known that he had fathered a child, becomes Elena's confidant so that he may hear news from Armando, with whom he is secretly in love, thinking that like his father he is also a homosexual.

As the story unfolds we see that Don Bonifacio has a sordid past when a wealthy mysterious woman, Omaira, arrives in the town and tells the mayor's wife that her husband is not really from the island but is Dominican and had to leave that country when he was a young man because he had an affair with the wife of an Argentinian poet, and that this led to bloodshed. The mayor's wife, Doña Gertrudis, has a nervous breakdown and ends up in the hospital where she is cared for by Dr. Garza, a one time secret admirer, unhappily married to, although he doesn't know this, Omaira's half-sister, Blanca. Omaira, it turns out, had been secretly in love with Dr. Garza in her youth.

Lauro, the gardener, overhears a conversation between Don Bonifacio and Omaira in which Omaira threatens to expose his previous life in the Dominican Republic unless the mayor romances her half-sister, Blanca, so that she may have clear sailing in her attempts to snare Dr. Garza. As the days go by and Doña Gertrudis, the mayor's wife, sinks deeper into madness, the good doctor falls more deeply in love with her.

The bank president, Don Arsenio, is overcome with grief when he learns that the mayor's wife Doña Gertrudis, with whom he's carried on an affair for the last thirty years, is in the hospital and totally mad. Don Arsenio, the bank president, begins making costly mistakes and soon is being sued by a number of clients for mismanagement. He begins drinking heavily and confesses to his wife, Doña Fulgencia, that he's always loved Doña Gertrudis, the mayor's wife. Doña Fulgencia, not to be outdone, attempts to commit suicide by swallowing half a bottle of sleeping pills, but is saved when a fire of suspicious origin takes place in her home and she is rescued by the maid, a stately old Indian woman by the name of Magdalena, who pulls her out of bed and drags her out of the house, and with the help of her nephew, Bartolomeo, a seventeen year old idiot, takes Doña Fulgencia, the bank president's wife, to her humble, but spacious hut, where she nurses her back to health.

It turns out that Magdalena and Doña Fulgencia share a secret. Elena, it turns out is the daughter of Doña Fulgencia, the bank president's wife, whom she had conceived out of wedlock with the mayor, Don Bonifacio, while the bank president, Don Arsenio, was in the Army and she, Doña Fulgencia, was supposedly in Madrid studying. Elena has been raised by Magdalena, believes she is Magdalena's daughter and, although Elena is grateful for the love that Magdalena has given her, she is ashamed of her Indian background.

Meanwhile, Lauro goes to Elena and tells her about Omaira, the mystery woman, threatening to expose the mayor, Don Bonifacio, not only because of the scandal back in the Dominican Republic, but because he is the father of an illegitimate child, which of course is Elena, although Elena doesn't know this.

We further learn that Armando, Elena's jailed beloved, is Omaira, the mystery woman's illegitimate son, who has also been raised by Magdalena, the stately old Indian woman, in another part of town. In her confusion Elena succumbs to the advances of Mario, the bank president's son, and loses her honor. She goes to the jail and tells Armando that she is dishonored and cannot marry him. He demands to know the identity of her lover. In the throes of an asthma attack she tearfully reveals Mario's name. Armando vows to avenge himself even if he has to wait until he is old and gray.

Elena, now in love with Mario learns that he is engaged to Cora, Dr. Garza's voluptuous daughter, who returns from her studies in Buenos Aires where she's had a torrid affair with Carlos, the son of an Argentinian poet, who in reality, although Cora doesn't know it, is the son of Don Bonifacio, the mayor, from his affair with the poet's wife in the Dominican Republic. Elena and Cora have a brutal verbal confrontation in which Cora calls Elena a sickly, worthless peasant. Elena returns to her humble home and prays for forgiveness. Prayer does not help and one night she walks out of her house, determined to go into the sea and drown.

Lauro follows her and watches as she walks, crying and wheezing from her asthma, into the surf. He cannot contain himself and calls her name. Elena dives in and disappears under the waves, but Lauro swims out and rescues her. In a moonlit scene he covers her face with kisses and realizes that he does not suffer from his father's sexual preference. He later finds out that his mother has lied to him and that he is not the son of a homosexual American artist but the illegitimate son of Don Eustaquio, a wealthy lawyer from the capital.

After three days I could no longer watch the soap opera. So engrossed had I become in the complications and the emotional outpouring of the actors that each time the credits came on I switched cassettes and did not read the credits. Although Magdalena, the maid, had looked familiar, her appearance had been brief and it wasn't until the last episode that I realized that the actress was no other than my own beloved, Esperanza. I watched the credits to make sure.

Elena
Lucía Manrique

Armando
Rafael Gutiérrez

Mario
Pablo Porrata

Lauro
Pascual Campos Torres

Omaira
Teresa Vizcarrondo

Don Bonifacio
Tomás Vega

Doña Gertrudis
Babette Rivera

Don Arsenio
Luis Antonio Echevarría

Doña Fulgencia
Alicia Betancourt

Magdalena
Esperanza De León

Bartolomeo
Edgardo Fuentes

Blanca
Iris María Collazo

Cora
Marisol Lugo

Don Eustaquio
Francisco Sabattini Morales

Carlos
David Coll

Padre Leandro
Fausto Hidalgo

Amazing, I thought. I was a jumble of emotions. Why hadn't Esperanza written and told me that she had finally, after nearly forty years of frustration, landed a part. My joy was short lived when further on in the credits I saw that this travesty, which perhaps should have been called "All Whose Children?" had been written by none other than Guillermo Bauza, my rival for Esperanza's affections since we were both at N.Y.U., who even then deemed himself worthy enough to cross literary swords with me and wrote execrable poetry in his moronic attempts to win favor with Esperanza. He had finally, after forty years of trying, triumphed and had seduced my Esperanza. Not given to violence, I nevertheless saw myself flying down to the island, purchasing a revolver and confronting Bauza, perhaps even catching him and Esperanza in desperate geriatric gropings. I would have no choice but to shoot them both and then put the gun to my head in order to end my suffering.

I suddenly caught myself racing madly through the labyrinths of my mind, tapping some primal instinct which was calling for me to be involved in jealousy, intrigue, unfaithfulness, revenge and lifelong bitterness because of love. Without considering the matter further I immediately understood that I was under the spell of the soap opera and that I was beginning to see my life in those terms. If that were the case then Dorcas Conde, Bobby's mother, was under the same spell and her feeble mind and uneventful life were being directly affected by the *novela* and she saw herself as part of the story line, creating for herself unnecessary complications.

My next question made me shudder. Was Rogelio Valenzuela also caught in that spell? If so, I had no choice but to intervene. If not for their sake, for that of their children. I determined at once to speak to Rogelio directly as soon as possible and confront him with the possible consequences of his actions. Under the pretext that it was imperative I speak to him about a mutual acquaintance, I obtained his work telephone number from Awilda.

Rogelio, a certified public accountant, worked for a large accounting firm in Lower Manhattan. I called him and he was actually flattered to hear from me. I suggested that we have lunch the following day. He agreed to meet me and we went to a quiet Chinese restaurant. After we had finished our soup I asked him if he watched much television. He told me he watched Masterpiece Theater, the Boston Pops, Nova and financial programs, all on public television.

"During the baseball season I watch the Mets," he said.

"No *novelas*?" I said, looking directly into his eyes.

He was obviously insulted, but perhaps out of respect for my status he did not let on. Instead, he said that his wife enjoyed watching *novelas* but was too caught up in them, so that half the time he wasn't sure whether she was talking about the soap opera or their own life. I tried another approach and asked him how he felt about his daughter's upcoming marriage.

"He's a wonderful young man," Valenzuela said. "Because of God's mercy and the blood of the Lamb Jesus, my daugther's very lucky to have found such an industrious and respectful mate."

"Very handsome too," I said.

"Yes," Valenzuela said, picking up a forkful of egg foo young.

"Like his mother." I said.

Valenzuela blushed and looked nervously around him.

"Yes, of course," he said.

"She's extremely attractive," I said. "A wonderful figure, a beautiful smile and lovely eyes. What North Americans call bedroom eyes."

This time he choked on his food and turned beet red. I pushed on relentlessly, knowing that in the next instance he would confess his illicit affair with Dorcas Conde and for the sake of his daughter and future son-in-law would desist from his madness. When he finished coughing, he wiped his mouth and drank some water. He told me that she was indeed attractive and that his wife had accused him on several occasions of paying too much attention to her. I thought to myself, here it comes. He's about to unburden himself.

"I don't know if you noticed it," he said. "But I did not speak to her during that Christmas dinner. In fact, I hardly looked at her even though in the beginning, when we first met, I learned that we were both from the same hometown."

"Oh? Which one?" I said.

"Cacimar," he said.

"I see," I said, scrutinizing him for signs of deception. "My hometown also. What a pleasant coincidence," I added, not without a degree of irony, noting for myself that my poor hometown was still known for its loose morals and oversexed denizens.

"But we did not know each other," he said, perhaps a bit too quickly. "I was from the mountains and several years older than her. I never saw her until the children met and my daughter brought Bobby to visit."

"But you found that you had more in common than a hometown," I said.

"Oh, yes," he said, smiling happily. "She reads the Bible daily and teaches Sunday school like I do."

"Do you attend the same church?"

"No, although at times I've wished that we did,"

"Yes, of course," I said. "I think she finds you extremely attractive also."

This time he dropped his fork and as he attempted to retrieve it, hit the teapot and sent it crashing to the floor. The waiter came over and Valenzuela apologized profusely. The waiter smiled, swept up the broken teapot, mopped the floor and brought us more tea.

"I was afraid of that," Valenzuela said, shaking his head. "It is the workings of the Devil," he added. "We are both being tested. It is exactly as it is written in the scriptures."

Sure, I thought. Cover up the entire matter by avoiding personal responsibility and blaming the Devil, when it was blatantly obvious that they were carrying on their romance right under their spouses' noses. As I've said, I'm not prone to pointing the finger at others for their moral weaknesses, but when it comes to the noble institution of the family I feel it is my responsibility to act swiftly and decisively to maintain its integrity.

"My counsel to you," I said, "is that you be absolutely honest with yourself and with Dorcas. Before things get out of hand, take her somewhere where you can be alone and discuss the situation."

He was astounded that I would suggest such a thing, but trained to detect the merest of deceptions, I was able to see through his ruse and remained steadfast in my determination to put a stop to their clandestine attachment.

"She is a married woman," he said. "Where could I take her that we would not be seen?"

More deception, I thought. Oh, he was a sly one, this number shuffling Lothario. He probably knew every motel within a hundred mile radius and he was asking me for advice.

"You have a car, don't you?"

"Yes, of course," he said. "Some of our clients request that we work on their books in their place of business."

"Well then," I said. "Her husband is away a great deal of the time. Call her up and explain that you must speak to her urgently. Pick a deserted place somewhere in the city, meet her there after dark and then drive across into New Jersey. Find an unpopulated area, park and explain to her that the two of you must put an end to this illicit attraction."

What a superb actor he was. He feigned shock and attempted to extricate himself from the situation.

"What if I simply prayed and asked our Lord for forgiveness?" he said.

I was appalled by his hypocrisy. Even though I do not believe in a Supreme Being, I was forced to deal with Valenzuela on his own terms and invoke the fact that adhering to his religion also meant having conviction and being honest.

"Jesus Christ," I said, "was not a coward. Did He not go into the temple and drive out the money lenders?"

"Yes, He did, but . . ."

"Courage then, my friend," I said. "For the sake of these children you must confront the issue and deal with it as a man."

Rogelio Valenzuela became quite serious and then agreed that he must do exactly as I said. We finished eating, paid the check, went back out into the street and said goodbye. He thanked me and I went away convinced that because he was basically a good man he would stop seeing Dorcas Conde and their lives would return to some semblance of normalcy.

A month passed, then two more without my hearing from Valenzuela. One Tuesday afternoon in April I received a hysterical phone call from Awilda, Valenzuela's daughter, requesting to see me. I had made some progress with *The Duel*, so I agreed. We met in a coffee shop near Hunter College and I almost didn't recognize Awilda, such was her state of agitation. After ordering coffee I asked her if there was anything wrong.

"It's Bobby's mother," she said.

"Has there been an accident?" I said. "Is she ill?"

Awilda said that Dorcas Conde was fine and that Bobby himself had wanted to speak to me but was too ashamed.

"She's flipped out, Dr. Mendoza," Awilda said. "Totally gone."

"I thought you said she wasn't sick," I said.

Awilda explained that her future mother-in-law had undergone a personality change: that she had dyed her hair blonde, started going to exercise classes, had stopped going to church and was threatening to go to college.

"She's even started reading *Cosmo* in Spanish," Awilda said. "She's totally out there and she told Bobby that she had been a fool for too many years. She said that she was still a young woman and had no plans to let herself grow old without fulfilling her natural urges as a woman. She's reading about vitamins and listening to *salsa*. She even called up Gilda Miró, who gives advice to women on Spanish radio, asking her what she thought about extramarital affairs."

"Live, on the radio?" I asked, somewhat shocked.

"Yeah, live," she said. "So you could hear her voice, Bobby told me."

"What was the response from Gilda . . .?"

"Miró. Gilda Miró. She said that she ought to see a marriage counselor or talk to her priest or minister."

"Has she done that?"

"No, she hasn't. Now she's even talking about her G-spot."

"G-spot? I don't understand."

"You think I didı I hadn't even heard of it 'til I spoke to my girlfriend, Sharon Ramirez. She's a Psych major and knows about all the new sexual breakthroughs. She's like Masters ¿ Johnson all rolled up into one. You know, AC-DC. It's some sort of muscle inside the woman's . . ."

"That's all right, Awilda," I said, beginning to grow alarmed by her degree of openness with me. "I understand perfectly. I may be advanced in age but I keep up with science," I added, not having the slightest notion of what a G-spot was or what its function could be.

"Oh, good," she said. "Then you understand that she's in trouble and probably's gonna start experimenting sexually, if she hasn't already."

"It certainly seems very serious," I said, and without sounding as if I were prying, inquired about her father, knowing full well that now that the cat was out of the bag, now that he knew they had been found out by me, they were going to flaunt their affair. "Does he know about this?"

Awilda was not at all surprised by the question and said that was another matter which concerned her because suddenly her father had also begun acting strangely.

"What do you mean?" I said.

"Well, you saw him," she said. "I don't mean any disrespect but he dresses like you, very conservative, the way fathers are supposed to, right?"

"Yes, I suppose," I replied.

"Well, he's letting his hair grow, he's stopped using Yardley brilliantine and went and bought himself a hair dryer. He wanted to know how the Dry Look seemed on him. The thing that got me is that I've never seen my father in blue jeans and all of a sudden he walks in one day and he's wearing designer jeans and boots and talking about yoga and body auras and karma. He's a very bright man, but I think he's also flipped his lid. I found a book on sex in my father's briefcase. Not a dirty book, nothing like that, but something by a psychologist. Bobby and I don't know what to do. With the wedding coming up and everything and our parents acting like thisı What do you think's happening to them? Bobby's convinced that there's something going on between the two of them."

"That's preposterous," I said, sternly. "How can you jump to such a conclusion about your father and future mother-in-lawı Your father loves your mother, I'm sure."

"No, he doesn't," Awilda said. "He's very unhappy with her and in a way I don't blame him. She's my mother but she's caught in a time warp, back in my grandmother's time. I hope I'm not embarrassing you, Dr. Mendoza, but I think you're a liberal man and I can speak freely. I don't think my father and mother have sex with each other. Bobby and I discussed it. He says he can't imagine when his mother and father have any time either, with him driving those buses all the time. Like, Bobby and I don't even wanna get married. We're doing it just for the families. We're like experimenting with life. We love each other but we think marriage will probably interfere with our artistic development."

I didn't know how to respond. Everything had gone awry and I couldn't understand why. Awilda went on.

"Like, if the two of them, my father and Bobby's mother, have a thing for each other, should we like encourage them, or what? I mean, they're entitled to a sexual life, don't you think?"

"Yes, of course," I said. "But what about the breakup of the family?"

"That's just it," Awilda replied. "There's no need for it to happen. It's not too late. Maybe you could talk to my father again. He told me the two of you had lunch and that you're very perceptive, which I already knew from reading your books. But he really respects you. Please."

I told her I'd see what I could do and that perhaps it would be a good idea if I saw the two of them together. She said she'd talk to Bobby and see what he thought. We said goodbye and that evening I received a call from Valenzuela. He sounded totally different and said it was no problem at all. Conde was somewhere in the Rockies and why didn't he and Dorcas meet us at the Karma Kafe down in Greenwich Village.

"It's a health food place," he said.

Great, I thought. That's all I needed to really get my stomach in a state of total disarray. Raw food. I dressed as casually as I could, but my attire was no match for Rog and Dee, which is what they called each other all evening. Already quite a handsome man, he now looked like something out of *GQ* magazine. But it was Dorcas Conde who shocked me beyond description and probably added several years to my already failing body.

She had lost nearly twenty-five pounds, had what is called a punk type haircut, with nearly half of one side of her head practically shaved and the rest moussed into bizarre blonde spikes. Her clothes seemed mismatched, but overall they went well together: baggy pants, tucked into boots, a balkan peasant blouse and a wide belt with an enormous buckle. She had had one of her ears pierced three times and wore one hoop earring and two other smaller ones. Her makeup was subtle, giving her an even more exotic look. I must confess that after the initial shock I found her rather attractive and immediately questioned my own degenerating values.

But the one thing that immediately caught my attention was the fact that they had that same look of spent but readily regenerating ecstasy which I had noticed in Bobby and Awilda when I first met them. We sat down and they steered me through the menu, explaining about each item. I settled on some spinach dish and herbal tea, which I found surprisingly soothing.

I found their conversation rather aimless, filled with talk of modern music and videos, co-ops, credit cards, foreign films, sushi, the New School, Tarot cards, astrology, life styles and numerous other subjects quite unimportant to me. To top it all off they chose to speak English, which I was surprised to learn they spoke as well as their children. After we finished eating I finally broached the subject of their affair and asked them directly whether they had considered their children before adopting this, to use one of their newly discovered phrases, life style.

"That's why me and Rog decided to go ahead," Dorcas said.

"Yeah," Rogelio said. "I did like you said, Mendoza. I called Dee up and we met and talked."

"Yes, but my intent was for you to stop doing what you were doing, not to become brazen," I said, rather stridently. "It was obvious that you were having an affair."

Rogelio laughed and looked conspiratorially at Dorcas.

"But we weren't," he said, turning back to me.

"No, far from it," she said. "But when he told me how he felt, it was like I had been hit right in my G . . ., oh, I'm sorry."

"Oh, no," I said, pleased that I had done some research. "I know all about Mr. G. Please go on."

"Anyway, I told him I felt the same way," Dorcas said. "We were on some back road somewhere in Jersey. We tried praying, but one thing led to another and that was it. We started seeing each other every week."

"It was the *novelas*, wasn't it?" I said to Dorcas.

She laughed and looked at Rogelio, who smiled so passionately at her that I had to look away.

"Yes, in a way," she said.

"What do you mean?" I said.

She thought for a moment and then said that hardly a day had gone by in the past twenty-five years that she hadn't watched a soap opera, most of the time in Spanish, but in the past five years the ones in English also. And that she finally saw that most of her pleasure came from thinking about what was going to happen to the characters and that she hardly ever thought about her own life, but instead found herself wanting to be like the women in the soap operas.

I asked her if that is why that evening of the Christmas party at the Valenzuela home she had told me that she had asthma, and that I hadn't believed her and had asked her son and he'd said that I had probably misunderstood her and she was talking about the current *novela* she was watching, *Más allá del olvido* in which the heroine suffered from asthma.

"That's just it," she said. "I developed asthma from it."

"That's very hard to believe," I said.

"It's true," she said, excitedly.

She added that she'd gone to the doctor and he began treating her, but then one of Awilda's friends came over with her to wait for Bobby when he got home from work and Awilda wasn't feeling well and went upstairs to rest and that she and Awilda's girlfriend began talking and the subject of asthma came up.

"Sharon Ramirez," I said.

"Yes, Sharon," Dorcas said. "You know her, then."

Dorcas Conde then said that asthma was the direct result of repressed psychosexual feelings and that the best cure for it was a healthy sexual life and that oftentimes the repressed feelings were brought about by an idealization of romance between the sexes.

"I was shocked," Dorcas continued, "but it began to make sense. She said I should read some books and she told me the titles and where to get them."

"And you began reading," I said.

"Yes, and the asthma went away. It was like my mind had been locked up," she said. "And then after I started reading, it was like a wild horse had been let loose. I wanted to read everything and then I saw myself looking fat and ugly, not at all like those women in the *novelas* and I felt stupid and hopeless and the asthma came back."

She said she tried talking to her husband but he couldn't understand what she was talking about. And then she went to her minister and he said that she was sinning against God for wanting to enjoy life and that she must endure her sufferings in order to gain everlasting peace in the next life.

"Sounds like a good plot for a *novela*," I said.

Both Rogelio and Dorcas laughed and clapped their hands.

"That's pretty good, Mendoza," he said. "That's exactly what Dee said when she told me."

"Yes, that's what it sounded like to me, but I felt really guilty about what I was reading and the way I was feeling. You can't imagine the torture I felt."

"Was that before Rogelio . . ., I mean, Rog called you?" I said.

"Yes, but not too long before," she replied. "I guess it was meant to happen."

"Yeah, like it was our karma or something," Rogelio said.

"You said something about doing it for the children," I said. "I don't understand. They're pretty worried about the two of you. The family and everything. What's going to happen to your husband and wife?"

Dorcas said that she and Rogelio had talked it over and, because Sharon Ramirez had said that Bobby and Awilda were practically living with each other already and that they had an apartment down on the Lower East Side where they spent most of their time and were probably more husband and wife than either one of us was to our mates, they had decided not to put so much pressure on them.

"They're really good kids," she said.

"Great kids," Rogelio said.

"Anyway, I kind of sense that they don't really want to get married and are doing it just to please us," Dorcas said. "At first we started being far out just to show them that they were all right and could live their lives any way they wanted and then we started enjoying the life style and could understand much better why the kids lived and thought the way they did."

I was touched by their concern and told them that Awilda had voiced exactly the same sentiments concerning the wedding. I added that they both approved, but that I was concerned about their mates.

"We've fixed that," Dorcas said.

"How?" I said, startled by the look of mirth which came into their eyes. "Don't tell me that you've told them."

"Better than that," Rogelio said. "We convinced them that they could benefit from it."

"I don't understand."

"They're seeing each other," Dorcas said. "Pablo really likes Margarita, but she's having a tough time dealing with the whole thing and told me that maybe some women didn't have a G-spot, but at least she's open to finding out. We're supposed to meet them later and go to SOB's to listen to this great Brazilian band."

"Yeah, you wanna come?" said Rogelio.

"No, I don't think so, Rog," I said. "But thanks."

Outside in the street I said goodbye, wished them the best of luck and watched as they went off, arms around each other, blending into the crowd. Quite suddenly I felt angry and began thinking again about going down to the island, purchasing that revolver and confronting that bastard Bauza who had probably filled my poor Esperanza with promises of ecstatic G-spot induced pleasures.

My head down and my heart feeling an unusual rage as I dealt with this new dilemma, I bumped into someone and immediately excused myself. To my surprise the person into whom I had bumped was a somewhat plump but rather attractive woman some fifty years of age, very well dressed and vaguely familiar.

"You're Ernesto Mendoza, aren't you?" she said.

"Yes, I am, madam. Have we met?"

"Yes, of course we've met. Brooks Landing. You don't remember me and I don't blame you. The ladies were in a veritable tizzy that afternoon. I'm Hope Barnes."

"Oh, yes, now I remember," I said, recalling that she had been very solicitous of me on that occasion, one of the few women who understood the intent of my talk that day. "Are you on your way somewhere?"

"Home," she said.

"To New Jersey?"

"God, no," she said, laughing easily so that her eyes twinkled. "My husband left me for a younger woman two years ago and, to be perfectly honest, I was relieved. That marriage was one of the dullest experiences of my life. My children are all grown and I've taken an apartment here in the Village. I've opened an antique store."

"Antiques, really?" I said, feeling totally unhinged by her rather charming aggressiveness.

"Yes, antiques," she said, touching my arm. "Would you like to come up and have a drink? I read recently that you have a new book coming out. Perhaps you can give me a preview of what to expect. Do say you'll come up. It's just up the street."

"Well, why not," I said.

"You don't have to go anywhere, do you?" she said, as she hooked her arm into mine.

"Not really," I said.

"And I'm not taking you away from your writing, am I?"

"Not at all," I said.

"Good," she said, squeezing my arm.

"I hope you're not offended by what I'm about to ask you," I said, as she opened her purse and extracted a set of keys in front of a high rise building.

"I'm sure I won't be," she said.

"Do you ever watch soap operas?" I said, hesitantly.

"Oh, Godı Neverı" she said. "I don't even watch television."

"Great," I said, and then feeling bolder, as we emerged from the elevator on her floor, I asked her if she had ever heard of something called the G-spot.She let us into her apartment, turned on the light and closed the door. We were in a beautiful room, very tastefully decorated, but warm and cozy.

"Yes, of course," she said, and my breath went away. "It's a jazz club."

"Well . . ." I demurred.

"Oh, noı That was the Five Spot," she said. "How stupid of me. No, I haven't. You'll have to tell me all about it. Sit down, please."

Sinking into an armchair and feeling better than I had in years, I recalled my grandfather's axiom comparing romance and missed buses. "*Los amores son como las guaguas. Si se te va una, espera un ratito, que por ahí viene otra.*"

The Monument

I had just finished the outline for my historical saga of the Flying Batatinis, the world renowned aerialists who toured the island for six generations putting on their act, when I heard a commotion out in the street. Through a one hundred and seventy-five year haze of double somersaults, near misses, public adulation and danger I heard my name being called from below. I went to the window of my Lower East Side apartment with Leandro Batatini's words echoing in my ears: "I have never felt greater freedom than hearing someone, in the crowd below, whispering that he hoped I broke my neck." As I leaned out to see who was calling me I suddenly understood Batatini's cryptic statement, written from Barcelona to his wife, Lola, back on the island, awaiting the birth of their daughter, Beatrız, destined to become the greatest female flyer of her time.

Down below, looking like twin Volkswagens, were the Fonseca brothers and their cousin Pucho.

"We have to talk to you, Mendoza," Enrique Fonseca said, holding both hands cupped to his mouth. "He's at it again and it's only one o'clock."

"Well, com'on up," I said, stupidly cupping my own hands.

I put on a pair of pants and a shirt even though it was August and much too hot. Ever the conscientious host, I checked the refrigerator for beer. Two six packs. Not nearly enough for the Fonsecas. Pucho didn't drink, so that was one consolation. Something had always troubled me about Enrique and Gumersindo Fonseca. First of all, they were incredibly fat, and fat people have always frightened me. It is an unnatural fear, but one which has persisted my entire life. It is as if at some point, while in my presence, they will burst and splatter me with their innards.

This, by the way, was the fate of Nicanor Batatini, the youngest of Leandro's offspring, who, although terribly overweight, insisted on a career on the high wire. During a practice session in 1846 while preparing for a European tour, Nicanor fell, ripped through the net and splattered his brothers Wenceslao, Rodolfo and Cayetano and his sisters, Beatrız and Consuelo. None of the Batatinis truly mourned Nicanor's passing, since the father, Leandro, had instilled in them how closely they walked with death in their business. Nicanor was also an embarrassment to the svelte, muscular family. Most relieved of all was Lola Batatini, the matriarch of the clan, who had given birth to Nicanor exactly 280 days after a brief and clandestine romance with a corpulent circus empresario in Montevideo.

Besides their obesity, something else bothered me about the Fonseca brothers. They were twins. See, when someone thinks of twins it's generally as small children, cute and somewhat dazed by their dual presence, looking as if they had spent the previous four hours staring at a mirror, their clothes always matched to confuse other people, always together because they have to be taken care of and go to school. After twins grow up, however, they usually split up and you don't see them together as much.

Not these two. They were over forty and still together. They still bought the exact same clothes and did everything together, even getting into bed every two weeks with Tina Bilakov, the skinny Ukrainian on 7th Street. For twenty years they had worked in the stockroom of Greenberg's wholesale lamp store over on Canal Street and had acquired a sort of Hassidic austerity when dealing with people outside the neighborhood. One time when a merchant near Greenberg's burned down his store for insurance purposes and the police came to investigate, the Fonsecas dummied up, leaving the detectives to mutter and say things like: "To hell with the fat hebes. Let's go."

Dummying up was not difficult for Gumersindo because generally Enrique did all the talking. I've always suspected, however, that the former was the brains, if that's possible; my implication not being that they lacked brains, but that perhaps that they shared *one* and split the different functions in order not to tax it overly. As an aside, it may interest people to know that in six generations, the Batatinis never had an instance of multiple births.

When the Fonsecas knocked on the door and I opened it, I was confronted, as usual, by two panting walruses dressed in black suits and white shirts buttoned to the top, their standard work uniform. As if I were seeing double, they were both mopping their sweaty brown faces with identical red bandannas which were big enough to cover a child.

"He's at it again, Mendoza," Enrique said, pulling at his moustache, which was thick and drooping, identical to his brother's.

"Back in the lot," said Pucho, peeking out from behind Gumersindo.

"Well, come in and tell me about it," I said.

They waddled forward and turned sideways to come inside. I closed the door and asked them to sit down. Pucho remained standing, but my two immense friends took seats at the dinette table, their fat butts and broad backs obscuring the chairs, so that the two of them looked as if they were sitting on air.

"It's a disgrace," Enrique said, shaking his head and making the fat on his neck jiggle like brown jello.

"What is?" I said.

"Uncle Mingo," Enrique replied.

"Oh, what now?" I shot back, innocently, knowing full well that part of Domingo Fonseca's present condition had to do with my research on the Flying Batatinis. "Is he threatening to shoot the President again?"

"No, he's back in the lot," Pucho said. "We told him not to go there anymore, but he don't listen, Mr. Mendoza."

I nodded several times while I tried to find a suitable reply for Pucho. He appeared totally distraught. Pucho is just a kid, maybe sixteen or seventeen, and I've never figured out why he follows the Fonsecas around. Even when they visit Tina Bilakov, he goes along and stands guard outside Tina's apartment until they are finished, which sometimes takes several hours. He also does all the cooking for the twins and their uncle. He's a good looking kid, tall and muscular but a little slow. Or as Harold Greenberg put it when Enrique tried to get Pucho a job at the lamp store: "I'd like to help you out, but I can't. The kid's got good real estate potential between the ears. More troubles I don't need." That time I had to spend nearly six hours and more than a case of beer explaining the whole thing to the Fonsecas before they left.

"Well, don't worry, Pucho," I finally said. "We'll think of something to calm Uncle Mingo down."

"It sure is a hot pistol," Enrique said, taking out his miniature blanket. Gumersindo followed suit.

This was my cue and I took it. Out came the two six packs from the refrigerator. I apologized to Pucho for not having a soda and placed the six packs on the table, one in front of each of the Fonsecas. Enrique thanked me, Gumersindo grunted and almost simultaneously they opened a can of beer, gulped it down and opened another before they decided to tend to the business at hand. Before he spoke, Enrique took a gigantic breath and I backed off a few paces instinctively, my fear of explosion surfacing momentarily.

"You okay, Mr. Mendoza?" Pucho said.

"Oh, sure. I'm fine, Pucho," I said, chastising myself for my weakness. I, Ernesto Mendoza, raconteur and literato, privy to the deepest emotions and documenter of the vicissitudes of the spirit, fearful of a human explosion. "Just fine," I reiterated, steeling myself, pulling up a chair and reluctantly sitting at the table with the Fonsecas.

"It's a first class disgrace, Mendoza," Enrique said. "You understand that, don't you? I mean, you're a smart man. Isn't it a disgrace?"

"Well," I said, fudging. "These things are relative."

"Being a relative doesn't cut it," Enrique countered. "He could be our father and it wouldn't matter. Wrong is wrong."

"No, what I mean is that it depends on how you look at it," I said.

"Exactly. That's all you have to do is look at it and you come to the same point of view," Enrique said. "It's a fuckin', excuse my language, disgrace."

"Okay, okay, don't worry about it," I said. "What did he do this time?"

"Same thing he always does," Enrique shot back, disgusted with having to pass on information which he considered obvious. "Same old thing."

"Just standing out there in the yard?" I said.

"That's it," Enrique said and opened another can of beer, the snap of the lift-off and the hiss followed by Gumersindo's.

"In the same place, Mr. Mendoza," Pucho said.

"Same pose?" I said.

"Yeah, the same pose," Enrique said. "Like a friggin statue. Left hand on his crotch and his right hand up in the air, holding up that damn middle finger. It's an A-1 disgrace."

"Same finger?" I said, once again stating the obvious.

"You bet," Enrique said. "Same damn finger, like he's telling God to you know what. Old Mrs. Mantilla says she's gonna call the cops if we don't get him outta there. And she will."

"What the hell does she care," I said forcefully, trying to work up some enthusiasm and at least express some sympathy with their dilemma.

"Hell, I don't know," Enrique said, belching loudly and making the hairs on the back of my neck stand up.

"He should listen," Pucho said.

"I think Uncle Mingo useta dip his stick in the old bag in Cacimar," Enrique said. "Now that they're both old she thinks he's reminding her. He was a hell raiser back on the island. Had women all over the place."

"How long's he been out there?" I said.

"Well, Pucho here came to get me and Gume at eleven, but we couldn't get away until half an hour ago and Greenberg says he's gonna fire us if we don't get back right away. He says we gotta be back by three or that's it. So that's why we came to see what you could do. Me and Gume could go and pick up the old goat and carry him upstairs, but then we'd have to stay there with him. We figured maybe he'll listen to you. He respects you. Greenberg's gonna fire us sure as hell if we don't get back."

"He's making a lot of trouble, Mr. Mendoza," Pucho said.

"Who, Greenberg?" I said.

"No, Uncle Mingo," Pucho said. "I try to help him, but he just gets mad. Yesterday he shot me with one of his books."

"Shot you?" I said.

"Yeah, Mr. Mendoza. A thick Spanish book. It just missed my head and knocked down the statue of the Virgin. The arm broke off."

"I understand, Pucho," I said, remembering that the verbs shoot and throw were used interchangeably in English by kids who had grown up with both languages.

"He's lost his mind, Mendoza," Enrique said, waving at Pucho to be quiet. "Flipped out. It's the smoke and the music from hanging out with those kids from 6th Street."

"What kids?" I said.

"The American kids in the rock band," Enrique said.

"The hippies?" I said.

"Yeah, the ones with the orange and green bus," Enrique said.

"He listens to *them*," Pucho said. "They're teaching him bad things."

"Just shut up a minute, Pucho," Enrique said, banging on the table at the same time that, miraculously, Gumersindo's fist came down. "Let me explain. Go up on the roof and see if Uncle Mingo is still at it. Watch him for a while and let me know if he moves. Go."

"Okay, Enrique," Pucho said, and went out of the apartment.

When Pucho was gone Enrique shook his head for a long time. Gumersindo kept nodding. Not shaking his head but nodding in agreement with Enrique's disapproval. After a while Enrique stopped.

"He's a good kid," he said, "but he gets on my nerves sometimes. I think my aunt musta dropped him on his head when he was a baby. She was a hell of a basketball player, you know. When she was in high school on the island they wouldn't let her play on the team 'cause she was a girl, so right before a big game she snuck into the school's equipment room and put *pique* in all the players' shorts; just soaked them with the hot sauce and the next day they were dry but the *pique* was still on them and when the players started sweating you shoulda seen them. We didn't see them but Uncle Mingo told us. He said that by the end of the first half their nuts were the size of grapefruits. They looked like they had hard-ons and all game long they were scratching their dongs. But she was a helluva a basketball player."

I didn't know what to make of the story. Perhaps I was supposed to infer, from the information about Pucho's mother's athletic ability, that she had attempted to dribble him or even shoot him up against some secret backboard in her home. I knew very little about their aunt, Dilcia, Pucho's mother, except that she was working on a Japanese whaling ship. In what capacity I was never able to ascertain, although the Japanese are very sports minded and it's not inconceivable that she could be athletic director of the ship on which she sails.

I could never make much sense out of the Fonsecas. The more I thought about it the more convinced I became that they shared one brain and that it wasn't too large at that. They were on their last beer and I still hadn't figured out what they expected me to do. I was half hoping they had forgotten about the trouble with their Uncle Mingo and would leave once they finished off the beer. Just then Pucho knocked on the door.

"The cops came, Mr. Mendoza," he panted, even though all he'd done was run down one flight from the roof. "There's a big crowd in the street."

"That's it," Enrique said. "Old dick-face Mantilla blew the whistle on the old man." He stood up. They stood up, I should say, because their action was simultaneous. I moved away cautiously, not revealing what I had now categorized as acute obesophobia. "That's it," Enrique repeated. "Off to the Tombs. Serves him right for being a degenerate. Let's go back to work, Gume."

Gumersindo grunted and out the door they went with Pucho trailing. I didn't make a move, but Enrique turned and stared at me.

"Ain't you coming?" he said.

"For what?" I said.

"You gotta talk to the cops," he said. "You gotta tell 'em he's an old man, that he's a little off, but that he's not gonna hurt nobody. They ain't gonna listen to nobody else. C'mon, Mendoza. We gotta go back to work or Greenberg's gonna have our ass in a sling."

"That's right, Mr. Mendoza," Pucho said. "They'll listen to *you*."

Jesus! They meant it. The three of them were worried as hell. I told them I'd see what I could do. I locked the apartment and followed them downstairs. As I said, I felt partly responsible since it was in my conversations with Domingo Fonseca that the idea for the book on the Flying Batatinis first took form. I remember my grandfather talking about them back in Cacimar, but I had stored it away as another in a long list of anecdotes with which my grandfather, an accomplished raconteur in his own right, regaled us as children. In fact, until I began to talk to Domingo Fonseca about the subject, I thought my grandfather, Bonifacio Mendoza, had been making up the entire story, since he had such a funny way of pronouncing the name and it seemed to us ludicrous that anyone in his right mind would have an entire family carry a name like Batatini.

To North American readers the name means nothing. They read it and make, at the very most, two assumptions: one, the name is Italian or two, the family made up the name because they were circus performers. Reasonable and above average in intelligence. However, Spanish-speaking readers, particularly those from the island, will, upon seeing the name Batatini, smile to themselves as if they were sharing a private joke with the author, chuckle at the mere insinuation of the sound of the word, or laugh uncontrollably at the deeper implications of its root (no pun intended).

For you see, the thing which would cause such mirth in us would be the simple and rather ludicrous fact that no matter how much we try to restrain ourselves, the name Batatini, whether intended or not, has to be a derivative of the word *batata* or sweet potato. Not yam, but sweet potato. In the latest Funk & Wagnalls *New Comprehensive International Dictionary of the English Language* we find the following: sweet potato 1. a perennial tropical vine (Ipomea batatas) of the morning glory family, with rose-violet or pink flowers and a fleshy tuberous root. 2. The root itself, eaten as a vegetable. 3. Colloq. An ocarina. The vegetable or tuber *batata* forms part of the staple of most country people and indeed a great many city people on the island. Along with *yautía, ñame, guineos verdes, plátanos* (*maduros y verdes*) and *bacalao, aguacate, cebollas* and *aceite y vinagre* it constitutes a most delectable dish called a *serenata* or serenade. One would assume that it has this name because after such a meal one has no alternative but to head for bed to sleep off this culinary lullaby.

Of all these foods: tannier, *ñame* (no English translation is available, but for those who desire authenticity or are amateur botanists, its Roman Latin name is *Dioscorea alata; aculeata; sativa*) green bananas, plantains (ripe and green), codfish, avocado, onion (raw) and oil and vinegar, none rings of the ridiculous more than *batata*. If you're a Spanish speaker and have used the word you may have by now taken the word for granted or mastered its inherently incongruent sound. If on the other hand you speak solely English, try pronouncing it as it sounds in Spanish. Now don't muff it and say things like baytayra or bat-tara, but say BAH-TAH-TAH with the accent on the second syllable. Say it a few times and see if primal feelings of attempting to communicate with your mother as she changed your diaper don't spring forth from your subconscious mind.

Believe it or not there are also sexual connotations attached to the word since *batata* is used in describing the calf of the leg. This flori-sexual connection occurs mostly in older people who go back to the days of long skirts when the mere sight of a woman's ankle, not to mention the calf, sent men into prolonged and ardent panting.

The above inferences and connotations pale in comparison to the more common use of the word as a pejorative noun when describing a person of inept skills or slow wits. It is not uncommon, for example, for a baseball player with little aptitude to be described as a *batata*. The same thing is true for a person with a passive personality, although if a person suffers momentarily from lack of initiative, he is then said to be *aplatanao* or in a state of plaintainhood.

It might interest students of comparative culture to learn that Cubans call a *batata* a *boniato*, but that is another story and, had Cuba suffered in the days of Leandro Batatini what his beloved homeland was suffering and would continue to suffer to this day, and had Leandro been a citizen of Cuba, he may well have christened his family something which would describe the patriotic torpor which he saw besetting his fellow citizens. Because above all, above being a trapeze artist of consummate skill and daring, Leandro Batatini was a patriot. Domingo Fonseca, however, did not share Batatini's patriotic fervor. That he turned out to be a hero is in part the people's doing in their quest to find a rallying point for their grievances against injustice. That fortune had chosen him seems fitting since he was truly a rebel.

When we got out into the street there was already a considerable number of people gathered near the empty lot. Three squad cars had arrived and the six officers were in different states of confusion. Two of them were intent on keeping the crowd moving, an impossible undertaking since most of them lived on the block and nothing short of napalm was going to interfere with their inalienable right to experience whatever there was to experience. Another of the policemen, a young man with the hungry, ambitious look of a junior executive, and who had obviously taken courses in public relations and Spanish in night school, was chatting amicably with neighborhood people. Yet another, fixated on the drug problem and bucking for a promotion into plain clothes, was suspiciously eyeing everyone who happened onto the scene. The two other policemen were utterly confused, although one of them kept looking up to the rooves of the tenements as if he expected to be attacked from above, while the other was hell bent on making sure some kid would not open a fire hydrant.

There was no question about it. A potentially dangerous situation was developing. All it would take was one person bumping against another, a man saying the wrong thing to a woman within hearing distance of her husband or boyfriend, or an imagined dirty look from one of the policemen. It was at this point that I made one the biggest mistakes of my life. Rather than remaining the dispassionate observer that I've prided myself on being during pressure situations, I panicked and stepped into a phone booth to make what, at the time, I thought to be an innocent telephone call to my friend, Potatoes Rivera, the dean of street poetry. You probably know him best for his poem, "Dig Those Dudes Sitting on the Stoop," in which he goes out on a limb and attacks not only the lack of employment opportunities facing the people, but also the passive attitude with which they confront their own diminution of power. I told him what was going on and he immediately said he would take care of it.

I returned to the empty lot and much to my dismay noted that the crowd had more than doubled in the five minutes which transpired during my conversation with Potatoes Rivera. More police had arrived and the mood began to turn ugly. Because I was well known, I was allowed to go up to Domingo Fonseca and speak to him. He, of course, wasn't speaking, and stood almost statue-like, his eyes staring ahead as if they saw nothing. When the police saw that I was having no success, they began moving toward Fonseca. Word ran through the crowd that the police was about to remove him forcibly and people surged suddenly forward and formed a ring three or four deep around Fonseca. They seated themselves around him and began singing the island's national anthem, the verses of which most of them did not know. The police backed off and watched sullenly as the crowd continued to grow.

By this time, I learned later, Potatoes Rivera had contacted a number of community leaders all over the city. Word ran like wild fire that something was taking place in The Lower East Side or Loisaida, as the the people call the area. Within the hour everyone who considered him or herself a leader had shown up.

A committee was immediately formed with Potatoes Rivera as its chairman. The committee's first move was to clear everyone out of the empty lot, speak to Fonseca and learn from him the exact nature of his one man demonstration. Under duress, since I have always refused to be part of any organization, I was inducted into the committee.

I felt partly responsible for Fonseca's condition. It was he who explained how Leandro Batatini combined visits by his family's trapeze act with subversive acts against the Spanish government. He planted bombs in military installations, attacked convoys, stole munitions and created havoc for the Spaniards on the island, passing on to his sons and daughters the need that he saw for the island to be independent. With each generation, however, the spirit to combat injustice waned and after the invasion by the United States in 1898 only Mateo Batatini, now 78 years old, a great-grandson of Leandro's, remained a stalwart proponent of independence. The family, no longer connected with circus life, had splintered and Mateo Batatini was considered an eccentric and possibly senile old man because he spoke of space travel and harnessing the power of the sun. He nevertheless vowed to carry on the fight to gain independence for the island. He chose as his battlefield the Protestant Church which he joined in order to infiltrate its ranks and sabotage its efforts to convert the people. Soon he was not allowed to attend its services. He then took to displaying his fully erect penis during the singing of the hymn, "Onward Christian Soldiers," which in translation is rendered "*Firmes y Adelantes*" or firm and forward. Whether Mateo Batatini saw a sexual connection in the lyrics of the hymn is not known, but it is quite possible that, given our culture's sexual passions, the hymn may have provided such initiative.

The committee questioned Fonseca on all matter of subjects and finally learned that, just as his nephews had suspected, he had tried to renew his acquaintance with Amparo Mantilla, who, not wishing to repeat the mistakes of her youth, had rejected his advances and had joined a women's liberation discussion group at the urging of a young VISTA volunteer by the name of Nancy Robidoux from Baton Rouge, Louisiana.

All hell broke loose then because there was no way the committee was going to give voice to Domingo Fonseca's grievance on the basis of his being spurned as a lover. By now every civic and political organization in twenty-five different neighborhoods had sent representatives and they were not about to pass up the opportunity to make a point. It was agreed that the steering committee of the newly formed Committee to Defend the Rights of Domingo Fonseca would meet in executive session and come up with a more cogent explanation of the issue.

Four hours later the committee emerged from Galería Coco Seco, where there was a current exhibition of ghetto paintings by my good friend Francisco Pinto. Potatoes Rivera, as the spokesman, explained to everyone that Fonseca was protesting the treatment of the people by the U.S. government and it was our responsibility to show solidarity with him by supporting his courageous stand against oppression. And right there and then on the stoop of Galería Coco Seco, with all the representatives from twenty-five communities where the people sweat and cry and scream and writhe in an effort to free themselves from bondage, he reeled off his now famous anti-Reagan poem: "Oye, Ronnie, Baby, What Really Went on Between You and Juanito Gwayne?" which I include in part simply to illustrate how, given this beginning, things were destined to get out of hand.

Oye, Ronnie, what's this I hear that . . .
way back then . . .
in the days of los vaqueros
you and Juanito Gwayne,
that mucho macho marine
from the Halls of Montezuma to the Shores of

Tripoli,
eran amantes,
that you were lovers and . . .
that You, you sly devil,
Yes, You
and Juanito Gwayne, that dubious symbol of
North Amerikan imperialist
manhood, were playing with each other's
peepees
between takes and
that you let
Juanito Gwayne inseminate you with his
STAR SPANGLED BANANA
in that nether region where the sun don't
shine,
so that you could become pregnant with power
and go on to so called greatness
and oppress the people,
Ronald Reagan,
you
Madreflaca!

And on it went, one vituperation after the other until the people had been whipped up into a froth, and after it got dark, the people lit bonfires in the empty lot and set up an all night vigil. Domingo Fonseca would not move from his position. A committee was formed to feed Fonseca as he stood in open defiance of oppression, his left hand on his crotch and his right hand aloft, middle finger pointing straight up at the fifth floor window of Amparo Mantilla's apartment, as a symbolic gesture against the oppressive practices of the U.S. government.

Songs were composed and sung, paintings were painted and shown, slogans were created and chanted, speeches were drafted and delivered and more poems were written and recited, all of them depicting the people as oppressed and struggling, fighting, climbing to great heights of valor in order to liberate themselves.

I could no longer work, my time taken up by meetings and press conferences. I had moved to The Lower East Side to be closer to the Village now that it appeared that Hope Barnes and I were more than a passing thing. I hadn't heard from Esperanza for nearly a year. I had written asking for an explanation of her silence, but I surmised that her new found fame as a soap opera star did not permit her to correspond with me. It didn't matter,

Hope was making me forget Esperanza. At first I felt guilty about the feelings she aroused in me, but she was a good companion and did not pressure me to perform sexually. Hope was very thankful that I had made her aware of her G-spot. But now I had no time to work. I wished I were back in El Barrio.

Day after day went by with Domingo Fonseca still standing. A frame was constructed to enable him to hold his body up and his arm aloft while he caught a few hours of sleep. Anticipating the rain and cold weather that was sure to come in future weeks, a clear plastic shelter was built around him and flood lights were rigged up so that people, day and night, could draw inspiration from Fonseca's heroic stand against oppression.

Weeks went by and then months and Domingo Fonseca became so inspired by the determination of the people that he forgot about Amparo Mantilla. No one could talk him out of standing out there. Domingo and Gumersindo tried, by yelling at him that he was disgracing the Fonseca name, but members of the committee had them arrested. The police complied because they saw that everyone in the community had rallied around the issue and crime had decreased and the people were for once manageable.

And then in November there was a terrible snow fall and Domingo Fonseca caught a cold. There was a threat that the demonstration would come to an end when Fonseca was examined by doctors who found him to be very ill. Complications could arise and there might be a need to hospitalize him and thus bring the demonstration to an end. It was then that Nancy Robidoux, the feminist VISTA volunteer who dabbled in the arts, came up with the idea of making a latex mask of Domingo Fonseca's face and that way the people could take turns wearing the mask and standing out there in shifts.

The plan was approved, the mask made and the people began taking turns, women as well as men, with their left hand on their crotch and their right hand held aloft with the middle finger extended in a sign of defiance. But standing there for more than an hour became boring to the people and fewer and fewer volunteers showed up each day.

That was when the committee met in executive session and decided to solicit funds from foundations and arts councils for the erecting of a permanent statue to commemorate the struggle of Domingo Fonseca. All hell broke loose and Potatoes Rivera began writing caustic letters and drafting petitions. Proposals were written and a fund raiser hired and soon the State Council for the Arts and the National Endowment for the Arts agreed to the proposed monument, but they wanted to know who was going to execute this monument, which called for a statue in dark marble some thirty feet high with a ten foot base and a plaque with the names of the people who struggled and sweated and screamed to be released from bondage, and a mini-park with a groundskeeper, a curator and guards to prevent vandalism. And then everything came to a standstill until they came to me for advice and I told them that the only person I knew capable of such a work was Nemecio Peralta, but that I didn't know if he still worked in stone on that large a scale and that I would find out.

I had a difficult time finding Peralta but finally tracked him down in Cape Cod where he had gone to live with Constance Bickford. He said, yes, he was working in stone once again but that the job sounded as if it would take a year or more to complete. I returned to the committee with the information and they said that it had to be done in less time or the movement would lose momentum. I went back to Peralta and he suggested bronze. Back I went to the committee and they said no, it had to be stone.

With funds from a foundation, Peralta was brought to New York and the committee finally accepted the project as a time-consuming one. Peralta made some sketches and, working in clay, sculpted a three foot model of Domingo Fonseca with his hand on his crotch and his hand held aloft with his middle finger extended in a sign of defiance and the committee cheered and the statue was put on display in a glass case in the lot under twenty-four hour guard. A sign was hung announcing the creation of a monument to commemorate the people's struggle.

In January a huge block of marble some forty-five feet high was delivered to the empty lot and two weeks later Nemecio Peralta began working. Scaffolds were erected and over them a covered shed. Working so feverishly that his hands were bloody, Peralta chiseled away eighteen hours a day until the stone began to take form.

Of course when word got out about the project, certain sectors of the community were outraged, pointing out that no matter how difficult things were for the people, no matter how oppressive the system, creating such a statue would definitely brand the people as defiant. The detractors of the project threatened to picket, demonstrate, call the media and, if all failed, to sue. They were told they were free to do whatever they wanted, but that it was the people's will to have the monument erected and, if they wanted to go against the will of the people, then that was their business. After some further rhetoric the opposition quieted down and things moved forward again.

And then the following spring the statue was completed and an unveiling took place. Peralta had poured every ounce of his creative genius into the statue. All the heroic power of the people and their struggle came through in the lines of Domingo Fonseca's face and in the folds of his clothing and the muscles of his limbs. At night from a distance, the statue resembled a giant defying order and calling for the people to join in and place their left hand on their crotch and hold their right hand aloft with the middle finger extended in a sign of defiance. Domingo Fonseca attended the ceremony and was seemingly happy about the statue, but in my opinion appeared withdrawn.

The day after the unveiling ceremony, I received a lengthy letter from Esperanza. In it she announced that she would be coming to New York to act in a play and that she would like to see me. I felt reluctant to reply but a new longing for Esperanza began stirring in me. Considering Hope Barnes' feelings, I discussed the matter with her. She was very understanding and told me that she was sure we could work something out and that she would be happy to meet Esperanza and why didn't the three of us get together when she arrived. Kink. Nothing but pure kink awaited me and I saw myself sandwiched between Hope Barnes and Esperanza De León.

I said I would think about it and returned to my apartment and my work on the Flying Batatinis. From my window I could see the head of the statue of Domingo Fonseca. I settled in and was about to start writing when I heard my name being called. I opened the window and looked out. Pucho Fonseca was pointing to the other end of the block.

"Come down, Mr. Mendoza," he was shouting. "He's at it again."

I put on a sweater and jacket and down I went, wondering what sort of madness Domingo Fonseca was up to now. Pucho was sweating and nearly on the verge of tears. He said that Gumersindo and Enrique had tried to stop their uncle but that he was doing something really awful and he had learned it from the hippies on Sixth Street.

"He listens to them, Mr. Mendoza," he said. "They give him drugs and then he acts crazy. You gotta do something."

We hurried down the block and there was Domingo Fonseca in the middle of another empty lot, his pants down and his buttocks exposed, mooning, as young people say. I shook my head and gave Pucho a quarter and wrote down Potatoes Rivera's number.

"Call him up," I said. "He'll know what to do."

I returned to the apartment, drank seven straight shots of rum and tried to figure out how many empty lots there were in New York City, Philadelphia, Newark, Boston, Hartford, Chicago, Gary and all the other places where the people struggled and sweated and cried and fought to extricate themselves from the bonds of oppression.

Belisheva the Beautiful: A Tale From a Refugee Camp

Dionisio Rosa was a dreamer who worked as a doorman at the Belvedere Arms which is an exclusive apartment house no more than thirty blocks from El Barrio, but really light years away. It is so exclusive, in fact, that at times no one occupies the 200 or so apartments because its tenants are in their other homes in places like Nice, London, Paris, Shaker Heights, Palma de Mallorca, Boulder, Buenos Aires, San Francisco, Tokyo, Geneva or Athens. My own publisher, Mr. Layton, who seduced me with promises of literary fame and social prestige simply to get me to reveal the fiction of life in the ghetto, has a penthouse apartment in the Belvedere Arms, which he uses not for himself, but as a meeting place for love starved authors, whom he provides with love starved English majors, men or women, depending on the author's sex or preference.

In the beginning, when I was young and virile, I used the penthouse several times, but always brought my own. In each case it was my one and only Esperanza De León and on summer nights we would make love until early in the morning and then, exhausted but unable to sleep, we would stand naked in the garden, forty stories above Fifth Avenue, and await the rising sun, pretending that we were Adam and Eve in the Garden of Eden while we fed each other apple sauce and decried our vanishing innocence and the threat of decadence which we were inviting by spending time in such opulence.

After a time, we stopped using Layton's penthouse and returned to the ghetto, living in squalor so that I could write my novels and betray the trust of the people. But this year I had the opportunity of returning to the Belvedere Arms for a reception given by a benefactor of the arts after the opening ceremony of the PEN International Congress, for which I was asked to participate in a panel but declined, being at odds with my colleague, Norman Mailer, the United States PEN president. I had heard that Norman was inviting a government official to speak. The congress, I was told, hoped to determine whether the government had an imagination or some such drivel. I immediately called up Norman and told him what I thought of his harebrained idea.

"Ernesto," he said, "take it easy. It's all politics."

"Norman," I said, "be that as it may, you're making a mistake and in the process you're digging yourself an early grave in the soil of American letters."

He coughed discreetly as if he were mentally editing what I had said and then told me that he had a meeting with his board and that I should have a nice day. I retorted by saying that given my financial, psychological, emotional and sexual situation, not to mention my literary and political disenfranchisement, I had other plans. Nevertheless, when the time came, I put on my old suit and went to the opening, rubbed elbows with the giants of international literature, felt inadequate and thought that if there were giants of literature there were also dwarfs and that I, alas, could not be counted among either, but fell into that broad category of wordsmiths who labor very nearly anonymously their entire lives without any recognition except some adverse publicity, or else, like me, have their work, through their own cowardice, relegated to the field of sociology.

So I went to the opening at the New York Public Library and listened to the speeches and watched as Grace Paley and Alan Ginsberg stood up and yelled at Norman. Obviously bothered, Norman delivered his address as if he were in the boxing ring sparring with another aging fighter, his voice like gravel and the punctuation of his sentences mimicking a supposed arsenal of punches; feinting where paragraphs were intended, jabbing repeatedly when serial commas were necessary, throwing hooks to symbolize periods and generally dancing and not really engaging in true combat, but nonetheless going some ten rounds with the English language and consequently leaving both, the language and himself, bloodied, injured and swollen.

After a cocktail reception at which the primary activity was the maneuvering by minor writers to positions next to major writers in order to be photographed by the media, we left the museum(Mario Vargas Llosa and Carlos Fuentes excused themselves, claiming prior commitments) and cabbed to Fifth Avenue and the Belvedere Arms; went up to a sumptuous duplex apartment with its own elevator from one to the other floor; some fifteen rooms, one more garish than the next in its insistence that cultured folks lived therein; an apartment which an aging real estate and architectural writer told me was worth from 75 to 100 million dollars. He pointed out Rubenses, Da Vincis, Brueghels and Caravaggios so that the shrimp scampi, which has always been one of my weaknesses, tasted like lead and made me wish to leave, which I did shortly thereafter when some young, newly lionized "twit," I think the English would call him, thinking I was one of the waiters, asked me to refill his wine glass while I was talking to

Bannister Ogleby-Smith about his new detective novel set in a Glasgow seminary.

Feeling like an outcast, I went downstairs and, once out of the elevator, still feeling the shame of being so humiliated, I began going out the door when a voice ladened with years of speaking Spanish asked me if I wished a cab, sir.

I turned and saw myself as a younger man, perhaps thirty, slight physique, tan skin, moustache, a full head of black hair and dark suffering eyes. I greeted him in Spanish and he smiled sadly and told me he was Dionisio Rosa, "my servant": a very polite and regal greeting which has nothing to do with servitude in Spanish, but with fealty among nobility. There was an immediate understanding between us, much as if we had traveled the same cosmic road of uncertainties and empty dreams. I remained there, suffering anonymously, and speaking intermittently with him as the guests left and he obtained cabs for them, saying "goodnight, sir" in a most polite way so that he was at all times in command and only a couple of extremely sensitive people picked up on the definite integrity of Dionisio Rosa's nobility while the others behaved condescendingly and appeared embarrassed by their station in life, as if recognition in a very narrow sphere of human endeavor, that of shaping words, had assured them immortality.

I remained until everyone had left and then Dionisio and I traveled uptown to Florindo's Bar in El Barrio where he began telling me of his woes. Nobody being home at the Belvedere Arms is how Dionisio happened to meet Elisheva Horowitz, who came there one evening and told him about her sisters Malka, Fegi, Nurit and Osnat and how all of them were more beautiful than she. This made Dionisio wonder how that could be, since she was the most beautiful woman he had ever seen and looking at her he saw himself riding a stallion and wearing armor in the days of the Moors in Spain; this without any knowledge of the history of the Moors, since I asked him if he knew about El Cid and he said he did not, but was able to tell me about his dreams which obviously centered around that historical period when the Moors and the Jews were being driven out of Spain. He called her Belisheva and I did not want to correct him and make him feel uncomfortable.

He said he thought he was happily married, despite his wife being very fat and screaming a lot, qualities which to him were as signs of health and caring. But then he had met Belisheva, and he became unhappy. She had come to the Belvedere Arms looking for Chaim Pinsky, the film producer who had an apartment there, because he had promised her a part in his next film and she had flown from Tel Aviv, spending the last of her savings only to find that no one was answering the phone, neither at his office nor at the apartment.

Dionisio explained that Mr. Pinsky was at that time in Zurich and was not expected until the following month. When she heard this she began crying and Dionisio helped her to sit down in the lobby and he held her hand, which was smooth and the color of very light coffee, and when she could not stop crying, he took out his clean handkerchief and dried her tears and that's when he saw her eyes and looked into them and saw himself back in time.

"Please don't cry," he said. "Everything will be all right."

"But I have no place to stay and I can't go back home," she said.

And that's when he decided to open up Chaim Pinsky's apartment and let her stay there. He made keys for her and she settled in and every evening after he was finished working, Dionisio would go up to the Pinsky apartment and she would be on the phone.

"I couldn't understand what she was saying," he said.

"Yiddish," I said.

"No, it wasn't that," he said. "I'd heard people in the building talking Yiddish. It wasn't like that."

"Hebrew," I said, motioning Florindo to bring us another beer. "They also speak Hebrew in Israel."

"That's what I thought too," said Dionisio, draining the last of his beer before starting on his new one. "Everything was in the throat, but nice to listen to once you got used to it. One time I was there and the phone rang and she picked it up and said hello and then said 'Saalam.' "

"You mean, shalom," I said.

He shook his head and said that he had heard the word 'shalom' around the Jewish holy days when he first went to work at the Belvedere Arms and used it now around Passover and Yom Kippur for the Jewish tenants and that they always smiled and gave him bigger tips, but that it wasn't shalom.

"It was 'saalam,' Mr. Mendoza," he said.

"Arabic?" I said.

Dionisio Rosa looked around as if he were afraid someone were listening.

"That's right," he said. "I didn't know what to do."

I tried to reassure him that there was nothing unusual in the young woman speaking Arabic, because in her region of the world the two languages existed side by side. He shook his head and said he knew that, but that the reason she spoke Arabic was because she was Palestinian.

"A Palestinian Jew," I said.

"No, she wasn't Jewish," he said. "She showed me her passport and it was Jewish, but she's not."

"So she's not Jewish," I said.

"No, she's not," he said.

"And she's not there to wait for Pinsky," I said.

Dionisio said that she was there to wait for him and that she was an actress and had been promised a part in his movie, but that it was all a cover for something else.

I asked him what that something else was. He told me that at first he didn't know, but that as the days went by, she became more and more nervous and he thought she was losing her mind. She kept asking him when Mr. Pinsky was getting back, even though he had told her when just the previous day. He again told her not to worry, that Pinsky wouldn't be getting back for a while. Each day she had him get all the newspapers. One day he came into the apartment and she was on the phone talking Arabic and he thought he heard her mention Koch.

"Mayor Koch?" I asked, suddenly feeling apprehensive.

"I couldn't believe it either," he said. "But that's who she was talking about. I thought it was just another Arabic word, but when she got off the phone she was pale and her hands were shaking and she said they were going to kill her and what was she going to do."

"Who was going to kill her?" I said.

Dionisio said she wouldn't tell him at first, but then he told Elisheva how he felt and that no matter what the problem was, he was ready to die for her, he loved her so much. She said he reminded her of her cousin Mohamed, who had driven a car bomb, and she cried and he held her until she was calm and then she told him that her name was not really Elisheva Horowitz, but Rowaida Said and she had come to New York as a Jew to assassinate Ed Koch.

I was shocked. I have always abhorred violence and although Edward Koch is not one of my favorite people, I didn't wish him any harm.

"But why?" I said.

"I don't know and she doesn't either," Dionisio said. "But that's not the problem. They want her to shoot him out in the open and then she's supposed to commit suicide right there."

"Wait a minute," I said. "These people want her to assassinate the Mayor and then, after she does this, she has to take a gun to her head? Just like that?"

"That's what she said," Dionisio replied. "She told them that she could do the job, but that it would be better if it was done quietly and they said that would be no good. Out in the open."

"What do you mean 'out in the open?' " I said.

"You know, down at City Hall or something," he said. "It's crazy. She told them she wouldn't do it and they said she's as good as dead."

"You better be careful," I said. "I don't want to tell you what to do, but she sounds like what the papers call a terrorist."

"She says she's a freedom fighter," Dionisio said. "She asked me a lot of questions about where I lived and about the island and politics, but I don't know anything about that."

I don't often suggest calling the authorities on minor matters, but this seemed more serious than usual. As soon as I mentioned the police, however, Dionisio told me it was out of the question.

"What's she gonna tell them?" he said. "That she's here to kill the Mayor, but that she's changed her mind?"

I had to agree that perhaps it wasn't such a good idea, but that I didn't have much more of an answer. Dionisio said he had to come up with a solution quickly, otherwise that would be the end for Belisheva or Rowaida, or whatever her name happened to be. He said goodbye to me and went off into the night. I had wanted to give him my address and telephone number in case I could help him in any way, but I didn't get a chance to do so.

For the next two or three months I read the papers and listened to the radio obsessively. Ed Koch was still alive, so after a while I forgot about Dionisio Rosa and his beautiful freedom fighter or terrorist or whatever you want to call her. I can't tell anymore who's who. And then Reagan sent planes to bomb Libya and the incident got me thinking about Dionisio again. I began looking for him, but everyone I asked either didn't know Dionisio or hadn't seen him in a while. I even went to the Belvedere Arms. They said he had stopped working there sometime in late January.

In true form I started to worry and imagined the worst. They had tracked down the girl and caught her with Dionisio and they had executed both of them. I felt helpless. I was a useless, idealistic, old man whose time had passed without much consequence. The people were still struggling but not accomplishing much of anything and all I could do was string words together in the hope of leaving some sort of record of what I had experienced and seen. I became morose and withdrawn. Hope Barnes called several times and asked me to come to dinner, but I refused. Esperanza came to New York and we met, but she was vague and elusive. She had had a face lift, was in rehearsals for a play and then she was off to Mexico to act in a film. I hardly recognized her, but my heart still longed for her. I was torn between my love for her and the true friendship and companionship which I had found with Hope Barnes.

One late spring day when I was walking around the neighborhood, pondering my existence and wondering how many more years I had left to live, I heard someone call my name. I was on a block of burnt down buildings and empty lots so common in El Barrio. I turned around and it was Dionisio Rosa, looking happier than any man I had ever seen. His eyes shone with a brilliance which startled me at first, until I realized that a strange transformation had taken place in him. He was dressed in old, but clean clothes. His hair, however, was long and he now had a beard.

"Dionisio?" I said. "Dionisio Rosa?"

"Yes, of course," he said. "How are you, Mr. Mendoza?"

"I'm fine," I said. "I went back to look for you at the Belvedere four months ago but you were gone."

"I quit," he said.

"The girl?"

"Yes," he said, smiling.

"How is she?" I said. "Did she go home?"

He shook his head, smiled openly again and asked me to come with him. Suddenly I found myself crossing an empty lot and heading toward one of the squatters' houses which the people have built on abandoned real estate in El Barrio. The houses, exact replicas of the typical wooden houses one sees on the island, appear to spring up overnight in the neighborhood. They're small, perhaps the size of a large living room, but most of them have a slanted roof, a porch and shutters on the windows. They are painted light blue, pink or yellow and they have little gardens with plastic animals out in front. The people who live in them are generally the more enterprising street people, the ones who have no family or worldly possessions and band together to support each other in surviving.

In one corner of the lot there was one of these small houses, painted yellow and blue. As we approached, a young woman came out on the porch and waved to us. When we reached the house she smiled shyly. She was small and dark, with jet black hair and beautiful dark eyes.

"Mr. Mendoza, this is Aida Sanchez," Dionisio said, in Spanish. "Aida, this is my friend, Mr. Mendoza. The writer. Remember me telling you about him?"

The girl said in Spanish that she remembered and was glad to meet me. I was instantly confused. This could not be the same girl Dionisio had told me about. This was not Belisheva, the beautiful, as he had called her back then. Had he misunderstood me? This was a typical girl one sees in our neighborhoods or on the island, a mixture of Spanish and Indian with perhaps some African thrown in. Pleasant to look at, but beautiful? No, not by any stretch of the imagination. Dionisio had probably gotten tired of his fat, screaming wife and found a young, probably homeless girl to throw in with him. They had built the house and probably did odd jobs around the neighborhood to survive.

"Come inside," Dionisio said.

I went inside the one room of the house and was immediately struck by the cleanliness within. There was a rug on the floor and cushions to sit on. As the late afternoon sunlight streamed into the house the girl brought coffee. We sat on the floor. The coffee was dark and sweet. After a while I asked Dionisio what had happened, but he deftly changed the subject. I became impatient. If this was Belisheva Horowitz, whom he had sheltered in the producer's apartment at the Belvedere, I had to find out. No matter what, I had to find out.

"Reagan really showed Libya what this country's all about," I said, looking at the girl. "I guess the Colonel's gonna think twice before pulling any more of his terrorist tricks."

What I saw next will always stay with me. The girl remained impassive, but her eyes narrowed and for a fraction of a second she looked at me with deep, remarkably intense hatred. I felt as if at any moment I would empty my bladder, such was my fear. I knew then that this small, young woman was capable of assassinating the Mayor of New York City and much more.

"You don't mean that, do you, Mr. Mendoza?" Dionisio said, a trace of pain in his voice.

"No, I don't," I said. "I'm sorry, but I had to find out."

"Did you?" he said.

"Yes."

"We're the same people," he said. "She's one of us now."

"Yes, she is," I said. "Is that business with the Mayor over?"

Dionisio nodded.

"Is she safe here?" I said.

"No problem," he replied. "Even the Palestinians who have stores around here think she's one of us."

"What's going to happen?"

"I don't know," he said. "But she's teaching us a lot."

"I should leave," I said. "It's getting late."

I got up and went outside. Dionisio and the girl followed me out on the porch. I stepped down into the small flower garden which they had planted, and after I had taken a couple of steps, I stopped and turned around.

"Saalam Alecom," I said to the girl.

She looked at Dionisio and Dionisio nodded.

"Alecom Saalam," she said, her voice like a sweet, melancholy flute, the 'c' catching in her throat as if it had a hard 'h' following it, so that I was reminded of a gentle wind playing on the branches of a tree. With her dark eyes she smiled a daughter's smile at me and I felt tears welling up in my eyes.

The Pursuit of Happiness

There is little doubt that the United States of America is the land of opportunity. Men of humble background ascend to the highest and most influential positions in government, virtual unknowns become celebrities overnight, and ordinary men transform dreams into millions of dollars, quite often through the invention of useless gadgets. And yet the question remains unanswered as to how these miracles come to pass. It serves no purpose, however, to speculate on how success comes to men. Suffice it to say that in the United States of America good fortune can visit anyone when least expected and at times through the most unusual combination of events.

Take for example the case of my friend, Don Sinforoso Figueroa. In order to help his nephew finance his education, Don Sinfo, as he was affectionately known to his neighbors, purchased a goat and now lives in an elegant townhouse in one of the more exclusive sections of New York City, where, if I will not be judged vulgar for mentioning it, I am on occasion invited.

There, surrounded by fine paintings, beautiful furniture, and waited on by servants day and night, he muses and thanks Heaven for his good fortune. When not in the city, he travels to Long Island aboard his yacht and periodically journeys to Bermuda as the guest of some of the wealthiest and most prominent families of that island. To say that he is a member of the jet set would be an understatement. In every European capital his name is dropped frequently by people in high office, the fashion industry and the arts.

Don Sinfo's odyssey from virtual bankruptcy to unlimited wealth began some years ago. At that time, Don Sinfo owned *Bodega Cacimar*, a grocery store in East Harlem, or El Barrio, as the people call this section of New York City. Concerned with the rising cost of meat and in competition with a newly opened supermarket a block away, he accepted the challenge and decided to offer his customers *cabrito,* one of the true delights of the people's cuisine. The word, of course, means little goat, but in a culinary context stands for a richly seasoned fricassee. The meat can also be roasted and carry the name *cabrito*, but it is the fricassee which people generally conjure up in their minds when they hear this magical word.

And yet when Don Sinfo introduced the idea to his nephew, Felipe, who helped him in the store and would be the eventual beneficiary of this brainstorm, he found the young man opposed to his plan.

"Uncle Sinfo," Felipe said, respectfully, as he finished restocking the shelves with canned beans. "I know this is your store and you brought me up and everything, but I gotta tell you something. Getting a goat isn't such a good idea."

Don Sinfo was somewhat taken aback by his nephew's shortsightedness in business affairs. He came out from behind the counter and spoke encouragingly to him.

"Blessed be the Virgin, Felipe," he said, patting his nephew's back. "This is an investment. Please, don't worry."

"Uncle," Felipe replied. "You're not on the island anymore."

"That's true, Felipe," Don Sinfo said, understandingly. "But that shouldn't prevent us from raising a goat. Animals are raised in the city all the time."

"You don't understand, Uncle," Felipe said, growing impatient. "There's nothing to people raising a chicken or two on a fire escape. Calixto Correa, the baker, even raised three ducks in his bathroom a couple of years ago and then sold them to a Chinese restaurant on the West Side for Peking Duck. And if you remember, I told you that back in October I heard a turkey in Margarita's building. They were fattening it up for Thanksgiving. Me and Margarita was going up to the roof to look at the stars and heard it gobbling just as the lady was coming out of her apartment. I joked about it and the lady said it was the plumbing acting up again. She knew it was against the law."

"Many things are against the law, Felipe. Trying to improve one's situation is not one of them. We are not living in Russia. Castro doesn't run this country. The law doesn't punish honest men, and, in any case, there are ways of working around the law without breaking it."

"Oh, sure, when it's a small animal. But we're talking about raising a goat. Sixty or seventy pounds full grown."

"Felipe, Felipe," Don Sinfo said. "Listen to me. Fundador Contreras, the super of the building where they have the Hallelujah church of which he is a member, there on Lexington Avenue, raised his own pig. He bought it real small from Marichal y Agosto on Park Avenue and each night collected leftovers from Pinto's restaurant to feed that animal. He kept it in the basement until it was almost too big to fit through the door. A whole year they had that pig down there. When the time came, Fundador and his sons dragged it over to the butcher shop one night. I don't mean to be disrespectful and I am only relating what other people have said, but at first it was thought they were dragging Azucena, Fundador's fat wife, down the street."

Don Sinfo chuckled, but Felipe was not amused.

"In any case," Don Sinfo continued, "they pulled and tugged and muffled the sound of the pig's squealing by putting a sack over its head and they finally got it over to the butcher shop and had it slaughtered. Jacinto Torres then shaved it, scalded it, dressed it with salt, pepper and oregano and then cleaned out the intestines for *morcillas*."

"I know, I know," said Felipe. "His wife came here and traded some of that blood sausage for ten cans of Coco Lopez to make *coquito,* even though they profess to be of the religion and are nothing but drunks."

"Yes, yes, the world is full of hypocrites," said Don Sinfo, annoyed that his nephew was not paying attention to the importance of his point. "As I was saying, that was an enormity of a pig, but after it was ready, Fundador and his sons put a pole through its rear end and out of its mouth and carried it over to the same Calixto Pérez whom you mentioned, and he roasted it for *Nochebuena.*"

"Yes, I know," Felipe said, as he stuck his hands into his pockets, dejectedly. "They had it on a pole and it was snowing."

"That's right," Don Sinfo said. "It was snowing."

"The whole neighborhood smelled of *lechón asao*. For about a month all the birthday and wedding cakes tasted like roast pork."

Don Sinfo laughed and clapped Felipe on the back.

"Yes, that's true," he said. "But you see my point, don't you? It can be done. Believe me. We can do it. What is necessary is that we start and we'll find a way. Can't you see what this means?"

Felipe shook his head in despair.

"Uncle Sinfo, I know exactly what it means. Can't *you* see what you'd be getting into? This isn't Puerto Rico and, anyway, a pig is a pretty tame animal. He doesn't get crazy ideas like goats do. It'd be different if we was in P.R. 'cause over there if you got a house, you got a yard and you can let the goat run around or tie it up on the side of the road to eat grass. People don't have to worry about somebody coming along and stealing it."

Don Sinfo thought for a moment.

"You're right," he said. "New York is full of thieves. There's no telling when someone's going to come along and get sticky fingers. It's a shame but even our own people have bad habits."

"Then you agree with me," Felipe said.

"No, this only means that we have to be more careful in protecting our investment."

Felipe, who had been flattening cartons and was ready to carry out a pile and place it in front of the store for the garbage truck to pick up, dropped the cartons in disgust.

"Uncle Sinfo, it's no good," he said. "It's a bad idea. A goat's not an easy animal to live with. They don't listen and they suffer from nerves. You know that. It's a crazy plan."

Don Sinfo lowered his head.

"Felipe," he said, after a few moments. "I'm an old man. I've been on this Earth sixty-five years and almost every year has been filled with suffering. More than half of those years I have been in this country. Maybe it's too late, but I've learned one thing. In the U.S. anything is possible. Suffering, that's all I've known. My wife is dead going on five years, my children don't even come around on Christmas anymore, and most of my friends have gone back to the island. All I have is this store and now this masturbator of a supermarket, excuse my language, wants to ruin me. I have no choice. I have to fight back. Please understand that."

"I'm sorry, Uncle," Felipe replied. "A goat is not the answer."

Hitching up his baggy trousers, Don Sinfo went on.

"Let me tell you something. Sometimes I feel so old and stepped on by time that I wish I could go to sleep forever."

The words startled Felipe.

"Don't talk like that, Uncle," he said. "Please, take it easy."

"No, listen to me. That's the odd thing about it. I don't feel like that this time. I'm not letting no supermarket beat me. I got it all figured out." Don Sinfo went into his back pocket and pulled out the small notebook on which he kept his accounts. Down came the pencil from his ear. "Look at this. If we raise a goat, we'll sell the meat and with the money buy more goats. In time everyone in El Barrio will come to us for *cabrito.*"

Felipe looked at his uncle sadly.

"It won't work, Uncle Sinfo," he said.

"Sure it will," Don Sinfo insisted. "With the money we make you'll be able to go to college, get married to Margarita and raise a family. I'm not ready to die, but people don't have control over things like that and I'm not leaving this world without providing a good life for you. Please go and see my *compadre*, Nicanor Toro, about his truck. We're going to the country to buy the goat."

Felipe, barely eighteen years of age and an orphan for twelve of those years, was unmoved by his uncle's enthusiasm. Reluctantly, he agreed to follow his orders.

"Don't say I didn't warn you," he said. "I'll go and tell Don Nica, but don't say I didn't warn you." As he went out the door muttering, Don Sinfo continued to multiply figures and even thought about asking Mr.

Seymour, who owned the lot across the street, if he would allow him to keep a half dozen goats there during the warm weather. Perhaps he could build some sort of structure to protect the animals from the elements during the rest of the year. In his mind there was no end to the possibilities.

The very next day, early in the morning, Don Sinfo and Felipe rode in the cab of Nicanor Toro's old moving truck and visited a goat farm some fifty miles from New York City. The weather was uncommonly warm for March, the sky clear, the fields greening and some of the trees sprouting blooms. At the farm Don Sinfo purchased a male kid, the single offspring of a magnificent white ewe, which the owner of the farm called Ruffian because of her nasty temper. Don Sinfo was overjoyed and took the small brown and white animal in his arms.

We'll name you after your mother," he said.

"What?" Felipe muttered as he scratched at the hay of the goatpen with his shoes, "Calamity Joe?"

"We'll name you Rufino, like your mother," Don Sinfo said.

"Good name," Don Nica said.

"Like his mother," said the owner of the farm, smiling as he pocketed the one hundred dollars, a price double what he would've sold the goat for, except that he knew desperation when he saw it. "Pretty good choice."

"Look at him, Felipe," said Don Sinfo, placing young Rufino back on the ground. "Look how he butts my hand with his head."

"That's not all he's gonna butt before he's finished," Felipe replied angrily under his breath.

The kid was indeed a beauty. Barely five months old, its small horns gave it a menacing air betrayed only by the innocence of its large eyes. Don Sinfo was brimming over with hope at the prospect of raising his goat and selling the meat.

"This is the beginning of our good fortune, Felipe," he said. He secured a rope around the goat's neck and handed it to Felipe. "Put him up on the truck, please."

Reluctantly, Felipe hoisted the animal onto the bed of the truck and climbed up after it.

"Tie the rope to the slats," Don Sinfo said as Don Nica closed the truck's tailgate.

On the way back to the city Don Sinfo chatted openly with his friend Nicanor Toro.

"I don't know how to thank you, Nica. This is the start of a new life for us. How can I repay you?"

"Forget it, Sinfo. What are friends for!"

"Wait a minute, *compadre*. There are friends and then there are friends. I insist. Who was it that baptized my first son? Wasn't it you?"

"Yes, of course."

"And who was it that risked his life to call the police when the drug addicts attacked me?"

"What else could I do?"

"And it wasn't a ghost that sent that beautiful wreath for Josefa's funeral, may she rest in peace, was it?"

"No, it was no ghost."

"Then you have to let me offer you something. Maybe a few pounds of rice, some beans, and one or two cans of peaches. Anything you want."

"Well," Don Nica said, pulling at his moustache as he drove. "Everything you say is true, but I'm an old man and it makes me feel ashamed to ask this."

"Nicanor, man. We've been friends too long. There's no need to feel ashamed."

"Very well, *compadre*. You've always been honest with me and I with you. We share a grandson and there's no better man to team up for dominoes or *brisca* than yourself. Tell me one thing."

"Anything."

"Aren't you buying the goat to sell the meat?"

"Sure, why do you ask?"

Nicanor Toro sighed deeply.

"The world is a much better place when friends are honest with each other, Sinfo. I've seen many things in my life. Some were good and some were bad. But I have to tell you something. Of all the good things, few are better than *cabrito*. If you don't consider it an abuse of our friendship, it would be a privilege if you saved me a few ribs after you've slaughtered your goat. Not a lot. Maybe a pound or two for a stew. It's been a long time since I tasted *cabrito*."

Don Sinfo's heart sank for a moment. But how could he refuse? Nicanor Toro was more than a friend. He was like a brother. Any hint of an excuse would wound him forever.

"Consider it done, *compadre*," he said, smiling. "Naturally, it will be a while before Don Cabrito is ready for fricassee, but when it takes place, you'll have the pick of the ribs."

Back in the city Don Sinfo said goodbye to his friend. Grumbling, Felipe carried the young goat down into the cellar of the store. In a corner, well away from the rice, canned goods, and other stock which had been cleared away in preparation for Rufino's arrival, Felipe tied the goat to a water pipe. Frightened by the ride home and finding himself in this dark, odd-smelling place caused Rufino to begin crying for his mother. He backed up into the corner and stood there shaking his head. He continued his mournful cries until Felipe, opposed to the plan but not given to cruelty, brought him a head of lettuce and fed him by hand. He even found himself stroking the goat's smooth, even coat and playing the butting game which Rufino seemed to enjoy.

As the weeks went by and Rufino began growing, Don Sinfo dreamed of the day when quartered and dressed he could offer the various parts to his customers. April came and went, vanishing with the wind. May and June were a memory and before anyone knew it, July passed in the blinking of an eye. By early August the goat was quite large. It had developed into an imposing buck animal with thick curved horns, a small beard and eyes in which the innocence of youth had begun fading.

Anyone who had seen the goat on the occasions when, by way of advertising Don Sinfo brought him upstairs, commented on its strength and warned him.

"He's a mean looking animal," they said. "Be careful."

Don Sinfo had grown proud of Rufino and the two had developed an unusual fondness for each other.

"There's no need for alarm," he would say to those who feared Rufino. "He's a gentle soul. I'm going to miss him when he's gone," he would add, only half in jest. "Let me take him back downstairs."

"Don't go first, Don Sinfo," people would say. "It's not good to turn your back on a goat. They're treacherous and vengeful."

"Nonsense," Don Sinfo would say. "Come, my son," he'd say gently in Spanish while stroking Rufino's forehead. "You must return to your dwelling and await your destiny."

And with those words he would lead the growing animal back down to the cellar.

But all did not go well for Don Sinfo and Rufino. The relationship became strained. Somehow, Rufino seemed to sense his eventual fate. He bleated mournfully from time to time. This produced great sadness in the old man, but he stoically resisted what he knew were the wails of the condemned. He had heard the same anguish from animals about to be slaughtered. Guilt, therefore, began to play a role in the matter and Don Sinfo became partially disenchanted with his scheme. At times he wished he had never purchased the goat. In his waning years he had found kinship with all living beings. One thing was to buy meat already cut and ready for sale and another was to raise an animal and then kill it. But as strongly as he felt for Rufino, the specter of poverty hovering about Felipe's life steeled him in his resolve to see the enterprise through.

One afternoon, when the store's scales were being checked by a City inspector, Rufino chose to express himself the loudest.

"Hey, mister," the inspector said. "You got sheep down there?" Don Sinfo laughed nervously.

"Jez, asheep," he replied, without letting on that anything was amiss. "Das berrry fonny." He shook his head disapprovingly and tapped his temple with a pencil. "Is my granson. He a leettle crasy. Jew know, *loco*."

"Oh, yeah," said the inspector. "I get it." He laughed and smacked Don Sinfo on the back. "Your grandson is lowco."

"That's all," Don Sinfo said, smiling behind his white moustache, but cursing inside. "Jew know, tinager."

"I know, rock and roll and drugs."

"No, no drogas. Disco and karate."

"Oh?"

"Jez, karate. Black bell. Berrry serio. Practicin alla tine."

"I see," the inspector said, going out the door.

But Rufino grew louder each day and his bleating came with greater frequency. The noise became so unbearable that Don Sinfo went down into the cellar and in his sternest Spanish scolded the animal.

"You are an ungrateful beast, a disgrace to those of your race and a lunatic. Can't you see what you're doing? I've honored you by bringing you into my home for a noble purpose and you've chosen to behave in this abominable manner. What is the matter with you? Your crying is an impertinence which I cannot tolerate and my advice is that you heed my words and conduct yourself with more courtesy. Your mother would be greatly saddened and ashamed if she learned of your lack of discipline."

Rufino looked penitent enough as Don Sinfo shook his finger in his face. Don Sinfo was sure he had gotten through to him. However, no sooner had the old man returned upstairs and a customer come into the store, than once again Rufino took up his pleading.

That very evening, before he closed the store, Don Sinfo had a visit from a young, very polite and soft-spoken policeman. Always on good terms with the authorities, Don Sinfo welcomed the young Puerto Rican policeman, whom he had seen several times on patrol.

"I'm sorry to disturb you," the policeman said in Spanish. "I don't know how true it is, but we've gotten a complaint from the Health Department. They say you're keeping an animal in the cellar. They said it was a cow, but I don't believe it. Am I right?"

Don Sinfo was too drained to fabricate another lie, but he agreed with the policeman.

"No, there is no cow in the cellar," he said.

"Good, I'm glad to hear that," the policeman said. "I can report that there are no animals in the cellar." He paused for a moment. "I don't mean to be disrespectful, but if you don't mind, I'd like to check to make sure."

Don Sinfo's heart sank.

"It's no good," he said. "I can't lie to a member of the police, especially to one of our own race." His face flushed with shame as he explained his predicament. "It's important that I leave my nephew with a future after I'm gone. There's no crime in that, is there? This store is no longer able to provide for us. Just today Goya made their last delivery."

"I understand," said the policeman. "But what you're doing is against the law. It hurts me but I have to give you a summons. Tomorrow someone from the ASPCA will come to take the animal away."

The policeman's words shocked Don Sinfo. His face grew dark with worry and his heart pounded anxiously.

"But I've worked so hard to raise this animal. Don't you see what you're doing? So many people will be disappointed when they hear that there's no *cabrito*."

At mention of *cabrito* a look of apprehension came over the young officer's face.

"I know how you feel," he said. "I'm only doing my duty. I've never tasted *cabrito*, but my grandmother speaks about it from time to time. She'd be pretty upset if she knew I was doing this. Of course, if she knew there was a place where she could get the meat easily, she would bless me and tell me I'd have at least one son."

Although there was no bribe implied, Don Sinfo brightened immediately.

"Then no more need be said on the subject," he said. "You're a very wise young man. It makes an old man feel good to know that young people of our race are still considerate. By the end of the month everything will be settled. Come by after you get off work and I'll have a small gift for your grandmother. I'm sure she'll be pleased with you. I'll do everything I can to keep the goat quiet."

The policeman said goodnight and Don Sinfo, although relieved, was left with a feeling of profound contempt for Rufino. The next day was a replica of the previous ones, as Rufino kept up his wailing. That evening Don Sinfo spoke to Felipe.

"It's no use," he said. "The animal is trying to tell us something. Perhaps there's an evil spirit inside of him and whoever eats the meat will be harmed."

Felipe did not believe in such things, but perhaps if someone else went along with his uncle's concern they'd be rid of the goat.

"That's very possible," he said. "But what can we do?"

"I've been thinking about this all day," said Don Sinfo. "Tomorrow, first thing in the morning, go to Saint Cecilia and ask Father Pantoja if he can offer us advice on the matter."

The next day Felipe went to the church and returned with the priest.

"Good morning, Father," Don Sinfo said. "You shouldn't have bothered to come all the way up here."

"It's no bother, Don Sinfo," the priest replied. "It's a fine day and I haven't seen you in church for months. What seems to be the trouble? Felipe mentioned something about your goat."

Don Sinfo tried to find the right words.

"Well, it's hard to explain, Father. Let me ask you something. Is it possible animals can be invaded by evil spirits?"

The priest laughed amiably and nodded understandingly.

"Anything is possible," said Father Pantoja. "I don't think this is the case, but let's have a look at the animal. Although the goat is often associated with Satan, the belief is grounded on superstition. Show him to me."

Don Sinfo led the priest down the cellar stairs. Not a sound could be heard. Rufino was munching peacefully on some cabbage and nodded politely when he saw the two men. The priest looked the goat over for several minutes and then spoke.

"He's a fine healthy animal," he said. "He'll bring pleasure to many people. I'll tell you what I think is the problem."

"Not here, Father," Don Sinfo whispered, gesturing toward Rufino. "I don't want him to hear. Sometimes I think he understands everything people say, English or Spanish. I think he knows what's coming. Let's go back upstairs."

When Felipe, who had been minding the store, closed the cellar door, the priest explained.

"You must understand that I'm not speaking from personal experience, but from a general knowledge of life."

"Yes, of course," Don Sinfo nodded attentively.

"As you can see if you observe his maleness, the animal has reached maturity and is merely expressing his natural urges."

"You mean he wants to . . ., I mean he needs to . . ."

Don Sinfo couldn't find the right words to express himself properly in front of the priest.

"Exactly," the priest finally said. "It's an instinct which can't be explained, but which all animals have."

Don Sinfo laughed for the first time in weeks. He clapped the still glum Felipe on the back.

"How could we have overlooked such a simple fact," he said, and smacked his forehead in disbelief. "What else could it be! I remember the first time I brought Josefa a serenade. I was never much of a singer but that night I sang like a nightingale."

"That's what I'm talking about," the priest said.

"Thank you, Father Pantoja," Don Sinfo said. "I'm relieved it's only a matter of the heart and not of the soul. I'll be in church next Sunday. Please rest assured of that."

"That's a wonderful promise, Don Sinfo. But let me tell you something. As you know the priesthood is a labor of sacrifice and suffering."

"Yes, I understand," said Don Sinfo, thinking that perhaps the priest wished to reveal his longings for female companionship to him. "It must be quite difficult."

"Well, to be honest," the priest said, "I don't think the Lord would mind . . ."

"I don't know too much about those things, Father," said Don Sinfo nervously, looking uncomfortably to Felipe.

"What I'm saying is that I don't think He would mind if I added one more task. I'd consider it my responsibility and a great honor if, when you're ready to partake of that fine animal, you would allow me to say a prayer of thanks at your table."

Don Sinfo's heart jumped crazily in his chest. He wanted to explain that the animal was for sale and not for personal consumption, but the gesture would be a selfish one.

"Nothing would please me more, Father," he said. "I'll reserve the place at the head of the table for you."

The priest left and Don Sinfo and Felipe began their daily task of placing the boxes of plantains, tanniers and fruit in front of their store. But no sooner had the first customer come into the store than Rufino took up *his* serenade. By noon his cries were so unbearable that Don Sinfo was seriously tempted to send for the butcher so that he could begin parting Rufino from his hide.

Felipe read Don Sinfo's thoughts.

"Do you want me to go and get Jacinto Torres?" he asked.

"No, no, this is criminal, Felipe," he said, angrily. "I can't deprive poor Rufino of one of life's true pleasures. The only thing we can do is find a mate for him."

This time Felipe remained calm. No doubt existed now in his mind that his uncle had taken absolute leave of his senses.

"There are other ways," he said, knowingly.

"Felipe!" said Don Sinfo, sternly. "What are you suggesting! I will not have Rufino learn bad habits. And in any case, that is physically impossible for a goat."

"No, Uncle," Felipe said, still calm. "What I was thinking is that maybe Mama Laboy ought to take a look at Rufino. She knows about that kind of thing. They say that she cured Pedro, the plumber's son, of his passion for Ezequiel Moreno's daughter after she promised to marry him and then changed her mind and became a nun."

"Yes, yes, I've heard that. She's a powerful woman, Mama Laboy."

And so it was.

No more than an hour later, Encarnación Laboy, whose fame in matters of the heart was known from Guayama on the island to Newark, New Jersey, and some said as far as Chicago, arrived at *Bodega Cacimar*, trailed by her son, Lolo, who carried a small drum and a bag of leaves and roots. They went directly to the cellar, the woman's long skirts rustling as she moved. In ten minutes they were back up.

"It's exactly as you told me on the telephone, Sinforoso," said Mama Laboy, her black face splitting into a knowing grin.

"What's to be done, Mama Laboy?" Don Sinfo asked, worried by the woman's lack of concern with the matter. "This is a serious situation."

"It's done, old man," she said, laughing uproariously. "I have given your goat a double dose of Oil of Forgetfulness and purified the air with incense to drive away any female goat spirits which may be disturbing Rufino. It's the same with all *machos*. The slightest female scent will distract them."

"Will this cure him of his misery?" Don Sinfo asked.

"Only in part," Mama Laboy answered. "I have given Felipe a bottle of the oil. You must give the goat two drops with each meal, keep a red candle lit and burn incense at all times. But no cure works without the proper surroundings. You must take the goat for a walk each day. This will create a further distraction and his mind will not be as troubled."

"Thank you very much, Mam Laboy," said Don Sinfo. "Please take these steaks I've cut for you. I would pay you with cash but there is little of that. The Public Assistance checks have not arrived yet this month and I've given out more credit than usual."

"Forget it, old man. Save the steaks for your customers and when you kill the goat, save me a few neck bones."

"Yes, I will do just that," Don Sinfo replied without hesitation.

He was pleased that things would go well now, but it troubled him that the amount of meat he was to sell had further dwindled. Nevertheless, each day at two o'clock in the afternoon, rope in hand, he took his prize possession on a tour of the neighborhood. In order to keep Rufino calm, Don Sinfo talked to him. As they walked he explained the myriad complexities of city life.

"Rufino, my son, he'd say. "All that you see about you, the good and the bad, is New York. You must be careful because it's a place of many dangers. I must be frank with you. I haven't lost faith yet, but I'm troubled. I think you should know a few things before you fulfill the purpose for which God created you. I know you're young, but you should have this knowledge. You should know that you're not alone in this world. All of us must travel the path from birth to old age, to sickness and eventually to death. These are the stages of all living things. You, at least, will be spared the intermediary steps and for this you must be thankful. Myself, I harbor no ill feelings for those who have injured me."

Rufino looked up quizzically and Don Sinfo's heart skipped a beat.

"I urge you to humbly do likewise. We are all creatures of the Almighty. We live in a land of opportunity and each must make his way as best he can. But friends should speak honestly to each other. I, like yourself, have had nothing but problems in this great land. I'm not saying it's a bad land, but solely explaining a reality of life, a fact you will have soon to accept. I'm sure you understand what I'm talking about."

Rufino looked up at him again and then away. He was content to listen, never growing alarmed by the strange noises or the amount of human activity they encountered.

One day, as Don Sinfo walked with Rufino, he was stopped by a group of militant young men and women in berets and Army jackets. They explained who they were and asked for his help.

Don Sinfo listened patiently.

"Our concern is to retain the culture of our parents, but everything is working against us. We have instituted a community education program for our younger brothers and sisters so that they can learn who's their friend and who's their enemy. We'd like you to speak with them and explain how you run your store in true revolutionary spirit and how you're raising this goat in order to share it with the oppressed people of the community on Thanksgiving Day, and with that act reject the turkey as another tool of the American imperialist monopoly on our eating habits."

Don Sinfo tried to explain that the goat had nothing to do with Thanksgiving.

"I'm only a simple *bodeguero*," he said. "I'm raising the goat to help my nephew with his education."

"Exactly the spirit we're talking about," said a young man.

Don Sinfo protested.

"It's true that I extend credit to those people who depend on Public Assistance for their necessities, but any man with half a heart would do the same."

"This is true, comrade. But how many do? You're an inspiration to all of us and we want you to share your experiences with our children. They've never tasted *cabrito*. You'll be doing the community a great cultural service and young people will rededicate their lives to the struggle, knowing that our older citizens are willing to share as you do."

And so it was.

Don Sinfo went with the young radicals, spoke to the children, and, as they petted Rufino, promised them a fine meal. How could he refuse the love in their eyes. They reminded him of his own grandchildren whom he hardly ever saw.

When he returned to the store he sat down and figured out how much of the goat he would be able to sell. After much juggling of ciphers he decided he would just about break even and that in order to make a profit he would have to allow Rufino to reach full maturity. The meat would not be as tender and perhaps people would accuse him of selling *chivo*, which is the word for old goat, but it could not be helped. One had to make the best of things and Felipe's future was at stake.

During the last week in August a heat spell enveloped the city. Trains ran behind schedule, highways became clogged as people tried to reach the beaches, brownouts occurred almost nightly and the Mayor went on the air to appeal for cooperation in conserving electricity and water. In El Barrio the situation was unbearable. Waves of heat rose from the pavement and the tenements emptied out. Day and nigh the streets were full of activity. People argued constantly, children cried with greater frequency, lovers struggled with each other in vain, the beer was always warm and even when the hydrants were turned on, the police came quickly and turned them back off. Fire, police and ambulance sirens screeched at almost timed intervals, keeping everyone on edge.

At *Bodega Cacimar* the situation took a turn for the worse. Although the walks had reduced Rufino's anxiety over his eventual demise, they also had the effect of fanning the fires of freedom in his heart. The bleating resumed, this time with greater urgency and remarkable frequency. As if the reprieve was one more unbearable torture, every ten minutes he would let loose with a long series of heart-rending moans. The wailing not only produced greater guilt in Don Sinfo, but began annoying his neighbors. Rumors spread irresponsibly. They ranged from animal sodomy to Rufino being the center of Devil worship. Customers who had whetted their appetites for the fine delicacy came into the store daily to have their orders filled only to be told that it would be a few more weeks yet.

It was at this time that Don Sinfo decided to take matters into his own hands. What had he to lose? The goat belonged to them. He might as well let them have it. He brought Rufino up from the cellar, led him out onto the sidewalk and tied him to a parking meter. Perhaps someone would come along and steal the wretched animal and that would be the end of the affair. But he knew he felt this way solely because of his anger at the unfortunate circumstances. He no longer saw Rufino as meat. The fine vision of a new life was fading and the smells of *cabrito* in a fine red sauce with small round potatoes and pieces of green pepper were turning to acrid smoke. And yet the thing which disturbed him most was that he cared for Rufino and constantly watched the huge, proud animal, whose beard was the same color and texture of his own moustache. Every few minutes Don Sinfo would go outside and check on him.

Nothing of consequence happened the first day the goat was tied to the parking meter. Police cars came by several times, but it was too hot a day and the officers ignored the sight. Neighborhood people, although curious, generally steered clear of the menacing horns.

As for Rufino, he was quite happy with his new and relative freedom and as night approached, he appeared subdued, even introspective as he was returned to the cellar for the evening. This routine was repeated three days in a row without incident.

On the fourth day, however, an old junk wagon, drawn by a rather decrepit mare happened by and Rufino lost all sense of propriety. Bleating loudly, he stood on his hind legs, his male organ fully erect, and tried to get at the mare while the wagon was parked in front of Don Sinfo's store. Don Sinfo heard the commotion, came out on the sidewalk and with great authority slapped Rufino's face.

"You must stop this immediately," he said, through clenched teeth. "You're making a fool of yourself. I know that you're desperate, but that is only a horse. It's obvious to everyone except yourself that she is not of your race and that even among her own she would be considered a physical atrocity of such ugly magnitude that she could easily frighten a regiment of ogres. Your insane passion can only lead to more trouble. Someone will call the police and they will come and arrest us both for disturbing the peace or even parking illegally. I implore you to restrain yourself and think of Felipe's future. I'm an old man and will never return to my homeland. Give me at least the small satisfaction of raising you. I'm sorry if I've injured your feelings, but you're being totally unreasonable."

Rufino calmed down considerably after the wagon left, but to pass the time began chewing absentmindedly on the rope with which he was tied to the parking meter. The men playing dominoes in the shade of the store's awning were too busy with their game to notice as Rufino chewed his way through the thick rope and wandered leisurely down the sidewalk toward Lexington Avenue. Don Sinfo, who had gone down to the cellar to bring up a box of dried codfish, missed Rufino's latest attempt at tormenting him. Felipe, speaking on the telephone with Margarita and absorbed in making preparations to attend a *salsa* concert the following weekend, also missed Rufino's exit.

Rufino had walked no more than twenty feet before he stopped halfway down the block and began nibbling some blades of grass growing through a crack in the sidewalk. Meanwhile, a group of boys had been watching Rufino and attempted to make his acquaintance by pulling his tail. This bit of insolence not only insulted Rufino but angered him. Enraged at their poor manners, he turned, lowered his head and butted one of them in the stomach, knocking him to the ground.

Have it be known that one of the great tenets on which our culture is anchored is physical courage. Whether as an expression of fact or merely of rhetoric, every male is a man and a man fights back. From the time a male child can clench his fist he is encouraged to express his bravery. Seeing his friend thus abused, another of the boys armed himself with the top of a garbage can and a stickball bat and began menacing Rufino. This was too much for Rufino and once more he charged. The boy remained in Rufino's path until the very last moment and then stepped aside, leaving only the garbage can lid in the way, much as a bullfighter will use his cape. As Rufino went by and his horns clattered against the galvanized tin, the boy administered a sizeable blow to Rufino's large testicles. It should be pointed out that although throwing the bull is an honored tradition among the people, bullfighting is not. However, on the island as well as in New York, our community benefits immensely from foreign films, be they from Latin America, Europe or the United States.

The attack on Rufino's masculinity totally awakened his fury. More to the point is a little known fact but one of no small relevance. While the clatter of horns hitting galvanized metal is hardly ever melodious, it will inspire goats to great deeds. Veering sharply to his right, there went Rufino making a prodigious leap over the hood of Big Pancho's Cadillac, cruising slowly up the block on the way back from one of his *bolita* banks. Big Pancho swore mightily in Spanish and to hear him tell it later, he thought the Mob had awarded his contract to the Devil himself.

By this time someone had informed Don Sinfo of Rufino's escape. After instructing Felipe to mind the store, here he came. Rufino was now in a total dither, his mind a mass of confusion. On the north side of the street he met up with a fire hydrant, which although shorter than himself must have appeared to be a formidable opponent. He butted the fire hydrant four times in quick succession before realizing his opponent was adamant about retaining its place.

Frustrated, Rufino jumped in the air twice and went racing down the middle of the street with a half dozen boys in pursuit.

On Lexington Avenue Rufino began going down the subway stairs, heard the Jerome Avenue Express roaring past and changed his mind. Back out on the street he eluded a bus and began racing up the hill on 103rd Street. People seeing the goat coming at them either jumped out of the way or stood exactly in his path, petrified by the powerful charging animal and hoping that somehow the beast would swerve and avoid hitting them. Such was not the case. Rufino had had enough of human abuse. Anything that stood in his way was bowled over.

Occasionally, perhaps in deference to Don Sinfo's authority and age, he avoided old people and, rather than butting them, leaped clear over their ducking heads, causing two nearly fatal heart attacks and no less than eight involuntary urinations. Having recently had their first sexual experience and deciding that they were about to receive divine punishment for their transgressions by being escorted directly to hell by the Devil, several young women fainted at the sight of Rufino.

When he reached the top of the hill, Rufino himself was seeing demons everywhere he turned. He made menacing gestures with his horns at every moving object, but stood still several minutes as if to get his bearings. The air was hot and damp and charged with tension. Women were screaming and small children cried. A car had gone up on the sidewalk and the crowd of boys had grown to more than two dozen. At a safe distance they cursed in English and Spanish and threw garbage in Rufino's direction. As if this were not enough insolence, a large overfed German shepherd came up and sniffed Rufino's tail. This threw Rufino once more into a frenzy. Turning quickly, he butted the dog and sent him away yelping. Rufino crossed the street, grabbed a lettuce from a vegetable stand and paused for a small repast. When the owner of the store came at him with a broom, Rufino dropped the half-eaten lettuce and ran off.

As Rufino reached the top of the hill on Lexington Avenue and 102nd Street, Francis Xavier O'Brien arrived at his post on the corner below. O'Brien was overweight, tired and already bothered by the heat of the day. A peace-loving man, he had never received a citation for valor or even witnessed a crime more serious than the running of a traffic light. This was not the fault of the neighborhood which abounded with rogues galore, but a result of O'Brien's disposition. In fifteen years as a member of New York's finest, he had only drawn his gun once, but this was in order to hang upside down from a second floor fire escape to retrieve a little girl's kitten stranded atop a window cornice.

When O'Brien saw the mayhem Rufino had caused and the developing confusion, he ran to the police callbox and rang the station house.

"Right, Sarge, that's what I said. A goat. Right. Going like a bat outta hell up the hill on Lex. Yeah, I'm sure. He's got a head start, Sarge. No way I'm gonna catch up now. You better send a couple of squad cars and an ambulance. There's people laid out on the ground and a lot of screaming going on. I see. O.K. I'll do that and report back."

O'Brien hung up the phone, closed the callbox and walked laboriously up the hill. When he arrived, Rufino had just escaped the grocer's broom and was now in the middle of the street dodging traffic. A throng of people followed at a distance. Cars were honking their horns and a few community-minded people were shouting directions to anyone who would listen on how to rid the neighborhood of this latest nuisance. Notwithstanding the fact that a number of people knew the animal was Don Sinfo's goat, they were angered that they had been kept waiting so long for their meat and that now they would not have it at all.

As a person charged with the telling of our diasporic woes, I am often accused of fabrication. "Mr. Mendoza," I was asked recently, at no less an august institution than Harvard University, "what do you draw upon for your inspiration." "The people," I replied, knowing I spoke the truth, but chagrined by the knowledge that as a people we use very little of our brain. And yet we go on surviving and multiplying at what some people consider an alarming rate, but which to us is quite normal. "We are a brilliant people who aspire to life and little more," I said, as poetically as I could, given the setting.

In retrospect, perhaps I was not totally honest with those ingenuous Cantabrigians and, rather than draw inspiration from our people, all I do is record that which goes on in our collective psyche. We, as a people, if nothing else, have wild imaginations given to fantasy and invention of the most bizarre nature. There is little need for me to fabricate. My talent is too humble and meager to concoct plots and complications, to pull rabbits out of literary hats and mold and shape that imagination into plausible reality. All I do is record what I observe and what comes to me through conversations with others.

In the middle of that confusion, of that throng of sweating, screaming, fainting and angry people, someone very calmly explained that he had been in the merchant marine, had traveled all over the world and that he knew exactly what they were up against. People were astounded. Their eyebrows went up, their mouths hung open and when they recovered, the word spread quickly that Rufino was no ordinary goat but a man-eating ram from India. Needless to say, greater chaos ensued as people were torn between growing fear and acute curiosity.

O'Brien was torn between his duty and his better judgment. Should he attempt to restore order to this potentially dangerous situation or should he pursue the perpetrator of the disorder? Perhaps what he had overheard in the Detectives' room was true and this was another militant ploy. But again, plainclothes people always saw everything as a plot. Monahan said he'd seen the goat in their precinct. His choice was made for him when a group of irate citizens surrounded him and began to berate the police for their lack of vigilance. Choosing the latter of the alternatives, that of pursuit, he jumped into a cab waiting for the light to change.

"Follow that goat," he said from the back seat.

"Gimme a break, Mac," said the cabbie, engrossed in honking his horn and not even bothering to look into his rearview mirror. "It's too hot for that kinda baloney."

"I'm not joking, buddy," O'Brien said. "Up ahead."

The cabbie looked into the rearview mirror, turned around, saw the uniform and looked up the street. Through the crowd he could barely make out a pair of horns.

"Holy cow," he said. "Right away, officer," he added and began honking his horn more furiously than before as he inched his way through the crowd.

The chase, if it could be called that, was on. O'Brien ordered the cabbie to keep his hand on the horn to clear a path. This not only brought more people out into the street but angered Rufino further. On 99th Street and Lexington Avenue, near the bus terminal, Rufino turned east and was gone, racing toward Third avenue. He crossed Third, Second and First Avenue before O'Brien's cab could catch up. By the time O'Brien once again established visual contact with the goat, Rufino had entered the East River Drive and caused a multiple car accident.

Due to the astonishment of Aram Essegian, a one time Armenian goat farmer, upon seeing a goat for the first time in thirty years and then on an American highway, some twelve cars had piled into each other when Essegian braked suddenly.

"Beautiful, beautiful, beautiful," said Essegian, in utter rapture and oblivious to the crunching metal as he observed Rufino. "Just beautiful."

Rufino, by now completely disoriented, his eyes wild with fear, butted indiscriminately at imaginary targets. People rolled up their windows and remained inside their cars, restricting their activities to fanning themselves, honking their horns and swearing. Again this did nothing to help matters. In his confusion, Rufino now heard the voices of his ancestors. While he suspected all along he would be sacrificed, that being part of his racial memory and something which he had resigned himself to after listening to Don Sinfo, the idea did not sit well with him. What he found difficult to accept was the manner in which death was to come. More distressing yet was the fact that long departed relatives, their ghosts grown to tremendous proportions and dressed in outlandish costumes, belching fire and smoke from their nostrils, could be making such irresponsibly wild and totally disparaging remarks about his person.

Hurt, dishonored, and no longer concerned with ancestral authority, he picked out a cream colored Volkswagen, which seemed to him to be the leader of the flock, and ran full speed into its side, denting the door, causing its occupants to exit in mortal fear from the other side and climb atop the vehicle, as if it were their house and it had been caught in a flash flood.

Infuriated by its obstinacy in not giving ground, Rufino attacked repeatedly until, dazed, he reeled back on wobbly legs. At this point O'Brien arrived on the scene. He jumped out of the cab, dodged some traffic still moving in one of the lanes and was about to collar Rufino, when the goat came to his senses and bolted away. Capture meant further torture and eventual death. In a second, Rufino was racing downtown with the traffic, running along with the cars, as if in a herd. Upon seeing this latest maneuver on Rufino's part, the beleaguered O'Brien stopped a car, got in and ordered the driver to give chase. O'Brien was sweating profusely, his uniform sticking to every part of his overweight and unused body. His face was flushed and he was breathing so heavily that his heart beat irregularly and he feared the possibility of a heart attack. The driver of the car tried to engage him in polite conversation about the exciting nature of the assignments given to policemen these days.

"Just keep driving, pal," O'Brien responded, cursing under his breath. He leaned out the window and considered shooting the goat, but decided against it. It could very well be that it *was* a miniature Tibetan yak, as some people on First Avenue had said. If that was indeed the case and he managed to capture this rare animal, he would be a hero. His picture might even appear on the front page of a newspaper.

But Rufino was not to be caught so easily. At 96th Street he veered right, found the exit and got off the highway. He walked several blocks, found a patch of grass and began to graze, unaware that his next threat from the authorities was being masterminded no more than two hundred feet from where he stood.

You see, if you are familiar with the City of New York, you know that not far from where Rufino browsed, there is a low, red brick building with the letters ASPCA displayed prominently on its facade. The letters stand for American Society for the Prevention of Cruelty to Animals. As you can well imagine, having lived all your life among concerned neighbors, someone had called this benign institution and informed the personnel of Rufino's location. Within minutes of the call, two representatives of the Society, armed with nets, rope and cabbages, converged on him. Rufino smelled them as soon as they emerged from the building. Although intrigued by the prospect of fresh cabbage, he waited until the men were no more than twenty feet away before making his move. Keeping his head down as if he were still grazing, he charged directly at them. The two men, adept enough at coaxing pet raccoons down from trees, extracting boa constrictors from dank cellars, and tracking down full grown albino alligators in the New York City sewer system, were not prepared for Rufino's sudden aggression and landed on their backs.

Getting up quickly, the two men cursed Rufino and gave chase, hurling cabbages after him. He in turn, hurdled a fence in a nearby housing project, broke up a boys' roller hockey game by disabling one of the goalies, and headed up 96th Street.

No more than a half hour had elapsed from the time Rufino chewed through his rope. However, a number of important and relevant events had transpired. On Third Avenue and 101st Street someone had turned on a fire alarm. A nearby fire company responded to the call and, after ascertaining the absence of a fire in the vicinity, began its return trip to the fire house, when it was redirected to set up a road block. When the fire chief arrived he found seventeen patrol cars, at least a dozen pieces of fire fighting equipment and six garbage trucks already at the scene. Traffic had been stopped in all directions and rerouted away from the intersection. Large crowds had begun gathering at each of the four corners.

Down the street, ten policemen, among them an exhausted Francis X. O'Brien, were attempting to herd Rufino towards the ASPCA men. They moved cautiously, not out of fear that the goat would cause them physical harm, but fully aware that if it escaped this carefully prepared cordon and headed west, the next field of battle could be Central Park, where it would be virtually impossible to trap the animal without causing undue publicity and charges of incompetence or even police brutality.

Don Sinfo, at first dismayed by the unfortunate turn of events, had finally claimed responsibility for and ownership of Rufino. He now watched the efforts of the police and the activity surrounding the operation from the back seat of a hook and ladder truck. This privilege had been made possible through the political influence of the Honorable Fernando Picot, a retired District Court judge and a pillar of the Puerto Rican political community.

When the judge first heard of Don Sinfo's predicament from a flash bulletin over one of the Spanish radio stations, he immediately called City Hall. He complained bitterly about the poor conditions and lack of adequate services available to Puerto Rican people in New York City, citing in particular the case of Don Sinforoso Figueroa and his goat. One of the Mayor's assistants, of which he had many, none regrettably, he informed the judge, for tracking down goats, reassured him of the Mayor's concern for his standing among the people and promised immediate action.

The assistant then called the Fire, Police and Sanitation departments, informed them of the situation and the gravity of an incident such as the one developing. He quoted for each one of the commissioners the tragic events at Sarajevo, as well as other historical catastrophes which began over misunderstandings or seemingly minor occurrences that had quickly escalated into all out war. All three department went into action, causing this most southerly border of El Barrio to appear as if the *Wehrmacht* were about to march north.

Perhaps to mention the *Wehrmacht* is stretching a point, but some sort of Germanic invasion of El Barrio was a distinct possibility, being that south of 96th Street is the community of Yorkville, for years the hub of Manhattan's German-American population. As word traveled through the neighborhood, people began emptying out of the buildings and bars, brandishing beer bottles and chair legs. Even the entire hockey population of Yorkville, from nine to forty years of age, was waving hockey sticks menacingly from their side of the border at their Spanish speaking enemies. The Hispanics, observing the sport oriented nature of the aggression, opted for athletic equipment with which they were more familiar and baseball bats began appearing. It was later reported that sporting goods stores in both neighborhoods did a rather brisk business. Given these circumstances, a major riot might have ensued.

Such, however, did not take place and no small amount of gratitude belongs to Don Sinfo and his goat. The truth is that Rufino as a goat did not experience the remorse of a petty criminal, easily beset by guilt, cowed by public opinion and eager for his captors to accomplish their task. Although appearing subdued by the amount of human activity now surrounding him, he made another of his supercaprian leaps through the connection of a hook and ladder truck and its cab.

From his seat atop the truck, Don Sinfo watched the white and brown flash go by, legs tucked in and horns slashing the air like twin sabres. He crossed himself and closed his eyes in dismay. Rufino landed on the other side of the truck and, before anyone could react, was gone up 96th Street. Up the hill he went, past Third Avenue.

On Lexington Avenue Rufino had a vague notion, perhaps a memory of safety, a remembrance of his cellar home. He began going down the stairs of the IRT subway line, remembered the roaring of the trains on 103rd Street, thought better of it and instead turned and went leaping over the hood of a Checker cab, racing to make a traffic light. The cab swerved sharply and *it* went halfway down the subway steps, shearing off half of the protective railing to the entrance and in the process knocking a mailbox through the plate glass window of a drug store on the other side of the street. The newspapers explained later how the driver, a Mr. Isaac Rabinowitz of Brooklyn, sat in the vehicle for several minutes, muttering, before finally retrieving his day's earnings from the floor of the cab, got out, continued down the stairs and took a train home without once looking back.

Rufino continued up 96th Street. On Park Avenue the original group of Puerto Rican boys who had instigated his behavior had now swelled to more than a hundred. Seeing the goat once more, they resumed the chase, yelling, making obscene gestures and clattering garbage can tops as if they were cymbals. The latter again served to infuriate Rufino. He cut across the avenue, clearing the fences of the landscaped center dividers. He raced ahead blindly until he reached Madison Avenue where there is a hospital called Mount Sinai. At that moment, toward it, in all haste, there now proceeded on a mission of mercy, an ambulance. Siren wailing, it hurtled toward its destination as Rufino made ready to cross the street and race to freedom by crossing Fifth Avenue and entering Central Park. The flashing lights and ear splitting whining were suddenly too much for the harassed Rufino and he quickly shifted direction. Turning south, he raced blindly ahead, crossing streets with wild abandon and total disregard for traffic lights until he had gone some twelve blocks.

He was now in one of the more affluent and fashionable sections of the city. Having outrun his tormentors for the moment, he slowed down and took in the surroundings, the quaint little shops, shady trees and low buildings which allowed sunlight to filter through to the surprisingly clean streets. He could still hear the siren, the clattering of metal and the excited voices, but they seemed so distant. It was as if he had, somehow, crossed a barrier in time and found himself in another dimension. He watched people carefully for signs of hostility, but found none. In fact, they seemed unconcerned with anything but their thoughts. Their pace was slow, relaxed, as if they were walking in a dream. Even the heat seemed more bearable here and suddenly for Rufino a small repast seemed in order.

He had not finished his second bunch of jonquils when Alex Papadopoulos, the owner of Madison Florist, came out to investigate what he thought was an English sheepdog scouting the area for a place to relieve himself. When he saw the horns, his life flashed before him and he saw a boy walking with difficulty up the side of a hill while a herd of goats clambered easily ahead. He threw up his arms and cursed mightily in his native Greek.

Rufino did not recognize the language nor was he impressed by the severity of the tone. Instead, he lowered his head and butted, causing the startled Papadopoulos, long out of touch with the habits of goats, to land in a potted azalea bush in front of his shop. Rufino turned once more to the jonquils and would have continued his meal had it not been for Joe, the fruit and vegetable man from Gristede's Grocery, who came out and waved his apron menacingly at him. Once more Rufino charged. Joe, seeing his friend, Papadopoulos, wrestling to right the upturned azalea bush, and being a goat hater from his Sicilian youth, anticipated the charge and moved back into the store, leaving G. Howard Trenton, resplendent in yachting cap, white ducks and deck shoes, ladened with just purchased stores for a run to Newport, in Rufino's path.

"Look out, Mr. Trenton," Joe shouted, ducking into the store.

Too late. Canned goods, fruit, meats and several rolls of tissue paper flew into the air and G. Howard Trenton, dazed by the blow, hat askew, landed at the feet of Elissa Paddleford, the instant cake mix heiress, maidenly still at the age of fifty summers and at least ten forgotten winters, who had been standing in front of an antique shop, admiring some porcelain shepherds.

"Sir," she said, "what *are* you doing? Senility is no excuse for sexual perversion!"

So accustomed was Elissa to G. Howard Trenton's advances, having repulsed him ever since making her debut in 1929, that she imagined his lying at her feet staring dumbly up her dress was another one of his infantile pranks designed to attract her attention. Head haughtily raised, she walked majestically away.

Rufino had turned back to the flower shop, but at that very moment a crowd of people came around the corner in frenzied haste. The group was an odd mob composed of policemen and Puerto Rican people, led by militant young men and women, fully arrayed in their battle fatigues and berets. Sirens could be heard approaching and people began emerging from shops. Conditioned to avoid crowds, Rufino turned and raced in the opposite direction.

Tall, stately Elissa Paddleford having just left the still prone G. Howard Trenton, turned to investigate the source of commotion. She saw the goat bearing down on her too late to avoid its rush, with the unfortunate result that all she could do was raise her skirt and cover her face. Rufino barely grazed her as he went by, but Elissa screamed in terror. Two young patrolmen, the first on the scene, stopped to assist her.

"That animal," screamed Elissa, clutching the hem of her skirt at her chin, "attacked me. Do something, young man. Call the police.!"

"Sure, lady," said one of the policemen, "but pull your skirt down."

Realizing that she had been exposing herself, Elissa fainted and the other policeman caught her as she fell.

The mob had now arrived in full. Joe from Gristede's had helped G. Howard Trenton to his feet and was dusting him off, when Trenton caught sight of the militants. He straightened his back in military fashion and screwed up his face.

"Good God, Joe," he said. "It's the revolution. It's finally arrived."

As the militants came closer, Trenton raised his fists and assumed an old fashioned boxing stance.

"C'mon then, you wild-eyed radicals," he shouted. "I've been waiting more than thirty years for you."

The bright dark faces ignored the lanky, horse-faced old man and continued down the street.

"*Míralo, míralo*! *Por ahí va,*" they shouted.

This was not a revolutionary slogan, but simply meant: Look at him, look at him. There he goes, referring of course to Rufino.

The unruly mob now numbered several hundred, not counting policemen, firemen, ASPCA, sanitation men and several high ranking, very worried city officials, including the Mayor, who had been alerted to a possible urban holocaust. At the tail end of the crowd here came Don Sinfo, who, having alighted from his perch atop Fire Company 83's Hook and Ladder truck, was in a state of agitation and quite embarrassed by this latest problem with Rufino.

"He must do penance," he thought, as he searched for Rufino. "Death would be a gift for this ingrate. Not until I see him on his knees will I forgive the son of the Devil."

And then, all at once, the crowd, which up to this time had at least the semblance, chaotic as it was, of purpose and direction, turned into a mass of confusion. The goat was nowhere in sight. It had vanished into thin air. A near panic developed as each person attempted to establish what was next expected of him in the situation. Police officials thought they should prepare for a possible outburst of violence. As if to oblige their highly developed paranoia, the young revolutionaries, whose whole purpose in joining the chase was to safeguard their part in Don Sinfo's investment, considered the possibility that it had all been a CIA plot to entrap them. To prepare themselves for battle they began shouting insults at the ranks of police that had lined up along the sidewalk. Like squirrels searching for hidden nuts, groups of young Puerto Rican boys began going in and out of stores, commenting on the merchandise and gearing themselves for the eventuality that enough chaos would ensue for them to make off with something.

Such was the disorientation that firemen, for no apparent reason, began to unwind hoses from their trucks and to connect them to fire hydrants. Not to be outdone, sanitation men went to work dumping whatever they could into garbage dumpsters. The ASPCA, which up to this time had come up empty, managed, in a matter of minutes, to capture three poodles, two miniature greyhounds, one scottish terrier, a basenji, a Welsh corgi, an aging basset hound, and a very chic, rather outraged, white angora cat which had been sunning itself on one of the first floor windows of a brownstone.

The Mayor, as always, impeccably dressed and displaying the decorum which comes from spending no less than four years in New Haven, and it being an election year, borrowed a portable loudspeaker, climbed atop a police car and proceeded to deliver a campaign speech. No one paid the least bit of attention to the handsome Mayor. People were shouting orders to one another and several minor scuffles broke out. Traffic once again had been stopped and angry motorists and bus drivers, their patience exhausted by the heat, leaned on their horns and cursed. Some even got out of their vehicles and joined the floating urban seminars on such subjects as: "What's really wrong with New York City," or "When I was a kid people had respect." Some even began to circulate petitions to impeach the Mayor. The only thing which prevented a major urban upheaval at this point was the arrival of several television news teams and reporters, in whose direction the disparate elements of the crowd now turned in order to make their feelings known.

It is at precise moments like these, when there is a seemingly insignificant parenthesis in the time-space continuum and the world appears to pause in its eternal spinning to allow us to take stock of ourselves as men and women, that some say the gods, or whatever makes fortune smile on mortals, turn the tide of fate and change our lives forever. I, for one, give this theory little credence. However, if anything has validity concerning the pursuit of happiness, these moments when no one is quite sure about his role are perfect opportunities for a man of ingenuity and courage to make the best of an adverse situation.

Don Sinfo was such a man, although he would never explain it as such nor take credit for it.

But back to Rufino and his whereabouts. Immediately after his brief encounter with Elissa Paddleford, Rufino, truly fatigued by this time, turned the corner of Madison Avenue and 84th Street. Several houses down the tree-lined, elegant block he found the open gate of a townhouse and went in. He proceeded cautiously on a short, paved driveway and there, in the back of the house, he found the oasis he had been searching for. In the middle of the oppressive heat and unbearable noise, which for the better part of the last hour he had attempted to escape, he came upon a carpet of velvety grass, growing in the shade of a large tree by a miniature pond. A gentle breeze drifted by, rustling the leaves of the tree and making ripples on the surface of the green water. Rufino walked carefully toward the water, lest it be another trap. Ignoring for the moment the profusion of fragrances and colors lining the ivy covered wooden fence which protected the place from the outside world, Rufino lapped desperately at the surface of the water. Had he been able to sigh, he would have, such was the sweetness and freshness of the water. When he was finished sating his thirst, he walked carefully around the pond, helped himself to several miracle marigolds, returned to the shade of the tree and began nibbling at the sweet, succulent grass, his racial memory traveling back to a time when all goats were one with nature and human strife was absent from Earth.

And yet, were I, the highly acclaimed Ernesto Mendoza of whom volumes of glowing literary criticism of his ghetto works have been unfortunately penned, to sit up night after night attempting to decipher how Lady Luck operates, I could have never come up with the implausible coincidence that this place where Rufino had at last found respite from his travails was the garden of the very same Elissa Paddleford whom he, no more than five minutes prior, had nearly frightened to death.

Shortly after Rufino entered the gate, two policemen, each holding one of Elissa's arms, helped her up the steps of her townhouse. The housekeeper met them at the door. Frightened by the noise and commotion she had been hearing during the past fifteen minutes, and seeing her mistress escorted by the officers, she thought the worst.

"It's 'em riots again, in it, mum," she said, tripping lightly over the words as if they were London cobblestone.

"No, Frances," said Elissa. "It was really nothing. A Rocky Mountains goat escaped from the Central Park Zoo and they're attempting to retrieve it."

"Blimey, mum. A Rocky Mountains goat, you say?"

"Yes, Frances. Nothing to be concerned about."

Elissa thanked the policemen and sat down.

"Shall I call Dr. Armstrong, mum?" Frances inquired, returning to the spacious and tastefully decorated sitting room after seeing the two officers out and locking the door. "Are you hurt? It's the Negroes and their civil rights again, in it, mum?"

"No, Frances. it was nothing like that. Just let me rest a moment and then I'd like some tea."

"Upstairs, mum?"

"No, Frances. In the garden."

"In the garden, mum?"

"Yes, Frances. In the garden. Perhaps we'll get a breeze before evening."

After catching her breath, Elissa rose and went upstairs. When she returned she had changed into a pair of faded jeans and an old shirt. She let herself out of the back door, went down the stairs and into the garden. After her tea she would work on her flower beds. She unfolded a patio chair, placed it in the shade of the tree, sat down and closed her eyes.

No sooner had she done so than a slight breeze pirouetted across the garden, carrying in it a slightly familiar yet disconcerting odor. Having been a brilliant, Phi Beta Kappa, chemistry student during her undergraduate days at Radcliffe College, Elissa identified the smell as $C_{10}H_{20}O_2$, or capric acid and attributed its presence to her brief contact with the goat. She composed herself and put the experience out of her mind. But no more than a minuted passed before she heard a long bleat and then two short ones. She opened her eyes and there, at the end of her garden, was the insolent beast. Elissa froze in her chair and then screamed.

"Frances, Frances, it's the goat again," she shouted. "It's in here. Quickly, call the police."

The housekeeper, long in service but short in animal husbandry, came down the stairs carrying a tea kettle. She leaned back as if she were about to pitch a cricket ball back home and heaved the kettle in Rufino's general direction. Her aim was completely off and the kettle banged noisily against the wooden fence, once more altering Rufino's peace and tranquility. Instinctively, he made ready to charge his new tormentors.

Meanwhile, outside of Elissa's townhouse a crowd had begun gathering. The latest tactic of the Combined Task Force, formed and commissioned on the spot by the Mayor in order to quell interdepartmental quibbling brought about by unclear jurisdictional responsibility, was to make a house to house search of the area. Even the Fire Department felt it was its particular concern because the hair on the goat could easily rub against a similar surface, start a conflagration and cause a worst disaster than the one visited upon Chicago by Mrs. O'Leary's infamous cow.

As the search progressed the Combined Task Force found the gate of Elissa Paddleford's townhouse open. The rumor spread quickly that the goat had been found and soon the front of the townhouse was a mass of activity. As before, each city department went into action, hooking up hoses, donning gas masks, sweeping streets, and capturing innocent and blameless pets. Television cameras kept rolling and reporters, microphones in hand, continued asking questions and receiving a myriad of irrelevant responses about subway fares, house mortgages, unemployment rates, rent hikes, inadequate snow plowing services, police brutality, police corruption, too much welfare, too many taxes, no place to park, sexual repression, topless dancers, Richard Nixon, Vietnam, the New York Giants football team moving to New Jersey, the decline of the Yankees, homosexuals, heterosexuals, bisexuals, the stock market, violence on television, rock and roll, the legalization of marijuana, heroin addicts, the Black Panthers, the Young Lords, the Weathermen, group therapy, teenage prostitution, snuff movies, the Broadway stage, nudity on beaches, the threat of communism and a million other subjects over which New Yorkers fret and worry.

Don Sinfo, who had managed to make his way to the front of the crowd, was thoroughly ashamed by all the trouble which Rufino had caused. His patience nearly exhausted he pushed forward.

"Let me pass," he shouted, angrily in Spanish. "That is my goat in there."

By the time he reached the gate there were several policemen guarding the entrance, adding substance to the theory that Rufino had chosen this place for a hideout. Don Sinfo introduced himself, but the officers ignored him.

"Is my got," he said in English, pointing to himself. And then out of frustration at not being understood, launched into Spanish once more. "He is my animal, imbecile," he said, with momentary disregard for the law. "Let me pass so I can take him from here, you pubic hair."

Arms crossed, the policemen stood their ground. At this point the Honorable Fernando Picot once more came to the rescue. Noting that his countryman was again the victim of injustice, he ordered the policemen to let Don Sinfo through.

"Hail Mary Purest, yes," said Don Sinfo. "Let me pass. Do I look like a thief? All I want is my goat."

"Nobody goes through until the sergeant gives the word, Mac," said one of the officers.

Don Fernando produced his credentials.

"I'm not Mac, as you can well see," he said with a slight accent. "I am Judge . . ."

The officer was not impressed.

"I don't care if you're the Mayor's own guardian angel," he said. "Nobody goes through."

Judge Fernando Picot, shocked by the officer's tone of voice, but familiar with New York City Police Department protocol, took no personal offense. Instead, he resorted to intimidation.

"Are you aware that I can hold you in contempt of court?" he said.

"Right, Chief," said the officer, impassive in the performance of his duty.

This latest bit of insolence was too much for the judge and he expanded on his tactics.

"That's right," he said, looking back over his shoulder at the crowd, particularly at the group of young militants, stationed on the stoop of a brownstone to shout revolutionary slogans. "I'm the Chief and the Indians are just waiting for you to make the wrong move so they can attack. All of it will be on television tonight."

"Maybe you better let him through," said another of the officers.

The first policeman looked at the crowd and relented.

"Okay," he said. "The two of you go in, but no funny stuff."

Don Sinfo protested.

"No, no," he said, holding back the Judge and speaking in English so that the officers would not consider his aims suspicious. "I go alon. Got get escare," he added.

"What did he say, Kelly?" said one of the officers.

Kelly shrugged his shoulders.

"Don't worry about it," he said.

"Are you sure you want to go in alone, Sinfo," said the Judge.

"Yes, I am sure, Don Nando," Don Sinfo said. "This faggot of a goat is as impertinent as he is big. He may even turn on you if he chooses to ignore that you are one of our race."

And then there was one long bleat and two short ones followed by a scream, some shouting and a loud clattering noise. The crowd moved forward and a squad of policemen rushed to block the gate. Don Sinfo quickly stepped through the opening provided by the police, went down the driveway and into the garden.

What Don Sinfo saw when he entered the garden both angered and dismayed him. Rufino had backed two elderly, defenseless women into a corner of the garden and was threatening them with his horns. Don Sinfo stopped short of the scene, coughed once and Rufino turned in his direction. A look of surprise crossed Rufino's eyes as Don Sinfo stepped forward.

"You look as if you cannot understand how I have finally caught up with you, son of the great whore," he said, angrily in Spanish.

Rufino let out one of his most mournful bleats.

"Quiet, you villain," said Don Sinfo. "You have betrayed me, you hypocrite. And not only myself but all of us. All the progress achieved by our people in the last twenty-five years has been destroyed because of your infantile behavior. Tomorrow it will be in all the newspapers: PUERTO RICAN GOAT ATTACKS CITIZENS IN A FIT OF LATIN FURY! How do you think people of our race will feel, idiot? You do not understand how these things work. All of us will be blamed for your disorder and lack of respect for the law. And do not think for one moment that things will go unnoticed by our own. Luisa Quintero will mention it in her column and other Latins will cluck their tongues and talk about us as if we were nothing but ill-bred peasants."

Rufino bleated helplessly once more.

"No, sir, I will not be taken in this time," Don Sinfo said, growing angrier with each word. "Nothing will save you this time. You are truly an idiot to think that you could get away with this. More than that, you lack common sense and I am convinced that somehow, I don't know how, you have been influenced by hippies, communists and drug addicts. I should have never let you out of the cellar."

Rufino put his head down and emitted a weak, quivering bleat.

"Look at me and stop your falseness," Don Sinfo said, sternly. "Go to the other side of the garden and remain there while I excuse myself to these ladies."

Feeling the sting of Don Sinfo's words, Rufino walked slowly and penitently away and stood by the fence. The old man now turned his attention to the two women, who had been watching him with a mixture of relief and trepidation. The noise out in the street was about to reach a crescendo and there was no telling what would happen next. Don Sinfo took several steps forward, removed his Panama hat and bowed to Elissa Paddleford and her housekeeper.

"An berry sorree," he said. "Fors tine and lass tine." He brought his right index finger to this throat, made a slashing motion and let his tongue hang limply out of his mouth. The ladies gasped. "Finis," Don Sinfo said. "No mor got. We keel tomoro."

Elissa Paddleford looked at the goat and then at this curious man standing before her. Not given easily to anger, it suddenly dawned on her that her privacy had been severely violated and that this man was the cause of it all.

"You say this animal belongs to you?" she said.

"Jez," Don Sinfo replied, pointing at himself. "My got."

"Very well," said Elissa. "We have established that, and that being the case, I want both you and your goat to leave here immediately. I have had enough foolishness for one day."

And with those words she pointed to the driveway.

Don Sinfo felt the words cut through him, shaming him more than anything that had happened up to that moment.

"Escuse me, ladee," he said, crestfallen. "You hab rop?"

"I beg your pardon," said Elissa.

"Rop."

"Rope?"

"Yes, rop."

"Frances, see if you can find a rope in the cellar," Elissa said, turning to Frances, who had not quite recuperated from the experience and hesitated.

"Don gworry, ladee," Don Sinfo said, reassuringly. "The got behabe now."

"Yes, go ahead, Frances," said Elissa.

"Very well, mum," said Frances, and moved cautiously toward the house.

When Frances had gone into the house, Don Sinfo moved away from Elissa and tried to understand how all his dreams had come to be destroyed. The police undoubtedly would fine him and take Rufino away. A great sadness darkened Don Sinfo's heart and he thought of his youth, recalling the clear mountain air of his beloved town of Cacimar on the island; of his long departed wife's freshly brewed coffee, the aroma drifting through the house in the early morning when the mist had not yet lifted and the crops seemed to rise from the light grayness. He thought of the sadness of love and of walking in the dark countryside at night with only the stars for light and off in the distance hearing the laughter of young women, reaching him as would celestial music, and then seeing not them but the green in their hair where they had pinned fireflies.

At this moment and while Don Sinfo decided that this fine lady was absolutely correct in treating him so harshly, he saw someone climbing over the fence. Like himself, he was an old man, except that he was dressed all in white as if he worked in a hospital or a bakery. When the man had let himself down to the ground, he spoke to someone on the other side and a rifle was handed over.

Although Don Sinfo had no way of knowing who he was, you, as a perceptive reader and observer of detail, by this time, have established the identity of the intruder.

As you've guessed, the intruder was none other than G. Howard Trenton, who had hurried home to his penthouse apartment to survey the obvious beginnings of the revolution. This matter of the revolution had concerned Trenton for well over thirty-five years. Back then Brendan Stillwell, the brilliant American impressionist painter, had literally stolen Elissa's affections from him before going off to fight in the Spanish Civil War. He was killed somewhere outside Madrid, plunging Elissa into a life of total sexual abnegation. Trenton had cursed Stillwell and watched through binoculars as Don Sinfo had entered the gate. He then asked his trusted butler, Gilliam Ashe, descendant of the famous Creighton Ashe, black man-servant to General George Washington's *aide de camp*, Lieutenant Sylvester Enderly, to assist him. Gillian Ashe loaded the gold-plated shotgun, carried it downstairs and through the backyard adjoining Elissa's garden. The trusted Gilliam Ashe was aware that no good would come from his master's actions but obeyed dutifully. When he had handed the shotgun over the fence he returned to the penthouse to observe the scene below.

Don Sinfo was intrigued by the strange, gaunt figure of the man. He was even more puzzled when, without the slightest hesitation, the man came directly to him with an air of such authority that Don Sinfo considered the possibility that this might be the woman's husband.

"All right, sir," said Trenton, the shotgun at the ready. "It's quite obvious you're one of the leaders of this revolt and are using that animal as a diversionary measure to ransack this house. Put your hands in the air. Both you and your goat are under arrest."

G. Howard Trenton's entrance into the backyard having been obscured from Elissa Paddleford's sight by the large tree, she was shocked when she heard his voice. She took three steps, saw Trenton and stiffened. Her voice and manner became that of the coldly angered matron who lives by rigid social standards from which a deviation is tantamount to dishonor.

"Mr. Trenton, I've had just about enough of your pranks," she said. "You are at this moment trespassing on private property, carrying a firearm, and uninvited. While the first two are against the law, the third is simply boorish and I suggest that being a Yale man does not excuse such behavior. Please oblige me by leaving immediately."

"Stand back, Elissa," Trenton replied. "I've watched you make a shambles of your life once before and I won't let it happen again. There is more at stake now than your flirtation with a revolutionary cause. Stillwell should be here to see the fruits of his madness."

Elissa Paddleford was irate.

"You leave him out of this, G. Howard Trenton," she said.

"He was a wastrel, a bohemian and a hopeless romantic," replied Trenton. "He lured you away from me with his liberal facade."

"No one lured me away from you, you old fool," Elissa countered.

"All he wanted was your money, Elissa. He only wanted to finance his insane adventure and his warped sense of reality."

"At least he believed in something. That is far more than you've ever done. Aside from that dreary Newport race business, you do nothing. You, sir, are a moral newt."

"Elissa, Elissa," Trenton pleaded. "Stop this pretense. It's gone on too long. Right now the same revolutionaries who won Stillwell over are ready to dismantle your house, rob and pillage the neighborhood and establish their own form of government. Can't you hear them out there? I've come to show you that I too can be of use in a crisis. I'm going to march this anarchist and his goat out of here."

"You *are* mad," said Elissa. "This man simply came to get his goat. He's not a revolutionary. As for the crowd, I'm sure they simply followed the fire engines, thinking there was a fire."

"I won't hear of it, Elissa. I've seen it all too clearly before but didn't have the courage to act. Oh, what a fool I was to think that a woman like yourself, so independent, so full of life, could be won with urban gentility. No, beneath that polished, well-bred exterior lurks a wild, sensual, she-animal waiting to be ravished, mounted, dragged off to a nuptial cave."

Elissa looked at Trenton through narrowed eyes.

"G. Howard Trenton, that is the most obscene thing I've ever heard," she said. "Please leave now before you force me to call the police."

Don Sinfo watched G. Howard Trenton with great interest and although he understood little of what he was saying to Elissa Paddleford, it was obvious that Trenton was in a profound state of agitation. The gun, which was no more than ten feet away, was still trained on Don Sinfo's stomach.

"Pliss, sir," said Don Sinfo. "Put de gon down. This is a berry dangeros thin you al doin."

"Quiet, you rabble rouser," Trenton snapped. "I have a mind to execute you on the spot."

"Howard, go home," said Elissa. "I'm warning you."

"No, Elissa. This time *I* will be the moving force. Not Brendan Stillwell, not painting, not incipient bohemianism, not the Spanish Civil War, but G. Howard Trenton. And not only for us, but for the values and principles on which the republic was founded. I refuse to see this great country go up in smoke because of anarchists and foreigners. Stand back."

For the first time since she had known G. Howard Trenton, Elissa was frightened by his manner. Nevertheless, she was determined to stand her ground.

"Howard, darling," she said, adopting a new tack. "This gentleman is my guest. I'm sure you understand that. He is here at my request. His goat happened to wander into the garden and he was kind enough to come for it. Nothing more."

Trenton was beyond being charmed.

"Don't lie to me, Elissa," he said. "It was enough that you told me that the affair with Stillwell was just a friendship. And if it is true that this man is your guest, then I have no recourse but to also place you under arrest. You're harboring an enemy of our country. As much as my heart tells me it's wrong, the dictates of my conscience tell me otherwise. Elissa, raise your hands."

"I'll do no such thing," said Elissa.

"Raise them or I'll be forced to take more drastic measures," Trenton said, grabbing Elissa's wrist.

Aging brings on maturity, tolerance and wisdom, but if there was something which the gentle Don Sinfo could not permit, it was to see a woman abused and ill-treated by a man. Whether through tradition, love of mother or chivalry, Don Sinfo's code of honor did not allow certain situations to go unanswered.

"Jew are no a yentleman," Don Sinfo countered. "Jew hab dishonor jewlself. We mus hab a dual."

"A what?" said Trenton, screwing up his face.

"A dual. Is de only gway. Jew hab insultated dis gwoman an she can no defen hersel. Put de gon down an fie. If we hab pistolas we do it right, but it no matta. A man fie anee gway."

Don Sinfo was quite angry and his voice rose in menacing tones, daring Trenton to accept the challenge. But nothing would come of the matter. At the very moment when the showdown seemed imminent, Rufino, who had heard his master's voice, looked up. He was surprised that the angry words coming from Don Sinfo were not directed at him. In looking up he caught a glint of light from the shiny surface of the shotgun. The flash blinded him momentarily and he recalled his previous encounters with metal. This time he did not wait for the sound but charged directly at the source.

Filled with mature energy, Rufino's attack was a classic, stylized charge transmitted genetically and perfected through millenia of natural selection, true in every respect, esthetic but violent. The outcome could have been tragic, were it not for the good fortune which, all at once and unbeknownst to Don Sinfo, had begun coming his way.

The moment of impact was sheer perfection of motion. As Rufino passed Elissa she moved away, seemed to stumble and was caught by Don Sinfo, who placed a comforting arm around her. Trenton reacted much too slowly. At the last moment he turned the shotgun on Rufino, but it was too late. Measuring the distance to the millimeter, Rufino lowered his head, tucked in his front legs and, propelled by his powerful hindquarters, sprung forward at an upward angle, hitting G. Howard Trenton flush in the stomach with his lowered horns. The force of the blow propelled Trenton backwards into the pond. As he hit the shallow bottom the gun discharged and flew backwards out of his hands and beyond his reach.

The roar of the gun startled Rufino anew, but rather than fleeing, this time he seemed possessed. It was as if something which had been repressed in him had been suddenly released. He began racing madly around the pond at breakneck speed, stopping every so often to paw at the ground, his nostrils opening and closing as if daring Trenton to stand up and resume battle. Such would not be the case, for G. Howard Trenton had been knocked nearly unconscious and lay in the shallow pond in a state of undignified mortification, his always impeccably white clothes covered with brown mud and green slime. Mind muddled, vision somewhat blurred, his thoughts alternated between observing his execution by a firing squad and suing Elissa Paddleford.

Elissa was totally unhinged by the gunshot. She clung to Don Sinfo and began crying. In a matter of seconds the garden was full of police. A captain took command of the situation.

"Who discharged this weapon?" he asked, pointing at the shotgun, which had been carefully retrieved by one of the officers.

G. Howard Trenton stood up shakily in the pond, the green slime clinging to his clothes.

"I did, Captain," he said. "I was trying to make a citizen's arrest of this man when his goat attacked me. Please arrest him now that you're here."

"Just hold on a minute, buddy," said the captain. "Let me understand something. You break the law and you're telling me to arrest someone else? You can't go around shooting guns off in the city."

"Captain, I was doing my duty," Trenton explained. "If it hadn't been for the goat, the gun wouldn't have gone off."

"That's not true, Howard," Elissa interjected, shakily. "You know very well that you were threatening to shoot both this good man and myself. If it hadn't been for the goat, who knows what might have happened."

"You go along with that, Pop?" said the captain to Don Sinfo.

"Jez," said Don Sinfo, not understanding fully, but realizing that he was being asked to corroborate Elissa's side of the issue. "The ladee is spicking de true."

"Let's go, Mac," the captain said. "Cuff him, Sergeant Flaherty."

"I'll go quietly, Captain. There's no need for handcuffs."

"Yeah?" said the captain.

"That's right."

"Flaherty, cuff him."

Trenton was furious as he was turned around and ordered to put his hands behind his back.

"The Mayor will hear about this, Captain," he said. Before they took him away, he turned to Elissa and threatened her once more. "Miss Paddleford," he said, formally, "you can rest assured you'll be hearing from my lawyers in the very near future. We'll see if this ends up with the same romantic overtones of the Stillwell affair. This time I will emerge victorious and you'll wish that you had let me arrest this anarchist."

Elissa did not deem it important to offer a rejoinder and the police led Trenton away.

Outside, the young revolutionaries, having heard the shot, had begun scuffling with the police. The firemen, ever at the ready, were awaiting orders to discharge their hoses against them. The Mayor was still trying to get everyone's attention with the usual results. TV crews were busy filming the action. Guns had yet to be drawn, but the time was no more than a few seconds away since the Brooklyn contingent of the militants had arrived and were preparing a barrage of soda bottles intended for the policemen standing in front of the townhouse gate.

Just before the barrage was to begin, the police brought G. Howard Trenton out. Cheers went up from the crowd. No one knew the man, but wet, disheveled and his face contorted by the indignity of arrest and public humiliation, he looked like the typical run of the mill criminal, finally apprehended after a furious battle. Word quickly spread that the man had been holding Don Sinfo and his goat hostage.

"*Viejo cagao! Racista! Imperialista! Capitalista! Hijo 'e puta! Opresor del proletariado! Muérete, viejo maricón*!"

These were the things being shouted by the militants. The words were a mixture of curses and revolutionary rhetoric. Satisfied that some justice had prevailed, they pounded each other's back in congratulatory fervor.

In the garden of the townhouse, Elissa Paddleford had undergone a remarkable transformation. It was as if in recalling those times of unfulfilled ardor with Brendan Stillwell so many years ago, followed by the shot from Trenton's shotgun had once again opened her heart. Although weathered by the years, her eyes were now those of a young woman in love. The clear violet tint in them shone as she smiled at Don Sinfo. Her Spanish, which had been flawless back then as she prepared to be a nurse in the battlefields of Spain, returned suddenly to her.

"*Señor*," she said, touching Don Sinfo's arm. "You could have been killed. Why did you do it?"

The accuracy of her Spanish, the lisping quality of that which our people call, with self-deprecation, Spanish Spanish, that is, the language spoken in Madrid, together with the curious admiration with which colonials seem to regard North Americans who speak our language, endeared Elissa to Don Sinfo immediately.

"It was a matter of little importance," he said. "I am an old man and it was the only thing to be done. In any case, it was Rufino's bravery which caused an end to that lunatic's behavior."

"Yes, but had it not been for your initial courage, your goat would not have found it in himself to obey your subtle command. You have trained him well."

"He is a smart animal, *señora*."

"*Señorita*," said Elissa, proudly.

"Oh yes, of course. Pardon me. What are you called?"

"Elissa Paddleford."

"Sinforoso Figueroa, your servant," said Don Sinfo, extending his hand.

"Would you like to come inside and rest?" said Elissa, taking his hand. "Why don't you tie Rufino near the stairs. He will get plenty of grass there."

"Very well," said Don Sinfo. "I am tired. You are very kind to invite me."

But no sooner were they inside than Frances came to them in the living room to explain that a policeman was at the door with, as she put it, another Spanish gentleman.

"Shall I let 'em in, mum?" she inquired.

"By all means, Frances," Elissa replied.

The Spanish gentleman was Judge Fernando Picot and he directed himself to Don Sinfo after bowing to Elissa.

"The people want you, Sinfo," he said. "You are their hero and they want to make sure you're safe. Please come outside and bring the fine lady with you."

Don Sinfo could do nothing less. He looked at Elissa and ever so subtly she assented. It was as if they had known each other for years and the slightest signal was sufficient for them. He gave Elissa his arm and together they went to the porch of the townhouse. From there he waved to the crowd.

"*Qué Viva Don Sinfo*," the people shouted. "*Qué Viva Puerto Rico*. Speech. Speech. Speech."

Both the Judge and Elissa urged Don Sinfo to speak to the crowd.

"My friends," Don Sinfo began, as the crowd grew still for the first time. "I have been very lucky today in finding my goat. A tragedy could have taken place were it not for the good work of the police, the firemen and other city workers. I want to thank them. I also want to thank my friend, the Honorable Fernando Picot for all he has done. And I want to especially thank the owner of this house, who did not hesitate to defend the rights of a humble *bodeguero* and his property from the wanton attack of a raving lunatic. Thank you, my friends, for your support."

Don Sinfo raised his hand in salute and the crowd applauded and cheered. And then, almost as if Don Sinfo had summoned the heavens, a great rumbling was heard overhead. The sky turned dark and long streaks of lightning cracked the gray cover. Heavy drops of rain began falling and within seconds a tremendous downpour had sent the crowd running for shelter.

The rain fell heavily. It was warm summer rain, making the air charged with a freshness that released the pent up anger of the people into a dance. Young and old, cop and militant splashed through the puddles, laughing. Huddling in doorways and under awnings, they spoke with each other without suspicion, the lines of fear and resentment washed away by the rain, each one, although not ready to admit it publicly, glad that nothing harmful had taken place. Tomorrow they may well return to their same entrenched positions, but for now they enjoyed the rain.

The downpour continued for the next hour and then became a fine drizzle. Soon after, everyone had gone and the street in front of Elissa Paddleford's townhouse was back to normal. Don Sinfo was not allowed to leave even after a cab was called for the Judge. Reassured that the danger had passed, Fernando Picot bid Don Sinfo goodbye. Elissa and Don Sinfo were left alone in the upstairs library. Here among priceless volumes of great literature, regrettably none authored by me, Elissa poured out her heart to Don Sinfo. Her tale stirred a passion in him as great as he had felt for his wife in their youth. What a miserable, selfish wretch he had been for only seeing his own suffering when this gentle being, so honest and good had endured such agony.

"I swore once I would never love another man," Elissa said. "I am too old to be thinking of such things, Sinfo, but if you want me I am yours. Do with me what you wish, my heart."

Elissa's body was aflame with desire. The slightest caress would have been sufficient to send her into prolonged ecstasy. The beauty of the Spanish language lends itself aptly to such passionate scenes, but nothing is more dramatic than its counterpart in the form of chivalry.

"We must do nothing until our wedding night," Don Sinfo said. "It is something which is proper and in the long run the best course of action. We must wait. Although we are both in the winter of our lives it is no excuse for us to act with abandon and perhaps make a costly mistake."

The proposal made Elissa swoon and in the dim light she let her head tilt back, profiling, if not a beautiful face, at least a face filled with long awaited satisfaction. Marriage was not mentioned again that evening. After dinner Don Sinfo borrowed an umbrella and, along with Rufino, made his way back to El Barrio. The sky had cleared and a few stars ventured out in the clear night. Don Sinfo walked the rain-slick streets, enraptured by Elissa's gentleness.

During the next few weeks he visited her regularly. They took long walks in the park, talked and became better acquainted. With each day their love and respect for each other grew. The wedding was attended by a number of Elissa's friends and relatives. At the reception they took Don Sinfo into their circle as if he were one of their own, finding that he possessed an old world charm which fascinated them. This gentle and well mannered person was the perfect match for their friend, Elissa, over whom they had worried for years. Apprehensive at first, they were soon relieved that their fears about the people they so much heard about in newspapers and on television were unfounded. They were so different, they all remarked.

Don Sinfo's family, as well as many of his friends, were also in attendance. Don Cipriano Reyes, a cousin of Don Sinfo's, who, in spite of his years, loved dancing, brought his musician friends and accompanying them on the accordion, set the mood for the party.

Before long the wedding reception moved from the Plaza Hotel to the garden of Elissa's house where it became an old fashioned, down to earth, island feast, complete with roasted pig on a spit and homemade *pitrinche* rum, smuggled up from the mountains of the island for the occasion. The garden, strung with garlands of colored lights, suddenly became for Elissa's friends, too long fettered by convention but ever open to adventure, a place to let loose and be. As Countess Gloria Worthington de Cointreau, Elissa's roommate during her years at Radcliffe, said, "Isn't it marvelous going native for an evening." The party, loud from the outset for that section of the city, turned into a ribald fantasy. At one point Lady Cynthia Wiggins, the Bermuda socialite, removed her dress and did a topless dance to the tantalizing music of "*Tintorera del Mar*," that famous Puerto Rican *plena* which tells of the demise of a U.S. strike-breaking lawyer whose disappearence was attributed to a female shark.

Tintorera del mar
tintorera del mar
tintorera del mar
se comió el abogado de la Guánica central.

Even Frances, who had rarely smiled since leaving her native land, was in a state of extended hilarity and ended up in the cellar of the townhouse with Don Cipriano, minus his accordion. During the height of the festivities, Don Sinfo and Elissa made their escape and began their honeymoon trip to Spain.

And so it was that my good friend, Don Sinforoso Figueroa's fortune took a turn for the best. He now finds himself in an enviable position. His nephew, Felipe, is married, the father of a son and finished with not only his undergraduate education, but law studies in order to handle his uncle's estate. Don Sinfo has been asked to write his autobiography by one of the biggest New York publishing houses (which shall remain nameless, since it has done nothing but scorn my literary efforts for years) and there is even a rumor that Don Sinfo will, in the near future, run for public office.

Elissa Paddleford, in a state of prolonged bliss after so many years of solitude, rarely leaves Don Sinfo's side. Having overcome the last obstacle to her happiness by a countersuit which nearly ruined G. Howard Trenton, she contents herself with making of her husband's life a paradise.

As for Rufino, no small amount can be said on his behalf. He too has become lord and master of his destiny. Somewhere in Long Island, on a rambling four hundred acre estate, he manages to keep himself busy looking after some ten female companions and their offspring, at latest count numbering thirty-nine, the eldest eight having left home to work in children's zoos all over this great land. Rufino is cared for by a Swiss family, who for generations have looked after goats and their peculiar needs.

From time to time Don Sinfo visits Rufino and the two of them pass the time, neither concerned about the future nor reminiscent of the past, but quietly enjoying the present, thankful each one that he is alive.

Such is the fabric of this great land.

When one least expects it, there is a break in an otherwise bleak existence and life begins anew.

And yet, as much as one may look for Lady Luck, she is elusive and only fools will attempt to find a moral in this tale.

To sleep.

Good night.